. . . his ear caught a sound on the stairs, followed by the clanking of swords. . . .

"I demand admittance," said a loud voice outside the room, "in the name of the law!" The door was opened, and a magistrate entered, followed by four soldiers and a corporal.

"What is the reason for this unexpected visit?" asked M. Morrel, who evidently knew the magistrate. "There must be some mistake."

"If that is so," replied the magistrate, "you will receive my deepest apology. Meanwhile, I bear an order of arrest. Which of you is Edmond Dantes?"

Every eye turned towards the young man who, in spite of the terror he could not help but feel, advanced with dignity. He said in a firm voice, "I am he. What is your business with me?"

"Edmond Dantes," replied the magistrate, "I arrest you in the name of the law."

A Background Note about
The Count of Monte Cristo

The Count of Monte Cristo begins in February 1815. At the request of his dying captain, French sailor Edmond Dantes has delivered secret documents to Napoleon Bonaparte. Doing so has placed Edmond at risk. Why?

Having ruled France from 1799 to 1814, Napoleon was in exile on the Mediterranean island of Elba. King Louis XVIII now ruled France. However, French people were divided as to whom they wanted to lead their country. Some, called Royalists, supported King Louis; others, the Bonapartists, wanted Napoleon to return to power. Because Napoleon was the king's enemy, any communication with him would be considered a crime—namely, treason.

Napoleon Bonaparte did return to France on March 1, 1815. By March 20 he had gathered such a large army of Frenchmen that he was back in power, but only briefly. Great Britain, Prussia, Austria, and Russia gathered forces against him, and Napoleon's troops were decisively defeated in the Battle of Waterloo on June 18. Napoleon was permanently exiled to the remote island of Saint Helena, where he died. King Louis XVIII returned to the French throne and ruled until his death in 1824.

Because the characters in *The Count of Monte Cristo* are French, their names and titles are different from ours. Men were called *Monsieur* (meaning "Mr."), abbreviated as *M.* Married women's names began with *Madame*, abbreviated *Mme.*, while unmarried women were called *Mademoiselle* (*Mlle.*). French priests had a special title before their names: *Abbé*, meaning "Father."

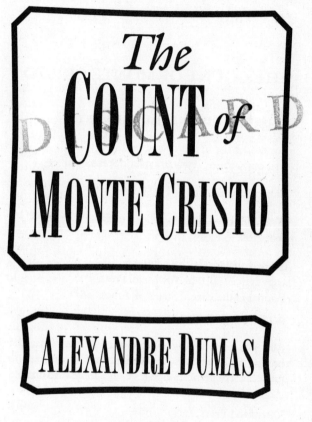

The COUNT of MONTE CRISTO

ALEXANDRE DUMAS

Edited by
Jothi Ravindran and Martin E. Goldstein,
with an Afterword by Martin E. Goldstein
and Janet M. Goldstein

 THE TOWNSEND LIBRARY

THE COUNT OF MONTE CRISTO

TP **THE TOWNSEND LIBRARY**

For more titles in the Townsend Library,
visit our website: www.townsendpress.com

Illustrations © 2010 by Hal Taylor

Note: This book has been edited to make it more
accessible to today's readers.

Townsend Press, Inc.
439 Kelley Drive
West Berlin, NJ 08091
permissions@townsendpress.com

ISBN-13: 978-1-59194-216-0
ISBN-10: 1-59194-216-0

Library of Congress Control Number:
2009943317

CONTENTS

CHAPTER 1
Marseilles—The Arrival

As the sailing ship Pharaon *pulls into port, Edmond Dantes, the captain's mate, tells the ship's owner, Pierre Morrel, that a tragedy has occurred during the voyage.*

On February 24, 1815, during the reign of King Louis XVIII, the lookout at the port of Marseilles, France, signaled the appearance of the sailing ship named the *Pharaon*, arriving after a long voyage. Spectators immediately rushed to the docks to watch the ship come into port.

One of the spectators, 36-year old Pierre Morrel, the ship's owner, did not wait for the ship to reach the dock. Instead, he jumped into a small rowboat and ordered it alongside the *Pharaon*.

"Ah, is it you, Edmond Dantes?" Morrel called out to the *Pharaon*. "What's the matter? Why does everyone look so sad?"

"We lost our brave Captain Leclere," Edmond replied. He was a fine, tall, slim young fellow of eighteen or twenty, with black eyes and hair as dark as a raven's wing. He had the calm and resolute appearance often found in men who contend with danger.

1

"And the cargo?" inquired the owner, eagerly.

"The cargo is all safe, M. Morrel. You need not worry. But poor Captain Leclere—"

"What happened to him?" asked the owner.

"He died of brain-fever in dreadful agony." Turning to the crew, he said, "Bear a hand there! Take in sail!"

Eight or ten seamen sprang to their stations. The young sailor gave a look to see that his orders were carried out and then turned again to the owner.

"If you will come on board, M. Morrel," said Edmond, "your cargo officer, M. Danglars, will give you every detail. I must look after the anchoring and dress the ship in mourning."

The owner seized a rope which Edmond flung to him and climbed up the side of the ship. The young man left the conversation to Danglars, who now came toward the owner. He was the sort of man who is overly polite to his superiors but insulting to men under him.

"Well, M. Morrel," said Danglars, "you have heard of our misfortune?"

"Yes, poor Captain Leclere! He was a brave and honest man."

"And a first-rate seaman, one with many years of honorable service," replied Danglars.

"But," replied the owner, watching Edmond direct the anchoring of his vessel, "it seems to me that a sailor does not need to be so old to be an expert. Our friend Edmond seems to understand his business thoroughly."

"Yes," said Danglars, glancing at Edmond with hatred. "He is young, and youth is always self-confident. The breath had barely left the captain's body when Edmond Dantes took command, without consulting anyone. Worse, he caused us to lose a day at the island of Elba, instead of heading directly for Marseilles."

"As to taking command," replied Morrel, "that was his duty as captain's mate. But as to losing a day off Elba, that was wrong, unless the vessel needed repairs."

"The vessel was in as good condition as I, and as I hope you are, sir. That day was lost because of his own pleasure and nothing else."

"Edmond," said the ship owner, turning toward the young man, "come this way!"

"I'll be with you in a moment, sir," answered Edmond. Then calling to the crew, he said—"Let go!"

The anchor was instantly dropped, and the chain rattled across the deck. He added, "Put the flag at half-mast."

"You see," said Danglars, "he acts as though he is captain already."

"And so he is," said the owner.

"But he has not yet gotten your signature on his documents, M. Morrel."

"He will have it soon enough," said the owner. "True, he is young, but he seems a thorough seaman, and well experienced."

A cloud passed over Danglars' forehead.

"Pardon me, M. Morrel," said Edmond,

approaching. "The vessel is anchored, and I am at your service."

"Edmond, why did you stop at the island of Elba?"

"I do not know, sir. It was the last wish of Captain Leclere. As he lay dying, he gave me a packet for Marshal Bertrand there."

"Did you see the marshal, Edmond?"

"Yes."

Morrel drew Edmond to one side, asking in a voice barely above a whisper, "And how is former Emperor Napoleon?"

"Very well, as far as I could judge."

"You actually saw the emperor, then?"

"He entered the marshal's apartment while I was there."

"And you spoke to him?"

"Why, it was he who spoke to me, sir," said Edmond, with a smile.

"And what did he say to you?"

"He asked me questions about the vessel: when she left Marseilles, the course she had taken, and her cargo. But I told him I was only the captain's mate, and that she belonged to the firm of Morrel & Son. 'Ah, yes,' he said, 'I know them. The Morrels have been ship owners from father to son; a Morrel served with me when I was at Valence.'"

"By God, that is true!" cried the owner, delighted. "That was Policar Morrel, my uncle. Edmond, you must tell my uncle that the emperor remembered him, and you will see it will bring tears into the old soldier's eyes. Come, come," he continued, patting Edmond's shoulder kindly, "you did right to stop at Elba. However, if people discovered that you had taken a packet to the marshal, and had talked with the emperor, it might bring you trouble."

"How could that bring me trouble, sir?" asked Edmond. "I did not know what I was carrying, and the emperor only asked questions as he would of any visitor." And the young man went to the gangway.

As he departed, Danglars approached Morrel and said, "Well, has he given you satisfactory reasons for his landing at Elba?"

"Yes, most satisfactory, my dear Danglars."

"Good," he replied, "for it is not pleasant to think that a comrade has not done his duty."

"It was Captain Leclere who gave orders for this delay," replied the owner.

"Talking of Captain Leclere, hasn't Edmond Dantes given you a letter from him?"

"To me? No. Was there one?"

"I believe that, besides the packet, Captain Leclere entrusted a letter to his care."

"Of what packet are you speaking, Danglars?"

"Why, the one Dantes left at Elba."

"How do you know he had a packet to leave at Elba?"

Danglars turned very red.

"I was passing close to the half open door of the captain's cabin, and I saw him give both to Dantes."

"He did not speak to me of it," replied the ship owner, "but if there is any letter he will give it to me."

Danglars thought for a moment. "Then please don't mention it to Dantes. I may have been mistaken."

At this moment Edmond returned, and Danglars walked away.

"Well, my dear Edmond, are you free to dine with me tonight?" inquired the owner.

"I am greatly honored, M. Morrel, but I must decline. I must see my father."

"Quite right, Edmond. You are a good son."

Edmond smiled. "My father is proud, sir. If he was starving, I doubt he would ask anything from anyone but Heaven."

"Well, then, after this we shall expect you."

"I must again excuse myself, M. Morrel, for after this visit I have another I am anxious to pay."

"True, Edmond. I forgot the young lady waiting for you at least as impatiently as your father—your lovely sweetheart, Mercedes."

Edmond blushed. "She is not just my sweetheart. We are engaged."

"Well, dear Edmond," continued the owner, "don't let me delay you. You have managed my affairs so well that I ought to give you all the time you require for your own. Do you need any money?"

"No, sir. I have saved nearly three months' wages."

"You are a careful fellow, Edmond."

"I have a poor father, sir."

"Yes, yes. I have a son too, and I would be very angry with anyone who kept him from me after a three months' voyage. Captain Leclere did not, before he died, give you a letter for me?"

"He was too weak to write, sir. But that reminds me that I must ask for a leave of absence for some days."

"To get married?"

"Yes, and then to go to Paris."

"Take what time you require, Edmond. It will take weeks to unload the cargo. But be back in three months, for the *Pharaon*," added the owner, patting the young sailor on the back, "cannot sail without her captain."

"Without her captain!" cried Edmond, his eyes sparkling with joy. "You intend to make me captain of the *Pharaon*?"

"If I were sole owner we'd shake hands on it now and call it settled. But, I have a partner, and I must gain his consent. Rely on me; I will do my best."

"M. Morrel, I thank you on behalf of my father and my fiancée, Mercedes."

"That's all right, Edmond. Heaven watches over the deserving. Go to your father, to Mercedes, and afterward come to me. I shall look over the accounts with Danglars. Have you been satisfied with him this voyage?"

"Do you mean is he a good comrade? No, for I think he has disliked me since the day when I was silly enough, after a quarrel, to propose that we stop at the island of Monte Cristo to settle the dispute. But if you are asking if he is a responsible officer, there is nothing to say against him."

"That's right, Edmond. I see you are a

thoroughly good fellow, and I will detain you no longer."

"Then, M. Morrel, a thousand thanks!"

"I hope to see you soon, my dear Edmond. Good luck to you."

The ship owner, smiling, watched him until he saw him spring out on the dock and disappear into the crowd. On turning round, the owner saw Danglars behind him, also watching the young sailor. There was a great difference in the expression of the two men.

CHAPTER 2
Father and Son

After visiting his elderly father, Edmond sets off to visit his fiancée, Mercedes.

Edmond entered a small apartment house, climbed up to the fifth floor, and paused before a half-open door. Inside the small room he could see his father looking pale and shrunken.

"Father—dear father!" exclaimed Edmond.

The old man uttered a cry.

"What ails you, my dearest father? Are you ill?" inquired the young man.

"No, no, my dear Edmond—my boy—my son! I did not expect you. I am overjoyed to see you. Come, tell me all the good fortune that has befallen you."

"The good Captain Leclere is dead, father, and it is probable that I shall have his place. Imagine—a captain at age nineteen, with a captain's pay! Is this not more than a poor sailor could have hoped for?"

"Yes, my dear boy," replied the old man, "it is very fortunate."

"Well, with the first money I get, I am going to buy you a little house."

9

Suddenly the old man collapsed into a chair.

"What's the matter, father? Are you ill?"

"It's nothing; it will soon pass."

"Let me get you a glass of wine."

"No, thank you. It is no use," said the old man. "There is no wine."

"No wine?" said Edmond, turning pale, looking first at his father's hollow cheeks and next at the empty cupboards. "Do you need money, Father?"

"I need nothing now that I have you," said the old man.

"Yet," stammered Edmond, "I gave you two hundred francs when I left."

"Yes, Edmond, but you forgot your debt to our neighbor, Caderousse. He reminded me of it, telling me if I did not pay, he would go to M. Morrel. I paid him."

"But," Edmond exclaimed, "I owed a hundred and forty francs!"

"Yes," stammered the old man.

"So you have lived for three months on sixty francs," muttered Edmond.

"You know how little I need," said the old man.

"Heaven pardon me," cried Edmond, falling on his knees. "Take this," he said, emptying his pockets. "Buy what you need immediately." Old Dantes's face brightened. "But, hush, here comes somebody."

The bearded face of Caderousse the tailor appeared at the door.

"Edmond, you're back again?" he said, with a grin that displayed his ivory teeth.

"Yes, Caderousse, and ready to be helpful to you in any way," replied Edmond, barely able to hide the coldness under this cloak of good manners.

"Thanks. Fortunately, I do not need anything. I lent you money, and you returned it. We are even."

"We are never even with those who help us," Edmond replied, "for when we do not owe them money, we owe them gratitude."

"Let us talk instead of your happy return, my boy. When I heard you were here, I came as fast as I could, so I could have the pleasure of shaking hands with a friend."

"Good Caderousse!" said the old man. "What a good friend you are."

"I love and esteem you, because honest folks are so rare. But it seems you have come back rich, my boy," continued the tailor, looking at the bills on the table.

The young man noticed the greed in the dark eyes of his neighbor. "Oh," he said carelessly, "this money is not mine. I was expressing my fears to my father that he had run out of money while I was gone. To convince me otherwise, he emptied his wallet on the table. Come, Father," added Edmond, "put this money back—unless Caderousse wants anything, and in that case it is at his service."

"No, my boy," said Caderousse. "I am not in need, thank God."

"Well, Father, now that I know you are well, I ask your consent to visit Mercedes."

"Go, my dear boy," said old Dantes. "Heaven bless you in your wife, as it has blessed me in my son!"

"His wife!" said Caderousse. "How fast you go, Father Dantes. She is not his wife yet."

"No, but with Heaven's help she soon will be," replied Edmond.

"Yes, yes," said Caderousse. "But you were right to return as soon as possible, my boy, because fine girls never lack admirers."

"Really?" answered Edmond, with a smile that showed his uneasiness.

"Ah, yes," continued Caderousse, "and tempting offers, too. But you will be captain, and who could refuse you then?"

"Come, come," said Edmond. "I have a better opinion of women in general, and of Mercedes in particular. I am certain that, captain or not, she would love me."

"Excellent!" said Caderousse.

"I will go see her directly," was Edmond's reply. Embracing his father, he left.

Caderousse lingered for a moment. Then, saying goodbye to old Dantes, he went downstairs, where he met Danglars.

"Well," said Danglars, "did you see Edmond?"

"I have just left him," answered Caderousse.

"Did he mention his hope of being captain?"

"He spoke of it as a settled thing."

"Indeed!" said Danglars. "He is in too much of a hurry. If we play our cards right, he will remain what he is, and perhaps even less."

"What do you mean?"

"Oh, nothing—I was speaking to myself. Is he still in love with Mercedes, the beautiful Catalan maiden?" asked Danglars.

"Head over heels. But unless I am mistaken, there will be a storm in that quarter."

"What do you mean?" demanded Danglars.

"Well, every time I have seen Mercedes come into the city, she has been accompanied by a tall, strapping, black-eyed Catalan, very fierce-looking. She calls him cousin."

"And you think this cousin is in love with her?"

"What else can a strapping man of twenty-one want with a fine girl of seventeen?"

"And you say Dantes has gone to see Mercedes?"

"He went before I came down."

"Let us go the same way. We can stop at a café."

"Very well," said Caderousse.

In response to their questions, the café owner said he had seen Edmond pass by not ten minutes before. He assured the men that Edmond had gone to see the girl. And so they sat down.

CHAPTER 3
The Catalans

Mercedes welcomes Edmond. Meanwhile, her rejected suitor, Fernand, joins Danglars and Caderousse at a nearby café.

Beyond a bare, weather-worn wall, about a hundred paces from the spot where the two friends sat drinking their wine, was the section of town where the Catalans, a separate nationality, dwelled.

A young and beautiful girl, with hair as black as jet, her eyes as velvety as a deer's, was leaning in a corner. Her arms, bare to the elbow, were brown and as beautiful as those of a marble statue. Impatiently she tapped the earth with her arched foot, displaying her well-shaped leg. A few feet from her was a tall young man in his early twenties. He stared at the girl with a mixture of irritation and uneasiness.

"And so, Mercedes," said the young man, "here it is Easter again. Isn't it finally the moment for our wedding?"

"I have answered you a hundred times, Fernand, and really you must be very stupid to ask me again."

"Well, say it again, and perhaps I can begin to believe it! Tell me for the hundredth time that you refuse my love, which your mother wished you to accept. I have dreamed for ten years of being your husband, Mercedes, now I must lose that hope!"

"You know I never encouraged you in that hope, Fernand," replied Mercedes. "I love you as a brother, but do not ask from me more than that, for my heart belongs to another."

"You have been cruelly frank with me. But do you forget that among the Catalans it is a sacred law to intermarry?"

"It is not a law, but merely a custom," answered Mercedes. "You are the son of my father's brother. I appreciate that you sometimes give me fish that you catch, so I can sell them to earn the money for the flax that I spin. Be content with my friendship, for I tell you once more, that is all I can promise."

"I understand," replied Fernand. "Maybe if I were a sailor, you would love me. But perhaps the one you wait for is not as faithful as you think."

"Fernand," cried Mercedes, "I believed you were good-hearted, and I was mistaken! You are wicked to try to plant jealousy in my heart! Yes, I will not deny it, I do love him of whom you speak. If he does not return, instead of believing that he has forgotten me, I will know that he died loving only me." The young girl made a gesture of rage.

Fernand did not reply, nor did he try to stop the tears which flowed down Mercedes's cheeks. He arose and paced up and down. Suddenly he came to a halt. With his eyes glowing and his hands clenched, he said, "Mercedes, once for all, is this your final decision?"

"I love Edmond Dantes," the young girl calmly replied, "and none but Edmond shall ever be my husband."

"And you will always love him?"

"As long as I live."

Fernand let his head fall forward like a defeated man. Then, suddenly looking her full in the face, he said through clenched teeth, "But if he is dead or has forgotten you . . ."

"Mercedes!" called a joyous voice from the street. "Mercedes!"

"Ah," exclaimed the young girl, blushing with delight, "you see he has not forgotten me, for here he is!" And rushing toward the door, she opened it, crying, "Here, Edmond, here I am!"

Fernand, pale and trembling, drew back like a traveler at the sight of a serpent, and collapsed into a chair. Edmond and Mercedes threw their arms around each other. Suddenly Edmond saw the gloomy, threatening face of Fernand in the shadows. Instinctively, the young Catalan placed his hand on the knife at his belt.

"Ah, I beg your pardon," said Edmond, frowning. "I did not notice that there were three of us." Then, turning to Mercedes, he asked, "Who is this gentleman?"

"One who will be your best friend, Edmond. It is Fernand—the man whom, after you, I love the best in the world. Do you not remember him?"

"Of course!" said Edmond, and without letting go of Mercedes's hand, he extended the other pleasantly to the Catalan. But Fernand, instead of responding to this friendly gesture, remained silent and trembling. Puzzled, Edmond looked at the excited, embarrassed Mercedes, and then again at the gloomy and menacing Fernand. He understood all, and his anger flared.

"I did not know, when I came so hastily to see you, that I was to meet an enemy here."

"An enemy!" exclaimed Mercedes, with an angry look at her cousin. "An enemy in my house, Edmond! If I believed that, I would take your arm and go with you to Marseilles, leaving this house forever."

Fernand's eyes flashed with lightning. "And if any misfortune befell you, dear Edmond," she continued, proving to Fernand that she had read his innermost thoughts, "if misfortune should occur to you, I would climb to the highest point of the Cape de Morgion and throw myself down off the cliff."

Fernand turned deadly pale. "But you are mistaken, Edmond," she continued. "You have no enemy here—there is no one but Fernand, my cousin, who will shake your hand and be your devoted friend."

With these words, the young girl fastened a commanding look on the Catalan. As if hypnotized, Fernand came slowly toward Edmond, and gave him his hand. But scarcely had he touched Edmond's hand than he felt he had done all he could do, and he rushed hastily out of the house.

"Oh!" he exclaimed, running furiously and tearing his hair. "Who will deliver me from this man? How miserable I am!"

"Hello, Fernand! Where are you running to?" called a voice.

The young man stopped suddenly, looked around, and saw Caderousse sitting at a table with Danglars.

"Well," said Caderousse, "come join us. Are you in such a hurry that you cannot pass the time of day with your friends?"

"Particularly when they have a full bottle in front of them?" added Danglars. Still stunned, Fernand stared at them but did not say a word.

"He seems very disturbed," said Danglars, nudging Caderousse with his knee. "Are we mistaken? Has Edmond won, in spite of everything?"

"Why, we must ask," Caderousse replied.

Fernand wiped away the perspiration from his brow as he walked into the café. The cool shade seemed to restore some calmness to his senses.

"Good day," he said. "You called me, didn't you?"

"I called you because you were running like a madman, and I was afraid you would throw yourself into the sea," said Caderousse, laughing. "When a man has friends, they should not only offer him a glass of wine, but prevent his swallowing three or four pints of water unnecessarily!"

Fernand gave a groan, which sounded like a sob.

"Well, Fernand, I must say," said Caderousse, his curiosity destroying all his tact, "you look uncommonly like a rejected lover. Come, come, Fernand," he went on, "tell us what is the matter."

"I'm all right," said Fernand, clenching his hands without raising his head.

"Ah, you see, Danglars," said Caderousse, "this is how it is. Fernand is a good and brave Catalan, one of the best fishermen in Marseilles, and he is in love with a very fine girl, named Mercedes. But it appears, unfortunately, that the girl is in love with the mate of the *Pharaon*, and as the *Pharaon* arrived today—why, you understand!"

"No, I do not understand," said Danglars.

"Poor Fernand has been rejected," continued Caderousse.

"Well, and what of it?" said Fernand, lifting his head and looking like a man who wants to find a target for his anger. "Mercedes owes nothing to me, does she? Is she not free to love whomever she chooses?"

"But," said Caderousse, "I thought you were a Catalan, and they tell me Catalan men do not allow themselves to be beaten by a rival. Indeed," Caderousse continued, "Fernand is not the only person inconvenienced by the arrival of Edmond, is he, Danglars?"

"Indeed he is not," answered his friend in an angry tone.

"Well, never mind," answered Caderousse, pouring out a glass of wine for Fernand, and filling his own for the eighth or ninth time. "When is the wedding to be?" he asked Fernand.

"It is not yet scheduled," grumbled Fernand.

"No, but it will be," said Caderousse, "as surely as Edmond will be captain of the *Pharaon*—eh, Danglars. Let us drink to Captain Edmond Dantes, husband of the beautiful Catalane!"

Caderousse raised his glass to his mouth with an unsteady hand, and swallowed the contents at a gulp. Fernand dashed his on the ground.

"Ho, ho!" exclaimed Caderousse. "What do I see down there by the wall, in the direction of the Catalans? Look, Fernand, your eyes are better than mine. Perhaps wine is making me imagine things, but I should say it was two lovers walking side by side, and hand in hand."

"Yes," was the reply, in a low voice. "It is Edmond and Mercedes!"

"Indeed it is!" said Caderousse. "Hello, Edmond! Hello, lovely girl! Come tell us when the wedding is to be."

Fernand, as irritated as a bull is by the bullfighter, rose from his seat. He seemed to be preparing to attack his rival, when Mercedes, smiling and graceful, lifted her lovely head, and looked at them with her clear, bright eyes. At this, Fernand remembered her threat of dying if Edmond died, and he dropped again heavily on his seat. Danglars looked at the two men, the one brutalized by liquor, the other overwhelmed with love.

"I shall get nothing from these fools," he thought. "One is an envious fellow making himself drunk when he ought to be making plans. The other is a fool who sees the woman he loves stolen from under his nose, and he behaves like a big baby. Yes, Edmond's star is rising, and he will marry this splendid girl, and be captain, too, and laugh at us all, unless"—a sinister smile passed over Danglars' lips—"unless I take a hand in the matter."

"Well," continued Caderousse, "what about the wedding?"

"The happy event will take place as soon as possible," Edmond replied with joyful enthusiasm. "Today all the preparations are being made at my father's, and tomorrow, or next day at latest, the wedding festival will take place. I hope you will attend, M. Danglars, and you, Caderousse."

"And Fernand?" asked Caderousse with a chuckle.

"My wife's cousin is my cousin," said Edmond, "and we, Mercedes and I, would be very sorry if he were absent at such a time."

Fernand opened his mouth to reply, but his voice died on his lips.

Danglars continued the conversation. "Today the preparations, tomorrow or the next day the ceremony! You are in a hurry, Captain!"

"Danglars," said Edmond, smiling, "Do not give me a title which does not yet belong to me. That may bring me bad luck."

"I beg your pardon," replied Danglars. "I merely said you seemed in a hurry, and we have lots of time. The *Pharaon* cannot sail again in less than three months."

"We are always in a hurry to be happy, M. Danglars. Besides, I must allow time to go to Paris."

"Ah, really! To Paris! Will it be the first time you have ever been there, Edmond?"

"Yes."

"You have business there?"

"Not of my own, but related to the last request of poor Captain Leclere. You know of what I am speaking, Danglars—it is my sacred duty. I shall only take the time to go and return."

"Yes, yes, I understand," said Danglars, and added to himself, "To Paris, no doubt to deliver the letter which the grand marshal gave him. Ah, this letter gives me an idea—a wonderful idea! Ah, Edmond, my friend, you are not yet captain on board the good ship *Pharaon*."

Then turning toward Edmond, who was walking away, he said, "A pleasant journey."

"Thank you," said Edmond with a friendly nod. And the two lovers continued on their way, as calm and joyous as if Heaven smiled upon them both.

CHAPTER 4
Conspiracy

Danglars and Fernand devise a plot.

Danglars noticed Fernand's pale face and trembling hands.

"Well, my dear sir," said Danglars to Fernand, "here is a marriage which does not appear to make everybody happy."

"It drives me to despair," said Fernand.

"Do you love Mercedes, then?"

"I adore her!"

"And you sit there, tearing your hair, instead of seeking a way to improve the situation. I did not think that was the way of the Catalans."

"What would you have me do?" asked Fernand.

"How do I know? Is it my affair? I am not in love with Mademoiselle Mercedes."

"I would stab the man, but the woman told me that if any misfortune happened to her betrothed, she would kill herself."

"Pooh! Women say those things, but never do them."

"You do not know Mercedes. What she threatens, she will do."

"Idiot!" thought Danglars. "Who cares whether she kills herself or not, as long as Edmond is not captain?"

"I could do nothing that would harm Mercedes," replied Fernand stubbornly. "I would rather die myself."

"That's what I call love!" cried Caderousse, more tipsy than ever. "That's love, or I don't know what love is."

"My dear fellow," replied Danglars, "you are three-quarters drunk. Finish the bottle, and do not meddle with what we are discussing, for it is a matter that requires brains and cool judgment."

"Me, drunk!" said Caderousse, "that's a good one! I could drink four more bottles. Waiter, more wine!" he demanded, rattling his glass upon the table.

"You were saying, sir?" said Fernand.

"What was I saying? I forget. This drunken Caderousse has made me lose my train of thought. Oh yes, the marriage may easily be prevented, I think, without Edmond dying."

"Death alone can separate them," remarked Fernand.

"Absence will separate a couple as well as death," said Danglars. "If the walls of a prison were between Edmond and Mercedes, they would be as effectively separated as if he lay under a tombstone."

"Yes, but one gets out of prison," said Caderousse, who was listening eagerly to the conversation. "And when one gets out and one's name is Edmond Dantes, one seeks revenge. And besides, why should they put Edmond in prison? He has not robbed or killed or murdered."

"We can find a reason to arrest Edmond, I think," said Danglars. "Waiter," he called out, "bring me pen, ink, and paper." The waiter did as he was asked.

"What I think," said Caderousse, letting his hand drop on the paper, "is that this right here is more dangerous than an assassin waiting at a dark street corner. I have always had more dread of a pen, a bottle of ink, and a sheet of paper, than of a sword or pistol."

"The fellow is not so drunk as he appears," said Danglars. "Give him some more wine, Fernand." Fernand filled the glass, and Caderousse, like the confirmed drunkard he was, lifted his hand from the paper and seized the glass.

"Now," continued Danglars, "given the evidence of Edmond stopping at the island of Elba, someone could easily denounce him as a Bonapartist agent."

"I will denounce him!" exclaimed Fernand hastily.

"Yes, but they will make you sign your declaration. Edmond cannot remain in prison forever. One day he will leave, and the day he comes out, he will seek out the man who sent him there."

"Oh, I could wish for nothing better than that he would come to fight me."

"But what about Mercedes? Mercedes will detest you if you so much as scratch the skin of her dearly beloved Edmond!"

"True!" said Fernand.

"No, no," continued Danglars. "It would be much better to write out the accusation like this." With these words, he dipped the pen in the ink and wrote with his left hand, in a style completely unlike his usual one, the following lines,

> The king's attorney is informed by a friend to the throne and that one Edmond Dantes, second in command on board the *Pharaon*, is the bearer of a letter from Murat to the usurper Napoleon, and of another letter from the usurper to the Bonapartist club in Paris. Ample corroboration of this statement may be obtained by arresting the above-mentioned Edmond Dantes, who either carries the letter for Paris about with him, or has it at his father's abode.

He handed the paper to Fernand and said, "See, now there is no way that your revenge can be traced back to you. There is nothing to do now but fold the letter as I am doing, and write upon it, 'To the king's attorney,' and it's all settled." Danglars wrote the address as he spoke and gave it to Fernand to deliver.

CHAPTER 5
The Marriage Feast

Edmond's engagement party is rudely interrupted..

The wedding feast had been prepared in the café. Although the feast was scheduled to begin at twelve o'clock, by eleven the café was filled with impatient guests. They included Edmond's favorites from the crew of the *Pharaon* and other friends of the bride and groom. They were all dressed in their finest clothes.

When M. Morrel appeared, the crew of the *Pharaon* greeted him with enthusiastic applause. Soon afterward the engaged couple, a party of young girls attending the bride, and Edmond's father entered the main dining room. Trailing the group was Fernand, wearing a sinister smile, as well as Danglars and Caderousse. Edmond's father was impressively dressed in a suit of glistening silk, beautifully trimmed with polished steel buttons.

With his handsome face radiant with happiness, the bridegroom was as fine a specimen of manly beauty as could be imagined. With her bright, flashing eyes and ripe coral lips, Mercedes was lovely as a dream.

27

M. Morrel added to the joyfulness by announcing that Edmond would be the captain of the *Pharaon*. Edmond respectfully placed Mercedes's hand in the arm of M. Morrel, who led her up the flight of wooden steps leading to the banquet room. They were followed by the guests.

"Father," said Mercedes to old Dantes, "please sit at my right hand. On my left I will place him who has ever been a beloved brother to me." She pointed with a gentle smile to Fernand, but her words were torture to him.

Edmond, at the opposite side of the table, sat with his most honored guests. M. Morrel was at his right hand and Danglars on his left. Once they had been seated, the other guests sat where they wished.

Edmond exclaimed to no one in particular, "I cannot believe myself worthy of being the husband of Mercedes."

"Careful, now!" cried Caderousse, smiling. "You have not attained that honor yet. Mercedes is not yet your wife. Just try to order her about like a husband, and see how she will remind you that she is not yet yours!"

The bride blushed, while Fernand, restless and uneasy, seemed to jump at every new sound. From time to time he wiped away the large drops of perspiration that gathered on his forehead.

"It's true that Mercedes is not actually my wife," Edmond remarked, "but in just an hour she will be."

An exclamation of surprise ran through all

the guests. Mercedes looked pleased and gratified, while Fernand grasped the handle of his knife under the table.

"In an hour?" inquired Danglars, turning pale. "But surely the actual wedding is tomorrow at the earliest? What do you mean?"

"Thanks to the influence of M. Morrel, to whom, next to my father, I owe thanks for every blessing, we have received permission to bypass the usual delay. At two-thirty the mayor of Marseilles will be waiting for us at the city hall."

Fernand closed his eyes, and he actually had to grip the table to prevent falling from his chair.

"So, what we thought was the engagement feast turns out to be the actual wedding dinner!" said Danglars.

"No, no," answered Edmond. "Don't imagine I am going to treat you all so shabbily. Tomorrow morning I start for Paris. I shall be back by the first of March, and on March second I will give my real marriage feast."

Danglars now looked as pale as Fernand. Unable to sit still, Fernand was among the first to leave the table.

"Shouldn't we set forth?" asked the sweet, silvery voice of Mercedes. "Two o'clock has just struck, and you know we are expected in a quarter of an hour."

"To be sure!" exclaimed Edmond, eagerly leaving the table. "Let us go at once!"

His words were echoed by the whole party, with hearty cheers.

At this moment Danglars saw Fernand stagger and fall back into a seat placed near one of the open windows. At the same instant, his ear caught a sound on the stairs, followed by the clanking of swords. Finally came the hum and buzz of many voices, so noisy as to deaden even the cheerful mirth of the bridal party. Almost instantly the room took on a deathlike stillness.

The guests looked at one other in confusion.

"I demand admittance," said a loud voice outside the room, "in the name of the law!" The door was opened, and a magistrate entered, followed by four soldiers and a corporal.

"What is the reason for this unexpected visit?" asked M. Morrel, who evidently knew the magistrate. "There must be some mistake."

"If that is so," replied the magistrate, "you will receive my deepest apology. Meanwhile, I bear an order of arrest. Which of you is Edmond Dantes?"

Every eye turned toward the young man who, in spite of the terror he could not help but feel, advanced with dignity. He said in a firm voice, "I am he. What is your business with me?"

"Edmond Dantes," replied the magistrate, "I arrest you in the name of the law."

"Me!" repeated Edmond, slightly changing color. "With what cause?"

"I cannot inform you, but you will be told the reasons at the preliminary examination."

Edmond surrendered to the officer saying, "Do not worry, my good friends. There's been some little mistake, that's all. Very likely it will be cleared up before I reach the prison."

"Quite right!" responded Danglars, who had now approached the group. "Nothing more than a mistake, I feel quite certain."

Edmond descended the staircase, trailing the magistrate and followed by the soldiers. A carriage awaited him at the door. He got in, followed by two soldiers and the magistrate, and the vehicle drove off.

"Goodbye, goodbye, dearest Edmond!" cried Mercedes, stretching out her arms to him from the balcony.

The prisoner heard the cry, which sounded like the sob of a broken heart. Leaning from the coach, he called out, "Goodbye, Mercedes—I shall be back soon!" Then the vehicle disappeared around a corner.

"Wait for me here, all of you!" said M. Morrel. "I will hurry to Marseilles and return with information."

"That's right!" exclaimed a multitude of voices. "Go, and return as quickly as you can!"

Morrel went to obtain news about Edmond's imprisonment. Not long after, Morrel reappeared. Mercedes and old Dantes rushed to meet the ship owner at the door. He was very pale.

"What news?" exclaimed a general burst of voices.

"Alas, my friends," replied M. Morrel, "the thing is more serious than I expected."

"Oh, but sir—sir! He is innocent!" sobbed Mercedes.

"That I believe!" answered M. Morrel. "But still he is charged with being an agent of the Bonapartist faction."

A cry escaped Mercedes's lips. Edmond's father sank into a chair.

Caderousse quickly made a hasty departure. After he left, Fernand, who acted as the friend and protector of Mercedes, led the girl to her home. The friends of old Dantes conducted the half-fainting man home as well.

"Meanwhile," observed M. Morrel, "here is the *Pharaon* without a captain."

"Oh," replied Danglars, "we cannot leave this port for three months. Let us hope that before that period ends, Edmond will be free."

"No doubt, but in the meantime?"

"I am entirely at your service, M. Morrel," answered Danglars. "You know that I am as capable of managing a ship as the most experienced captain. I beg you to accept my services. Then when Edmond is released from prison, he and I can resume our usual posts."

"Thanks, Danglars. That will be a great help. I authorize you to assume command of the *Pharaon* at once and to oversee to the unloading of her freight. Private misfortunes must never be allowed to interfere with business."

"Do not worry about a thing, M. Morrel. But when do you think we shall be permitted to see our poor Edmond?"

"I will let you know that as soon I have seen the king's attorney, M. de Villefort. But for now, please

go to the *Pharaon*, and I will join you there soon."
With these words, the ship owner walked off toward
the city hall.

"All has gone as I had hoped," said Danglars
to himself. "I am, temporarily, commander of the
Pharaon, and that will become permanent. My only
fear is that Edmond will be released. But he is in the
hands of justice!" Smiling, he leaped into a rowboat
and ordered himself taken to the *Pharaon*, where
M. Morrel had agreed to meet him.

CHAPTER 6
Another Engagement Party

Gerard de Villefort, king's attorney, also has to leave his engagement party.

In one of the finest mansions in Marseilles, another engagement was being celebrated, almost at the same hour as the one given by Edmond. This one, however, bore little resemblance to that assembly of sailors, soldiers, and other ordinary people. It was made up of the flower of Marseilles society—judges, high-ranking officers, and others who were united by their hatred of Napoleon Bonaparte.

An old man rose and proposed a toast to the present king, Louis XVIII. The gentleman who offered the toast was the bride-to-be's father, the Marquis de Saint-Meran. This toast was met with enthusiasm. Glasses were thrust high in the air, and the ladies tore the flowers from their hair and dresses to scatter on the table. Remarks about "Louis the well-beloved" were heard as often as those referring to "Napoleon the accursed."

"Don't you agree, Villefort?" asked one distinguished older woman—in fact, the Marquise de Saint-Meran—who had been speaking to the young man at her side, her future son-in-law.

"I beg your pardon, madame," he replied. "Forgive me, but I was not paying attention to the conversation."

"Madame, madame!" said the old marquis to his wife, "let the young people alone. On one's engagement day there are more agreeable topics of conversation than politics."

"Dearest mother," said a young and lovely girl, with a mass of light brown hair and eyes that seemed made of liquid crystal. "It's my fault for keeping M. de Villefort from listening to what you said. But there, now take him."

"If you wouldn't mind repeating what you just said, I would be delighted to answer," said M. de Villefort.

"Never mind, Renee," replied the marquise, looking with tenderness upon her lovely daughter. "I forgive you. What I was saying, Villefort, was that the Bonapartists never possessed our sincerity, enthusiasm, or devotion."

"Dear mother," interrupted Renee, "please, at least today, can't we set those disagreeable memories aside?"

"Allow me, madame," added Villefort, "to add my request that you kindly forget the past. For my own part, I have given up even the name of my father, and I completely disown his political beliefs. He was—in fact, he probably still is—a Bonapartist, and is called Noirtier. I, on the contrary, am a strong supporter of the king, and have adopted the name de Villefort."

"Bravo, Villefort!" cried the marquis. "Well said! All I ask," the marquis continued, "is that Villefort be firm and inflexible in his political principles. Remember also, Villefort, that we have recommended you to His Majesty as a person of complete loyalty, and that the king has consented to forget the past, as I do now. But bear in mind, if anyone comes before you who is guilty of conspiring against the government, you must be especially strict against him, since you belong to a suspected family."

"Alas," Villefort answered, "my profession, as well as the times in which we live, forces me to be severe. Marseilles is full of people loyal to Napoleon and who seek his return to power."

A servant entered the room and whispered a few words in his ear. Villefort turned to his fiancée, Renee, and declared, "I cannot call a day my own, not even the day of my engagement."

"What business calls you away?" asked Renee.

"A very serious matter, one which could make work for the executioner."

"How dreadful!" exclaimed Renee, turning pale.

"If my information proves correct, a Bonapartist conspiracy has just been discovered," explained the young man. "Edmond Dantes has been charged with delivering a packet from Murat, the king of Naples, to Napoleon and with taking a letter from Napoleon to Bonapartist agents in Paris. I must go to the police station at the city hall, where Edmond Dantes is being held, at once."

"Oh, Villefort!" She clasped her hands as if in prayer. "Be merciful today, the day of our engagement."

Villefort smiled kindly at her and proceeded to the police station.

CHAPTER 7
The Examination

Villefort learns about a letter Edmond brought from Elba.

As Villefort left the mansion, he assumed the grave air of a man who holds questions of life and death in his hands. This was no easy task, for in general, Gerard de Villefort was as happy as a man could be. Although he was only twenty-seven, he was already rich, and he held a high official position. He was about to marry a charming woman whom he loved, not passionately, but reasonably, as became one of the king's attorneys. Besides her personal attractions, which were very great, Renee de Saint-Meran's family had great political influence, which they would, of course, use in his favor. His fiancée had a dowry of fifty thousand francs, and her fortune would increase to half a million when her father died. All these things, naturally, gave Villefort a feeling of contentment.

At the city hall he met the police captain, who was waiting for him. He immediately said, "Tell me what you have discovered concerning the accused and the conspiracy."

"We know nothing as yet of the conspiracy, monsieur. All the evidence is on your desk."

At this moment, a man approached. It was M. Morrel.

"Ah, M. de Villefort," he cried, "I am delighted to see you. Some of your people have committed the strangest mistake—they have arrested Edmond Dantes, mate of my vessel."

"I know, monsieur," replied Villefort, "and I am now going to question him."

"Oh," said Morrel, carried away by his friendship, "you do not know him, and I do. He is the best, the most trustworthy creature in the world, and there is not a better seaman in all the merchant service. Oh, M. de Villefort, I beg your mercy for him."

Villefort, as we have seen, belonged to the aristocratic society of Marseilles, and Morrel to the common people. The aristocrats supported the king; the commoners supported Napoleon. Morrel, therefore, was suspected of championing Napoleon. Villefort looked disdainfully at Morrel and replied, "You are aware, monsieur, that a man may be trustworthy in private life. He may even be the best seaman in the merchant service, and yet be, politically speaking, a great criminal. You may be sure that I shall perform my duty fairly."

He now coldly said goodbye to the ship owner and entered his office. The foyer was full of policemen. The prisoner, calm and smiling, stood among them. Villefort took the package an officer handed him and said, "Bring the prisoner into my office."

After an instant Edmond entered. He was pale, but calm and collected. After greeting the prosecutor with easy politeness, he looked around for a seat, as if he had been a guest in someone's home. It was then that he encountered for the first time Villefort's cold and steady look.

"Who and what are you?" demanded Villefort.

"My name is Edmond Dantes," replied the young man calmly. "I am mate of the *Pharaon*, belonging to Morrel & Son."

"Your age?" continued Villefort.

"Nineteen," answered Edmond.

"It is reported that your political opinions are extreme," said Villefort. He had never heard anything of the kind, but it was a useful sort of accusation.

"My political opinions!" replied Edmond. "Sir, I never had any opinions. I am barely nineteen. I have only three opinions: I love my father, I respect M. Morrel, and I adore Mercedes." As Edmond spoke, Villefort gazed at his open, friendly face. He remembered the words of Renee, who had begged Villefort to show mercy.

"By God," thought Villefort, "this is a noble fellow. Perhaps I shall gain Renee's favor easily by obeying the first command she ever gave me." Filled with this idea, Villefort's face became soft, and Edmond smiled in return.

"Sir," asked Villefort, "do you have any enemies?"

"Enemies?" replied Edmond. "My position is not high enough for that."

"But there may be those who are jealous of you. You are about to become captain at nineteen—an important post. You are about to marry a pretty girl who loves you. These two pieces of good fortune may have created envy in someone."

"You may be right. You know men better than I do."

"Edmond Dantes, you seem a good young man. I will try to help you discover the author of this accusation. Here is the paper on which it is written. Do you know the writing?" As he spoke, Villefort presented to Edmond the note written by Danglars. Edmond read it. A cloud passed over his brow.

"No, monsieur, I do not recognize the writing."

"Now," said the king's attorney, "answer me frankly. What truth is there in the accusation contained in this unsigned letter?"

"None at all. I will tell you the facts. When we left Naples, Captain Leclere was attacked with a brain fever. We had no doctor on board. He grew more and more ill. At the end of the third day, feeling he was dying, he called me to him. 'My dear Dantes,' he said, 'swear to perform what I am going to tell you, for it is a matter of the deepest importance.'

"'I swear, Captain,' I replied.

"'When I die, take command, and head for the island of Elba. Ask for the grand marshal there, and give him this letter. Perhaps he will give you another letter, and direct you to deliver it.'

"'I will do it, Captain,' I said. The next day he died."

"And what did you do then?"

"I sailed for the island of Elba, where we arrived the next day. I gave the letter to the grand marshal. As the captain had told me, the grand marshal gave me a letter to carry to a person in Paris. I accepted it because it was what my captain had asked me to do. I landed here, arranged the affairs of the vessel, and hurried to visit my fiancée. I was arrested at my engagement feast, just an hour before I was to get married. Tomorrow I intended to start for Paris, had I not been arrested on this charge, which you now see to be unjust."

"Ah," said Villefort, "you seem to be telling the truth. Give me this letter you have brought from Elba, and promise me you will appear if I should need to see you again. Then go and rejoin your friends."

"I am free, then, sir?" cried Edmond joyfully.

"Yes, but first give me this letter."

"You have it already. It is among the papers taken from my house while I was attending my engagement celebration."

"Stop a moment," said Villefort, as Edmond reached for his hat and gloves. "To whom is it addressed?"

"To M. Noirtier, Coq-Heron Street, Paris." If a lightning bolt had fallen into the room, Villefort could not have been more astonished. He sank into his seat, hastily turning over the packet, and drew forth the fatal letter. He looked at it with an expression of terror.

"M. Noirtier, Coq-Heron Street, No. 13," he murmured, growing still paler.

"Yes," said Edmond. "Do you know him?"

"No," replied Villefort. "A faithful servant of the king does not know conspirators. Have you shown this letter to anyone?" asked Villefort, becoming still more pale.

"To no one, on my honor."

"So no soul is aware that you are the bearer of a letter from the island of Elba, and addressed to M. Noirtier?"

"Not a soul, except the person who gave it to me."

Villefort's expression darkened more and more. His lips grew white, and he clenched his teeth. He then read the letter, set it down, and covered his face with his hands. After a few moments, he said to Edmond, "You say that you don't know what this letter says?"

"I give you my word of honor, sir," said Edmond.

Villefort fell back on his chair, passed his hand over his sweating forehead, and once more read the letter.

"Oh, if he knows what this says!" he murmured to himself, "and that Noirtier is my own father, I am lost!" In a voice he tried to keep steady, Villefort said, "Sir, I am no longer able, as I had hoped, to free you immediately. Before doing so, I must consult the trial judge. I must keep you a bit longer, but I will make it as short as possible. The principal charge against you is this letter, and you see—" Villefort approached the fire, threw the letter in, and waited until it was entirely consumed, "you see, I have destroyed it."

"Oh," exclaimed Edmond, "you are goodness itself."

"Listen," continued Villefort. "You can now have confidence in me after what I have done."

"Oh, command, and I will obey."

"This is not a command, but advice I give you."

"Speak, and I will follow your advice."

"I will keep you until this evening here in the city hall. If anyone else questions you, tell him what you have told me, but do not breathe a word about this letter."

"I promise." It was Villefort who seemed to beg, and the prisoner who reassured him.

"You see," he continued, glancing toward the grate, where fragments of burned paper fluttered in the flames, "the letter is destroyed. You and I alone know of its existence. Therefore, if you are questioned, deny all knowledge of it—deny it boldly, and you are saved."

"I will deny it."

Villefort rang the bell. A police officer entered. Villefort whispered some words in his ear, and the officer nodded.

"Follow him," said Villefort to Edmond. Edmond saluted Villefort and left the room. The door had barely closed when Villefort threw himself into a chair, nearly fainting.

"Oh, my God," he murmured, "if the king's lead prosecuting attorney himself had been in Marseilles, I would have been ruined. This accursed letter would have destroyed all my hopes. Oh, my father, must you always interfere with my successes?"

Suddenly a light passed over his face, and a smile played round his set mouth.

"This will do," he said, "and this letter, which might have ruined me, will make my fortune. Now to work." The king's attorney hurried back to the house of his fiancée.

CHAPTER 8
The Chateau d'If

Edmond is taken to an island fortress, the Chateau d'If.

The police captain made a sign to two officers, who placed themselves at Edmond's sides. A door opened, and they went through a long range of gloomy halls. After innumerable turns, Edmond saw a door with an iron lock. The door opened, the two officers gently pushed him forward, and the door closed with a loud clank behind him. He was in prison.

Edmond waited uneasily in his cell for several hours. At the slightest sound, he rose and hurried to the door, convinced they were about to free him. However, each time the sound died away, and Edmond sank again into his seat. At last, about ten o'clock, steps were heard in the corridor, a key turned in the lock, the massive oaken door flew open, and a flood of light from two torches filled the room. By the torchlight Edmond saw the glittering rifles of four officers.

"Are you here to fetch me?" he asked.

"Yes," replied an officer.

"By the orders of the king's attorney?"

"I believe so." The knowledge that they came

from M. de Villefort relieved all Edmond's fear. He advanced calmly, and the escort closed around him. A carriage waited at the door. The coachman was on the seat, and a police officer sat beside him.

"Is this carriage for me?" said Edmond.

"It is for you," replied an officer.

Edmond was urged forward. He mounted the steps and was seated inside between two officers. The two others took their places opposite, and the carriage rolled heavily over the stones.

The prisoner glanced at the windows. They were heavily barred. Through the bars, however, Edmond saw they were approaching the port.

The carriage stopped, and a detachment of soldiers escorted Edmond to a small boat. They all got on board and boat shoved off, four sturdy oarsmen rowing it rapidly.

The prisoner's first feeling was of joy at again breathing the pure air—for air is freedom. But he soon sighed, for he passed by the café where he had that morning been so happy. Edmond folded his hands, raised his eyes to heaven, and prayed deeply.

The boat continued its voyage.

"Where are you taking me?" he asked.

"You will soon know."

"But still—"

"We are forbidden to give you any explanation." Edmond knew there was no point in questioning these men, and so he remained silent.

The boat went on, but the prisoner thought only of Mercedes. A jutting cliff hid the light, and Edmond turned and realized that they had gotten out to sea. While he had been absorbed in thought, they had stored their oars and hoisted sail. The boat was now moving with the wind.

After some time, Edmond looked around. He saw, rising within a hundred yards, the black and forbidding rock on which stands the stone fortress called the Chateau d'If. This gloomy stronghold looked to Edmond like a house of death.

"The Chateau d'If?" he said, surprised. "What are we going there for?"

The officer smiled.

"I cannot be going there to be imprisoned," said Edmond. "It is used only for political prisoners. I have committed no crime. Are there any magistrates or judges at the Chateau d'If?"

"There are only a governor, a warden, turnkeys, and good thick walls," said the officer.

The prisoner asked, "Am I being taken to the Chateau d'If to be imprisoned?"

"It is probable."

"In spite of M. de Villefort's promises?"

"I do not know what M. de Villefort promised you," said the officer, "but I know we are taking you to the Chateau d'If."

At those words, Edmond sprang forward in an attempt to throw himself into the sea, but four muscular arms seized him. He fell back, cursing with rage.

"Good!" said the officer, placing a knee on his chest. "If you move, I will blow your brains out." And he leveled his gun at Edmond, who felt the muzzle against his temple. Edmond gnashed his teeth and wrung his hands with fury.

The boat landed with a violent shock. His guards seized him by the arms and coat collar and dragged him toward the steps leading to the gate of the fortress. The soldiers escorted him up some stone stairs and into a dimly lit room that seemed built partially underground. A grim-faced man entered and stated, "You'll stay here tonight. It is late, and the governor is asleep. Tomorrow he may move you. In the meantime there is bread, water, and fresh straw to sleep on. That is all a prisoner can wish for. Good night."

Edmond was alone in darkness and in silence. With the first light of dawn, the jailer returned with orders to leave Edmond where he was. He found the prisoner standing in the same position, as if paralyzed there, his eyes swollen with weeping.

"Didn't you sleep?" asked the jailer.

"I do not know," replied Edmond. The jailer stared.

"Are you hungry?" he continued.

"I do not know."

"Do you want anything?"

"I want to see the governor." The jailer shrugged his shoulders and left the room.

All of Edmond's emotions then burst out. He cast himself on the ground, weeping bitterly, at a loss as to what crime he was being punished for.

The day passed. He ate nothing, but walked around the cell like a wild beast in its cage.

The next morning at the same hour, the jailer came again.

"Well," said the jailer, "are you more reasonable today?"

Edmond did not answer.

"Come, cheer up. Is there anything that I can do for you?"

"I wish to see the governor."

"That is impossible."

"Why is it impossible?"

"Because it is against prison rules."

"What is allowed, then?"

"Better food, if you pay for it. Books, and permission to walk about."

"I do not want books, I am satisfied with my food, and I do not want to walk about. I wish to see the governor."

"If you annoy me by repeating the same thing, I will not bring you any more to eat."

"Well, then," said Edmond, "if you do not, I shall die of hunger."

The jailer saw that Edmond would be happy to die. As he gained his pay according to the number of his prisoners he tended, he replied more gently, "What you ask is impossible. But if you are very well behaved, you will be allowed to walk about, and some day you might meet the governor."

"How long shall I have to wait?"

"Oh, I cannot say. A month—six months—a year."

"That is too long. I need to see him at once."

"Ah," said the jailer, "do not obsess about what is impossible, or you will go mad in no time."

"You think so?"

"Yes. I will give you an example. The priest who was in this room before you was always offering the governor great sums of money in exchange for his freedom. That eventually drove him mad."

"Was he freed, then?"

"No, he was put in a dungeon."

"Listen!" said Edmond. "I am not a priest, and I am not mad, although I may be soon."

"Wait a moment," said the jailer, who walked away from the cell. Edmond's hopes rose.

Soon the jailer returned with four soldiers. "Take this prisoner to the dungeons," he ordered. "The madman must be with the others of his kind." The soldiers seized Edmond, who went with them without protest.

He descended fifteen steps. One of the soldiers unlocked the door of the dungeon and thrust Edmond in. The door closed, and Edmond advanced with outstretched hands until he touched the wall. He sat down in the corner until his eyes became accustomed to the darkness. The jailer was right. Edmond was very close to being mad.

CHAPTER 9
The Evening of the Betrothal

Mercedes and Morrel try to obtain Edmond's release.

Villefort had hurried back to the home of his fiancée. He found the guests gathered over their coffee in the library. All were anxiously awaiting his arrival, and a chorus of excited comments greeted him.

"Marquise," said Villefort, approaching his future mother-in-law, "forgive me for leaving you so abruptly. Sir," he said, addressing the marquis, "may I have a few moments' private conversation?"

"It is really a serious matter, then?" asked the marquis.

"So serious that I must leave you for a few days." Turning to Renee, he added, "You know I would not do so if I could avoid it."

Once the two men were alone, the marquis anxiously asked, "Well, tell me. What is it?"

"An affair of the greatest importance, which demands my immediate presence in Paris. I must see the king. I tell you, marquis, my fortune is made if I reach his majesty promptly. He will not forget the service I can do for him. I must leave immediately. Please present my excuses to the marquise and

Mademoiselle Renee, whom I leave on such a day with great regret."

Villefort hastily left the mansion and went to his own house to gather up some necessities for the journey. At the door of his house, he noticed someone waiting for him in the shadows. It was Mercedes. Hearing no news of Edmond, she had come to inquire after him.

As Villefort drew near, she stepped out before him and asked about her fiancé.

"The young man you speak of," said Villefort coldly, "is a great criminal. I can do nothing for him, mademoiselle."

Mercedes burst into tears. "At least tell me where he is, that I may know whether he is alive or dead," she begged.

"I do not know. He is no longer in my hands," replied Villefort.

He pushed by her and closed his door, as if to shut out the pain he felt. But remorse is not so easily banished. The first pangs of an unending torture had seized his heart. The man he had sacrificed on the altar of his ambition appeared in his mind's eye. Here was an innocent man whose happiness he had destroyed.

Meanwhile, Mercedes had met Fernand as she returned home, where she had despairingly collapsed on her couch. Fernand, kneeling by her side, took her hand and covered it with kisses that Mercedes did not even feel. She sat like that all night. The lamp burned its store of oil and went out, but she did not notice. Dawn came, but she did not see the light. Grief had made her blind to all but one object—Edmond.

M. Morrel had not readily given up the fight. He had learned that Edmond had been taken to prison. He went to all his most influential friends to get him released, but they would do nothing to free a suspected Bonapartist conspirator. M. Morrel returned home in despair, declaring that nothing more could be done.

Caderousse was equally restless and uneasy. But instead of seeking to aid Edmond, he shut himself up with two bottles of black currant brandy, in the hope of drowning his thoughts. He did not succeed.

Only Danglars was content and joyous. He had gotten rid of an enemy and made his own situation on the *Pharaon* secure. He went to bed at his usual hour, and slept in peace.

CHAPTER 10
The Hundred Days

Time passes. Villefort prospers; others are not so fortunate.

The history of what happened next is well documented. Villefort informed King Louis XVIII of a plot to return Napoleon to the throne. In fact, Napoleon did return and unseated Louis, but only for one hundred days. After Napoleon lost the Battle of Waterloo in 1815, Louis regained the throne of France. Villefort obtained a high position in the city of Toulouse. Two weeks later, he married Renee de Saint-Meran, whose father, the marquis, was now extremely influential at court.

And so, after the Hundred Days and Waterloo, Edmond remained forgotten in his dungeon. Upon Napoleon's brief return to power, Danglars' courage failed him. He lived in constant fear of Edmond's return. He left M. Morrel's employ and entered the service of a Spanish merchant.

All that Fernand knew was that Edmond was gone. What had become of him, he did not want to know. He watched constantly for Edmond's reappearance on a mission of vengeance. His devotion to Mercedes, and the compassion he showed for her misfortunes, made her grateful to him. When he was at last called to active military service, she spoke fondly to him. "My cousin," she said, as she placed his knapsack on his shoulders, "take care of yourself, for if you are killed, I shall be alone in the world." These words carried a ray of hope into Fernand's heart. If Edmond did not return, perhaps Mercedes might one day be his.

Mercedes was left alone. Often she stared at the sea, wondering if it would not be better to throw herself in. Caderousse was, like Fernand, drafted into the army. Old Dantes, who had been surviving only on hope, lost his will to live when Napoleon fell. Five months after he had been separated from his son, he died, penniless and starving, in Mercedes's arms. M. Morrel paid the expenses of his funeral and the few small debts the poor old man had contracted.

For M. Morrel, there was more than kindness in this action. There was courage, too. In these troubled times, to assist the dying father of an accused Bonapartist such as Edmond Dantes was regarded as a crime.

CHAPTER 11
Number 34 and Number 27

It is six years later. Edmond hears unusual sounds from a neighboring dungeon.

The old governor of the prison was transferred and a new one took his place. This one found it too troublesome to learn the names of the prisoners, so he gave them numbers instead, corresponding to the numbers of their cells. Edmond Dantes no longer was Edmond Dantes. He was now Number 34.

Now in his sixth year of confinement, Edmond had passed through all the usual stages that prisoners endure, finally turning to religion. He remembered the prayers his mother had taught him, and he discovered a new meaning in every word. He prayed aloud, no longer terrified at the sound of his own voice, and his prayers sometimes brought him serenity. He laid every action of his life before the Almighty, and ended every prayer by saying, "Forgive us our trespasses as we forgive them that trespass against us." But in spite of his earnest prayers, Edmond remained a prisoner.

Losing all hope, Edmond said to himself, "I wish to die." He even chose how he would die. "When my meals are brought," he promised himself, "I will throw them out the barred window into the sea, and they will think that I have eaten."

He kept his word. Twice a day he threw out the food his jailer brought him. He did it at first cheerfully, then gravely, and finally with regret. Hunger made the repulsive prison food seem desirable. Once, he held the plate in his hand for an hour, gazing thoughtfully at the morsel of bad meat, spoiled fish, and moldy bread. His instinctive yearnings for life urged him to eat. He was still young, only 24 or 25. He had many years to live.

What unforeseen events might open his prison door and free him? He raised the food to his lips, but he did not eat. He starved himself until, at last, he did not have the strength to get up and throw his food out the window. The next morning he could not see or hear. Edmond hoped he was at death's door.

The day crept on. Edmond felt a stupor creeping over him. The feeling was almost like contentment. The gnawing pain in his stomach had eased. His thirst had lessened. When he closed his eyes, he saw lights dancing before them. He felt as though he were crawling toward the doorway of death.

Suddenly, about nine o'clock in the evening, Edmond heard a hollow sound in the wall next to his bed. So many disgusting furry animals lived in the prison that he rarely noticed their noises anymore. But hunger had sharpened his hearing, or perhaps the noise was really louder than usual. Edmond raised his head and listened. It was a continual scratching, as if made by a huge claw, a powerful tooth, or some iron instrument attacking the stones.

The noise continued for nearly three hours. He then heard something fall, and all was silent.

Some hours later it began again, nearer and more distinct. Edmond was intensely interested.

"There is no doubt about it," he thought. "It is some prisoner, working to free himself. Oh, if only I could help him!" Then another idea occurred to him. Perhaps the noise was only made by workmen repairing the neighboring dungeon. But how could he be sure? He was too feeble with hunger to think clearly.

There was only one way to make his mind clear again. He seized the soup which the jailer had brought, raised it to his lips, and drank it with indescribable pleasure. He no longer wanted to die. As strength began to return to his body, he was able to form a plan.

"I will knock on the wall," he said to himself. "If it is a workman, he will stop for a moment in order to find out who is knocking. But then he will continue. If, on the other hand, it is a prisoner, the noise I make will alarm him. He will stop working, and not begin again until he thinks every one is asleep."

Edmond staggered to his feet. He went to a corner of his dungeon, detached a stone, and with it knocked three times against the wall where the sound came. At his first blow the sound ceased.

Edmond listened intently. An hour passed, two hours, and no sound was heard from the wall—all was silent.

Full of hope, Edmond swallowed a few mouthfuls of bread and water. Thanks to his youth and strength, he soon found himself nearly recovered.

The day passed away in utter silence—night came without recurrence of the noise.

"It is a prisoner," said Edmond joyfully. The night passed in complete silence. Edmond did not close his eyes.

In the morning the jailer brought him more food. He ate, listening anxiously for the sound. He grew impatient at the silence of the other prisoner, who did not guess he had been disturbed by a captive as anxious for liberty as himself.

Finally, on the third evening, Edmond imagined he heard an almost imperceptible movement among the stones. He walked up and down his cell to collect his thoughts. Then he went back and listened.

There was no longer any doubt. Something was at work on the other side of the wall.

Encouraged by this discovery, Edmond decided to assist the laborer. He began by looking around for anything he could use to loosen the moist cement and displace a stone.

He saw nothing. He had no knife or sharp instrument. His furniture consisted of a bed, a chair, a table, a pail, and a jug—nothing with a sharp edge. Edmond raised the jug and let it fall on the floor. It broke into pieces. He concealed two or three of the sharpest fragments in his bed, leaving the rest on the floor.

When day came, the jailer entered. Edmond told him that he had dropped the jug while he was drinking. The jailer, grumbling, went to fetch another, without bothering to remove the fragments of the broken one. Edmond waited for the sound of the jailer's shuffling feet to die away. Then he began attacking the plaster that surrounded the stones of the floor.

The damp had made the plaster soft, and Edmond was able to break off small pieces. At the end of half an hour he had scraped off a handful. He calculated that in two years, supposing he did not run into rock, he might dig out a passage twenty feet long.

After three days of careful work, he had succeeded in removing some of the cement that covered the underlying stones. Now he had to figure out how to remove stones from their sockets. Edmond tried to do it with his nails, but they were too weak. The fragments of the jug broke, and after an hour of useless work, he paused in despair.

Was he going to be stopped at the beginning of his task? Could he only wait idly until his unknown fellow workman had completed the job? Suddenly an idea occurred to him—he smiled.

The jailer always brought Edmond's soup in an iron saucepan and poured it into a porcelain dish. The handle of this saucepan was of iron. Edmond would have given ten years of his life in exchange for it.

When evening came, Edmond put his plate on the ground near the door. As the jailer entered, he stepped on the plate and broke it. In disgust, the jailer told Edmond to keep the metal saucepan.

Edmond was beside himself with joy. He rapidly devoured his food. He then took the handle of the saucepan, inserted the point between the stones of the wall, and used it as a lever. At the end of an hour, he had removed a stone from the wall, leaving a hole a foot and a half in diameter.

Edmond carefully collected the plaster, carried it into the corner of his cell, and buried it in earth. Then he continued to work without ceasing. At dawn he replaced the stone, pushed his bed against the wall, and lay down pretending to sleep until the jailer arrived. Breakfast consisted of a piece of bread, which Edmond greedily consumed. He had noticed, however, that the prisoner on the other side seemed to have stopped working. No matter— if his neighbor would not come to him, he would go to his neighbor. All day he worked. By evening he had removed ten handfuls of plaster and fragments of stone.

When it was time for his jailer's visit, Edmond straightened the handle of the saucepan as well as he could, and put it in its usual place. The turnkey poured his ration of soup into it and left. Edmond wanted to know whether his neighbor had really ceased to work. He listened—all was silent, as it had been for the last three days. Edmond sighed. It was evident that his neighbor did not trust him. However, he worked on all night without being discouraged, but after two or three hours he encountered an obstacle. His iron tool had no effect on it. It was necessary to dig above or below it.

This discovery made Edmond very unhappy. He spoke aloud: "Oh my God, my God! I have so earnestly prayed to you that I hoped my prayers had been heard. After having denied me my liberty, after having denied me death, after having recalled me to life, my God, have pity on me. Do not let me die in despair!"

"Who talks of God and despair at the same time?" said a voice that seemed to come from beneath the earth.

Edmond's hair stood on end. "I hear a human voice," Edmond gasped. He had not heard anyone except his jailer for four or five years.

There was no response.

"In the name of heaven," cried Edmond, "speak again, though the sound of your voice terrifies me. Who are you?"

"Who are *you*?" said the voice.

"An unhappy prisoner," Edmond replied.

"Of what country?"

"A Frenchman."

"Your name?"

"Edmond Dantes."

"Your profession?"

"A sailor."

"How long have you been here?"

"Since the 28th of February, 1815."

"Your crime?"

"I am innocent."

"But of what are you accused?"

"Of having conspired to aid the emperor's return."

"What! For the emperor's return? The emperor is no longer on the throne, then?"

"He gave up his throne in 1814, and was sent to the island of Elba. But how long have you been here that you are ignorant of all this?"

"Since 1811."

Edmond shuddered. This man had been in prison four years longer than himself.

"Do not dig any more," said the voice. "Only tell me how high off the floor you are working."

"It is level with the floor."

"How is it hidden?"

"Behind my bed."

"Has your bed been moved since you have been a prisoner?"

"No."

"What does your cell open onto?"

"A corridor."

"And the corridor?"

"Onto a court."

"Alas!" murmured the voice.

"What is the matter?" asked Edmond.

"I have made a mistake. I took the wrong angle, and have come out fifteen feet from where I intended. I believed the wall that you are working on was the outer wall of the fortress."

"Then you would have been close to the sea?"

"That is what I hoped."

"And supposing you had succeeded?"

"I would have jumped into the sea, and swum to one of the islands near here. Then I would have been safe. But now all is lost. And you—you must hide your digging carefully. Do not work any more until you hear from me."

"Tell me, at least, who you are?"

"I am—I am Number 27."

"I am 34. But I see you do not trust me," said Edmond. He heard a bitter laugh come from the earth, and he was filled with fear that the man would abandon him. He continued hastily, "But do not leave me. Come to me, or let me come to you. We will escape, and if we cannot escape, we will talk. You will speak of those you love, and I of those I love. You must love somebody?"

"No, I am alone in the world."

"Then you will love me. If you are young, I will be your friend. If you are old, I will be your son. I have a father who is seventy if he is still alive. I love only him and a young girl named Mercedes. My father has not yet forgotten me, I am sure, but God knows if Mercedes still loves me. I shall love you as I loved my father."

"Very well," returned the voice. "Tomorrow."

Edmond rose, hid his rubble as before, and pushed his bed back against the wall. He then gave himself up to happiness. He would no longer be alone. He was, perhaps, about to regain his freedom. At the worst, he would have a companion.

The next morning Edmond heard three knocks on the stones.

"Is your jailer gone?" asked the voice.

"Yes," said Edmond. "He will not return until evening, so we have twelve hours."

"I can work, then?" said the voice.

"Oh, yes, yes! This instant. I beg you."

In a moment that part of the floor on which Edmond was resting his hands suddenly gave way. He leaped back, while a mass of stones and earth disappeared in a hole that opened beneath the area where he had dug. Then from the bottom of this passage he saw appear, first the head, then the shoulders, and finally the body of a man, who sprang lightly into his cell.

CHAPTER 12
A Learned Italian

Edmond meets a fellow prisoner, the Abbé Faria.

Edmond seized in his arms the friend he had so long
desired. He was a small man, with hair turned white
by suffering and sorrow rather than by age. His
eyes were deep-set and penetrating, almost buried
beneath the thick gray eyebrows. A long (and still
black) beard reached to his chest. His thin face,
deeply lined by care, and his strong features gave
him the look of one whose work was mental rather
than physical. Great drops of perspiration were
standing on his brow, and the garments he wore
were so ragged that one could only guess at their
original shape.

The stranger might have been sixty or sixty-
five, but a certain briskness in his movements
suggested that he was a younger man. He seemed
greatly pleased by the enthusiastic greeting
of his young acquaintance, although he must
have been bitterly disappointed to find another
dungeon where he had thought to find the
open sea.

"Let us first see," he said, "whether it is possible to hide the traces of my entrance here. Our future depends upon our jailers being ignorant of it." Going to the opening that Edmond had made, he stooped and fitted the stone back into place, saying, "You removed this stone very carelessly, but I suppose you had no tools to help you."

"Do you have tools?" asked Edmond with astonishment.

"I made myself some. Except for a file, I have all that are necessary—a chisel, pincers, and a lever."

"Oh, how I should like to see them."

"Well, in the first place, here is my chisel." He displayed a sharp strong blade, with a handle made of beechwood.

"And how did you make that?" inquired Edmond.

"With one of the clamps from my bed. This tool allowed me to hollow out the tunnel by which I came here, a distance of about fifty feet. To think that all my work has been in vain. And so the will of God be done."

"Tell me, who are you?" Edmond asked. "I have never met anyone like you."

"I am the Abbé Faria, and I have been imprisoned here since 1811. Before that I was confined for three years in a fortress. I have been in prison all these years because of my political views."

"How have you occupied your mind and kept your sanity?"

"I wrote or studied."

"They gave you pens, ink, and paper?"

"Oh, no," answered Faria. "I made my own."

"You made paper, pens and ink?"

"Yes."

Edmond stared with wonder and admiration.

"When you pay me a visit in my cell, my young friend," said Faria, "I will show you my work. It is the fruits of the thoughts and reflections of my whole life. My work is titled *A Treatise on the Possibility of a General Monarchy in Italy*."

"What have you written all this on?"

"On two of my shirts. I invented a preparation that makes linen as smooth and as easy to write on as paper."

"Are you a chemist, then?"

"An amateur."

"And how did you manage to write the work you speak of, if you had no pens?"

"I made myself some excellent pens. You know that we are served fish three times a week. I used material from the fish heads to create my pens."

"But the ink?" said Edmond.

"There was once a fireplace in my dungeon," replied Faria, "but it was closed up long before I came here. Still, it must have been in use for many years, for it was thickly covered with a coat of soot. I dissolved this soot in a portion of the wine I am given every Sunday, and I assure you I could not desire a better ink. For very important notes I pricked one of my fingers, and wrote with my own blood."

"And when may I see all this?"

"Whenever you please," replied Faria.

"Oh, then, let it be now!" exclaimed the young man.

"Follow me, then," said the priest, and he reentered his underground tunnel, followed by Edmond.

CHAPTER 13
The Abbé's Chamber

Edmond tells Faria his story.

After having crawled through the passage, the two friends were able to enter Faria's dungeon. Edmond looked around eagerly, but he saw nothing unusual.

"Where are all these writing items you just described?" Edmond asked.

Faria smiled. Moving to the unused fireplace, he used his chisel to pry up a large odd-shaped stone. Beneath that was a hole of considerable depth. This served as a vault for the articles he had mentioned to Edmond.

"What are you thinking about?" asked Faria with a smile, noting the absorbed expression on Edmond's face.

"In the first place, I was thinking how enormously intelligent you are. What might you have accomplished if you had been free?" replied Edmond.

"Possibly nothing at all," the priest replied. "In a state of freedom, I might have frittered everything away. Misfortune is needed to bring out the treasures of the human intellect. But you were thinking of something else as well, didn't you say?"

"I did!"

"Let me hear the other."

"It was this. You have told me something about your past life, but you know nothing about mine."

"Your life has been so short, my young friend."

"It has been long enough for me to suffer a great and undeserved misfortune. I want to know what man to blame, so that I can stop blaming heaven."

"Then you say you are innocent of the crime with which you are charged?"

"I do, indeed. I swear it by the two people most dear to me on earth—my father and Mercedes."

"Well, then, come," said the priest, closing his hiding place, and pushing the bed back to its original place. "Let me hear your story."

Edmond obeyed and began his tale. He went quickly over his past, until he arrived at the story of his last cruise, the death of Captain Leclere, and the receipt of a packet to be delivered to the grand marshal. He told of his visit to Elba and of receiving a letter there addressed to a M. Noirtier. He described his arrival at Marseilles, and his talk with his father. He dwelled about his affection for Mercedes, and described their engagement feast in great detail. And finally he came to his arrest and questioning, his temporary detention at the city hall jail, and his final imprisonment in the Chateau d'If. From that point on everything was a blank to Edmond—he knew nothing more, not even the length of time he had been imprisoned.

When his story was done, Faria thought long and hard. Finally, he spoke. "It is often fruitful, in trying to discover who is responsible for a bad action, to ask this: 'Who did this action benefit?'" said Faria. "Let us apply the question to your case. Who could have profited from your disappearance?"

"No one, by heaven! I was a very insignificant person."

"Not so! Everything is relative, my dear young friend. The king stands in the way of his successor, and the employee holds the job his assistant wants. Now let us think about your particular world. You say you were about to be made captain of the *Pharaon*?"

"Yes."

"And about to become the husband of a young and lovely girl?"

"Yes."

"Now, could anyone have benefited from preventing you from accomplishing these two things? Let us look at the first question—that of your being captain of the *Pharaon*. What do you say?"

"There was only one person among the crew who resented me. I had quarreled with him once and had even challenged him to fight me, but he refused."

"Now we are getting somewhere. What was this man's name?"

"Danglars."

"What rank did he hold on board?"

"He was the officer in charge of the cargo."

"Now then, tell me, was anyone present during your last conversation with Captain Leclere?"

"No, we were quite alone."

"Could your conversation have been overheard by anyone?"

"Perhaps, for the cabin door was open. Wait! Now I remember—Danglars himself passed by just as Captain Leclere was giving me the packet for the grand marshal."

"That's better," said Faria. "Now we are on the scent. Did you take anybody with you when you went on shore at Elba?"

"Nobody."

"Somebody there took your packet, and gave you a letter in place of it, I think?"

"Yes, the grand marshal did."

"And what did you do with that letter?"

"I carried it back on to the ship."

"So that when you went on board the ship, everybody could see that you held a letter in your hand?"

"Yes."

"Danglars, as well as the rest?"

"Danglars, as well as others."

Faria shrugged his shoulders. "The thing is clear as day," he said. "You must have a very trusting nature, as well as a good heart, not to have suspected where the whole affair originated."

"Do you really think so? Ah, that would indeed be wicked. But it was not in Danglars' handwriting. I would have recognized that."

"How was the anonymous letter written?"

"The letters leaned backwards."

Again the priest smiled. "Disguised. Let us proceed to the second question," he said.

"Oh, yes, yes!"

"Was there any person who might wish to prevent your marriage with Mercedes?"

"Yes, a young man who loved her."

"And his name was—"

"Fernand."

"Can you imagine him writing the letter?"

"No, I cannot. He would more likely have got rid of me by sticking a knife into me. Besides," said Edmond, "he knew nothing of the facts mentioned in the letter."

"You had never spoken of them yourself to anyone?"

"To no one."

"Then it is Danglars."

"I feel quite sure of it now."

"Was Danglars acquainted with Fernand?"

"No. But—wait, yes, he was. Now I recollect—"

"What?"

"I saw them sitting at a café table together the evening before the day I was to be married. They were talking earnestly. Danglars was joking in a friendly way, but Fernand looked pale and agitated."

"Were they alone?"

"There was a third person with them, a man I knew well. He had probably introduced them. He was a tailor named Caderousse, but he was very drunk. Oh! How strange that this should not have occurred to me before! Now I remember that on the table at which they were sitting, there were pens, ink, and paper. Oh, the heartless, treacherous scoundrels!" exclaimed Edmond, pressing his hand to his throbbing forehead.

"Is there anything else I can assist you in discovering, besides the villainy of your friends?" asked Faria with a laugh.

"Yes, yes," replied Edmond eagerly. "I beg of you, to whom the greatest mystery seems but an easy riddle, to explain something to me. Why was I never questioned a second time? Why was I never brought to trial? Why was I sent here without ever having been convicted of a crime?"

"That is altogether a more serious matter," responded the priest. "If you wish me to investigate the more difficult part of the business, you must assist me by providing the tiniest details."

"Please, ask me anything. Truly, you see more clearly into my life than I do myself."

"In the first place, then, who questioned you— the king's attorney, or a magistrate?"

"The attorney."

"Was he young or old?"

"Twenty-six or seven, I would say."

"So," answered Faria. "Old enough to be ambitious, but too young to be corrupt. And how did he treat you?"

"Very mildly."

"Did you tell him your whole story?"

"I did."

"Did his behavior change at all as you talked?"

"He seemed very disturbed when he read the

letter that had brought me into this trouble. He appeared quite overcome by my misfortune."

"By *your* misfortune?"

"Yes."

"You feel quite sure that it was your misfortune that disturbed him?"

"Indeed, he did something quite extraordinary as proof of his sympathy. He burned the only evidence that could have incriminated me."

"He burned the letter?"

"I saw it done."

"This changes everything. This man might be a greater scoundrel than you have thought possible."

"Upon my word," said Edmond, "you make me shudder. Is the world filled with tigers and crocodiles?"

"Yes. And remember that two-legged tigers and crocodiles are more dangerous than the others. But let us go on. You tell me he burned the letter?"

"He did. He said at the same time, 'You see I am destroying the only proof existing against you.'"

"This action is somewhat too heavenly to be natural. To whom was this letter addressed?"

"To M. Noirtier, No. 13 Coq-Heron Street, Paris."

"Now, can you think of any reason that your heroic king's attorney could have wanted that letter destroyed?"

"It is not impossible that he had a reason, for he made me promise never to speak of the letter to anyone. He assured me that this was for my own good."

"Noirtier!" murmured Faria. "Noirtier! I knew a person of that name—yes, there was a Noirtier. . . . And what was name of this king's attorney?"

"De Villefort."

Faria burst into a fit of laughter, while Edmond gazed on him in utter astonishment.

"You poor fellow! Poor, poor young man!" the priest exclaimed, nearly choking with mixed laughter and anger. "You poor short-sighted simpleton. Can't you guess who this Noirtier was, whose name he was so careful to keep concealed? Noirtier was Villefort's father."

If a thunderbolt had fallen at Edmond's feet, he could not have been more completely horror-struck than he was at these words. Jumping up, he clasped his hands to his head as though to prevent his brain from bursting, exclaiming, "His father! His father!"

"Yes, his father," replied the priest. "His original name was Noirtier de Villefort."

At this instant a bright light shot through Edmond's mind, clearing up all that had been dark and obscure before. He thought of the change that had come over Villefort during the interrogation; the destruction of the letter; the promises; the almost begging tones of the king's attorney—all returned with stunning force to his memory. He cried out and then hurried out of Faria's cell, saying, "I must be alone to think all this over."

Back in his dungeon, Edmond threw himself on his bed. During his evening visit, the jailer found him quiet and motionless as a statue. Eventually, the voice of Faria interrupted the younger man's thoughts, inviting Edmond to share his supper.

When the two returned to the priest's cell, Faria looked carefully at Edmond. "I am sorry now," he said, "that I gave you the information I did."

"Why is that?" inquired Edmond.

"Because it has implanted a new passion in your heart—the passion of vengeance."

Edmond smiled. "Let us talk of something else," he said. "You must teach me some of what you know, otherwise, you surely will grow bored with me."

Faria smiled. "My boy," he said, "when I have taught you mathematics, physics, history, and the modern languages that I speak, you will know as much as I do myself."

"Well, then," said Edmond, "I am in a hurry to begin. I want to learn."

That very evening the prisoners sketched out a plan of education, to be started the following day.

Edmond had a wonderful memory, combined with a quick and ready intelligence. At the end of a year, Edmond was a new man. Toward the end of that period, Edmond noticed that the Abbé Faria grew sadder and more troubled every day. Sometimes he would fall into long daydreams, sigh heavily, then suddenly rise and begin pacing the confined space of his dungeon.

One day much later, Faria asked Edmond, "Are you strong?" In reply, the young man picked up the iron chisel, bent it into the shape of a horseshoe, and then straightened it.

"And will you promise not to do any harm to the sentry, except as a last resort?"

"I promise on my honor."

"Then," said the abbé, "we may hope to put my plan of escape to work."

"How long will it take?"

"At least a year."

"Shall we begin at once?"

"At once." Faria then showed Edmond the notes he had made as he planned their escape. Edmond's eyes sparkled with joy. He rubbed his hands with delight at the idea of a plan so simple, yet seeming so likely to succeed.

That very day they began their work. Nothing interrupted their labors except the necessity of returning to the cells in time for the jailer's visits. At the end of fifteen months, the work was finished.

Edmond was busy arranging a piece of wood when he heard Faria call to him in a voice of anguish. Edmond rushed to his dungeon, where he found the priest standing in the middle of the room, pale as death, his forehead streaming with perspiration and his hands clenched.

"Gracious heavens!" exclaimed Edmond. "What is the matter? What has happened?"

"Quick! Quick!" answered Faria. "Listen to what I have to say." Edmond looked in fear and wonder at the priest's chalk-white face. His eyes, dull and sunken, were surrounded by purple circles, while his lips were pale as those of a corpse.

"Alas," Faria said weakly, "all is over with me. I am terribly ill. I can feel a seizure approaching."

So sudden was the seizure that the unfortunate prisoner was unable to complete a sentence. A violent convulsion shook his whole body. His eyes bulged from their sockets. His mouth was drawn down one side, and his cheeks became purple. He struggled, foamed at the mouth, and threw himself about, uttering the most dreadful cries. Edmond muffled the noise as best he could by covering the priest's head with his blanket.

The fit lasted two hours. Then, more helpless than an infant, and colder and paler than marble, Faria fell back, as rigid as a corpse.

Finally a slight flush of color appeared on the priest's cheeks. Light began returning to the dull, open eyes. A faint sigh came from the lips, and he made a feeble effort to move.

"He lives! He lives!" Edmond exclaimed in delight.

The sick man was barely able to speak. "My good Edmond," Faria gasped, "this attack has condemned me to be a prisoner forever. I cannot escape if I cannot walk."

"Well, we will wait—a week, a month, two months, if need be—and your strength will return. Everything is ready for our flight, and we can select any time we choose. As soon as you feel able to swim, we will go."

"I will never swim again," replied Faria. "My arm is paralyzed, not for a time, but forever. Believe me, I know what I am saying. Since my first attack,

I have expected another. It is a family inheritance. Both my father and grandfather died of it."

"No," cried Edmond. "As for your poor arm, what difference will that make? I can take you on my back and swim for both of us."

"My son," said Faria, "you know as well as I do that a man so encumbered would sink before he had done fifty strokes. Do not deceive yourself with impossible hopes, no matter how excellent your heart is. I shall remain here until the hour of my death. But for you, who are young and active, do not delay, not on my account. Go! Escape!"

"No, I shall also remain," Edmond declared. "By the blood of Christ, I swear never to leave you while you live."

Faria gazed fondly on his noble-minded young friend. He saw in his face every mark of sincerity and devotion.

"Thank you," murmured the invalid. "I accept your promise. You may one day be rewarded for your devotion. Do not return here tomorrow until after the jailer his visited me. I will have something of the greatest importance to tell you."

Edmond took the hand of the priest in his and affectionately squeezed it. Faria smiled encouragingly at him, and the young man went back to his cold damp cell.

CHAPTER 14
The Treasure

Faria shows Edmond a treasure map.

When Edmond returned next morning to Faria's cell, he found him seated and looking calm. The priest held a sheet of paper in his left hand. He did not speak, but showed the paper to Edmond.

"What is that?" Edmond inquired.

"This paper, my friend, this paper is my treasure. From this day forth, one-half belongs to you."

The sweat broke out on Edmond's forehead. Faria had never before mentioned the treasure to him. This was the subject that had caused the jailers to believe the priest was insane. Now these words seemed to indicate a relapse into madness.

"Your treasure?" stammered Edmond, his voice betraying disbelief.

Faria smiled. "Yes," he said. "I see what is passing in your heart at this moment. I am not mad, Edmond. This treasure exists, and you will possess it one day."

Faria then allowed Edmond to examine the yellowed, tattered piece of paper. "This piece of paper," he said, "contains the key to your future, my young friend. I came across it two days before I was arrested in 1807. It was concealed for over three centuries in a neglected, gold-bound Bible that had been in the family I worked for, known as the Spada family. This family had been extremely rich generations before. By the time I went to work for them as a tutor and steward of the family archives, they had fallen on hard times. One night I was paging through their long-neglected Bible, when I came across this piece of paper. See what it says."

Faria handed the paper to Edmond, warning him to handle it with the utmost care because of its fragility. Edmond read:

> On this 25th day of April, 1498 . . . I buried in a cave . . . the small island of Monte Cristo . . . contains . . . of gold, money, jewels, and . . . amounts to nearly two million francs . . . twentieth rock from the small creek . . . east in a straight line . . . openings have been made in these . . . in the farthest angle of the second opening . . . I bequeath and leave it all to . . . April 25, 1498. Caesar Spada.

"Now," Faria went on, looking at Edmond with a fatherly smile, "now, my dear fellow, you know as much as I do myself. If we ever escape together, half this treasure is yours. If I die here, and you escape alone, it all belongs to you."

"But," asked Edmond hesitatingly, "isn't there someone who has a greater legal claim on the treasure than us?"

"No, no, do not be concerned about that. The family is extinct. Furthermore, the last Count of Spada made me his heir. If we lay hands on this fortune, we may enjoy it without guilt."

"And you say this treasure amounts to—"

"Two millions francs back then—it would be nearly thirteen million today."

Edmond staggered at the enormous amount. He thought he was in a dream. He wavered between disbelief and joy.

"Well, Edmond, aren't you going to thank me?"

"This treasure belongs only to you, my dear friend," replied Edmond. "I have no right to it. I am no relation of yours."

"You are my son, Edmond," exclaimed the old man. "You are the child of my captivity." And Faria reached out the only arm he still had use of, and the young man embraced him and wept.

CHAPTER 15
The Third Attack

Edmond says farewell to Faria.

Now that this treasure could insure the future happiness of the young man whom Faria loved as a son, it had doubled its value in the priest's eyes. Every day he spoke at length about the amount, explaining to Edmond all the good which a man with thirteen million francs could do for his friends. As he spoke, Edmond thought about how much harm a man with thirteen million could do to his enemies.

And so, if these were not happy days, at least they passed quickly. As Faria had predicted, he remained paralyzed in the right arm and the left leg. He had given up all hope of ever enjoying the treasure himself.

One night Edmond woke suddenly, believing that he heard someone calling him. He opened his eyes to utter darkness. There it was again—a plaintive voice calling his name. He sat up in bed, and a cold sweat broke out upon his brow. Undoubtedly the call came from Faria's dungeon. "Oh, no," murmured Edmond. "Can it be?"

Edmond rushed to Faria and saw the old man, pale, but still erect, clinging to his bedframe. His features were distorted with the horrible symptoms which Edmond had seen once before.

"Alas, my dear friend," said Faria sadly. "You understand, don't you? I am dying. Now lift me onto my bed, for I can no longer support myself."

Edmond took the old man in his arms and placed him on the bed.

"And now, my dear friend," said Faria, "my only comforter; you were a priceless gift of heaven. At this moment of leaving you forever, I wish you all the happiness and prosperity you so well deserve. Bless you, my son." Edmond fell to his knees, leaning his head against the old man's bed. A violent convulsion coursed through the old man's body. Edmond raised his head and saw the whites of Faria's eyes grow red. It seemed as if his blood had risen from his chest to his head.

"Goodbye, goodbye!" murmured the old man, clasping Edmond's hand convulsively.

Several hours passed as Edmond sat by the bedside of his friend. Putting his hand on Faria's chest, he felt the body grow colder, and the heart's beating become more and more deep and dull, until at last it stopped. It was six o'clock in the morning, and dawn's feeble light had come into the dungeon. Edmond saw that he was alone with a corpse. He tried to close the poor man's staring eyes, but in vain. He put out the lamp, carefully hid it, and then went away, closing behind him the entrance to the secret passage.

It was time for the jailer to bring the morning meal. He began with Edmond's cell, then went on his way to Faria's. Seized with an indescribable desire to know what was happening, Edmond scrambled back into the underground tunnel, halting inches from Faria's dungeon. He arrived in time to hear the turnkey calling out for help. Other jailers came, and finally the governor himself arrived.

Edmond heard the creaking of the bed as they moved the corpse. He heard the voice of the governor demand that they splash water on the dead man's face. Then, seeing that the prisoner did not revive, they sent for the doctor.

The doctor examined Faria's body and then declared that he was dead.

"Despite your certainty that he is dead," said the governor to the doctor, "I must ask you to go through the formalities required by law."

"Very well, although it is quite unnecessary," said the doctor. "Let the irons be heated."

"Here you are, sir." There was a moment's silence, and then Edmond heard the crackling of burning flesh as a nauseating smell penetrated behind the wall where he was listening in horror.

"You see, he is quite dead," said the doctor. "No living man could withstand his foot being burned so."

Edmond now heard other footsteps, going and coming, and the noise of rustling canvas. The bed creaked, and he knew they were sewing the poor abbé into his shroud.

"Bury him this evening," said the governor when the task was completed.

Then the steps retreated, and the voices died away in the distance. The noise of the door, with its creaking hinges and bolts, ceased, and an awful silence took its place. Edmond raised the flagstone cautiously and looked around the room. It was empty except for the shroud-covered body of his friend. Edmond emerged from the tunnel and entered the priest's cell.

CHAPTER 16
The Cemetery of the Chateau d'If

Edmond learns how funerals are conducted at the Chateau d'If.

On the bed lay a sack of canvas, and within it was the outline of the priest's body.

"I must not die now, after having lived and suffered so long and so much! No, I want to live! I shall struggle to the very last. I will win back the happiness which has been taken from me. I have much to do. Before I die I have my executioners to punish, and perhaps, too, some friends to reward. I must get out of here." As Edmond said this, he became silent. He stared straight ahead, overwhelmed with a strange and amazing thought.

"Dear God!" he muttered, "has this thought come from you? If only the dead leave this dungeon, let me take the place of the dead!" He bent over the shroud, opened it with Faria's knife, lifted the corpse out, and took it through the tunnel to his own room. There he laid it tenderly on his bed. He tied his own rag around its head, pulled the blanket high, kissed the ice-cold forehead, and tried again to close the staring eyes. Then he returned to the other cell. After climbing inside the sack, he sewed it closed from the inside.

After a while, the door opened, and a dim light penetrated the coarse sack that covered him. He saw two shadows approach his bed. A third remained at the door with a torch in his hand. The two men seized the sack at either end and placed him on a stretcher.

"He's heavy for a thin old man," remarked one as he lifted the head.

"They say every year adds half a pound to the weight of the bones," said another, lifting the feet.

The group, led by the man with the torch, went up the stairs. Suddenly, for the first time in many years, Edmond felt the fresh, sharp night air. The men went on for twenty paces, then stopped, putting the stretcher on the ground.

"Bring the torch over here," said one man, "or I'll never find it."

"What can he be looking for?" thought Edmond. "The spade, perhaps?" A satisfied grunt indicated that the man had found the object of his search. He walked back toward Edmond, who suddenly felt a cord fastened tightly around his feet.

"Have you tied the knot?" inquired the one who was watching.

"Yes, and pretty tight too, I can tell you," was the answer.

"What's the knot for?" thought Edmond.

"Let's go, then." The stretcher was lifted once more, and they proceeded.

They continued for about fifty paces, stopped to open a door, then went forward again. Edmond clearly heard the noise of waves dashing against the rocks.

"Bad weather!" observed one of the bearers. "Not a pleasant night for a dip in the sea."

"Why, yes, the priest might get wet," said the other, and there was a burst of brutal laughter. Edmond's hair stood erect on his head.

"Well, here we are," said one of them.

"No, a little farther," said the other. "Don't you remember that the last one was dashed against the rocks, and the governor wasn't at all pleased!"

They climbed five or six more steps. Then Edmond felt them take him, one by the head and the other by the heels, and swing him to and fro.

"One!" said the leader. "Two! Three!" And at the same instant Edmond felt himself flung into the air like a wounded bird, falling, falling, with a speed that made his blood curdle. Pulled downward by a heavy weight, it seemed to him that the fall lasted for a century.

Edmond had been flung into the ocean, where he was dragged down into its depths by the weight tied to his feet. The sea was the cemetery of the Chateau d'If.

CHAPTER 17
The Island of Tiboulen

A nearby uninhabited island becomes Edmond's refuge.

Although stunned and choking on the seawater, Edmond kept his wits enough to hold his breath. With the knife he held clenched in his right hand, he rapidly ripped open the sack and freed his arm, then his body. One desperate sweep of the knife was all it took to cut the cord holding the weight. With a mighty kick, he rose to the surface of the sea.

Edmond drew one mighty breath and then dived, in order to avoid being seen. When he reached the surface a second time, he was fifty paces from where he had first sunk. Over him he saw a black and stormy sky. Before him was the vast expanse of waters, dark and terrible, whose waves foamed and roared. Behind him, blacker than the sea, blacker than the sky, rose the huge stone cliffs of Chateau d'If. On the highest rock were two figures, lighted by a torch. It seemed to him that they were looking at the sea. Edmond dived again and stayed beneath the water a long time. When he came up again, the light had disappeared.

He tried to get his bearings. He knew the two islands nearest to the Chateau d'If had people living on them. Further away were two deserted islands, Tiboulen and Lemaire. Uninhabited islands were surely safer for him. He began to swim for Tiboulen.

Hours later the sky became even darker, and heavy clouds seemed to sweep down toward him. Suddenly he felt a sharp pain in his knee. He thought for a moment that he had been shot, but there had been no sound of gunfire. Then he reached out his hand and encountered a rock. He realized that he had reached the shore and had bumped his knee against a large stone.

Edmond staggered out of the water and fell into the deep, sweet sleep of utter exhaustion.

Later that night, he woke up. A flash of lightning revealed a fishing boat not too far off shore. It was approaching the rocky coast with frightful speed. Moments later, he heard a violent crash and cries of distress. From his rocky perch, Edmond saw the shattered vessel. Among its fragments floated the bodies of the unlucky sailors. Not a single body reached shore. Then all was dark again.

Slowly the wind died away. Vast gray clouds rolled toward the west, and a deep blue sky became visible. A red streak appeared on the horizon and light played over the waves, touching them with gold. Day had dawned.

As Edmond uttered a prayer, he saw a small ship skimming the sea like a gull in search of prey.

He knew exactly what it was: a smugglers' ship. She was coming out of the Marseilles harbor and making rapid progress in his direction. "Perhaps I can pass myself off as one of the sailors from last night's shipwreck," Edmond thought. "There is no one left to contradict me."

Edmond looked toward the spot where the fishing vessel had been wrecked. The red cap of one of the sailors dangled from a rock. Some timbers from the wrecked ship floated nearby. In an instant Edmond's plan was formed. He grabbed the cap, placed it on his head, seized one of the floating timbers, and began paddling desperately in the direction of the little ship. As he neared the vessel, he used the last of his strength to rise half out of the water, waving his cap, and shouting his loudest. He was heard! The ship changed direction and steered straight at him. Two sailors lifted him out of the sea and laid him on deck. One of the sailors held a glass of rum to his mouth as the captain joined them.

"Who are you?" asked the captain in bad French.

"I am a sailor from Malta," replied Edmond, in equally bad Italian. "We were coming from Syracuse with a load of grain. Last night's storm overtook us, and we were wrecked on these rocks. You have saved my life."

"To be honest, we weren't sure we should, though," the captain admitted. "You look more like a pirate than an honest man, with your beard and your hair a foot long." Edmond realized that his hair had not been cut all the time he was at the Chateau d'If.

"Now what are we to do with you?" said the captain.

"Anything you please. Leave me at the first port you touch. I can surely find a job."

"Do you know the Mediterranean?"

"I have sailed it since my childhood."

"You know the best harbors?"

"There are few ports that I could not enter or leave with a blindfold over my eyes."

"Well, Captain," said a sailor, "if what he says is true, why shouldn't he stay with us?"

"If what he says is true, well enough," said the captain doubtingly. "Now, Jacopo"—he was addressing one of the sailors—"find this fellow a shirt and a pair of trousers."

Then he turned to Edmond and said, "Is there anything else you need now?"

"A piece of bread and another glass of that excellent rum, please," answered Edmond. Food and drink were brought to him.

Jacopo sat down beside Edmond. "What is today's date?" Edmond asked him.

"The 28th of February."

"And what year?"

"You don't know what year it is?"

"I got such a fright last night," replied Edmond, smiling, "that I have almost lost my memory."

"It is the year 1829," replied Jacopo. It was fourteen years to the day since Edmond's arrest. He was nineteen when he entered the Chateau d'If. He was now thirty-three. He asked himself what had become of Mercedes, who had surely given him up for dead. Then his eyes lit up with hatred as he thought of the three men who had caused him so much agony. He renewed his oath of vengeance against Danglars, Fernand, and Villefort.

CHAPTER 18
The Smugglers

Edmond joins the crew of the smugglers' ship.

Edmond soon showed himself to be an excellent sailor and a handy man to have aboard the ship, so the captain was content.

At the first port, Edmond quickly visited the barber and a shop where he acquired a complete set of sailor's clothes. When he returned to the ship, the captain offered him a permanent position as a member of the crew. However, Edmond had his own plans to attend to, and he agreed to serve for only three months.

Two and a half months passed. He had passed the island of Monte Cristo twenty times but had never had a chance to land there. But then fortune smiled. The captain of the ship announced that they would stop at the island of Monte Cristo for fresh meat and water. At the prospect of finally reaching the island, Edmond trembled with joy.

CHAPTER 19
The Island of Monte Cristo

After the ship reaches the island of Monte Cristo, Edmond goes hunting.

One night later, the ship anchored off Monte Cristo. Edmond could not restrain himself. He was the first to jump on shore. Had he dared, he would have kissed the rocky earth.

The next day Edmond took a shotgun and announced his intention to hunt some of the wild goats that were seen springing from rock to rock in the hills above them. This gave Edmond a chance to explore the island and perhaps locate signs leading to the treasure. However, he did not wish to share the treasure with the smugglers. How could he get away so he could explore carefully and dig up the treasure, assuming he could even find it?

While reflecting on this serious problem, Edmond succeeded in shooting a goat. He delivered the dead animal to his shipmates and set off to hunt another.

Meanwhile, his comrades had gotten fresh water from a spring, spread out fruit and bread, and roasted the young goat. Just as they were taking the meat off the fire, they saw Edmond high over their heads, springing carelessly from rock to rock. They fired into the air to alert him that the meal was ready. As they watched, Edmond's foot slipped. He staggered at the edge of a rock, then disappeared. They all rushed toward him.

They found Edmond, bleeding and semi-conscious. When the sailors poured a little rum down his throat, Edmond opened his eyes, groaning with unbearable pain. When they attempted to lift him up and carry him to the campsite, he begged them to stop, saying he could not bear to be moved. "Go back and eat," he insisted. "Let me rest. I am sure I will feel better soon." The sailors did not require much urging. They were hungry, and the smell of the roasted goat was very tempting. An hour later they returned. Instead of feeling better, Edmond appeared to be in greater pain then ever.

"You must go and make your journey," he said to the captain. "Leave me a little food and a weapon and a few other things," which he enumerated. "And give me a spade and an axe, so that I'm able make a shelter if you cannot come back for a while. I will wait here for your return."

The smugglers provided Edmond with what he asked for and set sail. When they had disappeared, he leaped to his feet, as light and agile as one of the island goats. He took his gun in one hand, his spade in the other, and set out to find the chest of jewels and gold.

CHAPTER 20
The Secret Cave

Edmond makes an exciting discovery in an underground cave.

Following the directions Abbé Faria had made him memorize, Edmond found himself in front of a huge round rock. The rock weighed several tons. How could it have been lifted to this spot to conceal treasure buried beneath it?

Suddenly an idea flashed across Edmond's mind. "The rock wasn't lifted," he said aloud. "It was lowered here." He investigated the area and confirmed that the rock now lay at the foot of a steep slope—down which it could have been rolled. But how could he remove the boulder to get at the treasure lying beneath?

Instantly Edmond went to work. His eyes fell upon the container of gunpowder which Jacopo had left him. Using his spade, he dug a space below the rock and filled it with powder. Then he made a fuse out of his handkerchief. He lit it and ran back several hundred feet. The explosion soon followed. The large rock was lifted from its base by the terrific force of the powder. Thousands of insects escaped from the site, and a huge snake, like the guardian demon of the treasure, slithered out and disappeared.

On the spot where the rock had rested was an iron ring attached to a square flagstone. Edmond uttered a cry of joy and surprise. Using the handle of the spade as a lever, Edmond lifted the flagstone out of the ground. He found himself staring at steps that descended until they were lost in the darkness of an underground cave.

Down he went. Edmond could see to the farthest corners of the cave. He then recalled the words of the document. "In the farthest angle of the second opening," it had said. He had only found the first cave. He now had to seek the second. Edmond continued his search. He examined the stones all around him and struck against the walls with his spade, listening for a hollow sound that could indicate an opening. Eventually he was rewarded with a dull sound that made beads of perspiration break out on his forehead. He struck the wall with greater force. Pieces of stucco, which had been painted to resemble granite, broke away, exposing a wall of small stones. These were not cemented together but merely rested on top of one another, so they fell away easily.

He soon had created an opening large enough to allow him to enter the second cave. It was gloomier than the first, and the air was thick and stale. At the left of the opening was a deep, dark corner. The treasure, if it existed, was buried here.

Edmond advanced toward the corner. Summoning all his strength, he attacked the ground with the spade. Soon the spade struck something made of iron. Edmond turned deadly pale, then dug some more. He again encountered resistance, but not the same sound.

He dug out a space three feet long and two feet wide. There before him was an oaken chest, bound with metal. In the center of the lid he saw a silver plate, still untarnished, which bore the family crest of the Spadas.

Edmond seized the handles and tried to lift the trunk. It was impossible. He attempted to open it, but the padlock held tight. He inserted the blade of the shovel between the trunk and its lid and pressed on the handle with all his force, bursting the fastenings. The hinges broke, and the chest was open.

Edmond was seized with dizziness. He closed his eyes for a moment, then reopened them, and stood motionless with amazement. Three compartments divided the trunk. In the first, piles of golden coins glittered. In the second, there were bars of solid, unpolished gold. Edmond plunged his hands into the third, grasping handfuls of diamonds, pearls, and rubies. Jumping up, Edmond rushed out of the cavern like a madman. He leaped onto a rock, from which he could look at the sea. He was alone—alone with his fabulous treasure.

He held his head in his hands, as if to prevent his senses from leaving him. Then he rushed madly across the rocks of Monte Cristo, terrifying the wild goats and scaring the sea-birds with his wild cries and leaps. Still unable to believe the evidence of his senses, he rushed back into the cave. He fell on his knees, uttering a prayer intelligible to God alone. He slowly became calmer and happier, beginning to believe his incredible good fortune. Edmond saw that it was gradually growing dark. Fearing he might be surprised in the cave, he left it, his gun in hand. He had a few biscuits and a little rum for supper, then snatched a few hours' sleep, lying at the mouth of the cave.

It was a night of joy and terror, such as this most blessed and cursed of men had never experienced in his lifetime.

CHAPTER 21
The Unknown

Edmond purchases a yacht and sails back to Monte Cristo to retrieve the rest of the treasure.

The next morning, Edmond lowered himself into the cave. After filling his pockets with gems, he put the chest together as well as he could, sprinkled sand over the spot, and then stamped on the earth to make it look undisturbed. He erased every trace of his footsteps.

Six days later, the smugglers returned. Edmond spotted the ship and dragged himself with pretended difficulty toward the landing-place. He told his companions that he was better but still suffering from his accident.

With feigned difficulty, Edmond made his way onto the ship. As soon as the vessel arrived on the mainland, Edmond sold four of his smallest diamonds to a dealer in precious stones.

Edmond's term of service on the ship had expired, and he told the captain he would be moving on. Edmond said his final goodbyes and then left for Genoa. When he arrived, a small yacht was being tested in the bay. Edmond, struck with the beauty and speed of the little vessel, bought it with his new-found wealth.

After furnishing the boat with supplies, Edmond sailed it to Monte Cristo. He was relieved to find that the island was still deserted. His treasure was just as he had left it. Early on the following morning, he began the removal of his riches. By nightfall, all of his immense wealth was safely on board the boat.

In response to some inquiries that he made back on the mainland, Edmond learned that his father was dead and that Mercedes had disappeared. He had been prepared for his father's death, but he did not know what to make of Mercedes's disappearance.

He realized he had to go to Marseilles himself to learn the truth. One look in the mirror assured him he would not be recognized. Furthermore, he was rich enough to assume any disguise he chose. And so, one fine morning, his boat boldly entered the port of Marseilles. He anchored opposite the spot where he had been put on board the craft that carried him to the Chateau d'If.

The first person he noticed on the dock was one of the crew belonging to the *Pharaon*. Edmond was happy to meet this fellow, who had been one of his own sailors, as a sure test of whether he would be recognized. Going straight to him, he asked a variety of questions on different subjects, carefully watching the man's face as he did so. Not a word or look suggested that he had ever seen Edmond before. Giving the sailor a coin in return for his assistance, Edmond moved on.

His first stop was the house where his father had rented his apartment. The nasturtiums and other flowers which his father had loved to grow in front of his window were gone.

Edmond sighed sadly. His eyes filled with tears as he thought that it was here that his father had breathed his last, vainly calling for his son. Edmond asked whether Caderousse the tailor still lived there. He was told that the tailor had gotten into some sort of trouble and now kept a small inn on the road between Bellegarde and Beaucaire.

CHAPTER 22
The Pont du Gard Inn

Edmond, disguised as a priest, visits Caderousse to learn who had plotted against him.

The inn in question, known as the Pont du Gard Inn, was situated between the town of Beaucaire and the village of Bellegarde. Attracting few customers, the inn was rapidly heading for ruin.

On this particular day, a horse reached the Pont du Gard, from which a priest dismounted and tied his steed to a hitching-post. At that moment, the surprised host of the Pont du Gard appeared.

"You are welcome, sir, most welcome!" said the innkeeper, none other than Caderousse. "What can I offer you? I am completely at your service."

The priest gave him a long, searching look, and finally answered in a strong Italian accent, "You are, I presume, M. Caderousse?"

"Yes, sir," answered the host, more surprised than ever. "I am Gaspard Caderousse, at your service."

"Let me have a bottle of your best wine. Then let us continue our conversation."

"As you please, sir," said Caderousse, rushing off anxiously. When he returned five minutes later, he found the priest seated at the table, leaning on his elbow.

"Are you alone here?" inquired the guest, as Caderousse placed before him the bottle of wine and a glass.

"Quite alone," replied the man, "except for my poor wife, who is not feeling well."

"In the year 1814 or 1815, did you know a young sailor named Edmond Dantes?"

"Edmond? Did I know poor dear Edmond? Why, Edmond Dantes and I were intimate friends!" exclaimed Caderousse. "Do you know what has become of the poor boy? Is he alive and at liberty? Is he happy?"

The priest shook his head. "He died a wretched, hopeless, heartbroken prisoner."

Caderousse turned deadly pale. He turned away, and the priest saw him wipe his eyes with the corner of a handkerchief.

"You act as though you had kind thoughts about this young Edmond," observed the priest.

"I loved him," replied Caderousse, "although once, I confess, I envied him his good fortune. But I swear to you, sir, by everything a man holds dear, since then I have deeply lamented his unhappy fate." He grew silent, trying to control the sobs that had begun to shake him. Finally he continued, "You knew the poor boy, then?"

"I was called to see him on his death bed, that I might offer him the comforts of religion."

"What did he die of?" asked Caderousse in a choking voice.

"What do all young and strong men die of in prison? He died of his imprisonment. But the strangest part of the story is that Edmond, even in his dying moments, swore that he was utterly ignorant of the cause of his imprisonment."

"And so he was," murmured Caderousse. "Ah, sir, the poor fellow told you the truth."

"And for that reason, he begged me to solve the mystery and to clear his name, if any foul stain had fallen upon it."

The priest noticed with satisfaction the gloomy depression spreading over Caderousse's face. He continued speaking. "It so happens that Edmond was imprisoned with a rich Englishman, who was eventually released. Edmond had nursed the man through a severe illness. In gratitude, the Englishman gave him a large diamond. Edmond carefully kept that diamond, hoping that if he ever got out of prison, he could sell it and live on the money."

Caderousse's face turned bright and glowing. "It must have been an immensely valuable stone!" he said.

"Well, everything is relative," answered the priest, "but to someone like Edmond, certainly the diamond was of great value. You may judge for yourself, as I have it with me." He calmly drew forth from his pocket a little green box. Opening it, he displayed a large, sparkling diamond, set in an exquisite ring.

Caderousse's eyes fairly danced in delight. "But how did you get the stone, sir? Did Edmond make you his heir?"

"No, he merely asked me to carry out a bequest," the priest answered. "This is what he told me: 'I once had four dear and faithful friends, besides the girl to whom I was engaged,' he said. 'I know they have all suffered greatly over my loss. The name of one of them is Caderousse.'" The innkeeper shivered.

"'Another of the four is called Danglars,'" continued the priest. "'The third, despite being my rival in love, was my sincere friend. His name was Fernand. The name of the fiancée was—'" The priest stopped, thinking. "I have forgotten the girl's name."

"Mercedes," said Caderousse eagerly.

"That's it," said the priest, with a sigh, "Mercedes it was."

"Go on," urged Caderousse.

"Edmond told me, 'Go to Marseilles and sell this diamond. Then divide the money into five equal parts and give a portion to these good friends, the only people who have loved me upon earth.'"

"But why into five parts?" asked Caderousse. "You mentioned only four persons."

"Because I understand that the fifth is dead. The fifth was Edmond's own father."

"Too true, too true!" exclaimed Caderousse, almost suffocated by the contradictory emotions he was feeling. "The poor old man did die."

"I learned a good deal in Marseilles," replied the priest, trying to appear indifferent, "but I was unable to learn any details of the old man's death. Do you know anything?"

"Indeed I do," said Caderousse. "Why, I was old Dantes's neighbor. About a year after the disappearance of his son, the poor old man died."

"Of what did he die?"

"He starved to death."

"Starvation!" exclaimed the priest, jumping up from his seat. "Why, the lowest animals are not condemned to die like that. The dogs that wander homeless in the streets find someone who pities them enough to throw them a bone. Are you telling me that a man, a Christian, was allowed to perish of hunger among other men who call themselves Christians? It is too horrible to believe. Oh, it is impossible—utterly impossible!"

"Not everyone ignored him," explained Caderousse. "Mercedes and M. Morrel were very kind to him. But somehow the poor old man developed a profound hatred for Fernand—the very person," added Caderousse with a bitter smile, "that you named just now as being one of Edmond's faithful friends."

"And was he not a friend?" asked the priest.

Caderousse continued, "Can a man be faithful to another man when he covets that man's wife? But Edmond was so honorable and true-hearted that he believed everyone was the same. Poor Edmond was cruelly deceived. It was fortunate that he never knew, or he might have found it difficult, on his deathbed, to pardon his enemies."

"Do you know, then, what Fernand did to injure Edmond?" asked the priest.

"No one knows better than I."

"Please," the priest said, "tell me everything."

CHAPTER 23
The Story

Caderousse reveals the roles that Danglars and Fernand played in Edmond's arrest. We learn what has happened to them, and others, since Edmond was imprisoned.

"First, sir," said Caderousse, "you must make me a promise."

"What is that?" inquired the priest.

"If you ever make use of the details I am about to give you, you will never let anyone know that it was I who told them. The persons I will talk about are rich and powerful. They would cause me much harm if they knew."

"Be easy, my friend," replied the priest. "I am a priest, and your confession will die with me."

"Well, then," said Caderousse, "I will explain to you the 'friendship' which poor Edmond thought was so sincere."

"Begin with his father, if you please," said the priest. "Edmond talked to me a great deal about the old man."

"It's a sad story, sir," said Caderousse, shaking his head. The innkeeper then told of Old Dantes's grief at the disappearance of his son. "M. Morrel and Mercedes tried to comfort him, but to no avail," Caderousse said. "In time, the old man simply refused to eat, and so he died, overcome by sadness."

The priest rose from his chair and walked around the room. "This was, indeed, a horrid event," he said in a hoarse voice.

"Especially horrid as it was men's doing, and not God's," answered Caderousse.

"Tell me about young Dantes's so-called friends," said the priest.

"Two men were jealous of him, sir. One was jealous with love, and the other with ambition. They were Fernand and Danglars. In order to destroy Edmond, they denounced him as an agent of Napoleon."

"Which of the two actually denounced him?"

"Both, sir. One wrote the letter, while the other delivered it."

"And where was this letter written?"

"At a café, the day before the engagement feast. Danglars wrote the denunciation with his left hand, so that his writing would not be recognized. It was Fernand who delivered the letter."

"And what did you do, as you were there yourself?" asked the priest.

"I!" said Caderousse, astonished. "Who told you I was there?"

The priest saw he had said too much and might betray his true identity. So he added quickly, "No one. But you know so many details, I just thought you must have been an eyewitness."

"True, true!" said Caderousse in a choking voice, "I was there."

"And why didn't you stop them?"

"Sir," replied Caderousse, "they made me drink so much that I lost my senses. I was only dimly aware of what was going on. I objected to what I heard, but they insisted that they had only been joking."

"But the next day? You must have seen plain enough what was happening. You were present when Dantes was arrested."

"Yes, sir, I was there, and I wanted to speak, but Danglars stopped me. 'If he really is guilty,' he said, 'if he really did stop at the island of Elba and agree to deliver a letter for Napoleon, then anyone who supports him will be accused of being his accomplice.' I was afraid, and I held my tongue. What I did was cowardly, I confess, but not criminal."

"I understand. So you simply allowed matters to take their course."

"Yes, sir," answered Caderousse, "and I have regretted it every day since. I have begged God to pardon me, and I have no doubt that my cowardice is the reason that my life has gone downhill ever since."

"Well, sir," said the priest, "you have spoken honestly. You deserve pardon for having admitted your part in what happened." He thought for a moment. "You have mentioned a M. Morrel," he finally said. "Who was he?"

"The owner of the *Pharaon* and Edmond's employer."

"And what part did he play in this sad story?" inquired the priest.

"The part of an honest man, full of courage and compassion. He tried endlessly to see justice done for Edmond. Again and again, he came to see Edmond's father and begged him to come live in his own house. A night or two before the old man's death, Morrel paid the old man's debts. Later he saw that the old man was buried decently. I still have the purse that Morrel left with old Dantes—a large one, made of red silk."

"Is M. Morrel still alive?"

"Yes," replied Caderousse, "but nearly as poor and miserable as myself."

"What! I thought he was a rich and successful businessman!" exclaimed the priest.

"He was, but after twenty-five years of honest labor, and after establishing one of the most honorable names in Marseilles, M. Morrel is nearly destroyed. He has lost five ships in two years, and three of his largest clients have gone bankrupt. His only hope now is in the *Pharaon*, the very ship that poor Edmond commanded. It is soon expected from the Indies with a cargo of dyes. If this ship is lost, like the others, he is a ruined man."

"And what of his family?" inquired the priest.

"He has a wife who has behaved like an angel through all of this. He has a daughter who was about to marry the man she loved, but now his family will not allow him to wed the daughter of a poor man. His son is a lieutenant in the army. I believe if the ship owner were alone in the world, he would blow his brains out, and that would be the end."

"Horrible!" exclaimed the priest.

"And so this is how heaven rewards virtue, sir," added Caderousse. "All this, while Fernand and Danglars are rolling in wealth. Do not look surprised! Their deeds have brought them good fortune while honest men have been reduced to misery."

"Tell me first about Danglars. He thought up the plot, and therefore he is the most guilty."

"Well, he left Marseilles and went to work for a Spanish bank. Then during the war with Spain, the French army hired him as a purchasing agent. He made a fortune. He invested that money wisely and became even richer. He had married his banker's daughter, and after she died, he married a second time. His new wife is the daughter of the king's chamberlain, who is in high favor at court. So now he is a millionaire, and the king has made him a baron." He calls himself Baron Danglars.

"And Fernand?"

"Fernand? Why, much the same story. Just before the return of the emperor, Fernand was drafted. He was getting along well enough in the army.

Then, when France's war with Spain broke out, Fernand, being a Spaniard, was sent to Spain to spy on his fellow-countrymen. There he met Danglars and got to be very friendly with him. Thanks largely to Danglars, Fernand was made colonel and received the title of the Count de Morcerf. He was even awarded France's Legion of Honor."

"Destiny! Destiny!" murmured the priest.

"Yes, but listen . . . this was not all. When the war with Spain ended, Fernand's career was halted as well. But then Greece went to war against Turkey. Fernand obtained permission to go and serve in Greece, and he became a high-ranking aide to an important Greek leader. The leader was killed, but before that he rewarded Fernand with a considerable sum of money. He is a rich man now."

With an effort at self-control, the priest continued, "And Mercedes—they tell me that she has disappeared?"

"Disappeared?" said Caderousse, "Yes, as the sun disappears, only to rise again the next day with even more splendor. Mercedes is today one of the greatest ladies in Paris."

"Go on," said the priest.

"As I told you, Mercedes was in the deepest despair because of Edmond's arrest. In the midst of her agony, a new trouble arose. Fernand had to leave to take part in the war. She did not know about his evil actions against Edmond and still regarded him with brotherly affection. Fernand went to war, and Mercedes became extremely lonely. Three months later Fernand reappeared, dressed in the uniform of an army officer. He was not the one she wished for most, but it seemed as if a part of her past life had returned to her. Fernand pressed Mercedes to marry him, and eventually they were wed in the church of Accoules."

"The very church in which she was to have married Edmond," murmured the priest. "There was only a change of bridegrooms."

"After the wedding, Fernand was very anxious to get his wife away from Marseilles. There were too many unpleasant memories there, and, besides, he was terrified that Edmond might someday return. So eight days after the ceremony, they left the city."

"Did you ever see her again?" inquired the priest.

"Yes, during the Spanish war. She was busy attending to the education of her son."

"Her son?"

"Yes," replied Caderousse, "little Albert. Today, Mercedes might be a queen, if crowns were placed on the heads of the loveliest and most intelligent. As Fernand's fortune grew, she developed along with it. She learned reading, writing, drawing, music— everything. She, I should say Madame de Morcerf, is rich, a countess—and yet—" Caderousse paused.

"And yet what?" asked the priest.

"Yet, she does not seem happy," said Caderousse.

"And what do you know of M. de Villefort?" asked the priest.

"I know nothing. I never knew him."

The priest then took the diamond from his pocket. Handing it to Caderousse, he said, "Here, my friend, take this diamond, it is yours."

"What, for me only?" cried Caderousse. "Ah, sir, do not joke with me!"

"This diamond was to have been shared among his friends. I see that Edmond had only one friend, and so it cannot be divided. Take the diamond and sell it. It is worth enough to easily release you from your poor condition. In exchange, give me the red silk purse that M. Morrel left with old Dantes."

Caderousse, more and more astonished, went to a large oaken cupboard, opened it, and gave the priest a purse of faded red silk. The priest took it, and in return gave Caderousse the diamond.

"Oh, you are a man of God, sir," Caderousse said. "You could easily have kept the jewel for yourself."

"That," thought the priest, "is what you would have done."

The priest got up, mounted his horse, and continued on his way.

CHAPTER 24
The Prison Register

Now disguised as an Englishman representing the Thomson & French Bank, Edmond visits M. de Boville, an inspector of prisons who is also an investor in Morrel's firm.

The next day, a man in his early thirties, elegantly dressed and speaking with an English accent, presented himself before the mayor of Marseilles. "Sir," he said, "I am chief agent of the Thomson & French Bank, of Rome. We have been connected for many years with the house of Morrel & Son, of Marseilles. We have a fair amount of money invested with them just now, and we are a little uneasy at reports that the firm is on the brink of ruin. I have come, therefore, to ask you for information."

"Sir," replied the mayor, "during the last four or five years, misfortune has seemed to pursue M. Morrel. He has lost four or five vessels. He has also suffered from the bankruptcies of three or four companies that owed him a great deal of money. Personally, I can tell you that M. Morrel is a highly honorable man, who has never failed to honor a debt. This is all I can say, sir. But if you wish to learn more, I advise you to speak with M. de Boville, the inspector of prisons. Here is his address. M. de Boville is an investor in Morrel's firm, and I'm sure he will be better informed than I am."

The Englishman bowed and departed, heading straight for the address given him.

"Oh, sir," exclaimed M. de Boville, when the Englishman had explained his errand, "your fears are unfortunately well founded. I am in despair, for I have a great deal of money placed in the hands of Morrel & Son. That money was to be the dowry of my daughter, who is to be married in two weeks. The money was to be repaid to me, half on the 15th of this month, and the other half on the 15th of next month. Only half an hour ago, M. Morrel came here to tell me that if his ship, the *Pharaon*, does not come into port on the 15th, he will be unable to make this payment. I very much fear that M. Morrel faces bankruptcy."

The Englishman thought for a moment, then said, "And so, you consider your investment in great danger?"

"To tell you the truth, I consider it lost."

"Well, then, I will buy it from you," said the stranger.

"But at a tremendous discount, of course?"

"No, for exactly what you invested."

The Englishman drew from his pocket a large bundle of cash. A ray of joy passed across M. de Boville's face. Yet he made an effort at self-control and said, "Sir, I ought to tell you that, in all probability, you will lose most if not all of your investment."

"That's no affair of mine," said the Englishman carelessly. "That is the affair of the Thomson & French Bank, in whose name I act. All I know, sir, is, that I am ready to hand you over this sum, in exchange for a small commission."

"Of course, that is perfectly fair," cried M. de Boville.

"You are the inspector of prisons?"

"I am, and have been so for fourteen years."

"You keep the registers of prisoners' entries and departures, and reports on those prisoners?"

"I do."

"Well, sir, I was educated by an abbé, who disappeared suddenly. I have recently learned that he was confined in the Chateau d'If, and I would like to learn the details of his death."

"What was his name?"

"The Abbé Faria."

"Oh, I remember him perfectly," M. de Boville said. "He was crazy."

"So they said."

"Oh, he was, decidedly. He claimed to know of an immense treasure, and offered vast sums to the government if they would free him."

"Poor devil! And he is dead?"

"Yes, sir, five or six months ago—last February."

"You have a good memory, sir, to remember dates so well."

"I remember this, because the poor man's death was accompanied by a very odd incident."

"Indeed? What was that?" asked the Englishman.

"Well, sir, Faria's dungeon was forty or fifty feet

away from the cell of a very dangerous man. He was an agent of Napoleon Bonaparte."

"Indeed!" said the Englishman.

"Yes," replied M. de Boville. "I myself saw this man in 1816 or 1817, and we could only go into his dungeon with a heavy guard of soldiers. That man made a deep impression on me. I shall never forget his face!"

The Englishman smiled gently.

"So," de Boville continued, "these dungeons were separated by about fifty feet. But it appears that this Bonapartist, Edmond Dantes, had somehow gotten his hands on tools, for they found a tunnel between the two cells."

"This tunnel was dug, no doubt, with the intention of escape?" the Englishman inquired.

"No doubt, but unfortunately for the prisoners, the Abbé Faria died."

"That must have cut short the escape plan."

"For the dead man, yes," replied M. de Boville, "but not for the survivor. On the contrary, this Dantes saw a better method of escape. No doubt, he believed that prisoners who died in the Chateau d'If were buried in an ordinary cemetery. So he took the dead man into his own cell, crawled into the sack which had held the corpse, and awaited his own burial. However, the Chateau d'If has no cemetery," explained de Boville. "They simply throw the dead into the sea, after fastening a thirty-six-pound cannonball to their feet."

"Really! And so, this Dantes fellow was drowned?" exclaimed the Englishman.

"Obviously!"

"So the governor got rid of the dangerous and the crazy prisoners at the same time?"

"Precisely."

"I suppose some official document was drawn up to explain all this?" inquired the Englishman.

"Yes, indeed, there is a death certificate. But excuse me from straying from the original story, sir. You had asked about the poor priest, who was really the most gentle soul imaginable."

"I would very much like to see any papers you have relating to him."

"Come into my study here, and I will show you." Everything was there, arranged in perfect order. The inspector invited the Englishman to take a comfortable armchair and placed before him all the documents relating to the Chateau d'If. De Boville himself sat in a corner and was soon absorbed in his newspaper.

The Englishman—actually Edmond in disguise—easily found the documents concerning the priest, Faria. However, he quickly put aside the notes on Faria and began searching for papers about Edmond Dantes. There he found everything arranged in order: the accusation; the report of his interview with M. de Villefort; Morrel's petitions; de Villefort's notes. He folded up the accusation quietly and put it in his pocket. He read the account of his interview with Villefort and took special notice that the name of Noirtier was not mentioned.

"Thank you," said the stranger, closing the register with a slam. "I have all I want; now it is for me to keep my promise. Write me up a simple receipt, and I will hand you over the money." M. de Boville quickly drew up the required paper, while the Englishman counted out the money on the other side of the desk.

CHAPTER 25
The House of Morrel & Son

Still disguised, Edmond visits Pierre Morrel's warehouse. As he leaves, Edmond tells Julie, Morrel's daughter, that she will soon receive an important letter.

Someone who had visited Pierre Morrel's warehouse a few years previously, and then returned to that establishment on this day, would have noticed a great change. Gone were the busy clerks hurrying through the long corridors, the bales of goods filling the courtyard, the shouts and the jokes of porters. Taking their place was an air of sadness and gloom. Of the many clerks that used to fill the corridors and the offices, only two remained. One was a young man named Emmanuel Herbaut, who was in love with M. Morrel's daughter. The other was an old one-eyed cashier, known by everyone as "Cocles."

Since the end of the month, M. Morrel had passed many an anxious hour. In order to meet the payments then due, he had gone so far as to sell his wife's and daughter's jewelry and some of the family silver. By these means he had met his most recent payments, but those funds were now gone. Rumors about his misfortune made it impossible for him to borrow money. To meet his debts, M. Morrel had no hope but the return of the *Pharaon*.

This was the state of affairs when the agent of the Thomson & French Bank appeared at M. Morrel's door. Emmanuel was the first to meet him. This young man asked Cocles to take the stranger to M. Morrel's office. Cocles went first, and the stranger followed him. On the staircase they met a beautiful girl of sixteen or seventeen, who looked anxiously at the stranger.

"M. Morrel is in his room, is he not, Mademoiselle Julie?" said the cashier.

"Yes, I think so," said the young girl hesitatingly.

Cocles and the Englishman continued to the office. There they found M. Morrel, paging through an enormous book containing records of his liabilities. At the sight of the stranger, M. Morrel closed the ledger, rose, and offered him a seat. Cocles and Morrel exchanged a few whispered words, and then the cashier left.

M. Morrel was now fifty years of age. His hair had turned white. Time and sorrow had worn deep lines in his face.

"Monsieur," said Morrel, "you wish to speak to me?"

"Yes, monsieur. You know who sent me?"

"The Thomson & French Bank, so my cashier tells me."

"That is correct. The Thomson & French Bank had considerable debts to pay this month in France. Knowing your excellent reputation, we have bought up the accounts of many of your creditors. My employers have assigned me to present them, and collect the funds."

Morrel sighed deeply and passed his hand over his forehead. "You hold bills of mine, then. What is the total amount?" asked Morrel with a voice he tried to make firm.

The Englishman scrawled a number on a piece of paper and showed it to M. Morrel. The poor man's face turned deathly pale.

The stranger continued. "Although your reputation is faultless, I cannot deny that we have heard rumors that you are unable to pay your debts. As a man of honor, will you be able to pay these bills?"

Morrel shuddered. "You have asked a frank question, and I will answer as frankly. Yes, I shall pay—if my ship arrives safely. But if the *Pharaon* is lost . . ." The poor man's eyes filled with tears.

"Don't you have friends who can help you?"

Morrel smiled mournfully. "In business, sir," he said, "one has no friends, only correspondents."

"That is true," murmured the Englishman. "Then you have only one hope."

"Only one."

"And if that fails—"

"Then I am ruined, completely ruined!"

"As I was on my way here, a ship was coming into port," said the stranger.

"I know that. She is *La Gironde*, coming back from India, but she is not mine."

"Perhaps she has had contact with the *Pharaon*,

and brings you some news of her? But wait—what is that sound?" exclaimed the Englishman.

A loud noise was heard on the stairs. People were moving hastily, and there were half-stifled sobs. Morrel began to rise, but sank back into his chair. The two men sat opposite one another, Morrel trembling in every limb, the stranger gazing at him with profound pity. The door opened, and Morrel's daughter entered, her eyes streaming with tears. "Oh, Father!" she said, clasping her hands. "Forgive me for being the bearer of evil tidings."

"The *Pharaon* has gone down, then?" said Morrel in a hoarse voice. The young girl did not speak. She merely nodded, embracing him.

"And the crew?" asked Morrel.

"Saved," said the girl, "saved by the crew of the vessel that has just entered the harbor."

Morrel raised his hands to heaven with an expression of resignation and gratitude. "Thanks be to God," he said, "at least only I am struck with this misfortune." A tear came to the eye of the silently watching Englishman.

"Come in, come in," called Morrel, "whoever is out there in the hall."

As soon as he had uttered those words, Madame Morrel entered, weeping bitterly. Emmanuel followed her, and behind him were seven or eight sailors dressed in rags. At the sight of these former shipmates, the Englishman withdrew to the farthest corner of the room. Madame Morrel sat by her husband and took one of his hands in hers, while Julie kept her arms around her father's shoulders.

"How did this happen?" said Morrel.

"Come closer, Penelon," said Emmanuel, "and tell us all about it."

An old seaman, bronzed by the tropical sun, advanced and nodded politely to Morrel.

"It is a terrible day, Penelon," responded Morrel. "What happened?"

Penelon shifted his load of chewing-tobacco from one cheek to another and began. It was a sad story of unexpected tropical storms, the leaking of the aging ship, and the gallant efforts of the crew. But there was nothing to be done, and the *Pharaon* and its precious cargo now rested on the ocean floor.

"Well, well," said M. Morrel, "I know there was no one at fault but destiny. It was the will of God that this should happen. What wages are due to you?"

"Oh, don't let us talk of that, M. Morrel."

"Yes, but we will talk of it."

"Well, then, three months," said Penelon.

"Cocles, pay two hundred to each of these good fellows," said Morrel. "At another time," he added, "I would have said, 'Give them two hundred more as a bonus.' But times have changed, and the little money that I hold is not my own. And if you can find another employer, enter his service. I have no more ships, and therefore I do not need any sailors."

"At least, we shall see each other again, M. Morrel?" asked Penelon.

"Yes, I hope so." Addressing the other people

in the room, Morrel said, "Please go now. I need to speak with this gentleman." And he glanced toward the Thomson & French agent.

The two men were left alone. "Well, sir," said Morrel, sinking into a chair, "you have heard everything. I have nothing further to tell you."

"I see that a fresh and undeserved misfortune has come to you," replied the Englishman. "This only increases my desire to be of help to such a man of honor. Now, I believe I am one of your largest creditors."

"You are."

"Do you wish for additional time to pay?"

"A delay would save my honor, and consequently my life."

"How long a delay do you wish for?"

Morrel thought. "Two months," he said.

"I will give you three," replied the stranger. Today is the fifth of June. Let us renew these bills up to the fifth of September. At eleven o'clock that morning, I shall come for the money."

"I shall expect you," answered Morrel. Overwhelmed with gratitude, Morrel saw the stranger to the stairs and said goodbye. As the Englishman left the house, he encountered Morrel's daughter Julie in the hallway.

"Mademoiselle," said the stranger, "one day you will receive a letter signed 'Sinbad the Sailor.' Do exactly what the letter tells you, however strange it may appear."

"Yes, sir," returned Julie.

"Do you promise?"

"I swear to you I will."

"Then all is well. Goodbye, mademoiselle. Continue to be the good, sweet girl you are, and I have great hopes that heaven will reward you by giving you Emmanuel for a husband."

Julie blushed like a rose. The stranger waved his hand, and left the house. In the courtyard he found Penelon, who seemed unable to make up his mind to whether to stay or go. "Come with me, my friend," said the Englishman. "I want to speak with you."

CHAPTER 26
The Fifth of September

The Morrels receive some unexpected good news.

The three-month extension, provided by the Thomson & French Bank, was such a stroke of good fortune for the poor ship owner that he almost dared to believe that his luck was changing. The Englishman was not seen in Marseilles again. As to the sailors of the *Pharaon*, they must have found employment elsewhere, for they also vanished.

The family quickly conferred and agreed that Julie should write to her brother, who was in the army, and request that he come home as quickly as possible. Although Maximilian Morrel was only twenty-two, he was a strong, upright young man who had great influence over his father.

One evening, M. Morrel very quietly entered his bedroom. After a few minutes, his wife and daughter passed quietly along the hallway, to peer through the keyhole at him.

"He is writing," whispered Madame Morrel. The terrible idea that he was writing his will flashed across her mind, and she shuddered.

Over the next few days, M. Morrel seemed as calm as ever and unusually affectionate to his wife and daughter. However, on the evening of September 4, the day before he was to pay a large sum of money to the Thomson & French Bank, he became unusually quiet and withdrawn. The family was frightened, for it was known that he possessed two pistols.

The next morning, to the women's joy, Maximilian appeared at their door.

"Mother," said the young man, "what has happened? Your letter frightened me, and I have come home as fast as possible."

"Julie," said Madame Morrel, "go and tell your father that Maximilian has just arrived." The young lady ran to obey, but on the staircase she found a man holding a letter in his hand.

"Are you Mademoiselle Julie Morrel?" inquired the man, with a strong Italian accent.

"Yes, sir," replied Julie with hesitation. "Who are you? I do not know you."

"Read this letter," he said, handing it to her. Julie hesitated. "It concerns the best interests of your father," said the messenger.

The young girl hastily took the letter from him. She opened it quickly and read:

Go immediately to the address printed at the bottom of this page. Ask the porter for the key to the apartment on the fifth floor. Inside it, on the mantelpiece, you will find a red silk purse. Take it and give it to your father. It is important that he should receive it before eleven o'clock.

You promised to obey me. Remember your oath.

Sinbad the Sailor.

P.S. It is important that you should fulfill this mission in person and alone. If you go accompanied by any other person, or should anyone else go in your place, the porter will reply that he does not know anything about it.

Julie's joy was touched by fear. Was this some trap laid for her? Needing advice, she hurried to Emmanuel and told him everything.

"You must go, mademoiselle," said Emmanuel. "I will accompany you."

"But it says that I must be alone," said Julie. Emmanuel nodded his assent, and the young girl sped off.

While Julie was absent, Madame Morrel told her son everything. The young man knew that misfortunes had struck his father, but he did not know that matters had reached such a desperate point. He was thunderstruck. He raced upstairs, expecting to find his father in his study, but he knocked on the door in vain.

While he stood there, he heard his father's bedroom door open. Morrel uttered a cry of surprise at the sight of his son. He stood frozen in place, pressing his left hand against something hidden under his coat. Maximilian threw his arms around his father's neck, then pulled back in horror, placing his hand on the older man's chest. "Father," he exclaimed, turning pale as death, "what are you going to do with that pair of pistols under your coat? In heaven's name, what are these weapons for?"

"Maximilian," replied Morrel, looking straight at his son, "you are a man of honor. Come, and I will explain to you."

With a firm step Morrel went to his study, while Maximilian followed him, trembling. Morrel opened the door and closed it behind his son. He placed the pistols on the desk, then pointed to the open record-book that lay there.

"Here is what I owe," he said, pointing to a figure. "And here is what I possess." He pointed to a second number.

The young man was overwhelmed by what he read. "And you have done all that is possible, Father, to raise this enormous sum?" asked the young man, after a moment's pause.

"I have," replied Morrel.

"You have no money coming in on which you can rely?"

"None."

"You have exhausted every resource?"

"All."

"So in half an hour, when the agent for the Thomson & French Bank arrives," said Maximilian in a gloomy voice, "our name will be dishonored."

"But blood washes out dishonor," said Morrel.

"You are right, Father, I understand you." Then extending his hand toward one of the pistols, he said, "There is one for you and one for me— thank you!"

Morrel caught his hand. "No! Your mother—your sister! Who will support them?" A shudder ran through the young man's frame.

"Father," he said, "do you order me to live?"

"Yes, I order you to live," answered Morrel. "It is your duty. You have a calm, strong mind, Maximilian. I make no requests. I only ask you to examine my position as if it were your own, and then judge for yourself."

The young man reflected for a moment. An expression of sad resignation appeared in his eyes. "So be it, then, my father," he said, holding out his hand. "Die in peace; I will live." Maximilian caught his father in his arms, and their two noble hearts were pressed against each other for a moment.

"And now, my son, there is no more to be said. Go be with your mother and sister." With a sob, Maximilian obeyed his father's final words.

Morrel fell back in his chair, his eyes fixed on the clock. There were seven minutes left. The hand moved with incredible speed. He seemed to see its motion.

He was now counting time by seconds rather than by minutes. As he picked up his pistol, he heard the door on the staircase creaking open on its hinges. The clock's hands were a hair's-breadth away from eleven.

He placed the muzzle of the pistol between his teeth. Suddenly he heard a cry—his daughter's voice. He turned and saw Julie at the door. The pistol fell from his hands. "My father!" cried the young girl, out of breath, and half dead with joy.

"Saved, you are saved!" And she threw herself into his arms, holding in her hand a red silk purse.

"'Saved,' my child?" asked Morrel. "What do you mean?"

"Yes, saved—saved! See, see!" said the young girl.

Morrel took the purse, staring at it, as a vague memory told him it had once been his own. Inside it were two things: a receipt for the entire amount he owed to the Thomson & French Bank, marked, "Paid in full." The other was a diamond as large as a hazelnut, attached to a slip of paper bearing these words: "Julie's Dowry."

Morrel passed his hand over his face, feeling as if he were in a dream. At this moment the clock struck eleven. He heard each stroke as a hammer falling upon his heart. "Explain, my child—explain—where did you find this purse?"

Julie quickly told him about the letter given to her on the staircase and her journey to the house where she found the purse.

At this moment Emmanuel entered, his face shining with joy. "The *Pharaon*!" he cried. "The *Pharaon*!"

"What—what—the *Pharaon*! Are you mad, Emmanuel? You know the vessel is lost."

"The *Pharaon*, sir! The *Pharaon* is entering the harbor!" Morrel fell back in his chair. But now his son rushed in. "Father," exclaimed Maximilian, "how could you say the *Pharaon* was lost? The lookout has signaled her. They say she is coming into port."

"Impossible, impossible!" cried Morrel. "Come, dear ones," he said, "let us go and see!" They all went out, and in a moment they were at the harbor. A crowd was gathered on the pier, but the watchers parted when they saw the Morrels. "The *Pharaon*, the *Pharaon*!" they shouted.

And, wonderful to see, there was a ship bearing these words, printed in white letters: "The *Pharaon*, Morrel & Son, of Marseilles." She was the exact duplicate of the other *Pharaon*, and loaded, as that one had been, with dyes from India. She dropped anchor, and on her deck was the good old sailor Penelon, waving joyously to M. Morrel.

As Morrel and his son embraced on the pier, watched by the applauding crowd, a man stood concealed behind a stack of boxes, his face hidden by a black beard. He murmured quietly, "Be happy, noble heart. Be blessed for all the good you have done and will do. Let my gratitude remain a secret, like your good deeds."

And with a supremely contented smile, he left his hiding place. Without anyone noticing, he descended to the water's edge, shouting, "Jacopo, Jacopo, Jacopo!" Then a little boat came to shore, took him on board, and carried him to a splendid vessel. From its deck, he looked once more toward Morrel, who, weeping with joy, was shaking hands with all the crowd around him. Lifting his face to the sky, he seemed to be thanking his unknown benefactor.

"And now," said the black-bearded stranger, "farewell kindness, humanity, and gratitude!

Farewell to all the feelings that swell the heart! I have rewarded the good. Now the god of vengeance grant me power to punish my enemies!" At these words he gave a signal, and his boat quickly put out to sea.

CHAPTER 27
Roman Bandits

Edmond now calls himself the Count of Monte Cristo. Using this identity, he does a great favor for Mercedes's son, the Viscount Albert de Morcerf.

Near the beginning of the year 1838, two young men belonging to the highest society of Paris were in a hotel suite owned by the Pastrini family in Rome. They were the Viscount Albert de Morcerf, son of Mercedes and Fernand, who had assumed the title of Count de Morcerf, and the Baron Franz d'Epinay. They had decided to see the Carnival at Rome that year. They also had agreed that Franz, who had lived in Italy for the last three years, should act as Albert's guide. The remaining suite of rooms on that floor was occupied by "a very rich foreign gentleman."

Albert and Franz rented a carriage and went sightseeing in Rome. Late in the afternoon they returned to the hotel. They ordered the coachman to return for them at 8 p.m., so that they could travel outside the city gates to see the surrounding area by moonlight. When they mentioned their plan to the hotel owner, he said with urgency, "You mustn't do that! It's very dangerous to travel outside the city gates at night, because of Luigi Vampa."

"And who is this famous Luigi Vampa?" inquired Albert.

"He is a bandit, and a very dangerous one. After nightfall, you are not safe fifty yards from the gates of the city."

"All the better," replied Albert. "This will be a wonderful adventure! We will fill our carriage with pistols, knives, and double-barreled guns. When Luigi Vampa comes to capture us, we will capture him. We'll bring him back to Rome and present him to the Pope. We'll be heroes!"

"My dear Albert," returned Franz, "your idea is crazy. I'm not going to risk my life."

Albert poured himself a glass of wine. "M. Pastrini," he said, "how does this Luigi Vampa treat those he preys upon?"

"He holds them for ransom. If he doesn't get his money in time, he kills them."

Instead of traveling outside the city gates that night, Albert and Franz elected to view the landmark Coliseum by moonlight.

The next morning, the two young men were visited by a richly-dressed servant who said his name was Bertuccio. He explained that he was in the employ of the Count of Monte Cristo, who occupied the other rooms on the hotel floor. "The Count of Monte Cristo would like to make the acquaintance of Viscount Albert de Morcerf and Baron Franz d'Epinay," Bertuccio said. "The Count would be honored if they would visit him either now or some time later."

Franz replied, "Tell the Count that it will be our

great pleasure to visit him, and that we are prepared to do so right away." Bertuccio bowed and left.

After putting on better clothes, Albert and Franz crossed the landing to the Count's suite and knocked. Bertuccio opened the door, bowed, and invited them in. The two Frenchmen passed through luxuriously furnished rooms and were shown into an elegant parlor. Exquisite Turkish carpets covered the floor. Deeply cushioned couches and chairs filled out the chamber. Splendid paintings by famous masters decked the walls, as did costly tapestries. "If your excellencies will be seated," Bertuccio said, "I'll tell the Count you are here."

Franz and Albert were impressed with the apartment's magnificence. The Count entered, and the younger men rose to their feet. "Gentlemen," the Count said, "thank you for coming."

"Thank you for inviting us," Franz replied.

"Please sit down," the Count said. Will you join me for breakfast?"

"My dear Count, you are too kind."

"Not at all," the Count replied, and he signaled for a breakfast of several courses to be served.

After leaving the Count, the two youthful visitors spent the next two days observing the great Roman carnival. On the second day, Albert went on his own to a party at the mansion of the Duke of Bracciano. When the Viscount Albert failed to return to the hotel, Franz grew alarmed. After nightfall, M. Pastrini told Franz that a man was waiting for him outside with a message from Albert.

Franz went down to the street, where a man wrapped in a cloak came up to him. "Are you Baron d'Epinay?" he asked.

"I am," Franz answered.

"Here is a note for you."

"Will you wait for my reply?"

"Yes. I will wait here."

The note was written and signed by Albert. It said:

> My dear friend,
> The moment you receive this, take the letter of credit from my wallet, which you will find in the square drawer of the desk in our room. Add your own to it, if it is not sufficient. Run to Signor Torlonia, brother of the Duke of Bracciano, get four thousand piastres from him in exchange for the letters of credit, and give them to the messenger. It is urgent that I have this money without delay. I cannot say more, relying on you as you may rely on me.
>> Your friend,
>> Albert de Morcerf
> P.S. I now believe in Italian bandits.

Below this were a few added lines in Italian, written in different handwriting:

> If by six in the morning the four thousand piastres are not in my hands, by seven o'clock the Count Albert will be dead.
>> Luigi Vampa

Franz hurried over and opened the square drawer in the desk. He found the wallet and the letter of credit. It contained only three thousand piastres in credit. As for Franz, he had no letter of credit, but he did have 300 piastres available. He needed 700 more piastres. Franz panicked. Then he remembered the Count of Monte Cristo. Franz rushed to the Count's suite and was admitted immediately.

"Welcome, Baron," the Count said. "Will you dine with me?"

"Thank you, but I've come about an urgent matter."

"And what might that be?" asked the Count.

Franz handed him Albert's note. "Please read this."

The Count read the note and then turned to Franz. "Is the man who brought this note still here?" the Count asked.

"Yes. He is waiting outside the hotel," replied Franz.

The Count peered outside his window and saw the messenger standing below. When the Count gave a peculiar whistle, the man looked up, to Franz's surprise. "Come up here," the Count commanded. The man entered the hotel.

As soon as the messenger appeared at the Count's suite, the Count said, "Come in, Peppino." Peppino glanced anxiously at Franz. "You can speak in front of the baron," the Count said. "He is a friend of mine. How did Viscount Albert de Morcerf fall into Luigi's hands?"

"Excellency, Luigi has a mistress, Teresa, whom he is very fond of. The viscount has an eye for the ladies. While he was observing the Carnival festivities, Teresa attracted his attention and arranged to meet him later. When the viscount arrived, she had him get into her carriage. She told him they were going to a villa a mile from Rome. When they were just outside the city's gates, four members of Luigi's gang surrounded the carriage. They made the viscount get out and walk to the catacombs of Saint Sebastian, where Luigi and his men were waiting."

"I see," said the Count. "We must go to Luigi and release the viscount from captivity." Franz was surprised by the Count's confidence and familiarity with Luigi Vampa and his methods. The Count then ordered his carriage. The Count, Franz and Peppino got in, while one of the Count's servants, Ali, drove. They set off at a rapid pace.

When the carriage stopped, Peppino got out and opened the door for the Count and Franz. "We'll be there in ten minutes," the Count told Franz. He then took Peppino aside and gave him an order in a low voice. Peppino left, taking a torch with him. "Peppino is going ahead to warn the sentries of our coming," the Count told Franz.

For five minutes Franz and the Count stood and watched Peppino follow an uneven path through tall grasses and over uneven ground. "We'll follow him now," said the Count. He and Franz followed in Peppino's footsteps. The path led to the bottom of a small valley, where they saw Peppino talking with a bandit sentry. As the Count and Franz came forward, the sentry saluted them.

"Your Excellencies," Peppino said to the Count and Franz, "if you will both follow me, the entrance to the catacombs is nearby."

The three men reached a narrow passageway that sloped gently downward. They proceeded along it, forced to stoop. After 150 paces, someone demanded, "Who's there?" Peppino's torchlight gleamed on a rifle barrel.

"Peppino," answered the guide. He went alone up to the guard and whispered a few words to him. The guard waved on the three visitors. As they walked through a maze of dark corridors, the Count laid his hand on Franz's shoulder. "Would you like to see the bandit camp?"

"Very much," Franz replied.

"Come with me, then. Peppino, put out the torch." Peppino obeyed, and Franz and the Count were in utter darkness. They advanced silently, the Count guiding Franz as if he had the ability to see in the dark. Soon they stumbled onto the entrance of a chamber. Lamps, placed around the base of the walls, illuminated the room with pale and flickering flames. A peculiar scene presented itself to the eyes of the two visitors.

A man sat, leaning against a column, quietly reading a book. This was the chief of the band, Luigi Vampa. Around him slept at least twenty bandits, each having his rifle within reach. At the other end, silent, scarcely visible, was a sentinel walking up and down before a grotto.

When the Count thought Franz had gazed sufficiently on this scene, he raised his finger to his lips as a sign of silence and entered the chamber. He advanced toward Vampa, who was so intent on his book that he did not hear the noise of the intruder's footsteps.

"Who goes there?" cried the sentinel, who was less distracted, and who saw by the lamp-light a shadow approaching his chief. At this challenge, Vampa rose quickly, drawing a pistol from his belt. In a moment all the bandits were on their feet, and twenty rifles were leveled at the Count.

"Well," said the Count in a voice of perfect calm. "My dear Vampa, you certainly greet a friend with a great deal of ceremony."

The chief exclaimed, "Lay down your arms!" while he took off his hat respectfully. Turning to the Count, he said, "Your pardon, your excellency. The honor of your visit is so unexpected that I did not recognize you."

"It seems that your memory is equally short in other things, Vampa," said the Count. "Not only do you forget people's faces, but also the agreements you make with them."

"What agreement have I forgotten, your excellency?" inquired the bandit, with the air of a man who, having committed an error, is anxious to repair it.

"Was it not agreed," asked the Count, "that not only myself, but also my friends, should be respected by you?"

"And how have I broken that treaty, your excellency?"

"This evening you have kidnapped the Viscount Albert de Morcerf. This young gentleman is one of my friends, and yet you have taken him and have demanded a ransom."

"Why did you not tell me this?" the bandit chief demanded of his men, who all retreated before his glare. "Why have you caused me to break my word toward a gentleman like the Count, who has all our lives in his hands? By heavens, if I thought one of you knew that the young gentleman was the friend of his excellency, I would blow your brains out!"

"You see," said the Count, turning toward Franz, "I told you there was some mistake in this."

"You are not alone?" asked Vampa with uneasiness.

"I am with the person to whom this letter was addressed, and to whom I desired to prove that Luigi Vampa was a man of his word. Come forward your excellency," the Count added, turning to Franz. "Here is Luigi Vampa, who will himself express to you his deep regret at the mistake he has committed." Franz emerged from the shadows and approached the outlaw chief.

"You are welcome here among us, your excellency," Vampa said. "You heard what the Count just said, and also my reply."

"But," said Franz, looking around him uneasily, "where is the Viscount? I do not see him."

"Nothing has happened to him, I hope," said Monte Cristo with a frown.

"The prisoner is in there," replied Vampa, pointing to a doorway guarded by a bandit. "I will go myself and tell him he is free." The chief went toward the place he had pointed out as Albert's prison, and Franz and the Count followed him. "What is the prisoner doing?" inquired Vampa of the sentinel.

"On my word, captain, I do not know," replied the sentry, "I have not heard him stir for the last hour."

"Come here, your excellency," said Vampa. The Count and Franz climbed seven or eight steps after the chief, who drew back a bolt and opened a door. Then, by the gleam of a lamp, Albert could be seen, wrapped up in a cloak which one of the bandits had lent him, lying in a corner, deeply asleep.

The Count smiled his own peculiar smile and said, "Not so bad for a man who is to be shot at seven o'clock tomorrow morning."

Vampa looked at Albert with admiration and said, "You are right, excellency." Going to Albert, he touched him on the shoulder, saying, "Will your excellency please wake up?"

Albert stretched out his arms, rubbed his face, and opened his eyes. "Oh," he said, "is it you, Vampa? You should have let me sleep. I had such a delightful dream. I was dancing a waltz at the Duke's party with a beautiful woman."

Then he took his watch from his pocket, glanced at it and said, "Only half-past one? Why the devil have you awakened me at this hour?"

"To tell you that you are free, your excellency."

"My dear fellow," replied Albert, "please, in the future, remember Napoleon's words: 'Never awaken me only for bad news.' If you had let me sleep on, I would have finished my waltz, and have been grateful to you all my life. So, then, have they paid my ransom?"

"No, your excellency."

"Well, why am I free?"

"A person to whom I can refuse nothing has come to free you."

"Really? What a kind person he must be." Albert looked around and saw Franz. "What," he asked, "is it you, my dear Franz, who displays such devotion and friendship?"

"No, not I," replied Franz, "but our neighbor, the Count of Monte Cristo."

"Oh, my dear Count," said Albert cheerfully, arranging his clothes, "you are really most kind, and I hope you will consider me eternally grateful to you." Saying this, Albert extended his arm to shake the Count's hand. The Count secretly shuddered as he shook the hand of his mortal enemy's son. The bandit gazed on this scene with amazement.

"My dear Albert," Franz said, "if you will hurry, we shall still have time to finish the night at the Duke's. You may conclude your interrupted waltz and so have nothing to complain about to Signor Luigi, who has, indeed, acted like a gentleman."

"You are right. Come, gentlemen, let us go."

Albert, followed by Franz and the Count, crossed the square chamber, where all the bandits stood, hats in hand. "Peppino," said Luigi Vampa, "give me the torch."

"What are you going to do?" inquired the Count.

"I will show you the way back myself," said the captain. "That is the least I can do for your excellency." And taking the lighted torch, he preceded his guests, not like a servant who performs a dutiful act, but like a king who precedes ambassadors. On reaching the door, he bowed. "And now, your excellency," he added, "allow me to repeat my apologies, and I hope you will not retain any hard feelings for what has occurred."

"No, my dear Vampa," replied the Count. "Besides, you make up for your mistakes in so gentlemanly a way, that one almost feels grateful to you for having committed them."

"Now, my dear Count," said Albert, "let us hurry as much as possible. I am enormously anxious to finish my night at the Duke of Bracciano's." They found the carriage where they had left it. The Count gave a command to Ali, and the horses galloped off at great speed.

CHAPTER 28
The Compact

In gratitude for freeing him from Vampa, Albert invites the Count of Monte Cristo to visit him in Paris.

The following morning, the two young men went to the Count's apartments. After a servant showed them in, the Count himself soon joined them.

"My dear Count," said Albert, advancing to meet him, "permit me to repeat the poor thanks I offered last night, and to assure you that as long as I live I shall never forget the prompt and important service you rendered me. I am indebted to you for my life. Now I come to ask you whether I can in any way serve you. Although my father, the Count Fernand de Morcerf, is of Spanish origin, he possesses considerable influence in the French court as well as the Spanish one. I unhesitatingly invite you to take full advantage of any favors I can grant you."

"Thank you, Viscount. Actually, I would like to ask you a favor. I have never been to Paris, but I shall be going there soon. Could you or your family open to me the doors of that fashionable world?"

"With great pleasure," answered Albert. "Your timing is perfect. Just this morning I received a letter from my father summoning me to Paris to advance my proposed engagement involving a family of high standing. They are connected with the very cream of Parisian society."

"Wonderful," said the Count. "I have some business to attend to first. I plan to be in Paris in three months. Today is the 21st of February." Glancing at his watch, he added, "It is exactly half-past ten o'clock. I propose to call on you May 21 at this very hour."

"Excellent!" exclaimed Albert. "Your breakfast shall be waiting. I reside at No. 27 Helder Street."

"Well, since we must part for now," said the Count, holding out a hand to each of the young men, "allow me to wish you both a safe and pleasant journey." The young men rose, and bowing to the Count, left the room.

CHAPTER 29
The Breakfast

Albert's friends have been invited to the breakfast. When the Count arrives, Albert informs him of his engagement to Mademoiselle Eugenie Danglars, daughter of Baron Danglars.

On the morning of May 21, the de Morcerf servants prepared for the visit of the Count of Monte Cristo. In actuality, Albert did not believe the Count would actually appear.

"Is the countess my mother up yet?" Albert asked Germain, one of the servants.

"If you wish, I will inquire."

"Yes, ask her for a few bottles of liquor—my bar is incomplete. And tell her I shall have the honor of seeing her about three o'clock, and that I request permission to introduce someone to her." The valet left the room.

Albert threw himself on the sofa and glanced at two or three newspapers. The next moment, a carriage stopped before the door, and the servant announced M. Lucien Debray. This was a tall young man with light hair, clear gray eyes, and thin and compressed lips.

"Good morning, Lucien, good morning," said Albert. "Your being on time really alarms me. Has the government resigned?"

"No, my dear fellow," answered the young man, seating himself on the sofa. "Reassure yourself. We are tottering always, but we never fall. But I am hungry; feed me. I am bored; amuse me."

"It is my duty as your host," replied Albert, ringing the bell. "Germain, bring a glass of sherry and a biscuit."

"My dear Albert," replied Lucien, lighting a cigar, "how lucky you are not to have to work for a living. You do not know your own good fortune!"

"And what would you do, my dear diplomat," replied Albert, "if you did not work? You have an income of twenty-five thousand francs a year, quite aside from your career. You have a horse you've been offered eight thousand francs for and would not sell. You have a tailor who never disappoints you. Besides all that, with the opera, the jockey-club, and other diversions, can you not amuse yourself? Well, I will amuse you."

"How?"

"By introducing to you a new acquaintance. Ah, I hear Sebastian Beauchamp in the next room. Come in, come in!" said Albert, rising and advancing to meet the young man, a newspaper editor and a good friend of Albert's.

"My dear Albert! May I hope for breakfast?" Beauchamp inquired. I must be off soon, for I have work to do."

"Breakfast will be served as soon as two other

persons arrive. In the meanwhile, have a seat," Albert replied.

"And what sort of persons do you expect at breakfast?" said Beauchamp.

"A gentleman, and a diplomat."

"Then we shall have to wait two hours for the gentleman, and three for the diplomat. Oh well, I must do something to distract my thoughts. You see, this morning I shall hear M. Danglars make a speech at the Chamber of Deputies. And at his home this evening I shall hear more speeches yet."

"I understand," Albert responded. "We must attempt to amuse you well before that occurs. But remember, I expect to marry Eugenie Danglars. I cannot in good conscience let you insult the man who will one day say to me, 'Viscount, I give my daughter two million francs to share with you.'"

"Ah, this marriage will never take place," laughed Beauchamp. "The king has made Danglars a baron, but he cannot make him a gentleman. Your father, the Count de Morcerf, is too aristocratic to consent to such a mismatch for the modest sum of two million francs. You can't marry a woman whose rank is lower than marquise."

"Never mind what he says, Albert," said Debray, "you had better marry Eugenie Danglars. You marry for money, true, but you have enough aristocracy to share with her."

Just then the servant reappeared and announced two fresh guests: "Count Christopher de Chateau-Renaud and M. Maximilian Morrel."

"I was expecting Christopher, but I don't know this Morrel," Albert said to himself. As Albert finished this thought, Chateau-Renaud, a handsome young man of thirty, took Albert's hand. "My dear Albert," he said, "let me introduce to you M. Maximilian Morrel, a gallant officer, my friend as well as my hero." And he stepped aside to give place to a dignified young man with piercing eyes and a black mustache. The young officer bowed with easy and elegant politeness.

"Monsieur," said Albert with courtesy, "you are Christopher's friend, be mine also."

"Well said," interrupted Chateau-Renaud. "And you should hope that, if you were ever in such danger as I was, he would do as much for you as he did for me."

"What did he do?" asked Albert.

"Oh, nothing worth speaking of," said Morrel. "M. de Chateau-Renaud exaggerates."

"Not worth speaking of?" asked Chateau-Renaud. "We were on patrol in Africa. After rescuing me from the sword, he rescued me from the cold by giving me his cloak."

"The person I am expecting also saved *my* life," declared Albert. The viscount then recounted the story of his capture and rescue in Rome.

"And where does your hero come from?" asked Debray.

"He calls himself the Count of Monte Cristo," said Albert.

"There is no Count of Monte Cristo," said Debray. "I am familiar with all of Europe's nobility.

Where is this Monte Cristo?"

"I have heard of it," said Maximilian Morrel. "Monte Cristo is a small island. The old sailors my father employed spoke of it—a grain of sand in the center of the Mediterranean."

"Precisely!" cried Albert. "Well, the Count is the lord and master of this grain of sand."

"He is rich, then?"

"I believe so."

"Well, where is this Count of Monte Cristo?" added Debray. "It is half past 10, and he is late."

The sound of the clock had not died away when Germain announced, "His excellency the Count of Monte Cristo." All the young men rose from their chairs, and Albert himself was seized with sudden emotion.

The Count advanced, smiling, into the center of the room, and approached Albert, who hastened toward him, holding out his hand in a warm and cordial manner.

"My dear Count," replied Albert, "I was announcing your visit to some of my friends, whom I now present to you. They are the Count of Chateau-Renaud; M. Lucien Debray, private secretary to the Minister of the Interior; M. Beauchamp, an editor of an important newspaper; and M. Maximilian Morrel, an army captain who has served in Africa."

At this final name, the Count, who had saluted every one with formal courtesy, stepped a pace forward, a slight tinge of color in his pale cheeks, and checked out the young man more carefully.

"Gentlemen," said Albert, "Germain informs me that breakfast is ready. My dear Count, allow me to show you the way." They passed silently into the breakfast room, and everyone took his place.

The Count was a man who ate little but had varied tastes. "I have lived on pasta in Italy, curry in India, and swallows' nests in China. I eat everywhere and everything, only in small quantities," he explained to the other guests.

"And did you sleep well on your journey here?" asked one of the young men.

"Very well," replied the Count. "I am a tolerable chemist and have made up some excellent sleeping pills." He then drew from his pocket a magnificent pill-box, with a marvelous emerald on top, and closed by a golden lid. There were four or five little tablets in the box. He passed the container around the table. The diners were dazzled by the size and deep green color of the emerald.

"This is a magnificent emerald, and the largest I have ever seen," said Chateau-Renaud.

"I had three similar ones," returned Monte Cristo. "I gave one to the sultan of Turkey, who mounted it in his saber. I gave the other to our holy father the Pope, who had it set in his head-piece. The third I kept for myself."

"And what did these two sovereigns give you in exchange for these magnificent presents?" asked Debray.

"From the sultan, the freedom of a woman," replied the Count. "From the Pope, the life of a man."

"My dear Count, you have no idea what pleasure it gives me to hear you speak like this," said Albert. "I had described you to my friends as an enchanter out of the *Arabian Nights*, and now you show that I told the truth. But tell us, how did you persuade the bandit Luigi Vampa in Rome to spare my life?"

"Vampa tried to kidnap me once. Instead, it was I who captured him and a dozen of his band. I could have handed him over to the Roman police, but I did nothing of the sort. Instead, I allowed him and his band to go free on condition they would always respect my interests and, if necessary, help me and my friends."

"Well, now that you are in Paris," Albert said, "there is only one service I can provide, and that is to introduce you to my friends. I do not dare offer to share my apartments with you. My rooms are too small for anyone but myself, unless that visitor were female."

"Ah," said the Count, "that reminds me. I remember that at Rome you said something of a projected marriage. May I congratulate you?"

"The affair is still in the planning stage," answered Albert. "I hope, before long, to introduce you, if not to my wife, at least to my fiancée— Mademoiselle Eugenie Danglars."

"Eugenie Danglars," said Monte Cristo. "Tell me, is her father Baron Danglars?"

"Yes," returned Albert. "He just recently gained that title."

"And what did he do to merit this honor?" asked Monte Cristo.

Beauchamp answered him. "He negotiated a loan of six million francs for the king's younger brother. The king made him a baron and chevalier of the Legion of Honor. He is so proud of the honor that he wears the ribbon prominently displayed in his button-hole."

"Ah," interrupted Albert, turning to Monte Cristo. "You just now spoke the baron's name as if you knew him."

"I do not know him," answered Monte Cristo, "but I shall probably make his acquaintance soon, for I have a line of credit opened with Danglars' Bank through the Thomson & French Bank in Rome, as well as some other banks." As he pronounced the names Thomson and French, the Count glanced at Maximilian Morrel. Maximilian started as if he had been electrified.

"Thomson & French Bank!" he exclaimed. "How well do you know this bank, monsieur?"

"They are my bankers in Rome," returned the Count quietly. "Can my influence with them be of any service to you?"

"Oh, Count, perhaps you could help me to learn something I have been trying to discover for a long time. Years ago, this bank did my family a great service. But for some unknown reason, they have always denied any knowledge of it."

"I will assist you in any way possible," said Monte Cristo, bowing.

"But," continued Albert, "we have strangely wandered from the subject. We must find a suitable place for the Count of Monte Cristo to live. Where shall we lodge this new guest in our great capital?"

The young men suggested various neighborhoods where the aristocracy lived. The Count, however, showed no enthusiasm for any of these proposals. Then Maximilian Morrel spoke up. "I propose a suite of apartments in a charming hotel where my sister has lived for a year, in Meslay Street."

"You have a sister?" asked the Count.

"Yes, monsieur, a most excellent sister."

"Married?"

"Nearly nine years."

"Happy?" asked the Count again.

"As happy as can be," replied Maximilian. "She married the man she loved, who remained faithful to us in our fallen fortunes—Emmanuel Herbaut." Monte Cristo smiled imperceptibly. "I am living there now, during my leave of absence from the army," continued Maximilian.

"Thanks, monsieur," said Monte Cristo. "I shall content myself with being introduced to your sister and her husband, if you will do me the honor. But I cannot accept your kind offer. You see, I sent my valet to Paris ahead of me. By now he ought to have purchased a house and furnished it."

"So you have a valet who knows Paris?" said Beauchamp.

"It is the first time he has ever been in Paris, and he is unable to speak," returned Monte Cristo.

"It is Ali!" cried Albert, in the midst of the general surprise.

"Yes, Ali himself, the Nubian mute, whom you saw, I think, in Rome."

"Certainly," said Albert. "I remember him perfectly."

"He has been here a week, and he knows my preferences. He has arranged everything for me."

"What's your new address?" asked Beauchamp.

"Thirty Champs-Elysées Boulevard."

"Very princely," said Chateau-Renaud. He continued, "Since you have a staff and a residence in the Champs-Elysées, all you need is a wife." He was thinking of a lovely Greek girl he had seen seated next to Monte Cristo at several theaters.

"I have something better than that," said Monte Cristo. "I have a slave. I purchased her at Constantinople, after her father died and she was sold into slavery. Of course, she is free to leave me whenever she desires." This was, in fact, the beautiful Greek girl, named Haydee, whom he was looking after until she reached adulthood.

"My dear Albert," said Debray, rising, "it is half-past two. Your guest is charming, but one must sometimes leave the best company to go into the worst. I must return to the minister's. Goodbye all."

As he left the room, Debray called out loudly, "My carriage."

"What a story," said the journalist Beauchamp to Albert. "I shall have something better to offer my readers than one of M. Danglars' speeches." Beauchamp and the others departed, leaving Monte Cristo alone with Albert.

CHAPTER 30
The Presentation

Albert introduces the Count of Monte Cristo to his parents.

Albert immediately turned to the Count and said, "My dear Count, allow me to begin my services as guide by showing you an example of a Paris bachelor's apartment." Monte Cristo had already seen the breakfast room and the salon on the ground floor. As Albert gave him a lengthy tour of the two floors of his apartment, it became clear that Monte Cristo was very knowledgeable about archaeology, mineralogy and art.

From the salon they passed into the bed-chamber, which was a model of taste and simple elegance. One portrait in particular attracted the Count of Monte Cristo's attention. It was the portrait of a young woman of about twenty-five. She had a dark complexion and light and shining eyes, veiled beneath long lashes. She wore the picturesque costume of the Catalan fisherwomen, with a red and black top. She was looking at the sea, and her form was outlined against the blue ocean and sky. The light was so faint in the room that Albert did not see how pale the Count had become, or notice the nervous heaving of his chest and shoulders. Silence prevailed for an instant, during which Monte Cristo gazed intently on the picture.

"You have there a most charming lady-friend, viscount," said Monte Cristo in a perfectly calm tone.

"Ah, monsieur," returned Albert, "that is my mother. She had this portrait painted six or eight years ago for the benefit of my father. Strange to say, however, this portrait displeased my father. My mother, on the other hand, rarely comes here without looking at it. And when she looks at it, she almost always weeps. This disagreement is the only one between my parents in their twenty years of marriage."

"Now," said Albert, "please accompany me to the apartments of my father and mother. I wrote to them from Rome to tell them how you saved my life. Here we begin an initiation into Parisian life—a life of politeness, visiting, and introductions."

Monte Cristo bowed without making an answer. Albert summoned his servant and ordered him to inform M. and Madame de Morcerf of the arrival of the Count of Monte Cristo. Albert and the Count then proceeded to the main section of the house, occupied by Albert's parents.

"Father," said the young man, "I have the honor of presenting to you the Count of Monte Cristo, the man who saved my life in Rome."

"You are most welcome, monsieur," said the Count de Morcerf with a smile. Long ago, he had been known as Fernand, the Catalan fisherman who sent the letter that resulted in Edmond's imprisonment. He was now a man in his early forties, although he looked much older. His black mustache and eyebrows contrasted strangely with his almost white hair, which was cut short, in military fashion. He was dressed in plain clothes, but he was wearing some of the medals he had earned in the French army. "In saving our only son, Monsieur has rendered our family a service which insures him our eternal gratitude." As he said these words, Fernand pointed to a chair, while he seated himself in another opposite the window.

Monte Cristo took his seat. "The countess," said Fernand, "is still dressing and will join us in a few minutes."

"It is a great honor to me," answered Monte Cristo, "to meet a man whose merit equals his reputation. Have you not yet been made a general of the army in reward for your service?"

"Oh," replied Fernand, "I have retired from the military, monsieur. I have hung up my sword and thrown myself into politics."

"Ah, here is my mother," said Albert. Monte Cristo turned around hastily and saw Madame de Morcerf, whom he had known as Mercedes. She stood pale and motionless, and when Monte Cristo rose and bowed to her, she bowed her head without speaking.

"Good heavens, madame," said her husband, "are you ill? You look so pale."

"No," she replied, "but I feel some emotion on seeing the man who saved our son Albert's life."

Monte Cristo bowed again. He was even paler than Mercedes. "Madame," he said, "the count and you give me too much credit. To save a man, to spare a father's feelings, or a mother's heart, is not to do a good action, but a simple deed of humanity."

At these words, Fernand excused himself to attend a government meeting. Monte Cristo explained that he needed to supervise the arrangements in his new household. He too departed, stepping into a magnificent carriage, pulled by horses which their previous owner had, at one time, refused to part with for the enormous sum of 14,000 francs.

When Albert returned to his mother, he found her in her sitting-room, resting in a large velvet armchair. Albert could not see his mother's face, as she had put on a thin veil which fell over her features in misty folds. It seemed to him, though, that her voice had somehow changed. He noticed, amid the perfumes of the flowers in the vases, the sharp odor of smelling-salts, and he saw the bottle holding those salts on the countess's table. Knowing that people used smelling-salts to counter a feeling of dizziness or fainting, Albert exclaimed, "My dear mother, have you been ill?"

"No, no, Albert. You know how overpowering the scent of these flowers can be."

After making sure that his mother was all right, Albert returned to his rooms. "This is a devil of a fellow," he muttered, shaking his head. "I said he would create a sensation here, and I was correct. My mother has noticed him, and he must, therefore, be remarkable." He went down to the stables, feeling some slight annoyance that the Count of Monte Cristo had laid his hands on a set of horses which made his own look decidedly second-rate. "It is certainly true," he reflected to himself, "that all men are not created equal."

CHAPTER 31

Monsieur Bertuccio

Accompanied by his reluctant servant Bertuccio, the Count sets out for his new country house at Auteuil.

Meanwhile the Count of Monte Cristo had arrived at his house. It had taken him six minutes to travel the distance. But, these six minutes were enough to attract the attention of twenty wealthy young men who knew the price of his vehicle, which they themselves could never afford. They put their horses in a gallop in order to see the rich foreigner who could afford to pay 20,000 francs apiece for his horses.

The carriage stopped at the entrance, and two servants approached the carriage. One was Ali, who was smiling with an expression of the most sincere joy. The other bowed respectfully and offered his arm to assist the Count in descending. "Thank you, Bertuccio," said the Count. "Is the lawyer handling the house sale here?"

"He is in the small salon, excellency," returned Bertuccio.

"And the calling cards I ordered to be engraved as soon as you knew the number of the house?"

"Your excellency, it is already done. As you

ordered, I took the first card that was struck off to the Baron Danglars on Chaussee d'Antin Street. The others are on the mantelpiece of your excellency's bedroom."

Monte Cristo gave his hat, cane, and gloves to a footman, and then he passed into the small salon, preceded by Bertuccio. The lawyer awaited him there.

"You are the lawyer empowered to sell the country house that I wish to purchase, monsieur?" asked Monte Cristo.

"Yes, Count," answered the lawyer.

"Is the deed of sale ready?"

"Yes, Count. Here it is"

"Very well. And where is this house that I am buying?" asked the Count carelessly.

"The house you purchase is at Auteuil."

At these words Bertuccio turned pale. "And where is Auteuil?" asked the Count.

"Close by here, monsieur," replied the lawyer. "It is a charming place, well supplied with spring-water and fine trees. A very comfortable home, although abandoned for a long time. And the furniture, although old, is quite valuable."

"The deed, if you please, sir." The Count signed it rapidly, and said, "Bertuccio, give this man fifty-five thousand francs." The steward left the room with a faltering step, and returned with a bundle of bank-notes.

"I wish to see my new property this evening," the Count declared to Bertuccio. "Please arrange for my carriage to take us there."

"To Auteuil!" cried Bertuccio, his tanned face going white as paper. "I go to Auteuil?"

"Well, what is surprising about that? When I live at Auteuil, you must come there, as you are in my service. Get your hat and gloves now, and let us visit my new home."

"Am I to accompany you, your excellency?"

"Certainly, for I intend to remain at the house for a while." It was unheard of for a servant to dispute the Count's orders. And so the steward followed his master into the carriage, and they set off for Auteuil.

CHAPTER 32
The House at Auteuil

At the house at Auteuil, Bertuccio makes a confession to the Count.

As they approached the village of Auteuil, Monte Cristo noticed that Bertuccio crossed himself and muttered a short prayer. In twenty minutes they were at Auteuil. The steward's emotion had become more obvious as they entered the village. Crouched in the corner of the carriage, Bertuccio began to examine every house they passed with feverish anxiety.

The carriage stopped at 28 Fontaine Street, and the footman sprang off the box and opened the door.

Bertuccio got out and offered his arm to the Count, who leaned upon it as he descended from the carriage. "Knock," said the Count, "and announce me." Bertuccio knocked, the door opened, and the butler appeared. "What is it?" he asked.

"It is your new master, my good fellow," said Bertuccio.

"Good day," said the Count "and I hope I will give you no cause to regret the loss of your old master."

"Oh, monsieur," said the butler, "I shall not have much cause to miss him, for he came here very rarely. It is five years since he was here last."

"What was the name of your old master?" said Monte Cristo.

"The Marquis of Saint-Meran. "

"The Marquis of Saint-Meran!" returned the Count. "The name is known to me."

"He is an elderly gentleman," continued the butler. "He had only one daughter, who married M. de Villefort, who was the king's attorney." Monte Cristo glanced at Bertuccio, who became whiter than the wall against which he leaned to prevent himself from falling. "And is not this daughter dead?" asked Monte Cristo.

"Yes, monsieur, twenty-one years ago. Since then we have seen the poor marquis only three times."

"Thank you," said Monte Cristo. "Give me a light so I can see the rooms."

"Shall I accompany you, monsieur?" asked the butler.

"No, it is unnecessary. Bertuccio will do it. Take one of the carriage-lamps, Bertuccio," said the Count, "and let us see the rooms." The steward obeyed in silence, but it was easy to see, from the manner that the light trembled, how upset he was. They went through the house. Near one of the bedrooms, they came to a winding staircase that led down to the garden.

"Ah, here is a private staircase," said the Count. "That is convenient. Let's see where it leads to."

"Monsieur," replied Bertuccio, "it leads to the garden."

"And, pray, how do you know that?"

"It ought to do so, I meant to say."

"Well, let us be sure of that." The stairs did, indeed, lead to the garden. At the outer door, the steward paused. "Go on, Bertuccio," said the Count. But Bertuccio stood stock still. His eyes glanced nervously around, as if they recalled some terrible event. "Well?" inquired the Count.

"No, no," cried Bertuccio, setting down the lantern. "No, monsieur, it is impossible. I can go no farther."

"What does this mean?" demanded Monte Cristo.

"Sir, I must be frank with you. It was in this garden, this very spot, where I carried out my vengeance and committed a bloody murder. Did not Abbé Busoni, who heard my confession and recommended me to you, tell you I carried a heavy burden?"

"Well yes, but I thought that referred only to a bit of smuggling and some petty theft. Come, pull yourself together, and tell me everything."

"I will tell you all. But please, first, move away from that tree. The moon is just bursting through the clouds, and there, standing where you are, and wrapped in that cloak, you remind me of M. de Villefort."

" What!" exclaimed Monte Cristo, "your victim was M. de Villefort?"

"Your excellency knows him?"

"The king's attorney?"

"Yes."

"Who married the Marquis of Saint-Meran's daughter?"

"Yes."

"Who was known as the most severe, the most upright, the most rigid prosecutor on the bench?"

"Well, monsieur," said Bertuccio, "this man with this spotless reputation—"

"Well?"

"Was a villain."

"Bah!" replied Monte Cristo. "Impossible!"

"It is as I tell you. Allow me to begin."

CHAPTER 33
The Vendetta

Bertuccio tells the story of how he avenged his brother's death—and what he discovered when he opened a small box.

"The story begins in 1815," Bertuccio said. "I had an elder brother, who was in the service of the emperor Napoleon. This brother was my only friend. We became orphans—I at five, he at eighteen. He brought me up as if I had been his son, and in 1814 he married. When the emperor returned from the island of Elba, my brother instantly joined his army, was slightly wounded at Waterloo, and retreated with the army. One day we received a letter from my brother. He told us that the army was disbanded, and that on his way home he should pass the town of Nimes. He told me that if I had any money, I should leave it for him at Nimes, with an innkeeper with whom I had dealings.

"I possessed a thousand francs. I left five hundred with Assunta, my sister-in-law, and with the other five hundred I set off for Nimes. As I entered Nimes, I literally waded in blood. At every step, I encountered dead bodies and bands of murderers who killed, plundered, and burned. At the sight of this slaughter and devastation, I became terrified, not for myself but for my brother. As a soldier of Bonaparte, returning from the army in uniform, he had everything to fear.

"I hurried to the inn, where I discovered my worst fears realized. My brother had arrived the previous evening at Nimes and had been killed. I did all in my power to discover the murderers, but no one dared tell me their names, so much were they dreaded. I then went to the king's attorney."

"And this king's attorney was named Villefort?" asked Monte Cristo carelessly.

"Yes, your excellency. He came from Marseilles. I said to him, 'My brother was murdered yesterday in the streets of Nimes. I do not know who killed him, but it is your duty to find out. You are the representative of justice here, and justice must avenge those she has been unable to protect.'

"'Who was your brother?' he asked.

"'A lieutenant in Napoleon's army.'

"'A soldier of the enemy of the king, then?'

"'It would seem so.'

"'Well,' replied he, 'he lived by the sword, and he has died by the sword.'

"'You are mistaken, monsieur,' I replied. 'He has died by an assassin's dagger.'

"'What do you want me to do?' asked the king's attorney.

"'I have already told you—avenge him.'

"'On whom?'

"'On his murderers.'

"'How should I know who they are?'

"'Order an investigation!'

"'Why, no doubt your brother was involved in a quarrel and was killed in a duel. All these old soldiers commit excesses which were tolerated in the time of the emperor. In all probability, your brother deserved to die. Get out now, or I shall have you thrown out.'

"I looked at him for an instant to see if there was any hope for me to beg further. But he was a man of stone. I approached him, and said in a low voice, 'Let me tell you something. I will kill you. From this moment I declare a vendetta against you. Protect yourself as well as you can, for the hour that we next meet will be your last.' And before he had recovered from his surprise, I opened the door and left the room.

"From that moment he shut himself in his house and never went out alone. His agents searched for me high and low, but I was so well concealed that he could not find me. Then he became very frightened and did not dare stay any longer in Nimes. He asked for a change of residence and was assigned to Versailles, outside Paris. But I followed him there and watched.

"The most important thing was, not only to kill him—for I had an opportunity to do so a hundred times—but to kill him without being discovered. I no longer cared much about myself, but I had my sister-in-law to protect and provide for. For three months I watched M. de Villefort. For three months he did not take one step outdoors without my following him. I discovered that he made mysterious trips to Auteuil. I followed him there, and I saw him enter the house where we now are. However, instead of entering by the front door, he entered through the garden by the rear gate you see over there.

"If I wished to surprise him, this was the spot to lie in wait for him. The house belonged, as the butler informed your excellency, to M. de Saint-Meran, Villefort's father-in-law. M. de Saint-Meran lived at Marseilles. He rented the property to a young widow, known only by the name of 'the baroness.'

"One evening, as I was looking over the wall, I saw a handsome young woman walking alone in that garden, and I guessed that she was awaiting M. de Villefort. When she drew near enough for me to see her well, I perceived she was eighteen or nineteen years old, tall, and very fair. As she had a loose dress on, I saw she was pregnant. A few moments later, the garden gate opened, and a man entered. The young woman hurried to meet him. They threw themselves into each other's arms, embraced tenderly, and walked together to the house. The man was M. de Villefort."

"And," asked the Count, "did you ever find out the name of this woman?"

"No, excellency," returned Bertuccio.

"Go on."

"That evening," continued Bertuccio, "I could have killed Villefort, but I didn't know the neighborhood very well, and I had not planned my escape. I was afraid that if I did not kill him quickly, his cries for help might attract the police before I could get away.

"After I saw him leave that night, I made my plans. I returned the next day and rented a room across the street. After watching the house for three days, I saw some unusual activity. About seven o'clock in the evening, I saw a servant on horseback leave the house at full gallop and take off down the road to Versailles. Three hours later, the man returned with another man I recognized as Villefort. He left his horse outside the wall and went through the garden's small gate and into the house through this side door.

"I crossed the street and jumped over the wall and hid near the path Villefort would take through the garden back to his horse. Two hours passed. Midnight struck. As the last stroke of the clock died away, I saw a faint light shine out as the door opened. Villefort came out. I drew my knife and prepared to strike.

"He walked toward me, carrying a spade and a small box. He stopped close to where I was hiding, glanced around, and began to dig a hole in the ground.

"I wanted to see what he was going to do. I remained motionless, holding my breath. I watched as he placed the box, only two feet long and perhaps eight inches deep, into the hole he had dug. As he was covering up the box with dirt, I rushed out and plunged my knife into his heart.

"As he lay gasping on the ground, I looked him in the eye and snarled, 'I am Giovanni Bertuccio. Your death is for my brother's. Your treasure is for his widow. My vengeance is complete!' I watched his blood gush out of his body, and it seemed to refresh me. In a second, I dug up the box, filled the hole back the way it was before, and ran off."

"Ah," said Monte Cristo, "it seems to me this was nothing but murder and robbery."

"No, your excellency, it was a vendetta followed by restitution."

"And was there a lot of money in the box?" inquired the Count.

"It was not money," Bertuccio went on. "I hurried to the river, sat down on the bank, and with my knife forced open the lock of the box. Inside, wrapped in a fine linen cloth, was a new-born child. Its purplish face and hands showed that it had died from suffocation. As it was not yet cold, I hesitated to throw it into the water that ran at my feet. After a moment I thought I felt a slight pulse. I did what a doctor would have done—I inflated the lungs by blowing air into them. The infant began to breathe, and cried feebly. In my turn I uttered a cry, but a cry of joy."

"And what did you do with the child?" asked Monte Cristo.

"I did not think of keeping it. Instead, I took it to an orphanage in Paris. Before leaving it on the doorstep, I cut the linen surrounding the child into two pieces. This linen was marked with two letters. I left one piece containing a letter with the child and kept the other piece with its letter. Then I rang the bell and fled.

"Two weeks later, I was home in Rogliano. I said to my brother's wife, Assunta, 'Comfort yourself, sister. Your husband is dead, but he is avenged.' She asked what I meant, and after I told her, she said, 'Giovanni, you should have brought this child with you. We would have replaced the parents it has lost.' In reply, I gave her the half of the linen I had kept in order to reclaim him if ever we could."

"What letters were marked on the linen?" asked Monte Cristo.

"An H and an N, with a baron's coronet."

"What became of this little boy? For I think you told me it was a boy, Bertuccio."

"No excellency, I do not remember telling you that."

"I thought you did."

"Well, it was a little boy. As time passed, I had some successes as a smuggler, I am embarrassed to relate. Assunta took care of everything at home, and our little fortune increased. One day, when I returned after six weeks away, Assunta greeted me at the door and exclaimed, 'I have a surprise for you. Come this way.' The first thing I saw was a cradle, and in it was a baby seven or eight months old. Carrying the half of the linen, and armed with the day and hour at which I had left the child, she had gone to Paris and reclaimed it. I confess, your excellency, when I saw this poor creature sleeping peacefully in its cradle, I felt my eyes fill with tears. We called the child Benedetto.

"Alas, God made this infant the instrument of our punishment. Never have I seen a wicked nature develop at such an early age, and yet it was not owing to any fault in his upbringing. He was a most lovely child, with large blue eyes and fair skin. Only his hair, which was almost white, gave him an unusual appearance, and his smile was evil.

"Assunta's affection for Benedetto only seemed to increase as he became more unworthy of it. He spent all her money on things he wanted. When Benedetto was only eleven, his companions were young men of eighteen or twenty, the worst characters in Corsica. They had already run afoul of the law several times.

"I needed, at this time, to leave Corsica on an important expedition. With the hope of preventing more misfortune, I decided that Benedetto should accompany me. But when I spoke to Benedetto about this, he burst out laughing.

"'Are you mad, uncle? Do you think I am going to exchange the life I lead for the hard and dangerous work you do? You are out in the bitter frosts of night and the scorching sun by day. And when you are discovered, you are shot at like an animal. I have as much money as I want. Mother Assunta always gives it to me when I ask for it! I would be a fool to accept your offer.' Benedetto went back to join his friends.

"Not long after, I set off on a smuggling voyage. Unfortunately, when we docked, armed customs officers surrounded our boat. Terrified, I sprang into the water and was able to escape. I made my way to the nearby village of Beaucaire. I knew a man who had set up a little inn there."

"Yes," said Monte Cristo. "I think he was part of your smuggling operation."

"Yes," answered Bertuccio. "But my old colleague had, seven or eight years before this period, sold his inn to a tailor from Marseilles. Of course, we made the same arrangements with the new landlord that we had with the old. My plan was to seek shelter at this inn."

"What was his name?" inquired the count.

"Gaspard Caderousse. He had married a woman from the village of Carconte. She was suffering from malarial fever and seemed to be dying by inches. As for her husband, he was a strapping fellow in his early forties."

"And you say," interrupted Monte Cristo, "that this took place in what year?"

"1829, your excellency."

"In what month?"

"June."

"The beginning or the end?"

"The evening of the 3rd."

"Ah," said Monte Cristo "the evening of the 3rd of June, 1829. Go on."

"So I intended to demand shelter from Caderousse. Fearing that Caderousse might have some guests, I entered a shed in which I had often spent the night. This shed was separated from the inn only by a partition, in which we had made spy-holes that looked into the inn. My intention was, if Caderousse was alone, to let him know I was there and obtain a meal, for I was cold and hungry. Then, under the cover of the coming storm, I planned to return and check on the state of our vessel and its crew. I stepped into the shed, peered through the spy-hole, and saw Caderousse talking with a stranger.

"This man was one of those merchants who come to sell jewelry at the Beaucaire fair. Caderousse called to his wife and said, 'Carconte, the good priest has not deceived us. The diamond is real, and this gentleman, one of the finest jewelers of Paris, will give us 50,000 francs for it. Only, in order to satisfy himself that it really belongs to us, he wishes you to tell him about the miraculous way in which the diamond came into our possession. I have already done the same. In the meantime, please sit down, monsieur, and I will fetch you some refreshment.'

"'Tell your story, madame,' said the jeweler. He wanted, no doubt, to see if the two told the same tale.

"'Oh,' she replied, 'it was a gift from heaven. My husband was a great friend, in 1814 or 1815, of a sailor named Edmond Dantes. This poor fellow, whom Caderousse had forgotten, had not forgotten him, and when he died, he left this diamond to him.'

"'But how did Dantes obtain it?' asked the jeweler.

"'It appears that in prison he befriended a rich Englishman, and when this man fell sick, Edmond cared for him as if he were his own brother. When this Englishman was set free, he gave this stone to Edmond, and when Edmond died, he left it to us. He gave it into the charge of the excellent Abbé Busoni, who came here this morning to deliver it.'

"'The same story,' muttered the jeweler, 'and impossible as it seemed at first, it may be true. There's only the price we are not agreed about.'

"The two men spent much time haggling over the price and finally settled on 45,000 francs, an enormous sum. As a storm was by now raging, Caderousse invited the jeweler to stay the night. The visitor accepted."

CHAPTER 34
The Rain of Blood

Bertuccio continues his story, which ends with several deaths. Later that evening, the Count returns to his house in Paris, where he is joined by Haydee, a young and beautiful Greek woman.

"The Caderousses served dinner to their guest and then wished him a good night's sleep. As the jeweler ascended to his bedroom, the storm raged on. I myself, weary from the day's activities, lay down and fell asleep.

"I was suddenly aroused by the sound of a pistol shot, followed by a fearful cry. Above me I heard weak and tottering footsteps, followed by a dull thud. I had not yet fully awakened, when again I heard groans, as if from persons engaged in a deadly struggle.

"Looking through the spy-hole, I saw Caderousse. He was pale, and his shirt was all bloody. He was holding in his hand the small case that contained the diamond. He put this in his pocket and took from his cupboard the bank-notes and gold he kept there. Then he rushed out into the darkness of the night.

"Thinking that the unfortunate jeweler might

not be quite dead, I hastened to check on him. I made my way up the stairs. About halfway up, a body was lying across the stairs. It was that of La Carconte. The shot I had heard had most certainly been fired at her. She was stone dead. I strode past her and ascended to the sleeping chamber. The furniture had been knocked over in the deadly struggle that had taken place there. The murdered jeweler lay on the floor, his head leaning against the wall, and about him was a pool of blood which poured forth from three large wounds in his chest. There was a fourth gash, in which a long table knife was plunged up to the handle. In seeing if I could help him, I managed to get blood on my hands and shirt.

"I realized I could not help anyone, and I rushed down the stairs—right into the arms of a half dozen policemen. As I was covered in blood, they quickly assumed I was the killer. Despite my protests, they handcuffed me and took me to Nimes.

"While I was in prison in Nimes, my only hope was to find Abbé Busoni so that he could confirm my story. For two months the magistrate searched for him and for Caderousse. Three months after the incident, imagine my surprise when Abbé Busoni came to the prison. When I told him everything that happened, he confirmed it down to the tiniest detail. In addition, I asked him to hear my confession. He worked on my behalf. Soon thereafter Caderousse was caught, and he confessed everything. He was sent to the galleys for life, and I was set free."

"And then it was, I presume," said Monte Cristo, "that you came to me as the bearer of a letter of recommendation from the Abbé Busoni?"

"Yes," replied Bertuccio.

"I take pleasure in saying that you have served me faithfully, Bertuccio. But why did you never tell me about your sister-in-law and the adopted child?"

"Their story is a sad one. As soon as I was released from jail in Nimes, I was anxious to comfort my dear sister-in-law. When I arrived in Corsica, where she lived, I found a house of mourning. The widow had refused to comply with the unreasonable demands of Benedetto, who was continually tormenting her for money. One morning he had demanded money, threatening her with the severest consequences if she did not give it to him. She refused. In a fury, he stormed out of the house and did not return until 11 o'clock at night.

"He entered with a swaggering air, along with two of his companions. She welcomed him warmly, but they seized hold of her. Benedetto exclaimed, 'Torture her, and she'll soon tell us where her money is.'

"The two held Assunta, who, unable to imagine that any harm was intended, did not resist at first. They dragged her to the fireplace and placed her feet close to the fire in hopes of learning where she kept her money. In the struggle her clothes caught fire and Assunta was unable to escape and perished in the fire.

"The next morning the authorities found every drawer and closet in the house had been forced open, and the money stolen. Benedetto never again appeared, and I have neither seen nor heard anything concerning him."

"Do you know what happened to Benedetto?"

"Thank God, I have never heard his name mentioned by any person, and I hope and believe he is dead."

"Do not think so, Bertuccio," replied the count, "for the wicked are not so easily disposed of. And now leave me, Bertuccio, to walk alone here in the garden."

After spending some time in the garden, the count reentered his carriage. Bertuccio, who perceived the thoughtful expression on his master's face, took his seat beside the driver without uttering a word. The carriage proceeded rapidly toward Paris.

That same evening, when he reached his home in the Champs-Elysées, the Count of Monte Cristo inspected the whole building. Ali was his principal attendant during this survey. The Count, drawing out his watch, said to the attentive servant, "It is half-past eleven o'clock. Haydee will soon be here. She will be tired and will, no doubt, wish to rest."

Just at that moment voices were heard. The gate opened and a carriage stopped at the entrance. The Count hastily presented himself at the already opened carriage door and held out his hand to a young woman, completely enveloped in a green silk garment heavily embroidered with gold. She raised the hand extended toward her to her lips, and kissed it with a mixture of love and respect. Some few words passed between them in Greek. Then Monte Cristo summoned Ali to escort the new arrival to her suite of rooms. Meanwhile, the Count retired to his own rooms in another part of the house.

CHAPTER 35
Unlimited Credit

*The Count instructs Bertuccio to purchase Baron Danglars'
carriage horses. That evening, the Count visits Danglars and
requests a loan.*

About two o'clock the following day, a carriage
drawn by a pair of magnificent English horses
stopped at the door of Monte Cristo's mansion.
The passenger inside the coach was none other than
Baron Danglars. He directed his groom to inquire
at the porter's lodge whether the Count of Monte
Cristo lived there, and if he were at home.

The groom learned that the Count did indeed
reside there, but that he was not receiving visitors
on that day. Not used to such dismissal, the baron
called out to his coachman, "To the Parliament."

Monte Cristo had, from behind the blinds of
a room, observed the encounter. He summoned
Bertuccio and said, "You no doubt observed the
horses pulling that coach?"

"Certainly, your excellency. I noticed them for
their remarkable beauty."

"I have to pay a visit this evening. I desire that
these very horses, with completely new harness, be
at the door with my carriage."

"But your excellency, it will cost a fortune to purchase these animals."

"No matter," said the Count. "Pay whatever it costs."

Bertuccio bowed and retired.

At five o'clock, the new horses appeared, harnessed to the Count's elaborate coach. The Count directed the coachman to take him to the residence of Baron Danglars, one of the richest bankers in Paris. Danglars was proud to invite the Count into his drawing room, whose elegant furnishings of white and gold had caused a great sensation in Paris.

The baron got right down to business. "Permit me to inform you, Count," he said, bowing, "that I have received a letter from the Thomson & French Bank, of Rome. The letter states that Thomson & French will guarantee repayment of any loan my bank extends to you for an *unlimited* amount."

"I am glad to hear it, Baron."

"Tell me what sum you need."

"Why, truly," replied Monte Cristo, "my reason for desiring an 'unlimited' credit was precisely because I do not know how much money I might need."

"Suppose you were to require a million—"

"I beg your pardon," interposed Monte Cristo.

"I said 'a million,'" replied Danglars.

"But what could I do with a million?" retorted the Count. "That trifling sum I am in the habit of carrying in my wallet. Let us say six million francs."

"Six million!" gasped Danglars. "So be it."

"Then, if I should require more," continued Monte Cristo, "why, of course, I should draw upon you. Be kind enough, then, to send me 500,000 francs tomorrow."

"The money you desire shall be at your house by ten o'clock tomorrow morning, my dear Count," replied Danglars. "For the present, I would like to introduce you to my wife, the Baroness Danglars." Danglars rang and was answered by a servant in a showy livery. "Is the baroness at home?" inquired Danglars.

"Yes, my lord," answered the man.

"Ah, good. Please tell her I would like to introduce her to someone truly distinguished."

The servant departed and soon returned. "Her ladyship is waiting to receive you, gentlemen," said the servant.

"With your permission," said Danglars, bowing, "I will show you the way."

"By all means," replied Monte Cristo. "I follow you."

CHAPTER 36
The Dappled Grays.

The Count prevents a tragedy.

The baron, followed by the Count of Monte Cristo, traveled through the magnificent mansion till he reached the apartments of Madame Danglars. In contrast to the rest of the home, Madame Danglars' apartments were tastefully appointed. "Baroness," said Danglars, "give me leave to present to you the Count of Monte Cristo. He has decided to reside in Paris for a year. During that time he proposes to spend six million francs. That means balls, dinners, and lawn parties without end, in all of which I trust the Count will remember us."

"You have selected a most unfavorable moment for your first visit to Paris," said the baroness. "Paris is a horrible place in summer. Balls, parties, and celebrations are over. The only amusements left us are the tedious horse races at the Champ de Mars. Are you fond of horses, Count?"

"I have passed a considerable part of my life in the East, madame, and you are surely aware that the Orientals value only two things—the fine breeding of their horses and the beauty of their women."

"Nay, Count," said the baroness, "it would

have been somewhat more gallant to have placed the ladies first."

At this instant the favorite attendant of Madame Danglars entered the room. Approaching her mistress, she spoke some words in an undertone. Madame Danglars turned very pale, then exclaimed, "I cannot believe it. The thing is impossible."

"I assure you, madame," replied the woman, "it is as I have said." Turning impatiently toward her husband, Madame Danglars demanded, "Is this true?"

"Is what true, madame?" inquired Danglars, visibly agitated.

"What my maid tells me."

"But what does she tell you?"

"That when my coachman was about to harness the horses to my carriage, he discovered that they had been removed from the stables without his knowledge. What is the meaning of this?"

"Be kind enough, madame, to listen to me," said Danglars.

"Oh, yes! I will listen, monsieur, for I am most curious to hear what explanation you will give. Among the ten horses in the stables of Baron Danglars are two that belong exclusively to me—a pair of the handsomest and most spirited creatures to be found in Paris. Well, I had promised Madame de Villefort the loan of my carriage to drive tomorrow to the museum. But, when my coachman goes to fetch the grays from the stables they are gone—positively gone. No doubt, husband, you have sold them merely to fatten your wallet. How detestable!"

"Madame," replied Danglars, "the horses were not sufficiently calm for you. I was worried about your safety. My dear love, I promise you another pair exactly like them in appearance, only more quiet and steady." The baroness shrugged her shoulders with an air of contempt.

"This very morning I purchased an excellent pair of carriage-horses," said the Count, "and I do not think they were expensive. You can see them out this window."

As they walked toward the window, Danglars approached his wife. "I could not tell you in front of the others," he said in a low tone, "the reason for selling the horses. A most enormous price was offered me this morning for them. Some madman or fool, bent upon ruining himself as fast as he can, actually sent his agent to me to purchase them at any cost."

"Great heavens!" suddenly exclaimed the baroness, looking out the window. "There are my dappled grays!" Danglars looked absolutely stupefied. The baroness's frowning brow predicted a storm. Monte Cristo made a farewell bow and departed, leaving Danglars to endure the angry reproaches of his wife. This was the first step in the quest Monte Cristo had begun to make life unbearable for Baron Danglars.

"Excellent," murmured Monte Cristo to himself, as he left. "All goes according to my wishes. The domestic peace of this family is now in my hands. Now, I shall play another master-stroke, by which I shall gain the heart of both husband and wife—delightful!"

Two hours later, Madame Danglars received a most flattering letter from the Count, in which he begged her to take back her favorite "dappled grays." The horses were sent back wearing the same harness she had seen on them in the morning. By the Count's orders, in the center of each rosette that adorned either side of their heads was a large diamond.

That evening, Monte Cristo left Paris for his residence at Auteuil, accompanied by Ali. The following day, about three o'clock, Monte Cristo summoned the Nubian mute. "Ali," said his master, "you have frequently explained to me how skillful you are in throwing the lasso, have you not?" Ali drew himself up proudly and then returned a sign in the affirmative. "But do you believe you could stop a pair of carriage horses galloping out of control?"

The Nubian smiled and nodded. "That is good," said Monte Cristo. "Now listen to me. Before long, a carriage will dash past here, drawn by the pair of dappled gray horses you saw me with yesterday. At the risk of your own life, you must manage to stop those horses right in front of my door."

Ali fetched his lasso and went out to the street. Suddenly a distant sound of rapidly advancing wheels was heard, and almost immediately a carriage appeared, drawn by a pair of wild, ungovernable horses, while the terrified coachman strove in vain to restrain their furious speed.

In the vehicle were a young woman and a child. Terror seemed to have deprived them even of the power of uttering a cry. The carriage thundered and rattled as it flew over the rough stones, and the slightest obstacle under the wheels would have caused disaster. Ali suddenly took out his lasso and threw it so skillfully that it caught the forelegs of the near horse. The animal fell over, breaking part of the harness, and preventing the other horse from continuing its wild rampage. The coach came to a halt. A number of servants rushed from the house to assist the two passengers from the coach. They helped out a lady holding a young boy who had lost consciousness.

Monte Cristo directed that the servants bring them into his house. "Compose yourself, madame," he said. "The danger is over." The woman looked up at these words, and, with a glance, pointed to her child, who was still unconscious. "See how deadly pale he is! My child, my darling Edward! Speak to your mother—open your dear eyes and look on me once again!"

With a calm smile, Monte Cristo opened a vial containing a red liquid. He let a single drop fall on the child's lips. As soon as it had fallen on the boy, he opened his eyes and looked around. The mother was overjoyed. "Where am I?" she exclaimed.

"Madame," answered the Count, "you are under the roof of one who considers himself lucky to have prevented your continued sufferings."

"My wretched curiosity has brought all this about," continued the lady. "All Paris has sung the praises of Madame Danglars' beautiful horses, and I had the desire to know whether they really merited the high praise given to them."

"Is it possible," exclaimed the Count with pretended astonishment, "that these horses belong to the baroness?"

"They do, indeed. May I inquire if you are acquainted with Madame Danglars?"

"I have that honor. May I introduce myself? I am the Count of Monte Cristo."

"And I am Madame Heloïse de Villefort." The Count bowed. "How grateful will M. de Villefort be for all your goodness. How thankfully will he acknowledge that to you alone he owes the survival of his wife and child."

The Count replied, "I see you have quite recovered from your fright, and no doubt you wish to return home. I have arranged for the same horses you came with to be attached to one of my carriages. Ali will have the honor of driving you home, while your coachman remains here to attend to the necessary repairs of your carriage."

Ali quietly harnessed the pacified animals to the Count's carriage, took the reins in his hands, and drove Madame de Villefort and Edward back home.

CHAPTER 37
The Morrel Family

The Count pays a visit to the Morrel family. Maximilian Morrel tells the Count what his father, Pierre Morrel, revealed as he was dying.

The next day, the Count decided to pay a visit. The house that he pulled up to was of white stone fronted by two small beds full of beautiful flowers. Maximilian Morrel was superintending the grooming of his horse and smoking his cigar when the Count's carriage stopped at the gate.

Baptistin, the coachman for that day, sprang down and asked whether M. and Madame Herbaut and M. Maximilian Morrel would see his excellency the Count of Monte Cristo. "The Count of Monte Cristo?" cried Morrel, throwing away his cigar and hastening to the carriage. "I should think we would see him!" The young officer shook the Count's hand warmly.

"Come, come," said Maximilian. "My sister is in the garden plucking the dead roses, and her husband is reading his newspapers. They are so happy together. Wherever you see Madame Herbaut, you will always find M. Emmanuel Herbaut nearby."

At the sound of their steps, a young woman of twenty-five, busily engaged in plucking the dead leaves off a rosebush, raised her head. This was Julie. She uttered a cry of surprise at the sight of a stranger. "Penelon, Penelon!" she called out. An old man, who was digging busily at one of the beds, stuck his spade in the earth, and approached. "Penelon," said Julie, "go and inform M. Emmanuel of this gentleman's visit. I hope you will permit me to leave you for a few minutes," she said to Monte Cristo, and then she disappeared into the house.

"I am sorry to see," observed Monte Cristo to Morrel, "that I have caused such a disturbance in your house. Your family appears to be a very happy one," said the Count as they went inside.

"Oh, yes, they want nothing. They are young and cheerful, they are tenderly attached to each other, and with twenty-five thousand francs a year they fancy themselves as rich as can be." This account caused Monte Cristo's heart to swell with joy, for only he knew that he himself was the source of their wealth and happiness. Soon Emmanuel entered the room, followed by Julie, now suitably dressed for company. They all went inside.

"We are very happy, monsieur," said Julie. "But we have also known unhappiness. Thankfully, God sent us one of his angels." The Count's cheeks became scarlet.

Monte Cristo got up, took a step or two, and pointed to a crystal box, beneath which a silken purse lay on a black velvet cushion. "I was wondering what could be the significance of this purse, with the paper at one end and the large diamond at the other."

"Count," replied Maximilian, with an air of gravity, "those are our most precious family treasures."

"The stone seems very brilliant," answered the Count.

"Oh, my brother-in-law does not refer to its value, although it has been estimated at 100,000 francs. He means that the articles contained in this purse are the gifts of the angel I spoke of just now. These gifts came from a benefactor unknown to us."

"Ah, really," said Monte Cristo in a half-stifled voice.

"Monsieur," returned Maximilian, raising the glass cover, and respectfully kissing the silken purse, "this came from a man who saved my father from suicide, us from ruin, and our name from shame and disgrace." Maximilian drew a letter from the purse and gave it to the Count. "This letter was written by this unknown angel." Monte Cristo opened the letter and read it with an indescribable feeling of delight. It was the letter he had written to Julie and signed "Sinbad the Sailor."

"Unknown, you say, is the man who rendered you this service—unknown to you?"

"Yes, we have never had the happiness of thanking him," continued Maximilian. "My father, however, lying on his death bed, uttered his last words—'Maximilian, it was Edmond Dantes!'" At these words the Count's paleness, which had for some time been increasing, became alarming. He could not speak. He looked at his watch, insisted he was already late for an appointment, and hastily left.

"This Count of Monte Cristo is a strange man," said Emmanuel.

"His voice went to my heart," observed Julie. "And two or three times I thought that I had heard it before."

CHAPTER 38
Toxicology

While visiting Madame de Villefort, the Count cleverly suggests how she might poison someone.

The Count of Monte Cristo decided to pay a visit to Madame de Villefort. While seeming to pay no more than a social call, the Count actually intended to plant a murderous idea in the mind of the woman. We must remember that M. de Villefort played a key role in sending Edmond Dantes to prison.

As soon as the servant announced Monte Cristo's arrival, Madame de Villefort called her son, Edward, so that he could renew his thanks to the Count. After the usual civilities, the Count inquired after M. de Villefort. "My husband dines with the chancellor tonight," replied the young lady. "He has just left. Edward, what is your sister Valentine doing?" inquired Madame de Villefort. "Tell her to come here, that I may have the honor of introducing her to the Count."

"You have a daughter, then, madame?" inquired the Count."

"The daughter of M. de Villefort by his first marriage," replied the young wife. "She is a fine grown-up girl."

Valentine entered the room and greeted their guest warmly.

The assembly drank some tea and conversed until the clock struck six. "Valentine, will you and Edward go and see if your grandpapa, M. Noirtier, is ready for his dinner?" The younger members ran off.

"Count," Madame de Villefort said, "please allow me to thank you again for reviving my boy Edward after that terrifying carriage ride."

"Oh, think nothing of it," Monte Cristo replied. "I have long been interested in substances that heal the body. I am particularly interested in the theories of King Mithridates. Do you know about him?"

"No, but please tell me."

"Well, the king feared his rivals might try to poison him. So, he took a tiny amount of poison every day, allowing his body to build an immunity. At the end of a month, when drinking water from the same poisoned pitcher, you would kill the person who drank with you, without harming yourself."

"What about the wonderful remedy you administered to Edward?" the lady inquired.

"One drop will restore life, as you have seen. Five or six will inevitably kill. If it is poured into a glass of wine, it would not affect its flavor in the slightest. Tomorrow I will have some of this remedy sent to you." The clock struck half-past six, and a lady was announced, a friend of Madame de Villefort, who came to dine with her.

As he took his leave, she said, "Goodbye, sir, and do not forget the drug concoction."

Next morning, faithful to his promise, he sent the drug mixture requested. The Count could only hope Madame de Villefort would use it against her husband.

CHAPTER 39
A Flurry in Stocks

Albert de Morcerf confides to the Count that he would rather not marry Eugenie Danglars. The Count suggests an alternative.

Albert de Morcerf visited the Count of Monte Cristo at his house in the Champs-Elysées, which had already begun to look like a grand palace. Albert was accompanied by his friend Lucien Debray, the newspaper editor. After a servant offered the guests some food and drink, Monte Cristo addressed Albert. "Your marriage to Eugenie Danglars is still scheduled?"

"Alas, yes," replied Albert. "But I am not yet ready to marry. I am only twenty, and Eugenie is seventeen."

"Why don't you simply refuse to marry?" asked the Count.

"Oh, it will be too great a disappointment to my father if I do not marry Mademoiselle Danglars. He is as much in favor of the union as my mother opposes it."

"Is your mother really so very much against this marriage?"

"So much so that Madame Danglars very rarely comes to the house, and my mother has not visited Madame Danglars twice in her whole life."

"Then," said the Count, "I am emboldened to speak openly to you. I have, if agreeable to you, thought of inviting M. and Madame Danglars, and M. and Madame de Villefort, to my country-house at Auteuil. If I were to invite you and your parents to this dinner, I should give it the appearance of being a matrimonial meeting, especially if Baron Danglars did me the honor to bring his daughter. In that case your mother would be angry with me, and I do not at all wish that. Perhaps you could schedule a previous engagement that will make you unable to attend."

"I will do better than that," said Albert. "My mother is wishing to go to the seaside—what day is fixed for your dinner?"

"Saturday."

"This is Tuesday—well, tomorrow evening we leave, and the day after we shall be at the seashore. Really, Count, you have a delightful way of setting people at their ease. But you will come and call on my mother before tomorrow?"

"A thousand thanks," said the Count. "Your invitation is most gracious, but I regret that I cannot accept. I have a most important engagement. Major Bartolomeo Cavalcanti, a millionaire who ranks among the most ancient nobility of Italy, is coming to visit. He will be accompanied by his son, Andrea, a charming young man, about your own age, who is making his entry into Parisian society. The major will bring his son with him this evening—he gives him to my care. I will do what I can to advance his interests. Will you help me with that?"

"Most willingly. This Major Cavalcanti is an old friend of yours, then?"

"No, but he is a perfect nobleman, very polite, modest, and agreeable. I have met him several times at Florence, Bologna and Lucca. He has been in Paris only once before."

"You are a model mentor," said Albert. "If by any chance this Andrea should desire a wife who is very rich, very noble on her mother's side, and a baroness on her father's side, I will help you in the search. M. Paul Danglars' daughter, Eugenie, springs to mind."

"Nothing is impossible," replied Monte Cristo.

CHAPTER 40
Major Cavalcanti

The Count rehearses the men he has hired to play the roles of Major Cavalcanti and his son, Count Andrea Cavalcanti.

That evening a cab deposited a man calling himself Major Cavalcanti at the Count's door. The visitor was about fifty-two years of age. He wore trousers of blue cloth, boots tolerably clean, buckskin gloves, a hat, and a black necktie striped with white. In reality, the Count had hired a lower-class man to play the role of the rich Italian nobleman called Major Cavalcanti. A servant ushered the visitor into a simple and elegant drawing room, and the Count rose to meet him with a smile. "Ah, my dear sir, you are most welcome."

"Thank you, your excellency."

"Would you like a glass of port, sherry or wine?"

"Wine, thank you."

The Count rang, and Baptistin appeared. "Is the young man here?" asked Monte Cristo.

"Yes," Baptistin replied, "He is in the blue parlor."

"Good. Tell him to wait in the parlor. Bring us

some wine and crackers." Baptistin left and returned with a silver tray that contained wine, crystal glasses, and crackers on a china plate.

"Now," the Count said, "do you remember the story that we're going to follow?"

"Oh, yes. I am a nobleman of wealth and high reputation—Marquis Bartolomeo Cavalcanti, a descendent of an illustrious Florentine family. I'm also a former major in the Austrian army. My annual income is half a million francs. I married Marquise Oliva Corsinari, who died ten years ago. The marquise and I had one child, a son named Andrea, who is now twenty. I sent him to be educated at a college in a French province. Now I want him to complete his social education in Paris. Is that correct, my good Count?"

"Yes, very good. Here are 8,000 of the 40,000 francs I will be paying you. I have reserved rooms for you at the Princess Hotel on Richelieu Street. You will find suitcases in your hotel room. They contain the clothes you will need. On grand occasions, wear the military uniform, complete with the medals attached."

"Yes, your excellency. Thank you."

"Now I will fetch the young man who will be playing the part of your son." The Count entered the blue parlor, where he found Benedetto carelessly stretched out on the sofa. A handsome young man with blond hair and blue eyes, he was tapping his boot with a gold-headed cane. When the Count arrived, the young man immediately came to his feet.

"Let me hear you recite the agreed-on story," said the Count after he led the young man back to the drawing room and introduced him to his "father," the man playing "Major Cavalcanti."

"I am Count Andrea Cavalcanti, son of the Marquis Bartolomeo Cavalcanti, a descendent of a famous Italian family from Florence." Benedetto continued to recite the other fictitious facts.

"Good," said Monte Cristo. "You will have an annual income of 60,000 francs as long as you are in Paris."

"In that case, I think I'll stay here a long time," Benedetto commented.

"I have opened an account for you at Danglars' Bank. Every month I shall deposit 5,000 francs for you to draw on."

"And how long will the 'marquis' be staying in Paris?" Benedetto asked.

"Only a few months," said the Count. "Here is the birth certificate that proves you are Andrea Cavalcanti." Benedetto took the forged document.

"And now, gentlemen, I wish you good morning," said Monte Cristo.

"And when shall we have the honor of seeing you again, your excellency?" asked the older visitor.

"Yes," said Andrea, "when may we hope for that pleasure?"

"On Saturday, if you will. Yes, let me see— on Saturday I am to dine at my country house, at Auteuil, 28 Fontaine Street. Several persons are invited, and among others, M. Danglars, your banker. I will introduce you to him, for it will be necessary he should know you, as he is to pay you money."

"At what hour shall we come?" asked the young man.

"About half-past six."

"We will be with you at that time," said the major. The two "Cavalcantis" bowed to the Count and left the house. Monte Cristo went to the window and saw them crossing the street, arm in arm. "There go two trouble-makers," he said. "It is a pity they are not really related!"

CHAPTER 41
M. Noirtier de Villefort

M. Noirtier, elderly and paralyzed, learns that his beloved granddaughter Valentine is to marry Franz d'Epinay.

Around the same time, an important gathering occurred in the home of M. and Madame de Villefort. It will be recalled that M. de Villefort's original name was Noirtier. For political reasons, he dropped the name of Noirtier and chose to be known as de Villefort. He and his 25-year-old second wife supported his father, who had kept the name Noirtier. M. Noirtier lived in the home of the de Villeforts.

The old gentleman was paralyzed from the neck down. While he could hear and see, he could not speak. On this particular day, M. and Madame de Villefort entered the old man's chambers, where they found Noirtier along with his faithful attendant Barrois.

M. Noirtier was sitting in a wheelchair. He was placed before a large mirror, which reflected the whole apartment. That way he could see, without moving, all who entered the room and everything that was going on around him.

Only three people could understand the sign language of the poor paralytic. These were Villefort, his daughter Valentine, and Barrois. Villefort sent away Barrois and addressed his father. "Madame de Villefort and I have a communication to make to you. I trust it will meet with your approval." The invalid listened without moving a muscle.

"Sir," resumed Villefort, "we are thinking of arranging a marriage for Valentine." Had the old man's face been molded in wax, it could not have shown less emotion at this news.

"The marriage will take place in less than three months," Villefort continued. Noirtier's eyes still retained their inanimate expression.

Madame de Villefort now took her part in the conversation and added, "We thought this news would be of interest to you, sir, since you have always had great affection for Valentine. It therefore only now remains for us to tell you the name of the young man she will wed. It is one of the most desirable connections which could possibly be formed. He possesses fortune, a high rank in society, and every personal qualification likely to render Valentine supremely happy. His name, moreover, cannot be wholly unknown to you. It is M. Franz de Quesnel, Baron d'Epinay."

While his wife was speaking, Villefort had closely observed the old man's face. When Madame de Villefort pronounced Franz's name, the old man's eyelids trembled, and he darted a lightning glance at Madame de Villefort and his son. Villefort, who knew the political hatred which had formerly existed between M. Noirtier and the elder d'Epinay, well understood the agitation and anger which the announcement had produced. However, he immediately resumed the narrative begun by his wife.

"Sir," he said, "you are aware that Valentine is nineteen, which renders it important that she should form a suitable alliance quickly. Nevertheless, you have not been forgotten in our plans, and Valentine's future husband has consented that you should live with them. We know that you and Valentine are attached to each other, and you can enjoy each other's company even after Valentine is married."

Noirtier's look was furious. Something desperate was passing in the old man's mind, for a cry of anger and grief rose in his throat. The inability to form words appeared almost to choke him, for his face and lips turned quite purple with the struggle.

"This marriage," added Madame de Villefort, "is quite agreeable to young M. d'Epinay and his family. M. d'Epinay has no relations nearer than an uncle and aunt. His mother died at his birth, and his father was assassinated in 1815 when M. d'Epinay was two years old."

"That assassination was a mysterious affair," said Villefort. "The killer was never found. Now, father, Madame and I are leaving. Would you like us to send Valentine to you?"

It had been agreed that the old man should express his approval by closing his eyes, his refusal by blinking them several times, and if he had some desire or feeling to express, he raised them to heaven. If he wanted Valentine, he closed his right eye only, and if Barrois, the left. At Madame de Villefort's proposition, he instantly closed his eyes. M. and Madame de Villefort bowed and left the room, giving orders that Valentine should be summoned to her grandfather's presence.

When Valentine entered the room, one look told her that her grandfather was extremely upset.

"Dear Grandpapa," she asked, "what has happened? Are you angry?" The paralytic closed his eyes to indicate "Yes."

"Who has displeased you? Is it my father?"

"No."

"Madame de Villefort?"

"No."

"Me?" The listener closed his eyes. "What have I done, dear Grandpapa, that you should be angry with me?" cried Valentine.

Through a series of questions and answers, the soon-to-be married girl established that what displeased old Noirtier was the man she was going to marry.

"Well, listen," said Valentine, throwing herself on her knees, and putting her arm round her grandfather's neck, "I am upset, too, for I do not love M. Franz d'Epinay." An expression of intense joy illumined the old man's eyes. Noirtier's breathing came thick and short.

"Then the idea of this marriage really grieves you too? Ah, if you could but help me—if we could both together defeat their plan! But you—whose mind is so quick, and whose will is so firm are, nevertheless, as weak and unequal to the contest as I am myself."

At these words, there appeared in Noirtier's eye an expression of such deep meaning that the young girl thought she could read these words there: "You are mistaken. I can still do much for you."

"Do you think you can help me, dear Grandpapa?" said Valentine.

"Yes." Noirtier then raised his eyes. It was the signal that he wanted something.

"What is it you want, dear Grandpapa?" said Valentine, and she recited all the letters of the alphabet from A down to L. When she arrived at that letter, her grandfather made her understand that she had spoken the first letter of the thing he wanted. "Ah," said Valentine, "the thing you desire begins with the letter L."

"Yes, yes, yes," said the old man's eyes. In this manner, Valentine patiently learned that her grandfather wanted a lawyer to visit him.

"Shall my father be informed of your wish?"

"Yes."

"Do you wish the lawyer to be sent for immediately?"

"Yes."

"We will have him sent for directly, dear Grandpapa. Is that all you want?"

"Yes." Valentine rang the bell, and ordered the servant to tell M. and Madame de Villefort that they were requested to come to M. Noirtier's room. M. de Villefort entered, followed by Barrois.

"What do you want me for, sir?" he demanded of the paralytic.

"Sir," said Valentine, "my grandfather wishes for a lawyer." Barrois, with the fidelity of an old servant, went to fetch one.

CHAPTER 42
The Will

With Valentine's help, Noirtier communicates what he will do if Valentine marries Franz d'Epinay.

Barrois returned, bringing the lawyer with him.

"Sir," said Villefort, after the first greetings were made, "you were sent for by M. Noirtier, whom you see here. All his limbs have become completely paralyzed. He has lost his voice also, and we ourselves find much trouble in communicating with him."

Noirtier cast an appealing look toward Valentine. She answered immediately. "Sir," she said, "I perfectly understand my grandfather's meaning at all times."

"In order to render an act valid, I must be certain of the approval or disapproval of my client. Illness of body would not affect the validity of the deed, but sanity of mind is absolutely necessary," said the lawyer.

Valentine immediately spoke up. "Well, sir, by the help of two signs, with which I will acquaint you presently, you will determine that my grandfather is still in full possession of all of his mental faculties. M. Noirtier is accustomed to communicating his meaning by closing his eyes when he wishes to signify 'yes,' and to blink several times when he means 'no.' You now know quite enough to converse with M. Noirtier. Give it a try."

Noirtier gave Valentine such a look of tenderness and gratitude that the lawyer seemed convinced. "Have you have heard and understood what your granddaughter has been saying, sir?" asked the lawyer.

Noirtier closed his eyes.

"It was you who sent for me?"

"Yes."

"To make your will?"

"Yes."

"Well, sir," said the young girl, "do you understand now, and is your conscience perfectly at rest on the subject?"

Before the lawyer could answer, Villefort drew him aside. "Sir," he said, "do you suppose for a moment that a man can sustain a physical shock, such as M. Noirtier has received, without any damage to his mental faculties?"

"Let us proceed, and we shall see," replied the lawyer. "Valentine, who best seems able to understand her grandfather's wishes, can act as interpreter." The old man's eyes closed tightly.

"Well, sir, what do you require of me, and what document is it that you wish me to draw up?"

Valentine named all the letters of the alphabet until she came to "W." At this letter, Noirtier's eyes told her to stop. In this manner, the paralytic indicated that he wished the lawyer to prepare a new will for him.

The lawyer said, "When an individual makes his will, it is generally in favor or against some person."

"Yes," the eyes said.

"Have you an exact idea of the amount of your fortune?"

"Yes."

"I will name to you several sums which will gradually increase. Please stop me when I reach the one representing your savings."

"Yes."

The lawyer began at 300,000 francs, which proved to be too low. Noirtier signaled for the man to stop at 900,000 francs. "To whom do you desire to leave this fortune?" the lawyer asked.

"Oh," said Madame de Villefort, "there is not much doubt about that. M. Noirtier tenderly loves his granddaughter Valentine. She deserves to inherit his fortune."

"Is it, then, to Mademoiselle Valentine de Villefort that you leave these 900,000 francs?" demanded the lawyer.

The young girl looked away and tears came to her eyes. The old man looked at her with an expression of the deepest tenderness. Then, turning toward the lawyer, he blinked his eyes to say no.

"What," said the lawyer, "do you intend to leave Mademoiselle Villefort out of your will?"

"Yes."

Valentine raised her head, struck dumb with astonishment. But Noirtier looked at her with so much affectionate tenderness that she exclaimed,

"Oh, Grandpapa, I see now that it is only your fortune of which you deprive me. You still leave me the love which I have always enjoyed."

"Yes, that is true," said the eyes of the paralytic.

"Thank you, thank you," she murmured.

The old man's declaration that he did not intend to leave his fortune to Valentine excited the hopes of Madame de Villefort. She gradually approached the invalid and said: "Then, without a doubt, dear M. Noirtier, you intend leaving your fortune to your grandson, Edward de Villefort?"

The blinking of the eyes which answered this speech was most decided and terrible, and expressed a feeling of hatred.

"No?" asked the lawyer. "Then, perhaps, it is to your son, M. de Villefort?"

"No!" Noirtier blinked again.

Villefort and his wife both grew red, one from shame, the other from anger.

"What have we all done, then, dear Grandpapa?" said Valentine. "You no longer seem to love any of us." The old man's eyes passed rapidly from Villefort and his wife, and rested on Valentine with a look of unutterable fondness.

"Well if you love me, Grandpapa, explain yourself, please." Noirtier fixed his eyes on Valentine's hand. "My hand?" she asked.

"Yes."

"Her hand!" exclaimed everyone.

"Oh, gentlemen, you see it is all useless, and that my father's mind is truly impaired," said Villefort.

"Ah," cried Valentine suddenly, "I understand. It is my marriage you mean, is it not, dear Grandpapa?"

"Yes, yes, yes," signed the paralytic, casting on Valentine a look of joyful gratitude for having guessed his meaning.

"You are angry with us all on account of this marriage, are you not?"

"Yes!"

"Really, this is too absurd," said Villefort.

"Excuse me, sir," replied the lawyer. "M. Noirtier's meaning is quite evident to me, and I can quite easily connect the train of ideas passing in his mind."

"You do not wish me to marry M. Franz d'Epinay?" observed Valentine.

"I do not wish it," said the eyes of her grandfather.

"And you disinherit your granddaughter," continued the lawyer, "because she is engaged to someone contrary to your wishes?"

"Yes."

"So that, but for this marriage, she would inherit your money?"

"Yes."

There was a profound silence. Villefort was the first to break it. "I consider that I am the best judge of the marriage in question. I am the only person with the right to arrange my daughter's marriage. It is my wish that she should marry M. Franz d'Epinay—and she shall marry him." Valentine sank weeping into a chair.

"Sir," said the lawyer, "how do you intend to dispose of your fortune in case Mademoiselle de Villefort still marries M. Franz?"

The old man gave no answer.

"Will you give it to some member of your family?"

"No."

"Do you intend to give it to a charity?" pursued the lawyer.

"Yes."

Villefort then turned toward the door. Before leaving he addressed the lawyer. "My father, I can see, has made up his mind. Once he does so, he never changes it. I am quite resigned. These 900,000 francs will go out of the family in order to enrich some hospital. So be it. I will continue to act in the manner I think best for my family."

Having said this, Villefort left the room with his wife. That same day the will was made, the witnesses were brought, it was approved by the old man, sealed in the presence of all and given to the lawyer for safe keeping.

CHAPTER 43
An Invitation

The Count invites M. and Madame de Villefort to dine with him at his house in Auteuil.

M. and Madame de Villefort, upon returing to their chambers, found that the Count of Monte Cristo had come to visit them. A servant had ushered him into the drawing room, where he awaited them.

"How nice to see you," said Madame de Villefort.

"I feel the same about seeing you, madame," said the Count. "Unfortunately, I cannot stay long. I only came to remind you of your promise to join me for dinner on Saturday."

"Ah," said Villefort, "is it at your house in the Champs-Elysées?"

"No," said Monte Cristo, "it is at Auteuil."

"At Auteuil?" said Villefort. "And in what part of Auteuil do you reside?"

"Fontaine Street."

"Fontaine Street!" exclaimed Villefort in an agitated tone. "What number?"

"No. 28."

"Then," asked Villefort, "was it you who bought M. de Saint-Meran's house?"

"Did it belong to M. de Saint-Meran?" asked Monte Cristo.

"Yes," replied Madame de Villefort, "and, would you believe it, Count—"

"Believe what?"

"Well, the Saint-Merans were the parents of M. de Villefort's first wife, who died shortly after marrying my husband. They are also the grandparents of sweet Valentine. My husband would never live in that house."

"Indeed?" returned Monte Cristo, "that is a mistake on your part, M. de Villefort, for it is charming."

"I do not like Auteuil, sir," said Villefort, making an effort to appear calm.

"Nevertheless, I hope you will not deprive me of the pleasure of your company, sir," said Monte Cristo.

"No, Count—I hope—I assure you I shall do my best," stammered Villefort.

"Oh," said Monte Cristo, "let there be no excuses. On Saturday, at six o'clock. I shall be expecting you."

"I will come, Count—I will be sure to come," said Villefort.

"Thank you," said Monte Cristo. "Now I must leave you." And so he departed.

CHAPTER 44
Ghosts

At a dinner party at his house in Auteuil, the Count introduces the Cavalcantis to the Danglarses and the Villeforts.

At first sight, the exterior of the house at Auteuil gave no indications of splendor, nothing one would expect from the residence of the magnificent Count of Monte Cristo. At the direction of Monte Cristo, all the magnificence was lavished on the interior of the mansion.

One chamber alone had been left unchanged by Bertuccio. This was the bedroom at the top of the back stairs. It remained hung with red silk.

At precisely six o'clock, the first guest arrived. It was young M. Morrel. At the same minute, a carriage, accompanied by two gentlemen mounted on splendid horses, arrived. Lucien Debray jumped down and offered his hand to Madame Danglars to assist her from the carriage. The Count noticed that the woman secretly passed a note to the minister's secretary. She did so in a manner that indicated she had done this many times before. After his wife, the banker descended from the carriage.

Major Bartolomeo Cavalcanti and Count Andrea Cavalcanti were next to arrive, followed by Baron Chateau-Renaud.

The younger guests were talking together. On the entrance of the Cavalcantis, their eyes glanced from father to son.

"Cavalcanti!" said Debray.

"A fine name," said Morrel.

"Yes," said Chateau-Renaud, "these Italians are well named and badly dressed."

"You are too critical, Chateau-Renaud," replied Debray. "Those clothes are well cut and quite new."

"That is just what I find fault with. That gentleman appears to be well dressed for the first time in his life."

Monte Cristo intervened. "The son has been educated in a college in the South, I believe, near Marseilles. You will find him quite enthusiastic."

"Upon what subject?" asked Madame Danglars.

"The French ladies, madame. He has made up his mind to take a wife from Paris."

"A fine idea," said Danglars, shrugging his shoulders. Madame Danglars looked at her husband with an expression which, at any other time, would have indicated a storm, but at this moment she controlled herself.

"M. and Madame de Villefort," cried Baptistin, announcing the latest arrivals. M. de Villefort, trying to control his emotions, was visibly agitated. After all, this was the house that he had secretly visited to make love to a young woman, and where he had buried their illegitimate child.

After a short time, Bertuccio arrived at the Count's side. No sooner did he appear than he exclaimed, "Good heavens!"

"What is the matter?" said the Count.

"That woman—that woman!"

"Which?"

"The one with a white dress and so many diamonds—the fair one."

"Madame Danglars?"

"I do not know her name. But it is she, sir, it is she!"

"Whom do you mean?"

"The woman of the garden!" Bertuccio stood at the open door, with his eyes starting and his hair on end. "And there is the man she met!"

"What? Who?"

"Him!"

"Him?—M. de Villefort, the king's attorney? Certainly I see him."

"Then I did not kill him?"

"Really, I think you are going mad, good Bertuccio," said the Count.

"Then he is not dead?"

"No. You see plainly he is not dead. Instead of striking between the sixth and seventh left ribs, as your countrymen do, you must have struck higher or lower, and he lives. Now, take a close look at M. Andrea Cavalcanti, the young man in the black coat."

This time Bertuccio would have screamed out, had not a look from Monte Cristo silenced him. "Benedetto?" he muttered. "Unbelievable!"

Five minutes later, dinner was announced. The Count of Monte Cristo offered his arm to Madame de Villefort. "M. de Villefort," he said, "will you escort the Baroness Danglars?"

Villefort complied, and they passed on to the dining room.

CHAPTER 45
The Dinner

*The Count shows his dinner guests an unusual bedroom.
He then leads Villefort and a very nervous Madame
Danglars into the garden, where he makes a surprising
announcement.*

The dinner was magnificent. Every delicious fruit
that the four quarters of the globe could provide
was piled on platters from China and Japan.
Rare birds retaining their most brilliant plumage,
enormous fish, together with wines from all over
the world, graced the table.

"All this is very extraordinary," said Chateau-
Renaud. "It has been at least ten years since the
house had been occupied," he went on. "And it
was quite depressing to look at it, with the blinds
closed, the doors locked, and the weeds in the
court. Really, if the house had not belonged to
the father-in-law of Villefort, one might have
thought some horrible crime had been committed
there."

Villefort, who had not tasted the three or four
glasses of rare wine which were placed before him,
now took one and swallowed it in one gulp.

Monte Cristo waited a short time, and then said, "It is odd, Baron, but the same idea came across me the first time I came here. There was, above all, one room, very plain in appearance, hung with red silk, which appeared to me especially dramatic."

"Why so?" said Danglars. "Why dramatic?"

"It's hard to say," said Monte Cristo. "There are some places where we seem to breathe sadness. Since we have finished dinner, I will show it to you, and then we will take coffee in the garden."

Madame de Villefort rose, Monte Cristo did the same, and the rest followed their example. Villefort and Madame Danglars remained for a moment, as if rooted to their seats.

"Did you hear?" whispered Madame Danglars.

"We must go," replied Villefort, offering his arm.

At length they arrived at the room. There was nothing particular about it, except that everything in it was old-fashioned, while the rest of the rooms had been redecorated.

"Oh!" cried Madame de Villefort, "it is really frightful."

"Is it not so?" asked Monte Cristo. "Look at that large clumsy bed, hung with such gloomy, blood-colored drapery! And those two portraits, faded from the dampness. Do they not seem to say, with their pale lips and staring eyes, 'The terrible things we have seen here!'"

Villefort turned pale. Madame Danglars fell onto a large chair placed near the chimney.

"Oh," asked Madame de Villefort, smiling, "are you courageous enough to sit down upon the very seat upon which perhaps the crime was committed?" Madame Danglars rose suddenly.

"And then," said Monte Cristo, "this is not all."

"What, is there more?" said Debray, who had not failed to notice the agitation of Madame Danglars.

"This little staircase," said Monte Cristo, opening a door concealed by the drapery. "Look at it, and tell me what you think of it."

"What a wicked-looking, crooked staircase," said Chateau-Renaud with a smile.

"Can you imagine," said Monte Cristo, "some person, one stormy, dark night, descending these stairs step by step, carrying a parcel, which he wishes to hide from the sight of man, if not from God?"

Madame Danglars half fainted on the arm of Villefort, who was obliged to support himself against the wall.

"Ah, madame," cried Debray, "what is the matter with you? How pale you look!"

"I want air, that is all," she replied.

"Will you come into the garden?" said Debray, advancing toward the back staircase.

"No, no," she answered. "I would rather remain here."

"Are you really frightened, madame?" asked Monte Cristo.

"Oh, no, sir," said Madame Danglars. "But your imagination is so vivid."

"Ah, yes," said Monte Cristo smiling. "It is all a matter of imagination. Why should we not imagine this the apartment of an honest mother? And that mysterious staircase, the passage through which, not to disturb their sleep, the doctor and nurse pass, or even the father carrying the sleeping child?"

Here Madame Danglars, instead of being calmed by the soft picture, uttered a groan and fainted.

Shortly after she recovered, Monte Cristo proclaimed, "It is my opinion that a crime has been committed in this house."

"Take care," said Madame de Villefort, "the king's attorney, M. de Villefort, is here."

"Ah," replied Monte Cristo, "since that is the case, I will take advantage of his presence to make my case."

He then took Villefort's arm, and, at the same time, holding that of Madame Danglars under his own, he dragged them both out into the garden to the spot where Bertuccio had dug up the body of the not-yet-dead infant. All the other guests followed.

"Here," said Monte Cristo, "here, on this very spot," and he stamped his foot on the ground, "I had the earth dug up and fresh sod put in, to refresh these old trees." Embellishing the truth a bit, he went on. "Well, my man, digging, found an iron box that contained the skeleton of a newly born infant."

Monte Cristo felt Madame Danglars arm

stiffen, and saw Villefort seem to tremble.

"What is the punishment in this country for those who murder an infant?" asked Major Cavalcanti innocently.

"Their heads are cut off," said Danglars.

"I think so. Is that not right, M. de Villefort?" asked Monte Cristo of the king's attorney.

"Yes, Count," replied Villefort, in a voice now scarcely human.

Monte Cristo, seeing that the two persons for whom he had prepared this scene could scarcely endure it, and not wishing to carry it too far, said, "Come, gentlemen,—some coffee, we seem to have forgotten it," and he conducted the guests back to the table on the lawn.

This small procession enabled Villefort to whisper to Madame Danglars, "I must speak to you."

"When?"

"Tomorrow."

"Where?"

"In my office at the courthouse—that is the safest place."

"I will be there."

CHAPTER 46
A Conjugal Scene

Baron Danglars makes some serious accusations against his wife.

Back at her house, Madame Danglars was trying to recover after what had been an emotionally exhausting dinner at Monte Cristo's country home. She had just changed out of her party clothes and was preparing for bed when the door opened suddenly. M. Danglars appeared. Hermione Danglars turned around and looked upon her husband with an astonishment she took no trouble to conceal.

"Good evening, madame," said the banker.

"What are you doing here?" asked the baroness, with great annoyance in her voice.

"I saw you give Lucien Debray money at Monte Cristo's house. Given that you and I have not lived as husband and wife for four years, I don't mind your having a lover. I *do* mind your having a *gigolo.*"

"How dare you!" Hermione shot back.

"Either you stop giving Lucien Debray money, or he never sets foot in this house again. Do you understand, Madame?"

"Oh, this is too much!"

"I've never interfered in your love affairs, and you've treated mine the same way. But I won't have you spending my money on Debray. Furthermore," the baron continued, his voice rising, "I absolutely refuse to allow you to make me lose 700,000 francs, as you did so recently."

"I do not understand you, sir," said the baroness.

"In April you went to dine at the minister's. You heard a private conversation respecting Spanish affairs—on the expulsion of King Don Carlos. Based on what you told me, I bought some Spanish stock shares. The expulsion took place and I pocketed 600,000 francs the next day."

"Well, sir, that is good. What happened then?"

"Ah, yes, it was just after this that you spoiled everything."

"Really?"

"Well, three days after that you talked politics with M. Debray, and you fancied from his words that Don Carlos had returned to Spain. Again, based on your report, I sold my shares. But the next day I find the news was false, and by this false report I have lost 700,000 francs."

"For shame!" exclaimed the baroness. "Get away from me!"

Baron Danglars executed an abrupt about-face and stormed out of the room.

CHAPTER 47
Matrimonial Projects

When the Count tells Danglars that the Cavalcantis are rich, Danglars schemes to get Andrea Cavalcanti to join his family.

The following day Danglars told his coachman to drive to Monte Cristo's house in Paris.

A servant ushered Danglars into the parlor, and Monte Cristo appeared.

"What is the matter with you?" the Count inquired. "You look troubled. Really, you alarm me."

"I have had some bad luck for several days," said Danglars, "and I have heard nothing but bad news."

"Ah, indeed?" said Monte Cristo. "Have you had another loss at the Stock Exchange?"

"No, I am safe for a few days at least. But I am annoyed about the bankruptcy of one of my clients. Imagine a man who has transacted business with me to the amount of 800,000 or 900,000 francs during the year. Never a mistake or delay—a fellow who paid like a prince. He now owes me a million francs, but his bankruptcy has caused him to suspend payment!"

"Really?"

"In addition to that, I just lost 700,000 francs by purchasing Spanish stocks at the wrong time."

"So," said Monte Cristo, "you have lost nearly 1,700,000 francs this month. My dear M. Danglars, do you need money?"

"No, but while we are speaking of business," Danglars added, "tell me what I am supposed to do for Major Cavalcanti."

"Lend him money, if he is recommended to you, and the recommendation seems good."

"Excellent. He presented himself this morning with a check for 40,000 francs, payable at sight, and countersigned by you. I immediately handed him 40,000 francs."

Monte Cristo nodded his head in token of assent. "But that is not all," continued Danglars. "He has opened an account with my bank for his son."

"May I ask how much he allows the young man?"

"Five thousand francs per month."

"Sixty thousand francs per year. I thought I was right in believing that Cavalcanti to be a stingy fellow. How can a young man live upon 5,000 francs a month?"

"Do you trust the Cavalcantis?" asked the banker with a nervous twitch.

"I? Oh, I would advance six million on his signature."

"And with all this, how ordinary he is! I should

never have taken him for anything more than a common person, never a rich nobleman. By the way, noblemen marry amongst themselves, do they not?" asked Danglars with calculated indifference. "They like to unite their fortunes, I believe."

"Usually. But, Cavalcanti is an original who does nothing like other people. I cannot help thinking that he has brought his son to France to choose a wife."

"Do you think so?"

"I am sure of it."

"And you have heard his fortune mentioned?"

"My understanding is that they have buried their millions, the secret of which they have transmitted only to their eldest sons, who have done the same from generation to generation."

"I see," said Danglars. "This explains why they don't possess any land."

"Very little, at least. I know of none which Cavalcanti possesses, excepting his palace in Lucca."

"Ah, he has a palace?" said Danglars, laughing.

"Yes. He rents it to the minister of finance while he himself lives in a simple house. As I told you before, I think the old fellow is very odd."

"By the way—this is merely a simple question—when this sort of people marry off their sons, do they give them any fortune?"

"Oh, that depends upon circumstances. Should Andrea marry according to his father's views, he will, perhaps, give him one, two, or three million. For example, supposing it were the daughter of a banker, he might take an interest in the banking house of his son's new father-in-law. But do you wish to marry off your daughter, my dear M. Danglars? Is that why you are asking so many questions?"

"It would not be a bad business arrangement for her to marry young Cavalcanti, I fancy," said Danglars.

"But isn't she engaged to Albert de Morcerf?"

"Well, M. de Morcerf and I have talked about this marriage, but Madame de Morcerf and Albert—"

Here the Count interjected, "I should not think the Morcerfs would yield to the Cavalcantis."

"The Morcerfs!—My dear Count," said Danglars, "you are a man of the world, are you not?"

"I think so."

"And you understand heraldry?"

"A little."

"Well, look at my coat of arms. It is worth more than Morcerf's."

"Why so?"

"Because, though I am not a baron by birth, my real name is, at least, Danglars."

"Well, what then?"

"While his name is not Morcerf."

"What?—not Morcerf?"

"Not at all. I have been made a baron, so I actually am one. He made himself a count, so he is not one at all."

"Impossible!"

"Listen, my dear Count. M. de Morcerf has been my friend, or rather my acquaintance, during the last thirty years. Back when I was a clerk, Morcerf was a mere fisherman."

"And then he was called—"

"Fernand Mondego."

"You are sure?"

"I have bought enough fish from him to know his name."

"Then why did you think of giving your daughter to him?"

"Because Fernand and I, being both poor, both became noble. Now we are about equal in worth. However, people say certain things about him that were never said of me."

"What?"

"Oh, nothing!"

"Ah, yes. What you tell me recalls to mind something about the name of Fernand Mondego. I have heard that name in Greece."

"In conjunction with the affairs of Ali Tepelini, the Grand Vizier of Yanina?"

"Exactly so."

"This is the mystery," said Danglars. "I would give anything to find it out."

"I have many friends in Greece," said the Count. "I could find out for you. But perhaps you could inquire. Do you have friends in Yanina?"

"Most certainly."

"Well, write to your friends in Yanina and ask if any of them know about a Frenchman named Fernand Mondego and what part he played in the catastrophe of Ali Tepelini and the downfall of Yanina."

"Yes," exclaimed Danglars, rising quickly, "I will write today."

"And if you should hear of anything very scandalous—"

"I will communicate it to you."

"Thank you ever so much," said the Count.

Danglars rushed out of the room and leaped joyfully into his carriage.

CHAPTER 48

At the Office of the King's Attorney

Villefort and Madame Danglars have a painful conversation about their secret.

At half-past twelve o'clock, Madame Danglars arrived at the justice ministry, wearing a very thick black veil to conceal her face.

The instant she appeared, the doorkeeper came to her and conducted her by a private passage to M. de Villefort's office. The king's attorney was seated in an armchair, writing. As soon as the doorkeeper left the chamber, Villefort stood up, locked the door, closed the curtains, and examined every corner of the room. Then, when he had assured himself that he could neither be seen nor heard, he said, "Thank you, madame—thank you for coming," and he offered a chair to Madame Danglars. His visitor sat down abruptly, for her heart beat so violently that she felt nearly suffocated.

"It has been a long time since I have had the pleasure of speaking alone with you, madame. I regret that our conversation today will be painful. All our actions leave their traces—some sad, others

249

bright—on our paths. Every step in our lives is like the course of an insect on the sands—it leaves its track. Now, you must gather all your courage, for you have not yet heard all."

"Ah," exclaimed Madame Danglars, alarmed, "what more is there to hear? How chance has smitten us!"

"Chance, my dear Hermione?"

"Was it not by chance the Count of Monte Cristo bought that house? Was it not by chance he caused the earth to be dug up? Is it not by chance that the unfortunate child was disinterred under the trees?—that poor innocent offspring of mine, whom I never even kissed, but for whom I wept many, many tears."

"Well, no, madame—this is the terrible news I have to tell you," said Villefort in a hollow voice— "no, nothing was found under the trees. There was no child disinterred—no. You must not weep. No, you must not groan."

"What can you mean?" asked Madame Danglars, shuddering.

"I mean that this Count of Monte Cristo, digging underneath these trees, found neither skeleton nor chest, because neither of them was there!"

"Neither of them there?" repeated Madame Danglars, her staring, wide-open eyes expressing her alarm.

"No," said Villefort, burying his face in his hands. "No, a hundred times no!"

"Then you did not bury the poor child there,

sir? Why did you deceive me? Where did you place it? Tell me—where?"

"There! But listen to me—listen—and you will pity me who has for twenty years alone borne the heavy burden of grief I am about to reveal."

"Oh, you frighten me! But speak, I will listen."

"You recollect that sad night. The child was born, was given to me—motionless, breathless, voiceless. We thought it dead." Madame Danglars made rapid movements, as though she would spring from her chair, but Villefort stopped, and clasped his hands as if to implore her attention.

"We thought it dead," he repeated. "I placed it in the chest which served as the coffin. I went to the garden and dug a hole. I then placed the coffin in the hole. I had scarcely covered it with earth when the Corsican Bertuccio stabbed me. I felt a searing pain and wanted to cry out, but I stifled my voice. I thought I was dead. I will never forget your courage in nursing me back to health. We both decided to bury our secrets in our hearts. My work took me to the South. When I returned to Paris, I found that you were married to M. Danglars.

"I returned to the house in Auteuil and waited in the red room for night to fall. I was worried that the Corsican may have seen me dig the grave and may have found the child. I was afraid he would use it to blackmail you. It was very important to me that all traces of our past should disappear. Well, I waited until the dark of night and found my way to the garden.

"Hermione, I consider myself as brave as most men. However, when I opened the door, and saw the pale moon shedding a long stream of white light on the spiral staircase like a ghost, I leaned against the wall and nearly shrieked. I seemed to be going mad. At last I mastered my thoughts. I found my way from the red room to the lower door, which opened on to the garden. Outside this door a spade was placed against the wall. I took the spade and advanced toward the trees. I had provided myself with a lantern.

"I tied my lantern to a forked branch and went to work. How I struck every piece of turf, thinking to find some resistance to my spade! But no, I found nothing, though I had made a hole twice as large as the first. The chest was no longer there!"

"The chest no longer there?" gasped Madame Danglars, choking with fear.

"Then I thought," continued Villefort, "Why should that man have carried away the corpse? The child was, perhaps, alive, and the man who attacked me may have saved it!"

Madame Danglars uttered a piercing cry, and, seizing Villefort's hands, exclaimed, "My child was alive? You buried my child alive? You were not certain my child was dead, and you buried it? Ah—"

Madame Danglars had risen and stood before Villefort.

"I know not for certain," replied Villefort.

"Ah, my child, my poor child!" cried the baroness, falling on her chair, and stifling her sobs in her handkerchief.

"If this child lives, and someone knows it lives—someone is in possession of our secret. And since it was Monte Cristo who spoke of a child being disinterred, and we know that no child could be found, it must be him who is in possession of our secret."

"Just God, avenging God!" murmured Madame Danglars.

Villefort's only answer was a stifled groan.

"But the child—the child, sir?" repeated the agitated mother.

"How I have searched for him," replied Villefort, wringing his hands. "I asked myself again and again what the Corsican could have done with the child. Perhaps, on perceiving it was still alive, he had thrown it into the river."

"Impossible!" exclaimed Madame Danglars. "A man may murder another out of revenge, but he would not deliberately drown a child."

"Perhaps," continued Villefort, "he took it to an orphanage."

"Oh, yes, yes," exclaimed the baroness. "My child is there!"

"I ran to the orphanage. There I learned that the same night that I buried the infant, a newborn child had been brought there. They told me that the baby was wrapped in part of a fine linen napkin, purposely torn in half. This portion of the napkin was marked with half a baron's crown, and the letter H."

"Truly, truly," said Madame Danglars, "all my linens have this marking. Thank God, my child was not dead!"

"No, it was not dead," Villefort stated with finality.

"But where is the child?"

Villefort shrugged his shoulders and said, "Alas, I do not know. A woman, about six months later, came to claim it with the other half of the linen. This woman gave all the details, and the baby was given to her. I never ceased to search for our baby. But now I will begin with more determination and fury than ever, since fear urges me, not my conscience."

"But," replied Madame Danglars, "the Count of Monte Cristo can know nothing, or he would not seek our friendship."

"Oh, the wickedness of man is very great," said Villefort. "Did you observe that man's eyes while he was speaking to us?"

"No."

"Believe me, that man has hidden goals. Tell me," demanded Villefort, fixing his eyes more steadfastly on her than he had ever done before, "did you ever reveal to anyone our connection?"

"Never, to anyone."

"Do you talk in your sleep?"

"I sleep soundly, like a child. Do you not remember?" The color mounted to the baroness's face, and Villefort turned awfully pale.

"It is true," he said, in so low a tone that he could hardly be heard.

"Well?" said the baroness.

"Well, I understand what I now have to do," replied Villefort. "We must consider this Monte

Cristo as an enemy. I think he invited us to his Auteuil house to see our reaction. I don't know what he is planning to do—blackmail us, perhaps. In less than one week from this time, I will find out who this Count of Monte Cristo is, where he comes from, where he goes, and why he speaks of children that have been disinterred in a garden."

He then pressed the hand the baroness reluctantly gave him and led her respectfully back to the door.

CHAPTER 49
Madame de Saint-Meran

Valentine's grandmother, Madame de Saint-Meran, now living with the de Villeforts, suddenly becomes ill.

Some time later, the Marquis de Saint-Meran, father of Villefort's first wife, died suddenly. Seeking comfort from her granddaughter, the grieving widow came to the de Villeforts' home in Paris to visit Valentine. She had been in the house only one day when she, too, fell ill. Valentine and Madame de Villefort came upstairs and found the older woman in bed. She looked pale and was feeling very weak.

The next morning Valentine found her grandmother still in bed. She was feverish, and she appeared to be suffering from violent nervous irritability.

"Oh, dear Grandmamma, are you worse?" exclaimed Valentine.

"No, my child, no," said Madame de Saint-Meran. "But I was impatiently waiting for your arrival so I could send for your father."

"My father?" asked Valentine.

"Yes, I wish to speak to him," she said just as de Villefort entered the room.

"Sir," said Madame de Saint-Meran, "you wrote to me concerning the projected marriage of this child?"

"Yes, madame," replied Villefort, "it is not only projected but arranged."

"Your intended son-in-law is named M. Franz d'Epinay?"

"Yes, madame."

"Is he not the son of General d'Epinay who, like us, was a royalist opposed to Napoleon? And wasn't he killed some days before Napoleon returned from the island of Elba and tried to unseat our king?"

"The same."

"Does he not dislike the idea of marrying the granddaughter of a Bonapartist, M. Noirtier?"

"My father's political disagreements with me are a thing of the past," said Villefort. "M. d'Epinay was just a child when his father died. He knows very little about our family's former political views."

"Is it a suitable match?"

"In every respect."

"And the young man?"

"Everyone esteems him highly."

"You approve of him?"

"He is one of the most well-bred young men I know."

"Well, sir," said Madame de Saint-Meran, "the marriage must take place very soon, for I have but a short time to live."

"You, madame?" exclaimed M. de Villefort and Valentine at the same time.

"I know what I am saying," continued the marquise. "Since Valentine's mother is dead, she may at least have a grandmother to bless her marriage. I wish to see my son-in-law. I wish to tell him to make my child happy."

"It shall be as you wish, madame," said Villefort. "As soon as M. d'Epinay arrives in Paris, the marriage shall take place."

"When does M. d'Epinay return?" the old woman sputtered.

"We expect him any moment."

"That is good. As soon as he arrives inform me. Right now I wish to see a lawyer, so I may be assured that all our property goes to Valentine."

"Ah, Grandmamma," murmured Valentine, pressing her lips on the burning brow, "how feverish you are. We must not send for a lawyer, but for a doctor."

"A doctor?" she said, shrugging her shoulders. "I am not ill. I am thirsty—that is all."

"What are you drinking, dear Grandmamma?"

"The same as usual, my dear, my glass is there on the table—give it to me, Valentine." Valentine poured some liquid into a glass and gave it to her grandmother with a certain degree of dread. The marquise drained the glass in a single swallow. Then she turned on her pillow, repeating, "The lawyer, the lawyer!"

M. de Villefort left the room, and Valentine seated herself at the bedside of her grandmother. Two hours later the lawyer arrived, and Valentine left the room, weeping. At the door she found a servant, who told her that the doctor was waiting in the dining room. Valentine instantly ran down.

"Oh," said Valentine, "we have been waiting for you with such worry, dear Dr. d'Avrigny, for my poor grandmother. You know the calamity that has happened to us, do you not?"

"I know nothing." said Dr. d'Avrigny.

"Alas," said Valentine, restraining her tears, "my grandfather is dead."

"M. de Saint-Meran?"

"Yes."

"Suddenly?"

"From an apoplectic stroke."

"An apoplectic stroke?" repeated the doctor.

"Yes, and now my grandmother is strangely ill. Oh, Doctor, I beg you, do something for her!"

"Where is she?"

"In her room with the lawyer."

"And M. Noirtier?"

"Just as he was, his mind perfectly clear, but the same incapacity to move or speak."

"And the same love for you—eh, my dear child?"

"Yes," said Valentine, "he is very fond of me."

"What are your grandmother's symptoms?"

"Fever, an extreme nervous excitement, and a strangely agitated sleep. She also suffers from occasional delirium. She fancies that last night she saw a phantom enter her chamber and even heard the noise it made on touching her medicine glass."

"I will go and see her," said the doctor as he started up the stairs—passing the lawyer as he came down.

CHAPTER 50
The Promise

Valentine tells Maximilan, whom she loves, that she is being forced to marry someone else.

To clear her head, Valentine went into the garden. Waiting for her there was the man she loved, Maximilian Morrel.

"I am so happy to see you," she exclaimed. "But what brings you here at this hour?"

"I come to bring disturbing news."

"This, too, is a house of mourning," said Valentine.

"Dear Valentine," said Maximilian, trying to conceal his own emotion, "what I am about to say is very serious. When are you to be married?"

"This very morning the subject came up. My dear grandmother is anxious for it. As soon as M. d'Epinay returns to Paris, the contract will be signed."

The young man sighed as he gazed long and mournfully at the girl he loved. "My dearest Valentine, M. d'Epinay arrived in Paris this morning."

Valentine uttered a cry.

"Valentine, the time has arrived when you must answer me. And remember my life depends on your answer. What do you intend to do?"

Valentine held down her head. She was overwhelmed. The idea of resisting her father, her grandmother, and all the family, had never occurred to her. "Disobey my father's order, and resist my dying grandmother's wish? Impossible!"

"You are right," said Maximilian, with resignation.

"How can I do otherwise?"

"Valentine, I am free," replied Maximilian, "and rich enough to support you. I swear to make you my lawful wife before my lips even approach your forehead."

"You make me tremble!" said the young girl.

"Follow me," said Maximilian. "We will embark for Algiers, for England, for America, or, if you prefer, retire to the country and return to Paris only when your family accepts our union."

Valentine shook her head. "You are talking like a madman, Maximilian. That would be impossible!"

"Does that mean that you will submit to this awful fate?" asked Maximilian sorrowfully.

"Yes."

"Fortune has turned against me—I had thought to gain heaven, and now I have lost it."

"What are you going to do?" she asked.

"I am going to say goodbye, Valentine. I hope your life will be calm, happy, and so fully occupied that there is no place for me—even in your memory."

"Oh, Maximilian!" murmured Valentine.

"Goodbye, Valentine, goodbye!" Maximilian said, bowing.

"Where are you going?" cried the young girl.

"The moment you leave me, Valentine, I am alone in the world. I will wait until the very moment you are married. When my misery is certain, I will write a letter to my brother-in-law and the police, to acquaint them with my intention. Then, at the corner of some wood, I will put an end to my existence."

Valentine trembled convulsively. She fell to her knees and felt her heart almost bursting. She said, "Maximilian, my true husband in heaven, I entreat you, do as I do, live in suffering. Perhaps, one day, we will be united."

"Goodbye, Valentine," repeated Maximilian, slowly turning away.

"Oh God," said Valentine, raising both her hands to heaven. "Live, Maximilian, and I will be yours. Say when shall it be? Speak, command, I will obey!"

Maximilian, who had already gone some few steps, returned and, trembling with joy, extended both hands toward Valentine.

"Maximilian, I will follow you. I will leave my family home, I will give up everything, even my dear old grandfather."

"No," said Maximilian, "you shall not leave him. Before you leave, tell him everything. If he approves, then it would be your justification. As soon as we are married, he shall come and live with us."

"Listen to me, Maximilian. If by some means I can delay this marriage, will you wait?"

THE COUNT OF MONTE CRISTO **263**

"Yes, I promise you, as faithfully as you have promised me that this horrible marriage shall not take place, and that if you are dragged before a magistrate or a priest, you will refuse."

"I promise you by all that is most sacred to me in the world, namely, by my mother."

"We will wait, then," said Maximilian.

"Yes, we will wait," replied Valentine.

"Thank you, my adored Valentine, thank you. When I know the hour, I will rush to this spot and bring you to my sister's. You can stay there until we are married."

"Goodbye, then, till we meet again," said Valentine, tearing herself away.

The young man returned home. The following day, at ten o'clock in the morning, he received a note from the postman. It read:

> Tears, entreaties, prayers, have availed me nothing. Yesterday, for two hours, I was at the church of Saint-Phillippe du Roule, and for two hours I prayed. Heaven is as inflexible as man. The signature of the contract is fixed for this evening at nine o'clock. I have but one promise and but one heart to give, and they are both pledged to you. Meet me this evening at a quarter to nine at the garden gate.
>
> Your betrothed,
> Valentine de Villefort
>
> P.S. I think they have kept the contract signing secret from Grandpapa Noirtier.

Maximilian longed intensely for the moment when he should hear Valentine say, "Here I am, Maximilian. Come and help me." He had arranged everything for her escape.

At length the hour drew near. Maximilian went to the garden gate and waited.

The night gradually drew on, and the sky turned darker. Valentine failed to appear at the agreed time. The house remained in darkness. There was no sign that so important an event as the signature of a marriage contract was to take place. Maximilian's watch said nine-thirty.

All sorts of terrible thoughts went through his mind. Had Valentine fainted? Had she been discovered and stopped in her flight? Almost mad with grief, Maximilian drew closer to the dark house, when he suddenly heard voices.

He stepped back and concealed himself behind a bush. Maximilian saw Villefort come out, followed by a gentleman in black. Maximilian recognized the other gentleman as Dr. d'Avrigny.

"Ah, my dear doctor," said Villefort, "What a dreadful death—what a blow! Don't even try to comfort me. Nothing can ease so great a sorrow—the wound is too deep and too fresh! She is dead, dead!"

"My dear M. de Villefort," replied the doctor, "I have not led you here to comfort you. On the contrary—"

"What do you mean?" asked Villefort, greatly alarmed.

"I mean that behind the misfortune which has

just happened to you, there is another, perhaps, still greater."

"Can it be possible?" murmured Villefort, clasping his hands. "What are you going to tell me?"

"Are we quite alone, my friend?"

"Yes, quite. But why all these precautions?"

"Because I have a terrible secret to communicate to you," said the doctor. "Let us sit down."

Villefort took a seat on a bench. The doctor stood before him, with one hand placed on his shoulder. Maximilian, horrified, supported his head with one hand, and with the other pressed his heart, lest its beating should be heard.

"Speak, doctor—I am listening," said Villefort.

"Madame de Saint-Meran was, without a doubt, advancing in years, but she enjoyed excellent health."

"Grief has killed her," said Villefort. "Yes, grief, doctor! After living forty years with the marquis—"

"It is not grief, my dear Villefort," said the doctor. "We were both there during her last hours. The symptoms she experienced, my dear friend, were the result of poison. Someone murdered your mother-in-law!"

M. de Villefort started from his seat, then in a moment collapsed down again, silent and motionless.

Maximilian, overhearing this conversation, did not know if he was dreaming or awake.

"During the three-quarters of an hour that the struggle continued, I watched the convulsions and the death of Madame de Saint-Meran," the doctor said. "Not only am I convinced that her death was caused by poison, but I can also identify the poison."

"Can it be possible?"

"Madame de Saint-Meran succumbed to a powerful dose of brucine or strychnine, which someone gave to her, either deliberately or by mistake. Had Madame de Saint-Meran any enemies?"

"Not to my knowledge."

"Would her death affect anyone's interest?"

"It could not indeed, my daughter is her only heiress—Valentine alone. She would never do such a thing."

"May not Barrois, the old servant, have made a mistake, and have given Madame de Saint-Meran a dose prepared for his master?"

"For my father?"

"Yes."

"But how could a dose prepared for M. Noirtier poison Madame de Saint-Meran?"

"Nothing is more simple. You know poisons become remedies in certain diseases, of which paralysis is one. I have been giving M. Noirtier successive doses of strychnine in an attempt to alleviate his paralysis. This dosage which is harmless to M. Noirtier would be sufficient to kill someone else."

"But doctor, there is no communication between M. Noirtier's apartment and that of Madame de Saint-Meran, and Barrois never entered my mother-in-law's room."

"If this thing has been caused by negligence, watch over your servants; if from hatred, watch your enemies," said the doctor in a serious tone. "Let us keep this terrible secret to ourselves for now. Meanwhile, sir, watch always—watch carefully, for perhaps the evil may not stop here. And when you have found the culprit, if you find him, I will say to you, 'You are a magistrate, do your duty!'"

"I thank you, doctor," said Villefort. "I never had a better friend than you." The two men went back into the house, their heads bent low.

When they were gone, Maximilian was so mad with worry that he ran from his hiding place and quietly entered the house. He quietly climbed the stairs and heard a sob. He pushed open a door and entered. He saw the corpse, and beside it was Valentine, trembling and sobbing.

"My darling," she said, "how did you get here?"

"Valentine," said Maximilian with a trembling voice, "I have been waiting since half-past eight and did not see you come. I became frantic and—"

"But all will be lost if you are found here, love."

"Forgive me," replied Maximilian. "I will go away."

"Wait," said Valentine, "you can neither go out by the front door nor by the garden." Maximilian looked at her with astonishment. "There is only one way that is safe. It is through my grandfather's room. Come. He is my only remaining friend, and we both need his help—come with me."

As they entered M. Noirtier's room, they saw the old servant. "Barrois," said Valentine, "shut the door and let no one come in." She entered first. Noirtier, seated in his wheelchair, saw Valentine, and his eyes brightened. There was something grave and solemn in the approach of the young girl which struck the old man. "Dear Grandfather," she said hurriedly, "you know poor Grandmamma died an hour ago, and now I have no friend in the world but you." His expressive eyes showed the greatest tenderness. "To you alone, then, may I confide my sorrows and my hopes?"

The paralytic motioned "Yes."

Valentine took Maximilian's hand. "Look at this gentleman." The old man fixed his gaze on Maximilian. "It is M. Maximilian Morrel," she said, "the son of that good merchant of Marseilles, whom you must remember."

The old man signified that he remembered him.

"Well, Grandpapa," said Valentine, kneeling before him, "I love him and will be only his. Were I compelled to marry another, I would destroy myself."

The eyes of the paralytic expressed a mixture of conflicting thoughts.

"You like M. Maximilian Morrel, do you not, Grandpapa?" asked Valentine.

"Yes."

"And you will protect us against the will of my father?" Noirtier cast a glance at Maximilian, as if to say, "perhaps I may." Maximilian understood him.

"Mademoiselle," said the young man, "you have a sacred duty to fulfill in your deceased grandmother's room. Will you allow me the honor of a few minutes' conversation alone with M. Noirtier? You have explained to me how he communicates, so we can have a conversation."

"That is good," said the old man's eyes.

Valentine arose, tenderly embraced her grandfather, and went to her grandmother's room.

Maximilian explained to the old man how he had become acquainted with Valentine and how much he loved her. He told him his birth, his position, and his fortune. More than once the paralytic's eyes answered, "That is good, proceed."

Then Maximilian told him how they intended to flee together that night. When he finished, Nortier closed and opened his eyes several times, which was his manner of saying no.

"Am I to wait?"

"Yes."

"But delay may ruin our plan, sir," replied the young man. "I can scarcely hope for so good an opportunity to occur again. Do you authorize Mademoiselle Valentine to entrust herself to my honor?"

"No."

"Where will we get the help we need—from chance?" resumed Maximilian.

"No."

"From you?"

"Yes."

"You are sure of it?"

"Yes." There was so much firmness in the look which gave this answer that no one could doubt his will, even if they questioned his power.

"Oh, thank you a thousand times! But are you able to prevent this marriage while chained to that wheelchair and without the ability to speak?"

A smile lit up the old man's face as he indicated, "Yes."

"But what about the marriage contract with M. d'Epinay?" The same smile returned. "Will you assure me it shall not be signed?"

"Yes," said Noirtier.

"The contract shall not be signed!" exclaimed Maximilian. "Oh, pardon me, sir. I can scarcely realize so great a happiness. They will not sign it?"

"No," said the paralytic.

"Now," said Maximilian, "do you wish me to leave the house?"

"Yes."

"Without seeing Mademoiselle Valentine?"

"Yes."

Maximilian started to obey but as he was leaving turned and said, "First allow me to embrace you as your granddaughter did just now." The young man pressed his lips on the same spot, on the old man's forehead, where Valentine's had been. Then he bowed and retired. Outside the door he found Barrois, who guided him to the street by a back passage.

CHAPTER 51
The Villefort Family Vault

As Franz d'Epinay arrives at the Villefort residence to be married to Valentine, he is told that M. Noirtier wishes to speak to him.

No sooner had the marquise and the marquis (for his body had arrived shortly after the marquise's passing) been laid to rest in the family tomb, than M. Villefort decided to honor his mother-in-law's last wish.

After conversing with Baron d'Epinay, Villefort called his daughter and demanded that Valentine be present in the salon within a half hour for her marriage ceremony. He instructed her to be ready to receive M. d'Epinay and his two witnesses and the lawyer.

Soon Franz arrived with Chateau-Renaud and Albert. The lawyer, the same one who had arranged Noirtier's new will, pulled up at the same moment.

The lawyer, after arranging the marriage papers on the table, turned toward Franz and asked, "Are you M. Franz de Quesnel, Baron d'Epinay?"

"Yes, sir," replied Franz.

The lawyer bowed and said, "I must now inform you, sir, that your projected marriage with Mademoiselle de Villefort has changed the feeling of M. Noirtier toward his grandchild. He disinherits her entirely of the fortune he would have left her."

"Sir," said Franz, "I regret that such a question has been raised in the presence of Mademoiselle Valentine. I have never inquired about the amount of her fortune, which, however limited it may be, exceeds mine. All I seek is happiness."

Valentine thought to herself, "He is not after my money, but I still do not love him. I love Maximilian!" as two silent tears rolled down her cheeks.

At this very moment, the door opened, and Noirtier's servant Barrois appeared.

"Gentlemen," he said, "M. Noirtier de Villefort wishes to speak immediately to M. Franz de Quesnel, Baron d'Epinay."

The lawyer looked at Villefort. "It is impossible," said Villefort. "M. d'Epinay cannot leave the drawing room at present."

"It is at this moment," replied Barrois with the same firmness, "that M. Noirtier, my master, wishes to speak on important subjects to M. Franz d'Epinay."

"Excuse me, sir," said Franz, "since M. Noirtier has sent for me, I am ready to attend to his wish. Besides, I shall be happy to pay my respects to him, not having yet had the honor of doing so."

The young man arose and followed Valentine, who was running downstairs with the joy of a shipwrecked mariner who finds a rock to cling to. M. de Villefort followed them.

CHAPTER 52
A Signed Statement

Franz d'Epinay learns the truth about his father's death.

Noirtier was prepared to receive them, dressed in black, and sitting in his wheelchair. When the three persons he expected had entered, he looked at the door, which his valet immediately closed.

Villefort approached his father and said, "Here is M. Franz d'Epinay. After you speak with him, I am certain you will abandon your objections to Valentine's marriage."

Noirtier answered only by a look which made Villefort's blood run cold. He motioned to Valentine to approach. Thanks to her habit of conversing with her grandfather, she understood that he desired her to ask for Barrois. When the trusted servant entered, Noirtier signaled to him to open Noirtier's ancient desk and press a secret spring. When Barrois did so, out fell a bundle of papers tied with a black string.

"Is that what you wish for?" said Barrois.

"Yes."

"Shall I give these papers to M. de Villefort?"

"No."

"To Mademoiselle Valentine?"

"No."

"To M. Franz d'Epinay?"

"Yes."

Franz, astonished, advanced a step. "To me, sir?" he asked.

"Yes."

Franz took them from Barrois and, casting a glance at the cover, read out loud:

> To be given, after my death, to General Durand, who shall present the packet to his son, with instructions to preserve it as containing an important document.

"Well, sir," asked Franz, "what do you wish me to do with this?"

"To preserve it, sealed up as it is, without a doubt," said Villefort.

"No," replied Noirtier eagerly.

"Do you wish him to read it aloud?" said Valentine.

"Yes," replied the old man.

Franz untied the papers and, in the midst of the most profound silence, read:

> Extract from the Report of a meeting of the Bonapartist Club on Saint-Jacques Street, held February 5th, 1815.

Franz stopped. "February 5th, 1815 is the day my father was murdered." Valentine and Villefort were dumb. The eyes of the old man seemed to say clearly, "Go on."

"But it was on leaving this club," he said, "my father disappeared." Noirtier's eyes continued to say, "Read." He resumed:

The undersigned, Louis Jacques Beaurepaire, lieutenant-colonel, Etienne Duchampy, general of brigade, and Claude Lecharpal, keeper of woods, declare, that on the 4th of February, a letter arrived from the island of Elba, Napoleon's place of exile, recommending to the Bonapartist Club, General Flavien de Quesnel. The general, who had served the Emperor Napoleon from 1804 to 1814, was said to be devoted to the interests of Napoleon.

A note was addressed to General de Quesnel, asking him to attend a meeting of the Bonapartist Club the next day, the 5th. The note gave him neither the street nor the number of the house where the meeting was to be held. It bore no signature, but it announced to the general that someone would call for him at nine o'clock. At nine o'clock the president of the club presented himself to the general. The president informed him that one of the conditions of his introduction was that he should not know the place of meeting, and that he would allow himself to be blindfolded. General de Quesnel accepted the condition. "I have my carriage here," said the president.

The carriage stopped at an alley leading out of Saint-Jacques Street. The general alighted, leaning on the arm of the president. They went through the alley, mounted a flight of stairs, and entered the assembly-room.

The members were all in attendance. When in the middle of the room, the general was invited to remove his blindfold. He did so immediately and was surprised to see so many well-known faces. They questioned him as to his political beliefs—

Franz interrupted himself by saying, "My father was a royalist, a supporter of King Louis XVIII." He started reading again:

The president then told General Quesnel about the letter from Elba, which stated that the general was a supporter of Napoleon and could be trusted.

"Well," asked the president, "what do you say about this letter, general?"

"I say that it is too soon after declaring myself for King Louis XVIII to break my vow and support the ex-emperor."

"General," said the president, "we acknowledge no King Louis XVIII or an ex-emperor. We recognize only the proper emperor, Napoleon."

"Excuse me, gentlemen," said the general, "you may not acknowledge King

Louis XVIII, but I do. I remain forever loyal to him for making me a baron and a field-marshal."

"Sir," said the president, rising with gravity, "be careful what you say. It is clear we have been deceived. We have exposed ourselves to you, and now we discover our error. We will not force you to help us."

"By knowing your conspiracy and not calling the authorities, I am forced to become your accomplice," responded the general.

"Ah, my father!" said Franz, interrupting himself. "I understand now why they murdered him." Franz returned to the document, and continued:

"Sir," said the president, "we will ask you one last time. Are you for the king who reigns or for his majesty, the emperor?"

"I am a royalist," replied the general. "I have taken the oath of allegiance to King Louis XVIII, and I will stick by it."

These words were followed by a general murmur, and it was clear that several members of the group were thinking of making the general pay for his sentiments.

The president again arose, and having imposed silence, said, "Sir, your statements put us in a hazardous position. If the king's police learn about our devotion to Napoleon, they will execute us. You must swear on your honor not to tell anyone what has happened here."

"What is the oath you wish me to swear?" he asked.

"It is this: 'I swear by my honor not to reveal to anyone what I have seen and heard on the 5th of February, 1815, between nine and ten o'clock in the evening. And I plead guilty and deserve death should I ever violate this oath.'"

The general repeated the required oath.

"Now am I at liberty to leave?" asked the general.

The president arose, appointed three members to accompany him, and got into the carriage with the general after blindfolding him again.

"Where do you wish to be taken?" asked the president.

"Anywhere out of the damnable presence of you traitors to the king," replied General Quesnel.

"Beware, sir," replied the president, "do not insult us unless you wish to be held responsible."

But the general did not listen and went on, "You are brave in your carriage because you are four against one."

The president stopped the coach. They were at that part of the Ormes Boulevard where the steps lead down to the river.

"Why do you stop here?" asked General Quesnel.

"Because, sir," said the president, "you have insulted me, and I will not go one step farther without demanding a duel. Now, if you please, remove your blindfold."

The general tore the blindfold from his eyes and snarled, "At last I will be able to deal with you as my honor demands!"

They opened the door and all the men got out of the carriage.

Franz stopped once more and wiped the cold sweat from his forehead. Noirtier looked at Villefort with an almost sublime expression of contempt and pride. Franz continued:—

It was, as we said, the 5th of February. For three days the mercury had been five or six degrees below freezing, and the steps were covered with ice. The men carefully made their way down to the riverbank.

It was a dark night. One of the witnesses went for a lantern, and by its light they examined the weapons. The president's sword, which he carried in his cane, was five inches shorter than the general's. The general proposed to cast lots for the swords, but the president refused.

The lantern was placed on the ground, the two adversaries took their stations, and the duel began. The light made the two swords appear like flashes of lightning. It was so dark that it was hard to see the men.

General Quesnel was thought to be one of the best swordsmen in the army, but he was pressed so closely that he missed his aim and fell. The witnesses thought he was dead, but his adversary, who knew he had not struck him, offered him his hand to assist him to rise.

This circumstance irritated the general, and he rushed his adversary. But his opponent did not allow his guard to be broken. He defended himself with his sword, and three times the general drew back on finding himself too closely engaged.

He then returned to the charge, but after this rush he fell again. Everyone thought he had slipped again, but the witnesses, seeing he did not move, approached and endeavored to raise him. They then saw that his body was covered in blood.

The general lay motionless on the ground. The president approached the witness who held the lantern, and raising his sleeve, showed him two wounds he had received to his arm. Then opening his coat, he displayed his side, pierced with a third wound.

General Quesnel died five minutes later.

Franz read these last words in a voice so choked that it was hardly audible. After a moment's silence, he continued:

The president went up the steps. A track of blood on the snow marked his course. He had scarcely arrived at the top when he heard a heavy splash in the water. It was the general's body, which the witnesses had just thrown into the river after making sure that he was dead.

In proof of this, we have signed this paper to establish the truth of the facts, lest the moment should arrive when either of the actors in this terrible scene should be accused of premeditated murder or of infringement of the laws of honor.

Signed, Beaurepaire, Deschamps, and Lecharpal

When Franz had finished reading this account, he turned to Noirtier. "Sir," said d'Epinay to Noirtier, "since you are well acquainted with all these details, which are attested by honorable signatures, tell me the name of the president of the club, that I may at least know who killed my father." Villefort mechanically felt for the handle of the door. Valentine, who understood sooner than anyone her grandfather's answer, and who had often seen two scars upon his right arm, drew back a few steps.

"Please, sir," said Villefort, "do not prolong this dreadful scene. The names have been hidden all these years. My father himself does not know who this president was, and if he knows, he cannot tell you."

"Oh, misery," cried Franz. "Sir, sir," he pleaded, turning to Noirtier, "do what you can—make me understand in some way!"

"Yes," replied Noirtier.

"Oh, mademoiselle, mademoiselle!" exclaimed Franz, "your grandfather says he can identify the person. Help me." Noirtier looked at the dictionary. Franz took it with a nervous trembling, and repeated the letters of the alphabet successively, until he came to M. At that letter the old man signified "Yes."

"M," repeated Franz. The young man's finger glided over the words, but at each one Noirtier answered by a negative sign. Valentine hid her head between her hands. At length, Franz arrived at the word "MYSELF."

"Yes!"

"You?" gasped Franz, whose hair stood on end. "You, M. Noirtier—you killed my father?"

"Yes!" replied Noirtier.

Franz fell powerless on a chair. Villefort opened the door and fled.

CHAPTER 53

Progress of
Calvalcanti the Younger

Danglars tells the Count that Franz d'Epinay has broken off his engagement.

A short time after the events just recorded, Monte Cristo called on M. Danglars. M. Danglars was happy to receive his client and was quick to tell him the recent misfortunes that had affected the house of de Villefort. "You know the Marquis of Saint-Meran died a few days after he had set out on his journey to Paris, and the marquise a few days after her arrival. But that is not all. You know their daughter was to be married to M. Franz d'Epinay?"

"Has the engagement been broken off?"

"Franz declined the honor yesterday."

"Really! Is the reason known?"

"No."

"How extraordinary! And how does M. de Villefort bear it?"

"As usual. Like a philosopher. But Count Cavalcanti is a charming young man, is he not?" inquired Danglars. "Is he really a count?"

"I cannot answer that," said Monte Cristo, "but how does it matter to you?"

"I have promised to give my daughter Eugenie to a man who loves her. But Albert is cold as marble and proud like his father. If he were rich, if he had Cavalcanti's fortune, that might be pardoned. In truth, I haven't consulted my daughter. But if she has good sense—"

"Oh," said Monte Cristo, "my fondness may blind me, but I assure you I consider Albert Morcerf a charming young man who will make your daughter happy and will sooner or later attain a certain amount of distinction. Besides, his father's position is firmly established."

"Oh really?" said Danglars.

"Why do you doubt?"

"The past—certain rumors about his past."

"But that does not affect the son."

"Very true."

"But you cannot break it off so suddenly," said the Count. "The Morcerfs are depending on this union."

A servant came to Danglars and whispered something in his ear. "I shall soon return," said the banker to Monte Cristo. "Wait for me. I shall, perhaps, have something of interest to tell you." And he went out.

Danglars returned, visibly agitated. "I have just received my messenger from Greece," said Danglars. "Your advice was excellent," he said. "There is a whole history connected with the names Fernand and Yanina. Come visit me later, and I will tell you the whole story."

Monte Cristo assured him he would return.

CHAPTER 54
We Hear from Yanina

Maximilian receives some excellent news, but Fernand de Morcerf is not so fortunate.

If Valentine had seen how distraught Franz was when he left M. Noirtier's room, even she would have felt pity for him. Villefort muttered a few incoherent words and retired to his study. Two hours later he received the following note:

> After all the disclosures which were made this morning, M. Noirtier de Villefort must see the utter impossibility of any alliance being formed between his family and that of M. Franz d'Epinay.

Valentine, after having embraced and thanked the feeble old man for thus breaking with a single blow the chain which she had thought was unbreakable, went to the garden.

Maximilian had suspected that something very dramatic was happening. He was equally certain that Valentine would rush to meet him in the garden. He was not mistaken and soon saw Valentine. Her first words made his heart leap with delight.

"We are saved!" said Valentine.

"Saved?" repeated Maximilian, not being able to imagine such intense happiness. "By whom?"

"By my grandfather."

"But tell me, Valentine, what strange means has he used?"

"When I am your wife, I will tell you all about it."

Before leaving the garden, Maximilian received the promise of seeing Valentine again the next night.

Meanwhile, Madame de Villefort had gone to visit M. Noirtier. The old man looked at her with that stern and forbidding expression with which he usually greeted her.

"Sir," she said, "it is pointless for me to tell you that Valentine's marriage is canceled." Noirtier's countenance remained immovable. "Now that this marriage will not happen, I come to ask you, sir, to restore your fortune to your granddaughter."

Noirtier made a sign that he would do so. She then bowed to M. Noirtier and left.

The next day M. Noirtier, with the help of the lawyer, rewrote his will, leaving his entire fortune to Valentine, on condition that she should never be separated from him.

While these events were taking place at the house of M. de Villefort, Monte Cristo paid a visit to Count Fernand Morcerf. Monte Cristo told him, in complete confidence, that M. Danglars was considering preventing the marriage of his daughter to Morcerf's son Albert. Anxious to avoid such a development, Fernand decided to pay a visit to Baron Danglars. In order to impress his host, Fernand donned his uniform of lieutenant-general, which he ornamented with all his medals. Thus attired, he ordered his finest horses and set out for Danglars' residence.

On seeing his old friend, Danglars assumed a majestic air and settled himself in his chair.

"Well, Baron," said Fernand, "some time has elapsed since we discussed our plans for the future of our children. I think the time has come for us to formally agree to those arrangements." Making a low bow to M. Danglars, Fernand continued: "Baron, I have the honor of asking of you the hand of Mademoiselle Eugenie Danglars for my son, the Viscount Albert de Morcerf."

But Danglars, instead of welcoming this address, replied, "Monsieur, it will be necessary to reflect before I give you an answer."

"To reflect?" said Fernand, more and more astonished. "Have you not had enough time for reflection during the eight years which have elapsed since we first discussed this marriage?"

"Count de Morcerf," said the banker, "sometimes things occur which cause us to change our minds."

"I do not understand you, Baron," said Fernand. "Have you changed your mind?"

"I do apologize. I understand you must be surprised. But please understand that it is painful for me as well. Please understand that I am not without a good reason for my conduct," replied the banker.

"What do you mean to say?"

"It may be better for you if I do not give you any more details."

A tremor of suppressed rage shook Fernand as he said, "Enough sir, we will speak no more on the subject." And clutching his gloves in anger, he left the house.

The next morning, as soon as he awoke, Danglars asked for the newspapers. With a malicious smile on his face, he read a paragraph headed "We hear from Yanina." The report read,

> A correspondent at Yanina informs us of information which until now had remained hidden. The castle which formed the protection of the town was surrendered to the Turks, without a fight, by a French officer named Fernand Mondego. Ali Tepelini, the Grand Vizier of Yanina, had expressed the greatest confidence in this French officer. The French officer also sold his benefactor, Ali Tepelini, to the Turkish enemy. Since then, the French officer added to his Christian name a title of nobility and a family name. He now calls himself the Count de Morcerf, and ranks among the nobility.

CHAPTER 55
The Lemonade

The poisoner claims another victim.

Maximilian was very happy. M. Noirtier had just sent for him, and he was in such haste that he was running down the street. He was only thirty-one. Barrois, twice his age, was gasping from the heat and exertion.

After catching his breath, the old servant brought Maximilian into Noirtier's study. They were soon joined by Valentine. "Am I to say what you told me?" asked Valentine. Noirtier made a sign that she was to do so.

"M. Morrel," said Valentine to Maximilian, "my grandfather intends leaving this house. Barrois is now looking for a suitable apartment. I shall not leave my grandfather—that is understood between us. Once I am under my grandfather's roof, you can visit me in the presence of my good and worthy protector."

"Oh," exclaimed Maximilian, "what have I ever done in my life to have such happiness?"

"How hot you look, Barrois," said Valentine.

"Ah, I was running very fast, mademoiselle, trying to keep up with M. Morrel." Noirtier directed their attention to a table on which was placed a pitcher containing lemonade and a glass. The pitcher was nearly full, except for the little that M. Noirtier had drunk.

"Come, Barrois," said the young girl, "take some of this lemonade."

Barrois left with the lemonade. A few minutes later the front doorbell rang. Valentine looked at her watch.

"It is past noon," she said, "and today is Saturday. That must be the doctor, Grandpapa. He will come in here. Maximilian had better go—do you not think so, Grandpapa?"

"Yes," signed the old man.

"Barrois," cried Valentine, "Barrois!"

"I am coming, mademoiselle," he replied.

Addressing Maximilian, Valentine said Barrois would conduct him out by the back way.

At this moment Barrois entered. "Who rang?" asked Valentine.

"Dr. d'Avrigny," said Barrois, staggering as if he would fall.

"What is the matter, Barrois?" said Valentine. The old servant did not answer, but looked at his master with wild staring eyes, while with his cramped hand he grasped a piece of furniture to enable him to stand upright. His entire body began to convulse.

"What is the matter with me?" he shouted. "I am suffering—I cannot see. A thousand fiery darts are piercing my brain. Help, help!" Barrois turned around and with a great effort stumbled a few steps, then fell at the feet of Noirtier.

At this moment M. de Villefort, attracted by the noise, entered the room. Maximilian retreated to a distant corner of the room and hid behind a curtain. Barrois, his features convulsed, his eyes flushed with blood, and his head thrown back, was lying at full length, beating the floor with his hands, while his legs had become so stiff that they looked as if they would break rather than bend. A slight appearance of foam was visible around the mouth. He breathed painfully and with extreme difficulty.

Villefort sprang toward the door, crying out, "Doctor, doctor! Come instantly! Pray come!"

"Madame, madame!" cried Valentine, calling her stepmother, and running upstairs to meet her. "Come quick, quick!—and bring your bottle of smelling-salts with you."

"What is the matter?" said Madame de Villefort in a harsh and constrained tone.

"Oh, come, come!"

"Has he eaten anything lately?" asked Madame de Villefort, entering the room.

"Madame," replied Valentine, "he has not even had his breakfast. He took nothing but a glass of lemonade."

"Ah," said Madame de Villefort, "why did he not take wine? Lemonade was a very bad thing for him."

"Grandpapa's bottle of lemonade was standing just by his side. Poor Barrois was very thirsty and was thankful to drink anything he could find." Madame de Villefort started. Noirtier looked at her with a most deliberate glare.

"Madame," said Villefort, "I ask—where is Dr. d'Avrigny? In God's name answer me!"

"He is with Edward, who is not quite well," replied Madame de Villefort.

Villefort rushed upstairs to fetch him. Madame de Villefort followed him. Maximilian now emerged from his hiding place. "Go away as quick as you can, Maximilian," said Valentine, "and stay till I send for you. Go."

The young man pressed Valentine's hand to his lips and then left the house by a back staircase. At the same moment that he left the room, Villefort and the doctor entered by an opposite door. Barrois was now showing signs of returning consciousness. The crisis seemed past.

Dr. d'Avrigny and Villefort placed Barrois on a couch. The doctor prescribed some medication for the trusted servant and then asked to examine the pitcher of lemonade. On being told it was down in the kitchen, he raced down to fetch it. When he brought it back up, he asked Barrois what the drink tasted like.

"It had a bitter taste."

The doctor poured some drops of the lemonade into the palm of his hand, put his lips to it, and spat the liquid into the fireplace.

"Did you drink some too, M. Noirtier?"

"Yes."

"And did you also discover a bitter taste?"

"Yes."

"Then you feel pretty much as you generally do after you have had the dose which I am accustomed to give you every Sunday?"

"Yes."

"Barrois," said the doctor, "can you speak?" Barrois muttered a few unintelligible words. "Try and make an effort to do so, my good man," said Dr. d'Avrigny. Barrois reopened his bloodshot eyes. "Who made the lemonade?"

"I did."

"Did you bring it to your master as soon as it was made?"

"No."

"You left it somewhere, then, in the meantime?"

"Yes. I left it in the pantry, because I was called away."

"Who brought it into this room, then?"

"Mademoiselle Valentine." Dr. d'Avrigny struck his forehead with his hand. "Gracious heaven!" he exclaimed.

"Doctor, doctor!" cried Barrois, who felt another fit coming. In fact, this second attack proved much worse than the first. After writhing in agony, the good servant breathed his last and lay dead.

Villefort drew back a few steps and, clasping his hands, exclaimed, "Dead?—and so soon too!"

"Yes, it is very soon," said the doctor, looking at the corpse before him. "But that ought not to astonish you. M. and Madame de Saint-Meran died as quickly. People die very suddenly in your house, M. de Villefort."

"What?" exclaimed Villefort, with an accent of horror and concern, "are you still harping on that terrible idea?"

"Still, sir, and I shall continue to do so," replied Dr. d'Avrigny. "Now listen to what I am going to say. There is a poison which destroys life almost without leaving any visible traces. I recognized the presence of this poison in the case of poor Barrois as well as in that of Madame de Saint-Meran. There is a way of detecting its presence. It turns syrup of violets green. I have here some syrup of violets. Look," he said to Villefort, whose heart beat so loudly that it might almost be heard, "here in this cup is some syrup of violets. Watch as I mix it with the remainder of the lemonade which M. Noirtier and Barrois drank. If the lemonade is harmless, the syrup will retain its color. If, on the contrary, the lemonade is drugged with poison, the syrup will become green. Look closely!"

The doctor then slowly poured some drops of the lemonade from the pitcher into the cup. In an instant a light cloudy sediment began to form at the bottom of the cup. This sediment first took a blue shade, then it passed to that of opal, and from opal to dark green.

"The unfortunate Barrois has been poisoned," said Dr. d'Avrigny. Villefort said nothing. Overcome with horror, he sank into a chair.

CHAPTER 56
The Accusation

Villefort ignores the doctor's suspicions.

Villefort soon revived, declaring, "Oh, death is in my house!"

"Say, rather, crime!" replied the doctor.

"Dr. d'Avrigny," cried Villefort, "I cannot tell you all I feel at this moment—terror, grief, madness."

"Yes," said Dr. d'Avrigny, "but I think it is now time to act. I can no longer bear to be in possession of these secrets without seeing justice done. Do you suspect anyone?"

When Villefort did not reply, the doctor said, "'Seek whom the crime will profit'—that's an old axiom of law."

"Doctor," Villefort replied, "how often has man's justice been deceived by those fatal words. I know not why, but I feel that this crime is intended to affect me personally. I fear an attack myself, after all these disasters. The lemonade was intended for Noirtier. The other man drank it only by accident. Although Barrois is dead, it was Noirtier whose death was wished for. But tell me, doctor, why did it not kill my father?"

"Because his system is accustomed to that very poison. The dose was harmless to him, although fatal to another. No one knows, not even the murderer, that for the last twelve months I have given M. Noirtier brucine for his paralysis."

"Oh, have pity, have pity!" murmured Villefort, wringing his hands.

"Follow the culprit's steps; he first kills M. de Saint-Meran—"

"Oh, doctor!"

"I would swear to it. What I heard of his symptoms agrees too well with what I have seen in the other cases. He first kills M. de Saint-Meran," repeated the doctor, "then Madame de Saint-Meran—a double fortune to inherit." Villefort wiped the perspiration from his forehead. "Listen attentively."

"Alas," stammered Villefort, "I do not lose a single word."

"M. Noirtier," resumed Dr. d'Avrigny in the same pitiless tone,—"M. Noirtier destroyed his first will and made a second. Then, for fear he should make a third, he is targeted. This second will was made the day before yesterday, I believe. You see there has been no time lost."

"Have mercy on my child, sir," murmured Villefort.

"You see it is yourself who has first named her—you, her father."

"Have pity on Valentine! Listen—it is impossible! I would as willingly accuse myself!"

"No pity, Villefort. Mademoiselle Valentine herself packed all the medicines which were sent to M. de Saint-Meran, and M. de Saint-Meran is dead. Valentine prepared all the cooling drinks which Madame de Saint-Meran took, and Madame de Saint-Meran is dead. Mademoiselle de Villefort took from the hands of Barrois, who was sent out, the lemonade which M. Noirtier had every morning, and he has escaped by a miracle. Mademoiselle de Villefort is the culprit—she is the poisoner! To you, as the king's attorney, I denounce Mademoiselle de Villefort. You must do your duty."

Villefort, choking, pressed the doctor's arm. "Listen," he begged. "Pity me—help me! My daughter is not guilty. I will not drag her before a tribunal and hand her over to the executioner! The bare idea would kill me—would drive me like a madman to dig my heart out with my fingernails!"

"Well," said the doctor, after a moment's silence, "I will wait." Villefort looked at him as if he had doubted his words.

The doctor continued with a slow and solemn tone, "But if anyone else falls ill in your house, or if you feel yourself attacked, do not send for me, for I will come no more. I want nothing further to do with your family."

CHAPTER 57
The Burglary

In his Auteuil house, the Count surprises a burglar.

The next day, the Count of Monte Cristo received an unsigned message at his Auteuil house: "The Count of Monte Cristo is hereby warned that a man will attempt to rob his Paris house tonight at midnight. The man will enter by the bedroom window."

The Count sent word that the servants who remained at the Paris house immediately come to Auteuil. He himself, along with Ali, secretly set out for Paris, armed with a pistol.

By twilight he was opposite his Paris house, which was dark. One feeble light burned in the porter's lodge, which was 40 paces from the house. Monte Cristo, accompanied by Ali, hurriedly entered the house by a side door. He went to his bedroom and found that nothing had been disturbed. Then he waited.

As the church clock struck the last sounds of midnight, the Count saw a firm and practiced hand cutting a pane of glass with a diamond. A man put his hand through to unlock the window. Before he entered, Ali motioned to Monte Cristo to look at a young man standing guard in the street. By this time the thief had entered and was feeling his way around. He had brought a small lantern which he quietly pointed at various parts of the room. As the pale light revealed the man's face, Monte Cristo recognized him. The intruder began to pick the lock of a large cabinet.

After giving Ali strict instruction to stay concealed, Monte Cristo lit a candle and noiselessly walked into the room. The thief turned in response to the sudden illumination.

"Ah, good-evening, my dear M. Caderousse," said Monte Cristo. "What are you doing here, at such an hour? So you would rob me?"

"Please have mercy, sir!" Caderousse begged. Please let me go!"

"Why should I?" the Count demanded.

"This wasn't my idea. It was my companion's plan. Look out the window, and you'll see him standing guard in the street." The Count indeed did see someone lurking in the shadows.

"Tell me his name, and I'll consider releasing you."

"Are you the Count of Monte Cristo?"

"Yes," the Count replied.

"My companion is your illegitimate son," Caderousse said.

The Count was bewildered. "My son?"

"Yes. You've had him go by the name of Andrea Cavalcanti. You've been giving him money, and you've introduced him to Parisian society. So he must be your son. He has betrayed you. I simply went along with his plan."

The Count realized that Benedetto, now renamed Andrea Cavalcanti, had betrayed Caderousse. It must have been Benedetto who wrote the note warning of the burglary. He must have thought that Caderousse would be killed when he entered the house. For some reason, Benedetto wanted Caderousse dead.

As the Count was reflecting on these probabilities, Caderousse drew a knife from his waistcoat. Aiming the knife at the Count's breast, he declared, "You shall reveal nothing, sir!" To Caderousse's great astonishment, the Count seized the assassin's wrist and wrung it with such strength that the knife fell from his stiffened fingers. Caderousse uttered a cry of pain. But the Count, disregarding his cry, continued to wring the bandit's wrist, until, his arm being dislocated, he fell first on his knees, then flat on the floor. The Count then placed his foot on his head, saying, "I know not what restrains me from crushing your skull, you villain."

"Oh!" said Caderousse, groaning with pain.

"Take this pen and paper, and write what I dictate."

Caderousse sat down and wrote:

Sir—The man whom you are receiving at your house, and to whom you intend to marry your daughter, is a felon who escaped with me from confinement at Toulon. He was No. 59, and I No. 58. He was called Benedetto, but he is ignorant of his real name, having never known his parents.

"Sign it!" the Count demanded. Caderousse signed it. "The address, 'Baron Danglars, banker, Chaussee d'Antin Street.'" Caderousse wrote the address. The Count took the note. "Now," he said, "get out!"

"Which way?"

"The way you came."

"You wish me to get out at that window?"

"You got in very well."

Caderousse put his legs out of the window and stood on the ladder. "Now go down," said the Count, folding his arms. Understanding he had nothing more to fear from him, Caderousse began to go down. Then the Count brought the candle to the window, so that anyone standing in the street could see that a man was climbing out of the window.

As Caderousse's feet touched the ground, the Count saw Benedetto run over and stab him in the back and side. Benedetto stabbed him again, this time in the chest, and then ran off. Caderousse raised himself on his elbow, and with a dying voice cried out with great effort, "Murder! I am dying! Help, help!" Then Caderousse fell back with a groan.

The Count ran out to him. "Who has done this?" he asked, already knowing the answer.

In a weak voice Caderousse replied, "Your illegitimate son, the Corsican Benedetto, who calls himself Andrea Cavalcanti. He betrayed both of us."

"As *you* betrayed *me!*" the Count exclaimed.

"What? I don't even know you," Caderousse replied.

"Take a closer look," said the Count, removing his wig and placing the light near his face. "You used to know me and my father."

Caderousse peered closely at the face that hovered over him. "Edmond Dantes!" he gasped. He fell back with an agonized moan. He was dead.

"One," uttered the Count.

CHAPTER 58
The Trial

A surprise witness appears at Fernand's trial and tells what really happened in the Greek province of Yanina.

The following day, the morning papers carried several reports from the Greek province of Yanina.

One of the articles in question read:

> Our correspondent in the Greek province of Yanina has given us new information about Yanina's fall to the Turks. The fortress that protected the province was surrendered to the Turks by the French commander of Greek troops, namely, Colonel Fernand Mondego. The ruler of the province, Grand Vizier Ali Tepelini, had placed the greatest confidence in Mondego. It now appears that Mondego betrayed the grand vizier. Mondego now calls himself Count de Morcerf and is a member of the French parliament.

Unaware of the news, Fernand went to Parliament as usual. He arrived with a proud look and insolent expression. Passing through the corridors, he failed to observe the hesitation of the doorkeepers or the coolness of his colleagues.

The session had been in progress for about half an hour when he entered. Everyone held the accusing newspaper, but no one ventured to raise the issue. At length a member was recognized and read the accusatory report aloud. Fernand turned so pale that every member shuddered and fixed his eyes upon him.

The parliamentarians voted to conduct a formal inquiry and asked Fernand how much time he would require to prepare his defense. "I demand that the examination should take place as soon as possible, so that I can prove my innocence," he replied.

A committee of twelve members was chosen to examine the evidence Fernand would provide. The investigation would begin at eight o'clock that evening. Fernand asked permission to leave, so that he could prepare his defense.

At eight o'clock, all were in their places. Fernand held some papers in his hand. His face was calm and his step firm. He was dressed with great care in his military uniform, which was buttoned completely up to the chin.

At this moment one of the doorkeepers brought in a letter for the chairman of the Parliament. "You may begin your defense, M. de Morcerf," said the chairman, as he unsealed the letter. The count began his defense. He produced documents proving that Grand Vizier Ali Tepelini of Yanina had given him full confidence and authority to negotiate with the Turks. He produced the Grand Vizier's ring, Tepelini's mark of rulership, which the latter had given him as proof of Fernand's authority to negotiate on Ali Tepelini's behalf. Unfortunately, Fernand explained, the negotiation failed, and when he returned to defend his benefactor, Tepelini was dead. "However," said Fernand, "so great was the grand vizier's confidence in me, that on his deathbed he entrusted his favorite wife Vasiliki and their daughter Haydee to my care."

The chairman now stared at the letter he had just received. "Count de Morcerf, you say that Ali Tepelini, Grand Vizier of Yanina, entrusted his wife and daughter to your care?"

"Yes, sir," Fernand replied. "However, by the time I returned to Yanina, Visiliki and Haydee had both disappeared."

"Have you any idea what became of them?" the chairman asked.

"No, sir. I was in constant danger, so I couldn't search for them."

"Can you, sir, produce any witnesses to the truth of what you have said?"

"I'm afraid not, monsieur," replied Fernand. "All those who surrounded the vizier, or who knew me at his court, are either dead or gone away. I believe that I alone, of all my countrymen, survived that dreadful war. I have only the letters of Ali Tepelini, which I have placed before you, and the ring, a token of his confidence in me, which is here. The most convincing proof I can offer is the absence of any witness to call into question what I have said here."

Several of the lawmakers nodded their heads in agreement.

"Gentlemen," the chairman announced, "I have just received a letter that bears on this case. It reads,

Monsieur chairman, I can furnish this committee of inquiry with important information concerning the conduct of the Count de Morcerf while in Yanina. I am presently just outside your chamber.

Is the committee willing to hear this witness?"

"Yes, yes," they all said at once. The doorkeeper was called. "Is there anyone in the lobby?" said the chairman.

"Yes, sir. A woman, accompanied by a servant."

"Bring her in," said the chairman. The doorkeeper summoned a woman enveloped in a large veil, which completely covered her. The chairman requested her to throw aside her veil. She was dressed in Greek clothes and was remarkably beautiful.

Fernand looked at this woman with surprise and terror.

"Please tell us your name," said the chairman.

"I am Haydee, the daughter of Ali Tepelini and Vasiliki," she announced.

Fernand could not have been more overwhelmed if a thunderbolt had fallen at his feet and opened an immense gulf before him.

"Madamoiselle," replied the chairman, bowing with respect, "can you prove you are who you say you are?"

"I can, sir," said Haydee. From a satin satchel she withdrew her birth certificate and her certificate of baptism. Then she showed the chairman the record of the sale of herself and her mother to the Armenian merchant El-Kobbir. The document stated that the French officer, Fernand Mondego, sold Haydee and her mother to the merchant as slaves, for the sum of four hundred thousand francs. Another document, dated later, declared,

> **I, El-Kobbir, a slave trader, have received from the Count of Monte Cristo, an emerald valued at 800,000 francs. In return for this gem, I am turning a slave over to him: Haydee Tepelini, daughter of the late Vasiliki and Ali Tepelini, Grand Vizier of Yanina. Colonel Fernand Mondego, as French officer in Ali Tepelini's service, sold me Haydee and Vasiliki seven years ago.**
>
> **Signed, El-Kobbir**

A dreadful silence followed the reading of this document. Fernand stared at Haydee, his gaze a mixture of fire and blood.

"Mademoiselle," said the chairman, "can the Count of Monte Cristo confirm this account?"

"Sir," replied Haydee, "the Count of Monte Cristo, my foster father, has been in Normandy the last three days."

Fernand had not uttered one word the whole of this time. "M. de Morcerf," said the president, "do you recognize this lady as the daughter of Ali Tepelini, Grand Vizier of Yanina?"

"No," said Fernand, attempting to rise. "It is a base plot, contrived by my enemies."

Haydee shrieked, "You do not know me? . . . Well, I fortunately recognize you! You are Fernand Mondego, the French officer who led the troops of my noble father! It is you who surrendered the castle of Yanina! It is you who by trickery obtained my father's ring. It is you who sold us, my mother and me, to the merchant El-Kobbir! Murderer! Murderer! Murderer!"

"You positively recognize M. de Morcerf as the officer, Fernand Mondego?" asked the chairman.

"Indeed I do!" cried Haydee. "My mother told me, look at his right hand, on which he has a large wound." As she uttered these words, Fernand slid his mutilated right hand into his jacket. He then fell back on his seat, overwhelmed by wretchedness and despair. This scene completely changed the opinion of the assembly.

The chairman turned to Morcerf. "Have you really committed the crimes of which you are accused?"

Fernand raised his eyes toward the ceiling. Then, with a hasty movement, he rushed from the room like a madman. Soon the deputies heard the rattling of his carriage as he was driven away.

"Gentlemen," said the president, when silence was restored, "is the Count de Morcerf convicted of felony, treason, and conduct unbecoming a member of this House?"

"Yes," replied all the members of the committee of inquiry with a unanimous voice.

Haydee had remained until the close of the meeting. She heard Fernand's sentence pronounced without betraying an expression of either joy or pity. Then, drawing her veil over her face, she bowed majestically to the members of Parliament and left.

CHAPTER 59
Albert's Quest

Determined to avenge his father, Albert Morcerf visits Danglars.

The next morning, Albert Morcerf learned from his newspaper friend, Sebastian Beauchamp, that M. Danglars had asked a foreign correspondent about the Count de Morcerf's involvement in the Turkish takeover of Yanina where the fortress was surrendered without a fight.

Albert was resolved to kill the person who had struck this blow to his father. He asked his friend Beauchamp to accompany him on his quest.

The two young men entered the banker's mansion, pushed past the servant, and entered the banker's study. "Sir," cried Danglars, "am I no longer at liberty to receive whom I choose in my own house?"

"No, sir," said Albert, coldly. "Now tell me, is it true that you asked a foreign reporter to supply information about my father's involvement in the surrender of Yanina?"

"Why, yes. If you are to marry my daughter Eugenie, I have every right to know about your family's honor, or lack of it."

"Who led you to believe there was any reason to investigate my father's role in that matter?"

"Why, your friend, the Count of Monte Cristo."

"The Count of Monte Cristo told you to write to Yanina?"

"Yes."

"And did Monte Cristo learn what you found out?"

"Yes. I told him."

"Did he know my father's first name was Fernand and his family name Mondego?"

"Yes," Danglars replied.

Albert felt the blood rising to his head. In his mind, there was no doubt that Monte Cristo was in league with his father's enemies. Albert hastily left Danglars' residence to find Monte Cristo.

CHAPTER 60
The Insult

At the opera, Albert de Morcerf angrily accuses the Count of helping to bring about his father's downfall.

When Albert arrived at the Count's residence, the servants told him the Count was not at home. "However, he will be attending the opera tonight," one of the servants said.

Albert then arranged with his friends Sebastian Beauchamp and Christopher de Chateau-Renaud to meet him at the opera. Then he went to see his mother. Since her husband's public disgrace, she had refused to see anyone, keeping to her room. He found her in bed, overwhelmed with grief. When she saw her son, she pressed his hand and sobbed aloud.

"My dear mother," he said, "do you know if Father has any enemies?"

Mercedes started. "My son," she said, "persons in your father's situation have many secret enemies. Those who are not known are the most dangerous."

"What about the Count of Monte Cristo?"

Mercedes became paler than the sheet that covered her. "Do you suspect the Count of Monte Cristo?" she uttered in a breathless tone.

"Yes," replied the young man, and he left his mother's room.

Scarcely had he shut her door, when Mercedes called a trusted servant and ordered him to follow Albert wherever he should go that evening, and to come and tell her immediately what he observed. Albert went to his room and dressed with unusual care. At ten minutes to eight, Beauchamp arrived. The two men entered Albert's carriage and left for the opera.

Albert kept his eyes fixed on Monte Cristo's box, which to his surprise remained empty. At last, at the beginning of the second act, the door opened, and Monte Cristo entered with Maximilian Morrel.

At the intermission, Albert, accompanied by Beauchamp and Chateau-Renaud, entered Monte Cristo's box.

"Good evening, M. de Morcerf," said the Count in cordial tones. "Are you enjoying the opera?"

"We are not here, sir, to exchange hypocritical expressions of politeness, or false professions of friendship," said Albert, "but to demand an explanation."

"An explanation of the opera? Explanation of what?" said the Count.

Albert's face was apoplectic with rage. "An explanation of the disgraceful way you treated my father at Parliament this morning. I know who was responsible for Haydee's presence at the inquiry. I will be revenged," said Albert furiously.

"I don't like your tone, sir," replied Monte Cristo. "This is my box, and I insist that you leave at once."

"Not until you give me satisfaction," Albert cried out, waving his glove in Monte Cristo's face.

"Very well," said Monte Cristo quietly, "I see you wish to quarrel with me. I consider your glove thrown and will return it to you wrapped around a bullet. Now leave me, or I will summon my servants to throw you out."

Almost beside himself with fury, Albert stepped back, and Maximilian closed the door. Monte Cristo took up his glass again as if nothing had happened and gazed toward the stage. Maximilian whispered, "What have you done to him?"

"I? Nothing—at least not personally," said Monte Cristo.

"But there must be some cause for this strange scene."

"It was through Haydee that Parliament was informed of his father's treason."

"Indeed?" said Maximilian. "I had been told, but would not credit it, that the Greek girl I have seen with you was the daughter of Ali Tepelini."

"It is true."

"But what shall you do about Albert?"

"I shall kill him before ten o'clock tomorrow morning," the Count said with the utmost calm and certainty.

"Ah, Count," said Maximilian, "his father loves him so much!"

"Do not speak to me of that," said Monte Cristo, with the first sign of anger he had betrayed. "I will make that scoundrel suffer."

At the end of Act 3, a rap was heard on the door to the Count's box.

"Come in," said Monte Cristo with a voice that betrayed not the least emotion. Beauchamp appeared. "Good evening, M. Beauchamp," said Monte Cristo, as if this was the first time he had seen him that evening. "Be seated."

Beauchamp bowed and sat. "Sir," he said, "I've come about the matter of honor between you and Viscount Albert de Morcerf."

"Tell the viscount I shall see the color of his blood tomorrow before ten o'clock."

"Then all that remains for me is to make the arrangements for the duel," said Beauchamp.

"Tell your client that I leave him the choice of arms."

"Pistols, then, at eight o'clock, in the Bois de Vincennes," said Beauchamp.

"Very well, sir," said Monte Cristo. "Now that all is settled, do let me see the performance." Beauchamp left the box.

Monte Cristo turned to Maximilian. "Would you act as my second?"

"Certainly," said Maximilian. "I am at your service, Count."

"Who will be your other witness?" asked Maximilian.

"I know no one in Paris, Maximilian, on whom I could confer that honor besides you and your brother-in-law Emmanuel. Do you think Emmanuel would oblige me?"

"I know he will, Count."

"Thank you. Will both of you be with me tomorrow morning at seven o'clock?"

"We will."

"Hush, the curtain is rising. Listen! I never lose a note of this opera if I can avoid it."

CHAPTER 61
A Nocturnal Interview

Madame de Morcerf, once known as Mercedes, Edmond's fiancée, pleads with the Count to spare her son.

Later that night, Monte Cristo sat in his study, examining his pistols. His study door opened, and Baptistin entered. Before he had spoken a word, the Count saw in the next room a veiled woman, who had followed closely after Baptistin. Seeing the Count with a pistol in his hand, she rushed in. Baptistin looked at his master, who made a sign to him, and he went out, closing the door after him. "Who are you, madame?" said the Count to the veiled woman.

"Edmond, would you kill my son?"

The Count retreated a step, uttered a slight exclamation, and dropped the pistol he was holding. "What name did you just pronounce, Madame de Morcerf?" he said.

"Yours!" she cried, throwing back her veil. "Yours, which I alone, perhaps, have not forgotten. Edmond, it is not Madame de Morcerf who is come to you. It is Mercedes."

"Mercedes is dead, madame," said Monte Cristo. "I know no one now of that name."

"Mercedes lives and she remembers, for she recognized you when she saw you, and even before she saw you, she remembered your voice. Edmond, I know you are responsible for the disgrace that now befalls M. de Morcerf."

"Fernand! That is who you mean!" replied Monte Cristo, with bitter irony. Monte Cristo had pronounced the name of Fernand with such an expression of hatred that Mercedes felt a thrill of horror run through her veins.

"You see, Edmond, I am not mistaken, and so I have cause to say, spare my son! Albert has also guessed who you are. He attributes his father's misfortunes to you."

"Madame, they are not misfortunes—it is a punishment. It is not I who strike M. de Morcerf. It is providence which punishes him."

"What are Yanina and its vizier to you, Edmond? What injury has Fernand Mondego done you in betraying Ali Tepelini?"

"Ah, madame," replied Monte Cristo, "if I have sworn to revenge myself, it is not because he betrayed Ali Tepelini, but because he betrayed me. Why was I arrested many years ago? Why was I a prisoner those many years?"

"I do not know," said Mercedes.

"Well, I shall tell you. The day before I was to marry you, a man named Danglars wrote this letter, which the fisherman Fernand himself posted." Monte Cristo took an old letter out of his desk and handed it to Mercedes. It was Danglars' letter to the king's attorney. Mercedes read the following:

> The king's attorney is informed by a friend to the throne and that one Edmond Dantes, second in command on board the *Pharaon*, is the bearer of a letter from Murat to the usurper Napoleon, and of another letter from the usurper to the Bonapartist club in Paris. Ample corroboration of this statement may be obtained by arresting the above-mentioned Edmond Dantes, who either carries the letter for Paris about with him, or has it at his father's abode.

"How dreadful!" said Mercedes, passing her hand across her forehead, "and that letter—"

"I bought it for two hundred thousand francs, madame," said Monte Cristo. "But that is a trifle, since it enables me to justify myself to you."

"And the result of that letter—"

"You well know, madame, was my arrest. But you do not know how long that arrest lasted. You do not know that I remained for fourteen years within a quarter of a league of you, in a dungeon in the Chateau d'If. You do not know that every day of those fourteen years I renewed the vow of vengeance which I had made the first day!"

"Can it be?" cried Mercedes, shuddering.

"I have sworn to revenge myself on Fernand, and—I have revenged myself. Mercedes!" repeated Monte Cristo. "I have uttered your name with the sigh of melancholy, with the groan of sorrow, with the last effort of despair. I have uttered it when frozen with cold, crouched on the straw in my dungeon. I have uttered it, consumed with heat, rolling on the stone floor of my prison. Mercedes, I must revenge myself, for I suffered fourteen years,—fourteen years I wept, I cursed. I tell you, Mercedes, I must revenge myself."

"Revenge yourself, then, Edmond," replied the poor mother. "But let your vengeance fall on the culprits—on him, on me, but not on my son! Edmond," continued Mercedes, with her arms extended toward the Count, "since I first knew you, I have adored your name, have respected your memory. I, too, have suffered much!"

"Have you known what it is to have your father starve to death in your absence?" cried Monte Cristo. "Have you seen the woman you loved giving her hand to your rival, while you were perishing at the bottom of a dungeon?"

"No," interrupted Mercedes, "but I see him whom I loved on the point of murdering my son." Mercedes uttered these words with such deep anguish, with such intense despair, that Monte Cristo could not restrain a sob.

"What do you ask of me?" he said, "your son's life? Well, he shall live!"

Mercedes uttered a cry which made the tears start from Monte Cristo's eyes.

"Oh!" she said, seizing the Count's hand and raising it to her lips. "Oh, thank you, thank you, Edmond!"

"The duel will not take place, Edmond, since you forgive?"

"It will take place," said Monte Cristo, in a most solemn tone. "But instead of your son's blood on the ground, mine will flow." Mercedes shrieked, and sprang toward Monte Cristo, but suddenly stopped.

"Edmond," she said, "there is a God above us. Since you live and since I have seen you again, I trust to him from my heart." Mercedes extended her hand to the Count. "Edmond," she said, her eyes wet with tears, "how noble it is of you. Alas, I am grown old with grief more than with years, and cannot now remind my Edmond by a smile, or by a look, of that Mercedes whom he once spent so many hours dreaming about. I too have suffered much. It is sad to pass one's life without having one joy to recall, without preserving a single hope.

"But, Edmond, you will see that if my face is pale, if my eyes are dull, if my beauty is gone; if Mercedes, in short, no longer resembles her former self in her features, you will see that her heart is still the same. Thank you, Edmond. I have nothing more to ask of heaven—I have seen you again, and have found you as noble and as great as you were."

The Count did not answer. Mercedes opened the door of the study and left the house. Monte Cristo cried out, "What a fool I was not to have torn my heart out on the day when I resolved to avenge myself!"

CHAPTER 62
The Meeting

The Count and Albert de Morcerf meet at the dueling ground.

The next morning, Monte Cristo awoke in a deep gloom. As he was finishing his preparations for the duel, he heard a carriage approach. Maximilian and Emmanuel stepped down and entered the Count's residence. Ali escorted them into the Count's room. The Count rushed to his friends with open arms. "Maximilian," he said, "it is a happy day for me, to feel that I am beloved by such a man as you. Good morning, Emmanuel."

Turning to Ali, the Count handed him an envelope and said, "Take that to my lawyer. It is my will."

Maximilian looked at his friend with astonishment. "What?" said Maximilian, "you might die?"

"Yes. Must I not be prepared for everything, dear friend? M. de Morcerf might kill me. Let us depart for the dueling ground." Maximilian and Emmanuel joined Monte Cristo in the carriage, which brought them to the dueling site exactly on time. Another carriage was awaiting them.

"It seems to me," said Emmanuel, "that I see two young men waiting over there."

Maximilian advanced toward Beauchamp and Chateau-Renaud, who came to meet him. The three young men bowed to each other courteously, if not cordially.

"Excuse me, gentlemen," said Maximilian, "but I do not see M. de Morcerf."

"He sent us word this morning," replied Chateau-Renaud, "that he would meet us here." At that very moment, Albert arrived on horseback.

"How stupid," said Chateau-Renaud, "to come on horseback to fight a duel with pistols, after all the instructions I gave him."

Albert jumped from his horse and walked over. He was pale, and his eyes were red and swollen. He said, "I thank you, gentlemen, for joining me today. I have a few words to say to the Count of Monte Cristo."

"Ah," said Monte Cristo, "I trust he is not going to tempt me by some fresh insult!"

"I do not think that is his intention," said Emmanuel.

"Please come close, gentlemen," said Albert. "I do not want you to miss one word of what I am about to say to the Count of Monte Cristo."

"Sir," said Albert, "a short while ago I learned of the treachery of the fisherman Fernand Mondego toward you, and the almost unheard-of miseries which it caused. I say publicly, before all assembled here, that you were justified in revenging yourself on my father."

These words struck the spectators like a thunderbolt. Monte Cristo raised his eyes slowly toward heaven with an expression of infinite gratitude. He realized that Mercedes must have spoken to her son.

"Now, sir," said Albert, "if you think my apology is sufficient, shake my hand."

Monte Cristo, with wet eyes, extended to Albert a hand which the latter shook with a sentiment resembling respectful fear.

Albert said, "Gentlemen, the Count of Monte Cristo receives my apology. I had acted hastily toward him. Hasty actions are generally bad ones. I hope the world will not call me a coward for acting as my conscience dictated."

As for Monte Cristo, his head was bent down. He thought of that courageous woman who had come to plead for her son's life, to whom he had offered his, and who had now saved it. Yes, she saved his life by the revelation of a dreadful family secret, destroying forever the young man's feeling of love for his father.

CHAPTER 63
Mother and Son

Mercedes and Albert prepare to leave the Morcerf house forever.

The Count of Monte Cristo bowed to the young men and got into his carriage. Albert, too, took his leave and galloped home to Paris. Entering his own rooms, he cast one lingering look on all the luxuries which had rendered life so easy and happy. Then, with great care, he took down his mother's portrait and arranged all of his possessions, including his art and priceless artifacts. He then made an exact inventory of all his possessions and locked them in drawers. His preparations for leaving were nearly complete.

Albert then walked down the hall to his mother's rooms. Mercedes was doing the same thing in her apartment. Everything was in order— laces, dresses, jewels, linen, money, all were arranged in the sealed drawers, and the countess was carefully collecting the keys. Albert saw all these preparations and understood that Mercedes was also planning to depart. Albert threw his arms around his mother.

"I see we are both leaving," Mercedes said mournfully. "I had counted on you to accompany me. Am I wrong?"

"Mother," said Albert with firmness. "I cannot make you share the fate I have planned for myself. I must live from now on without rank and fortune. I will have to borrow money from a friend to start out."

"You, my poor child, suffer poverty and hunger? Oh, do not say so. It will break my heart."

"But not mine, Mother," replied Albert. "I am young and strong. No, Mother. From this moment I am done with the past and accept nothing from it—not even the name Morcerf. I cannot bear the name of a man who has behaved so shamefully."

"Albert, my child," said Mercedes, "do not despair. You have life before you, for you are barely twenty-two years old. Take my father's name—it was Herrera. I am sure, my dear Albert, whatever may be your career, you will soon render that name illustrious. Let me cherish these hopes, for I have no future to look forward to except the grave."

"I will fulfill all your wishes, my dear mother," said the young man.

"I am ready, my son," said Mercedes. Albert ran to fetch a carriage. At the moment he returned, a man approached and gave him a letter. Albert recognized the bearer. "From the Count," said Bertuccio. Albert took the letter and read it, then looked round for Bertuccio, but he was gone. He returned to Mercedes with tears in his eyes and heaving chest. Without uttering a word, he gave her the letter. Mercedes read:

Albert—I have learned that you and your mother are leaving your father's house. You will have a long struggle ahead of you. But spare your mother these hardships. Bear all the suffering alone. Spare her the trial of poverty which must accompany your first efforts, for she deserves not even the shadow of the misfortune which faces her.

Please pay particular attention to what I am saying here. Twenty-four years ago I returned from the sea, proud and joyful. I was returning to my fiancée, a wonderful girl whom I adored. As you now know, this treasure was your mother. Before my voyage, I saved up three thousand francs, which I painfully earned through ceaseless toil. I was planning to give this money to her. Knowing the treachery of the sea, I did not take the money aboard ship but buried it in my father's little garden at Marseilles, on the Allees de Meillan. Your mother knows that poor house well. A short time ago, I visited the old place, which revived so many painful memories. I took a spade and dug in the corner of the garden where I had concealed my treasure. The iron box was there—no one had touched it—under a beautiful fig tree my father had planted the day I was born. Please, Albert, urge your mother to accept this money, which was originally intended to assure her peace and comfort.

Albert stood pale and motionless, waiting to hear what his mother would decide after she had finished reading the letter. Mercedes turned her eyes toward heaven. "I accept it," she said. "I shall take it with me to some convent." Putting the letter in her purse, she took her son's arm and headed toward the carriage.

CHAPTER 64
The Suicide

Desiring revenge, Fernand de Morcerf appears at Monte Cristo's home.

In another quarter of Paris, as they rode in the carriage back from the dueling ground, Monte Cristo asked Maximilian Morrel to have breakfast with him.

"No, thank you. I must be elsewhere." was Maximilian's answer.

"You are having breakfast with someone else, then?"

"No, I am not hungry."

"Oh," said the Count, "I know only two things which destroy the appetite—grief and love. As I see you are very cheerful, might I presume you are in love?"

"Well, Count," replied Maximilian cheerfully, "I will not dispute it."

"Then go," said the Count. "Go, dear friend, but promise me, if you meet with any obstacle, to remember that I have some power in this world. I am happy to use that power to help those I love, and that includes you, Maximilian."

"I will remember it," said the young man, "as selfish children remember their parents when they want their aid. When I need your assistance, I will come to you, Count."

"Well, I rely upon your promise. Goodbye, then."

"Goodbye, till we meet again." They had arrived at the Count's house on the Champs-Elysées. Monte Cristo opened the carriage-door, and Maximilian sprang out onto the pavement. Bertuccio was waiting on the steps.

"Well?" asked the Count.

"She is going to leave her house," said the servant.

"And her son?"

"His valet thinks he is going to do the same," answered Bertuccio.

"Come this way." Monte Cristo took Bertuccio into his study, wrote the letter we have seen, and gave it to the steward. "Deliver this," he said quickly. "But first, tell Haydee that I am here."

"Here I am," said the young girl, who at the sound of the carriage had run downstairs and whose face was radiant. Both Haydee and Monte Cristo were ecstatic to see each other.

Monte Cristo was beginning to think something that he had not for a long time dared to believe—that he might yet be happy in love. Perhaps there was another women like Mercedes in the world. Perhaps he might yet be permitted to love again. As he was gazing at Haydee, the door opened. The Count frowned with displeasure.

"M. Fernand de Morcerf is here to see you," said Baptistin.

"Oh," exclaimed Haydee, "is it not yet over?"

"I do not know if it is finished," said Monte Cristo, "but I do know you have nothing to fear."

"But it is the wretched—"

"That man cannot injure me, Haydee," said Monte Cristo.

Monte Cristo smiled. "By my father's tomb," he said, extending his hand over the head of the young girl, "I swear to you, Haydee, that if any misfortune happens, it will not be to me. Ask M. de Morcerf into the drawing room," said the Count to Baptistin, while he led the beautiful Greek girl to a private staircase.

A moment afterward, Baptistin announced Fernand to Monte Cristo. Fernand was pacing the room the third time when he turned and saw Monte Cristo at the door. "Ah, it is M. de Morcerf," said Monte Cristo quietly.

"Yes, it is I," said the disgraced man.

"What brings you to my home?"

"Did you have a meeting with my son this morning?" asked Fernand.

"I did," replied the Count.

"I know my son had good reasons to wish to fight you."

"Yes, sir, he had very good ones. But you see that in spite of them he has not killed me, and did not even fight."

"Yet he considered you the cause of his father's dishonor."

"That is true, sir," said Monte Cristo with his dreadful calmness.

"You must have made some apology or explanation?"

"I explained nothing. It is he who apologized to me."

"Why would he do that?"

"Because there was one more guilty than I."

"And who was that?"

"His father."

Fernand smiled faintly and declared, "I came here to tell you that I also look upon you as my enemy. I came to tell you that I hate you with all my heart. That it seems as if I have always known you, and always hated you. Now, since the young people of the present day will not fight, it remains for us to do so. Don't you think so, sir?"

"Most certainly."

"So much the better. Are you prepared?"

"Yes, sir."

"You know that we shall fight till one of us is dead," said Fernand.

"Until one of us dies," repeated Monte Cristo.

"Let us start, then. We need no witnesses or seconds."

"Very true," said Monte Cristo. "It is unnecessary, since we know each other so well."

"On the contrary," said Fernand, "we know so little of each other."

"Indeed?" said Monte Cristo, with the same unflappable coolness. "Let us see. Are you not the soldier Fernand who deserted on the eve of the battle of Waterloo? Are you not the Lieutenant Fernand who served as guide and spy to the French army in Spain? Are you not the Captain Fernand who betrayed, sold, and murdered his benefactor, Ali? And have you not become a lieutenant-general with the title of Count de Morcerf?"

"Oh," cried Fernand, "I see you know me. But I know you only as an adventurer decorated with gold and jewelry. In Paris you call yourself the Count of Monte Cristo; in Italy, Sinbad the Sailor; in Malta, I forget what. But it is your real name I want to know, so that I may pronounce it when we fight, at the moment when I plunge my sword through your heart."

The Count of Monte Cristo reached into a nearby closet and put on a sailor's jacket and hat. He turned toward Fernand, who on seeing him felt his teeth chatter and his legs sink under him. "Fernand," he said, "of my hundred names, I need tell you only one. But you know what it is, do you not? I show you a face you must often have seen in your dreams since your marriage with Mercedes, my fiancée!"

Fernand ran to the door, calling out in one anguished cry, "Edmond Dantes!" When he reached home, he saw a hired carriage in the yard. He hid himself as he saw the two people he loved most, Mercedes and Albert, climbing into the vehicle. Fernand realized his wife and son were abandoning him. When he saw the carriage pull away, he reached into a desk drawer and took out a pistol. He fired one shot into his temple and slumped on his desk, dead.

CHAPTER 65
Valentine

Maximilian asks the Count for help in protecting Valentine.

After leaving Monte Cristo, Maximilian Morrel ran to inform Valentine that there had been no duel. After Maximilian had told Valentine and Noirtier of his morning adventures, Valentine motioned for him to sit near her grandfather.

She began, "You know, Maximilian, Grandpapa has thought of leaving this house, because he thinks this house is harmful to me."

"Do you feel you are in any danger?" asked Maximilian quickly.

"Not exactly danger. I feel a general uneasiness; that is all. I have lost my appetite, and my stomach is uneasy."

"Are you taking any medicine?"

"A very simple one," said Valentine. "Every morning I swallow some of the mixture prepared for my grandfather. It is very bitter—so much so that everything I drink afterward has the same awful taste." Valentine made a face to drive home the point.

"But," Maximilian said with much concern,

"this mixture was prepared for M. Noirtier, not for you. You need to consult Dr. d'Avrigny."

At the sound of a carriage in the courtyard, Valentine looked out the window. "It is Madame Danglars and her daughter Eugenie, who have come to call on us. I must go down and greet them, but I will come right back. Stay here."

True to her word, Valentine quickly greeted the Danglars and asked to be excused. As she was walking up the stairs, suddenly a cloud passed over her eyes. She missed a step, fell against the wall, and toppled to the floor. Maximilian heard the noise and quickly carried her to a chair. He and Noirtier were alarmed.

"Don't worry," she said, trying to smile. "I just feel dizzy, that's all." Valentine paused and took a breath. "Now, let me tell you some news. Eugenie Danglars is going to marry Count Andrea Cavalcanti in a week. In three days there is to be a grand feast. We are all invited—my father, Madame de Villefort, and me."

"When will it be our turn to think of these things?" Maximilian asked.

Before Valentine could respond, her arms stiffened and twisted, her head fell back on her chair, and she remained motionless. Maximilian rang the bell violently. The housemaid and the servant who had replaced Barrois ran in at once. Valentine was so pale and cold that they flew into the hallway crying for help.

"What's wrong?" M. de Villefort called from his study. Maximilian barely had time to hide in the closet before Villefort entered the room. Villefort ran to Valentine, took her in his arms, and cried, "Get Dr. d'Avrigny. No, I'll get him myself!" He raced from the room. A moment later, Maximilian darted out the other door. He had been struck to the heart by a frightful recollection—the conversation he had overheard between the doctor and Villefort the night of Madame de Saint-Meran's death. Valentine's symptoms were the same which had preceded the death of Barrois. At the same time, he recalled what Monte Cristo had said to him only two hours before, "Whatever you want, Maximilian, come to me. I have great power." He hurried to Monte Cristo's house.

At the same time, Villefort arrived at Dr. d'Avrigny's house. "Come, Dr. d'Avrigny! Please come! I know you said you would not come to my house any more, but the illness has struck Valentine now. So you see, she is innocent. Please save her."

"Each time you have come to me," said the doctor in a reluctant tone of voice, "it has been too late. Still, I will go. But let us make haste."

"Oh, thank you." The two men hurried to Villefort's home.

Not too far away, Maximilian rapped at Monte Cristo's door. A servant admitted him, and he breathlessly raced to the Count's study.

"Hello again, my good friend," said Monte Cristo. "Did you decide to take breakfast with me after all?"

"No, thank you. I need your help. Please listen to me. One evening I was in a garden. A clump of trees concealed me. No one suspected I was there. Two persons passed near me—allow me to conceal their names for the present. They were speaking in an undertone, and yet I was so interested in what they said that I did not lose a single word.

"Someone had just died in the house to which that garden belonged. One of the persons whose conversation I overheard was the master of the house. The other was the physician. The former was confiding to the latter his grief and fear, for it was the second time within a month that death had suddenly and unexpectedly entered that house."

"And what did the doctor answer?" asked Monte Cristo.

"He replied—he replied that the death was not a natural one, and must be attributed to poison."

"My dear friend," said Monte Cristo, "I think I know the house, or one very similar to it."

"It has started again, Count," exclaimed Maximilian. "Three months ago it was M. de Saint-Meran! Madame de Saint-Meran two months after! The other day it was Barrois, and today, young Valentine."

"And what is all this to me?" replied Monte Cristo, shrugging his shoulders with exaggerated indifference.

"But I," Maximilian protested, groaning with sorrow, "I love her!"

"You love?—who?" cried Monte Cristo, starting to his feet.

"I love Valentine de Villefort, who is being murdered at this moment! Do you understand me?

I love her, and I ask God and you how I can save her!"

"Unhappy man!" the Count exclaimed, wringing his hands. "You love Valentine—that daughter of an accursed man, a man whom I despise!" Maximilian drew back. Never had he seen the Count so angry.

Maximilian groaned. "Come now," continued the Count, "be a man, be strong, be full of hope, for I am here and will watch over you." Maximilian shook his head sorrowfully. "I tell you to hope. Do you understand me?" insisted Monte Cristo. "Listen, Maximilian—it is noon. If Valentine is not now dead, she will not die."

"How so?" cried Maximilian, "when I left her dying?"

"Maximilian," said the Count, "return home. Do not do anything. I will send you word when I am ready. Go."

"Oh, Count, have you power against death? Are you superhuman? Are you an angel?" And the young man, who had never shrunk from danger, shrank before Monte Cristo. But Monte Cristo looked at him with so sweet a smile that Maximilian felt tears filling his eyes.

"I can do much for you, my friend," replied the Count. "Go. I must be alone." Maximilian, subdued by the extraordinary power Monte Cristo exercised over everything around him, did not resist. He shook the Count's hand and left.

Meanwhile, Villefort and Dr. d'Avrigny had hurried back to Villefort's house. Valentine had not revived from her fainting fit, and the doctor examined her closely. At last Dr. d'Avrigny slowly uttered these words: "She is still alive!"

"Still?" cried Villefort. "Oh, doctor, what a dreadful word."

"Yes," said the physician, "I repeat it. She is still alive, and I am astonished at it."

"But is she safe?" asked the father.

"Yes, since she lives."

At that moment Dr. d'Avrigny's glance met Noirtier's eye. It glistened with such meaning that the physician was struck. "Sir," said d'Avrigny to Villefort, "go get Mademoiselle Valentine's maid, if you please."

Villefort went to find her, and the doctor approached Noirtier. "Have you something to tell me?" he asked.

The old man blinked his eyes expressively, "Yes!"

"Well, I will remain with you." At this moment Villefort returned, followed by the lady's maid. After her came Madame de Villefort.

The maid and Madame de Villefort carried Valentine away. She had awakened but could not move or speak. D'Avrigny wrote a prescription and ordered Villefort to go in person to the chemist to have it prepared. At last he was alone with Noirtier. After convincing himself that no one was listening, the doctor asked, "Do you know anything of this young lady's illness?"

"Yes," indicated the old man in his usual fashion.

"Did you see poor Barrois die? Do you know of what he died?" asked Dr. d'Avrigny.

"Yes," replied the old man.

"Do you think he died a natural death?"

A grim smile flashed across Noirtier's face.

"Did you think that Barrois was poisoned?"

"Yes."

"Do you think the poison was intended for him?"

"No."

"Do you think the same hand which struck Barrois has now attacked Valentine?"

"Yes."

"Then will she die too?" asked the doctor, fixing his penetrating gaze on Noirtier.

"No," he replied.

"Then you hope the poison will take no effect on Valentine?"

"Yes."

"Then how do you hope Valentine will escape?" Noirtier kept his eyes steadfastly fixed on the bottle containing the mixture which he took every morning.

"Ah, indeed?" asked Dr. d'Avrigny, struck with a sudden thought. "Did you prepare her system for poison?"

"Yes."

"By accustoming her by degrees?"

"Yes, yes, yes," said Noirtier, delighted to be understood.

"Of course. I had told you that there was brucine in the mixture I gave you."

"Yes."

"And by accustoming her to that poison, you have neutralized the effect of a similar poison. And you have succeeded!" exclaimed d'Avrigny. "Without that precaution, Valentine would have died."

At this moment Villefort returned. "Here, doctor," he said, "is what you sent me for."

"Well," said the doctor, "let us go to Valentine. I will give instructions to everyone, and you must see that everyone follows them strictly."

At this very moment, an Italian priest rented the house adjoining the house of M. de Villefort. No one knew why the three previous tenants left. There were rumors that the foundation was unsafe. However, the new tenant moved in immediately. The tenant was named Abbé Giacomo Busoni. Workmen were immediately called in and began repairing the lower part of the tottering house.

CHAPTER 66
The Marriage Contract

As the marriage contract between Eugenie Danglars and Andrea Cavalcanti is being signed, police officers arrive.

On the evening the marriage contract between Mademoiselle Danglars and Count Cavalcanti was to be signed, the Danglars' mansion was aglow with candlelight.

Every few minutes, in the midst of the crowd, the buzzing, and the laughter, the doorkeeper announced some name well known in the financial field, respected in the army, or illustrious in the literary world. Just as the clock struck nine, the Count of Monte Cristo was announced. As if by an electric shock, all the assembly turned toward the door.

Monte Cristo entered, greeted several ladies and gentlemen, and soon found himself with Danglars.

Soon the lawyers arrived and arranged the marriage papers on the table.

The contract was read during a period of silence. As soon as it was finished, the buzz quickly took over as everyone quickly started talking about the money that was to come into the hands of these young people. The officiating lawyer solemnly took the pen, flourished it above his head, and said, "Gentlemen, we are about to sign the marriage contract."

Baron Danglars took the pen and signed. Since Major Bartolomeo Cavalcanti had returned to Italy, a man representing him signed. Baroness Danglars took up the pen and, preparing to sign, remarked to Madame de Villefort, "It's a shame that Mr. de Villefort could not be here this evening."

"As the king's attorney, he had to attend to the murder and attempted robbery at the home of the Count of Monte Cristo a while ago," said Madame de Villefort.

"I regret," said Monte Cristo, standing nearby, "that I am the cause of his absence."

"Really?" said Madame Danglars, signing.

Standing not too far away, Andrea Cavalcanti looked extremely grave.

"You remember," said the Count, "that the person who came to rob me died at my house. It was assumed that his accomplice killed him when he left. The police undressed him to examine his wounds. Initially his clothes were overlooked. However, after a time, the police returned to his clothes." Andrea turned pale, and stepped toward the door.

"Well, today the police started to examine the bloodied clothes and found a paper in the pocket. It was a letter addressed to you, Baron."

"To me?" cried Danglars.

"Yes."

"But," asked Madame Danglars, looking at her

husband with uneasiness, "how could that prevent M. de Villefort—"

"In this simple way, madame," replied Monte Cristo. "The clothing and the letter were both what is termed circumstantial evidence and were sent to the king's attorney, M. de Villefort. Andrea looked steadily at Monte Cristo and disappeared into another room.

"Was this murdered man an old galley slave?"

"Yes," replied the Count, "a felon named Caderousse." Danglars turned slightly pale. Andrea moved further toward the exit from the house.

"But go on signing," said Monte Cristo. "I am sorry that my story has interrupted this event. I apologize to you." The lawyer called for Andrea, "Count Cavalcanti, Count Cavalcanti, where are you?"

"Andrea, Andrea," repeated several young people.

"Call Count Andrea. Inform him that it is his turn to sign," Danglars shouted.

Just as everyone was looking for Andrea, a sudden gasp came from a corner of the room. A high ranking police officer walked in, placed two officers at the doors to the drawing room, and started walking toward Danglars. Madame Danglars uttered a scream and fainted.

"What is the matter, sir?" asked Monte Cristo, advancing to meet the leading officer.

"Which of you gentlemen," asked the officer, "answers to the name of Andrea Cavalcanti?" A cry of astonishment erupted from the crowd.

"Just who is this man, Andrea Cavalcanti?" asked Danglars, amazed.

"A galley slave, escaped from confinement at Toulon."

"And what crime has he committed?"

"He is accused of having murdered the man named Caderousse, his former companion in prison, at the moment he was making his escape from the Count of Monte Cristo's house," said the policeman.

Monte Cristo cast a rapid glance around him. Andrea was gone.

CHAPTER 67
The Apparition

The Count tells Valentine that he has been protecting her.

Young Valentine had been confined to her bed and did not witness the dramatic events at the Danglars. The entire story had been retold to her, but she was still too weak to engage in very much conversation. At night she was plagued with delirious visions. Sometimes she thought she saw her stepmother threatening her; other times she thought she saw Maximilian, and there were even times she thought she saw strangers like the Count of Monte Cristo. Her nighttime visions often left her raw and exhausted during the day.

One evening after the doctor had left, Valentine's thoughts wandered in a confused maze. Suddenly, Valentine thought she saw the door of her library open slowly.

At any other time Valentine would have cried out for help, but she assumed that it was simply another delusion. From behind the door, a human figure appeared. Valentine hoped that it would be Maximilian. The figure moved closer to Valentine. She realized it was not Maximilian and waited, convinced that it was a dream. She remembered that the best method of dispelling such illusions was to drink the potion that the doctor had left for her. Valentine therefore reached her hand toward the glass. Moving swiftly, however, the visionary figure stopped her arm from reaching the glass. The figure then took the glass to the lamp and held it up to look at it. Every minute Valentine had expected that the figure would vanish and another vision would take its place. However, rather than disappearing, the ghost-like figure said, "Now you may drink."

Valentine shuddered. It was the first time one of these visions had ever spoken to her. She was about to call out when the man placed his finger on her lips. "The Count of Monte Cristo!" she murmured.

"Do not call anyone—do not be alarmed," said the Count. "Listen to me, I have watched over you the last four days, for Maximilian's sake."

"Maximilian!—has he told you everything?"

"Everything. I have promised him that you shall live."

"But where have you been? I have not seen you."

The Count extended his hand toward the library. "I was hidden behind that door," he said, "which leads into the next house, which I have rented."

"But what have you seen?" asked Valentine, warily.

"During my long watch over you, I have observed everyone who has visited you, what food was prepared, and what drink was served. If the liquid appeared to be poisonous, I substituted something more healthy."

"Poison—death!" exclaimed Valentine.

"Hush," said Monte Cristo, again placing his finger upon her lips. The Count took a bottle from his pocket, containing a red liquid, and poured a few drops into the glass. "Drink this, and then take nothing more tonight."

"Thank you, sir, thank you!"

"This is how you have lived during the last four nights, Valentine," said the Count.

"Sir," said Valentine, "you say you saw the deadly poison poured into my glass. But if you saw this, you must also have seen the person who poured it."

"Yes," replied the Count.

"Is someone trying to murder me in my father's house?"

"Think, Valentine. Are you the first? You have seen M. de Saint-Meran, Madame de Saint-Meran, Barrois, all die. Your grandfather knows that a poisoner lives here. Perhaps he even suspects the person. He has been protecting you against the fatal effects of the poison."

"But who, then, is this assassin, this murderer?"

"Have you ever seen anyone enter your room at night?"

"Oh, yes. I have frequently seen shadows pass close to me, approach, and disappear. But I took them for visions."

"You shall know the murderer tonight," said Monte Cristo.

"How do you mean?" said Valentine.

"Because you are not feverish or delirious tonight, but thoroughly awake. Valentine," said the Count, "summon up all your courage. Pretend to be asleep, and you will see who enters your room. Goodbye," said the Count, walking toward the library door.

CHAPTER 68
The Poisoner

Valentine learns the poisoner's identity.

Valentine was alone, and her thoughts raced. Why would anyone want her dead? What had she done to anybody?

After a few more minutes, she thought she heard the creaking of the floor. The door handle turned, and the door slowly opened. Someone approached the bed. Valentine used all of her efforts to pretend to be in a deep sleep, not moving a limb. She heard something being poured into her glass. Valentine half-opened her eyes and saw that the person standing over her glass was Madame de Villefort. Valentine did not see her leave, but after a few minutes, the Count of Monte Cristo reappeared.

"Well," he said, "have you seen?"

Valentine groaned. "Oh, yes. I saw, but I cannot believe! How can I escape?"

"Valentine, death will pursue you."

"But didn't my kind grandfather's precaution neutralize the poison?"

"Yes, but not against a strong dose. The amount of poison has been changed—the quantity increased."

"But," exclaimed the young girl, "why me?"

"Your inheritance from both sets of your grandparents will total hundreds of thousands of francs. Your stepmother wants her son to have this money. She has been killing everyone who stands in the way. First, she murdered your grandparents, the Marquis and Marquise de Saint-Meran. Then, as soon as Noirtier changed his will so that you would inherit his fortune, she tried to kill him. The unlucky Barrois drank the poison instead. If she killed you, your father would inherit the money. When he died, the vast fortune would go to his only living child, his son Edward."

"Edward? Poor child! Are all these crimes committed on his behalf? I see that I am condemned to die!"

"No, Valentine, you will live, but you must trust me."

"My father is not part of this fearful plot, is he, sir?" asked Valentine.

"No, but your father should have suspected foul play, and he should have been in my place watching over you."

"Sir," said Valentine, "I will do all I can to live, for my grandfather and Maximilian."

"I will watch over them as I have over you."

"Well, sir, tell me what you want me to do."

"Whatever may happen, Valentine, do not be alarmed. Just remember that I am watching over you and protecting you."

"I will think of Maximilian!"

"I alone can save you, and I will," said the Count.

Then he drew from his jacket pocket the little emerald box, raised the golden lid, and took from it a pill about the size of a pea, which he placed in her hand. "Take this pill," he directed. "It will put you in a deep sleep, so deep that everyone will think you are dead. After you've been placed in a coffin, I will come and take you out. You will not awaken until I have fetched you and taken you to a safe place. Then I'll put some stones in the empty coffin, so everyone will think your body is still there. I will tell old Noirtier of this plan, so that he will not worry. All will be well." Valentine took the pill and swallowed it. "And now, my dear child, goodbye for the present. You are saved."

Valentine drifted into a deep sleep. Monte Cristo emptied the glass into the fireplace and slipped away.

CHAPTER 69
Valentine

Valentine's apparently lifeless body is discovered.

Not long after, Madame de Villefort came into Valentine's room to see the effects of her drink. Valentine had ceased to breathe. Her eyes were closed, and her lips were light blue. Madame de Villefort placed her hand over Valentine's heart. There was no movement there. She quickly stole away.

A few hours later, the nurse entered Valetine's room, saw the white lips and bluish pallor on Valentine's face, and quickly realized that something was very wrong. She ran to the door, screaming for help.

"What is it?" asked Villefort, rushing from his room. "Dr. d'Avrigny, come quickly! Call Madame de Villefort!"

Dr. d'Avrigny ran to Valentine and raised her in his arms. "What?—this one, too?" he exclaimed. "Oh, when will it end?"

Villefort rushed into the room. "What are you saying, doctor?" he exclaimed.

"I am saying that Valentine is dead!" replied d'Avrigny.

M. de Villefort staggered and buried his head in the bedcovers. Frightened, the servants all fled. Just then, Madame de Villefort entered the room. When she saw her grief-stricken husband moaning next to Valentine, she turned around and hurried out the door and disappeared.

"Dead! She's dead!" groaned Villefort.

After awhile, the two men turned around and saw Maximilian standing at the door, pale and terror-stricken. A few minutes earlier, Maximilian had entered the house of his beloved and rushed to Noirtier's room. When Maximilian heard all the commotion, he rushed to Valentine's chamber.

CHAPTER 70
Maximilian

Maximilian reveals his love for Valentine, and Villefort promises he will bring the murderer to justice.

Villefort lifted his head. "Who are you, sir," he angrily inquired, "to enter this house stricken with death? Go, sir, go!" But Maximilian remained motionless. He stared for a moment at the supposed corpse and then ran to Noirtier's room. Shortly thereafter, he brought Noirtier in his wheelchair into Valentine's room. Noirtier looked directly at Villefort with his wrinkled face and flaming eyes.

"See what they have done!" cried Maximilian, with one hand leaning on the back of the wheelchair, and the other extended toward Valentine. "Tell them," said Maximilian in a hoarse voice, "tell them that I am her fiancé. Tell them she was my beloved, my noble girl, my only blessing in the world. Tell them—oh, tell them, that the corpse belongs to me!" The young man, overwhelmed by the weight of his anguish, fell heavily on his knees before the bed.

At length Villefort said to Maximilian, "You say you loved Valentine, that you were engaged to her.

I knew nothing of this engagement, of this love. Yet I, her father, forgive you, for I see that your grief is real and deep. Take your last farewell, as all Valentine needs right now is a priest."

"You are mistaken, sir," exclaimed Maximilian, raising himself. "Valentine requires not only a priest, but an avenger. You, M. de Villefort, send for the priest. I will be the avenger."

"What do you mean, sir?" asked Villefort.

"I tell you, sir, Valentine has been murdered!"

Villefort looked steadily at Maximilian and said, "No one has committed murder in my house."

The eyes of Noirtier lit up with rage, and Dr. d'Avrigny prepared to speak. Maximilian, however, extended his arm and commanded silence. "And I say that murders have been committed here," said Maximilian. "I tell you that this is the fourth victim within the last four months."

"You are mad, sir," exclaimed Villefort.

"You think I am mad?" said Maximilian. "Well, then, I appeal to Dr. d'Avrigny himself. Ask him, sir." Villefort and d'Avrigny exchanged looks.

Then the doctor spoke. "I agree with this young man that murder has been committed, and justice must be done."

"Oh, God!" murmured Villefort.

Maximilian, glancing at Noirtier, waved his arm to demand silence. "M. Noirtier wishes to speak," he said.

"Yes," indicated Noirtier.

"Do you know who has committed these murders?" asked Maximilian.

"Yes," indicated Noirtier. The old man let it be known that he wished everyone to leave the room except his son.

"But can he understand you?" Maximilian asked Noirtier.

"Yes."

"Oh, yes," said Villefort, relieved to think that the inquiries were to be made by him alone. "I can understand my father."

Dr. d'Avrigny and Maximilian left the room. After fifteen minutes Villefort summoned them back. Villefort spoke. "Gentlemen," he said in a hoarse voice, "give me your word of honor that this horrible secret shall forever remain buried amongst ourselves!" The two men drew back.

"I entreat you," continued Villefort.

"But," said Maximilian, "the culprit—the murderer must be punished."

"Do not alarm yourself, sir. Justice will be done," said Villefort. "My father has revealed the culprit's name. He knows that Valentine will be avenged. Rest assured, gentlemen, that within three days, I shall have justice," declared the king's attorney. "Swear, then," said Villefort, joining the hands of Maximilian and d'Avrigny, "swear that you will spare the honor of my house, and leave me to avenge my child."

Dr. d'Avrigny turned round and uttered a very feeble "Yes." Maximilian, disengaging his hand, rushed to the bed, and after pressing the cold lips of Valentine with his own, left.

D'Avrigny asked Villefort if he had a particular priest that he wanted him to call.

"No," said Villefort. "Fetch the nearest one."

"The nearest," said the doctor, "is a good Italian priest who now lives next door to you. His name is Busoni."

"Bring him here," said Villefort.

Dr. D'Avigny brought the Italian priest— actually Monte Cristo in disguise—to Villefort's house. As they walked, the doctor spoke, "It is a young girl."

"I know it, sir. The servants who fled from the house informed me. I also know that her name is Valentine, and I have already prayed for her."

"Thank you, sir," said Dr. d'Avrigny." Come and watch by the dead, and all the wretched family will be grateful to you."

D'Avrigny brought the priest to Valentine's room. Noirtier was still there. Once the doctor left, the priest rose to bolt the doors, so that he could have privacy when tending to the needs of the dead and the living.

CHAPTER 71
Danglars' Signature

Danglars unwisely lends the Count of Monte Cristo five million francs.

The priest Busoni watched over Valentine till daylight, and then left without calling anyone. Dr. d'Avrigny returned about eight o'clock in the morning. He and Villefort went to Noirtier's room to see how the old man had slept. They found him sleeping calmly, with the suggestion of a smile on his face. Abbé Busoni had already told Noirtier how he planned to save Valentine.

Meanwhile Monte Cristo, no longer posing as Abbé Busoni, called on his banker, Baron Danglars. The banker greeted him with a sad smile. "Well," he said, extending his hand to Monte Cristo, "I suppose you have come to sympathize with me, now that I have been ridiculed with the shame of Andrea Cavalcanti and have also lost my daughter."

"Your daughter?"

"Yes. Eugenie left with Madame Danglars. I doubt whether her pride will ever allow her to return to France."

"Still, Baron," said Monte Cristo, "family griefs are endurable to a millionaire. As you well know,

358

money eases many misfortunes."

"Yes," he answered, "if a fortune brings comfort, I ought to be comforted. I am rich."

Monte Cristo chuckled inwardly. As part of his plan to exact revenge against Danglars, the Count had encouraged Danglars' bank to lend Bartolomeo Cavalcanti six million francs. The bank gave the money to a supposed representative of Cavalcanti, a representative who was actually one of Monte Cristo's servants. Cavalcanti had then returned to Italy and disappeared. The Count gave the fraudulently obtained six million francs to charity. The loss of six million francs placed Danglars' bank in serious financial difficulty. However, Danglars elected not to bring up the matter of the Cavalcanti loan, because Monte Cristo was reputed to be so rich that Danglars didn't want to lose his business.

Danglars motioned for Monte Cristo to take a seat. Danglars then explained, "When you were announced, I was in the process of preparing a bank check for a gentleman who will arrive soon. Will you allow me to finish making out that check?"

"Certainly," the Count replied.

Danglars resume preparing the check. "This check is for five million francs," he said.

"What a coincidence!" said the Count. I myself have come for a bank check for five million francs."

Danglars looked up with alarm.

"So far," the Count went on, "your bank has given me 900,000 francs on credit against my Thomson & French account. If you now give me the bank check for five million francs, I'll write your bank an IOU for a total of six million francs. You will profit by 100,000 francs, a tidy sum. Consider the 100,000 francs a token of my gratitude for your excellent service." The Count prepared the IOU, and Danglars gave him a check for five million francs.

Not long after Monte Cristo left the bank, the president of the Royal Hospital knocked on Danglars' door. The visitor explained that he was there to withdraw the five million francs he had previously advised Danglars he would require.

"My dear sir," Danglars said with embarrassment, "can it possibly wait a day?"

"You are joking, right?" replied the visitor.

"No, not at all. I will have your five million francs tomorrow at noon."

"Well, I suppose I could wait a day. The Countess de Morcerf and her son Albert just donated their entire fortune to the hospital."

"Really!" exclaimed Danglars. "Why?"

"They were unwilling to keep money acquired by dishonest means."

"But what will the countess and her son live on?"

"I've heard that the countess is moving to Marseilles, and her son Albert has enlisted in the army."

"How much was the fortune they donated?"

"A modest sum—twelve to thirteen hundred thousand francs."

"Wonderful. Now, can you come back tomorrow at noon for your money?"

"Yes, Baron Danglars, but I must have it at that time."

"Don't worry, you shall have every franc."

As soon as the hospital president left, Danglars rose and double-locked the door to his office. The banker knew that he would not be able to pay out any more money, for the firm was bankrupt. Danglars' Bank was ruined, and he was about to be disgraced.

The baron took the count's six million franc IOU, all the money from his safe—a total of 50,000 francs—and then burned several papers, finally taking his passport from his desk drawer. He then sat down and wrote a letter to his wife. After completing all these arrangements, Danglars slipped out of the bank by a little-used back door.

CHAPTER 72

The Cemetery of Pere-la-Chaise

After witnessing what he believes to be Valentine's burial, Maximilian no longer wishes to live.

A large crowd gathered at Valentine's gravesite at the cemetery of Pere-la-Chaise. Monte Cristo arrived with the sole purpose of searching out Maximilian. The Count had already removed Valentine's body, as planned. He quickly spotted Maximilian witnessing the burial from a small tree-covered hill overlooking Valentine's tomb. Once the mourners had finished with their eulogies and prayers, everyone left except Monte Cristo and Maximilian. The young man mournfully trudged to the freshly dug grave, knelt down, and murmured, "Oh, Valentine!"

The Count's heart was pierced by the utterance of these two words. He stepped forward and, touching the young man's shoulder, said, "I was looking for you, my friend. Would you like me to take you in my carriage back home?"

"No, thank you."

"Do you wish anything?"

"Leave me to pray."

The Count stepped away. However, concerned that Maximilian might commit suicide, Monte Cristo positioned himself so that he could see the young man's every move. At length Maximilian arose, brushed the dust from his knees, and turned toward Paris. The Count, dismissing his carriage, followed him about a hundred paces behind. Five minutes after Maximilian reached his house, Monte Cristo appeared. Julie was in the garden, where she was attentively watching Penelon. Penelon had become quite the gardener and was busy grafting some Bengal roses. "Ah, Count," Julie exclaimed with delight. "How good of you to come."

"I noticed that Maximilian has just returned," said the Count with unaccustomed abruptness. "May I go up and see him?"

"Please go ahead. Is anything wrong?"

"No. Everything will be fine." As soon as he was inside the house, the Count dashed up the stairs to Maximilian's room. The Count feared Maximilian might do something drastic any second. Monte Cristo knocked on the door. No answer. He tried to open the doorknob, but it was locked. "Maximilian!" he called. "Maximilian!"

Much to Monte Cristo's relief, Maximilian opened the door, but only enough to see who was there. Maximilian stood in the doorway so as to block the Count's entrance. "What do you want?" Maximilian asked in the most mournful of tones.

"I must speak to you."

"I don't wish to speak to anyone," replied Maximilian, and he started to close the door.

The Count, however, forced his way through the opening into Maximilian's room. "Excuse me," he said, "but I must speak to you urgently. I see your fingers are stained with ink. Were you writing?"

"Yes, I was writing. I do sometimes, soldier though I am."

Monte Cristo advanced into the room and looked around him. "Your pistols are beside your desk," said Monte Cristo, pointing with his finger to the pistols on the table.

"I am on the point of starting on a journey," replied Maximilian.

"A journey?" said the Count, "Let us both lay aside the masks we have assumed. I know that you wish to kill yourself because of Valentine."

"Well," said Maximilian, "what if I do? All my hopes are blighted, my heart is broken, my life is a burden, everything around me is sad and mournful. Life has become distasteful to me, and human voices distract me. It is a mercy to let me die, for if I live, I shall lose my reason and become mad."

"I tell you, sir, everything will turn out all right. Maximilian, for the sake of your father, you must not die!"

Maximilian appeared startled. "Why do you mention my father?" he stammered.

"Because I am the one who saved your father's life when he wished to destroy himself, as you do today. Because I am the man who sent the purse to your young sister, and the *Pharaon* to old Morrel. Because I am the Edmond Dantes who nursed you, a child, on my knees."

Maximilian took a step back, staggering, breathless, crushed. Then all his strength give way, and he fell at the feet of Monte Cristo. Suddenly he arose, rushed out of the room exclaiming energetically, "Julie, Julie—Emmanuel, Emmanuel!"

Julie, Emmanuel, and some of the servants ran up in alarm on hearing the cries of Maximilian. Maximilian seized their hands and exclaimed in a voice choked with sobs, "On your knees—on your knees—he is our benefactor—the saviour of our father! He is—"

He would have added "Edmond Dantes," but the Count prevented him. Julie threw herself into Monte Cristo's arms. Emmanuel embraced him as a guardian angel. Maximilian again fell on his knees. For a while nothing was heard in the room but a succession of sobs. Julie had scarcely recovered from her deep emotion when she rushed out of the room, descended to the next floor, ran into the drawing room, and raised the crystal globe which covered the purse given by the (until now) unknown benefactor. Meanwhile, the Count addressed Emmanuel in a low voice, "Watch over your wife's brother."

"Why so?" asked the young man, surprised.

"I cannot explain myself, but watch over him." Emmanuel looked around the room and caught sight of the pistols. Julie returned, holding the silken purse in her hands, while tears of joy rolled down her cheeks, like dewdrops on a rose.

"Here is the treasured purse," she said. "Do not think it will be less dear to us now we are acquainted with our benefactor!"

"My child," said Monte Cristo, coloring, "allow me to take back that purse. Since you now know my face, I wish to be remembered by that alone."

"Oh," said Julie, pressing the purse to her heart, "no, no, I beseech you, do not take it. After all, one unhappy day you will leave us, will you not?"

"You have guessed rightly, madame," replied Monte Cristo, smiling. "In a week I shall have left this country, where so many persons who merit the vengeance of heaven lived happily, while my father perished of hunger and grief. But for now, I must speak to Maximilian alone. Would you kindly leave us?" Emmanuel and Julie left the room.

"Come," said Monte-Cristo, touching Maximilian's shoulder with his finger, "are you feeling yourself again, Maximilian?"

"Yes, for I begin to suffer again."

The Count frowned and addressed Maximilian. "Listen to me. One day, in a moment of despair like yours, I also wished to kill myself. One day your father, equally desperate, wished to kill himself too. If anyone had said to your father, at the moment he raised the pistol to his head—if anyone had told me, when in my prison I pushed back the food I had not tasted for three days—if anyone had said to either of us then, 'Live—the day will come when you will be happy, and will bless life!'—we would have denied that possibility."

"Ah," exclaimed Maximilian, interrupting the Count, "you had only lost your liberty. My father had only lost his fortune, but I have lost Valentine."

"Look at me," said Monte Cristo. "Now, if I entreat, if I order you to live, Maximilian, it is in the conviction that one day you will thank me for having preserved your life."

"But," said the young man, "perhaps you have never loved! You see, I have been a soldier ever since I attained manhood. I reached the age of twenty-nine without loving. Well, at twenty-nine, I saw Valentine. For two years I have loved her. To possess Valentine would have been a happiness too infinite, too ecstatic, too complete, too divine for this world. Without Valentine, the earth is desolate."

"I have told you to hope," said the Count "You must stay with me. In a week we shall leave this country together."

"What! You think I suffer an ordinary grief, and you would cure it by a simple change of scene! Hah!"

"What more can I say?" asked Monte Cristo. "I have confidence in the remedy I propose, and ask you only to permit me to try it out."

"Count, you prolong my agony."

"Then," said the Count, "if I do not cure you in a month, to the day, to the very hour, mark my words, Maximilian, I will place loaded pistols in front of you along with a cup of the deadliest Italian poison—a poison more sure and prompt than that which has killed Valentine."

"Will you promise me?"

"Yes, for I have suffered like yourself and also contemplated suicide. I do not know whether you remember that this is the 5th of September. It is ten years today since I saved the life of your father, who wished to die."

"Well then," uttered Maximilian, "I promise not to take my life for one month."

Monte Cristo drew the young man toward him and pressed him to his heart. "And now," he said, "after today, you will come and live with me. You can occupy Haydee's apartment. My adopted daughter will at least be replaced by my son."

"Haydee?" said Maximilian, "what has become of her?"

"She departed last night."

"To leave you?"

"To wait for me. Make yourself ready to join me tomorrow at my house on the Champs-Elysées." Maximilian nodded in agreement, and the Count departed.

CHAPTER 73
Dividing the Proceeds

Madame Danglars requests an emergency meeting with her lover, while Mercedes de Morcerf receives some unexpected financial support.

The apartment building where Albert de Morcerf had selected a residence for his mother had another apartment that was rented to a very mysterious person.

It was a man whose face the doorman had never seen. In the winter his chin was buried in a large scarf, and in the summer he made a point of always blowing his nose just as he approached the door. His visits to the apartment began about four o'clock, though he never spent the night there.

Twenty minutes after he arrived, a carriage stopped at the house, and a lady in a black or dark blue dress alighted, She was always thickly veiled and proceeded directly to the second floor without a word to anyone. There she tapped at a door which, after being opened to admit her, was again quickly fastened. They used the same precautions in leaving the house. The lady always left first, so that they were never seen together. Twenty minutes afterward, the gentleman would depart.

The day after Monte Cristo had called upon the banker Danglars, the mysterious renter entered at ten o'clock in the morning instead of the usual time. Almost directly afterward, without the usual interval of time, a cab arrived, and the veiled lady ran hastily upstairs. The door opened, but before it could be closed, the lady exclaimed: "Oh, Lucien—oh, my love!"

"What is the matter, my darling?" asked the gentleman named Lucien. "You look so upset. Tell me, my sweetheart, what is the matter?"

"Oh, Lucien, can I confide in you?"

"Of course, you know you can. But what can be the matter? Your note this morning has completely bewildered me. Why this emergency meeting?"

"Lucien, a wonderful event has happened!" said the lady. "M. Danglars left last night!"

"Left?—M. Danglars left? Where has he gone?"

"I do not know."

"What do you mean? Has he gone, intending not to return?"

"I believe so. He left a letter for me."

"A letter?"

"Yes, read it."

Madame Danglars took from her pocket a letter which she gave to her lover, Lucien Debray. The letter read as follows:

Madame,

When you receive this, you will no longer have a husband, for I shall have left France. This morning I had to give a bank customer five million francs on credit. Almost immediately after, an account holder came and demanded the same amount from his account. I put him off until the next day, because I cannot pay the requested sum. This is because the imposter "Marquis Cavalcanti" made off with a "loan" of six million francs, despite Monte Cristo's avowals of his integrity. The Danglars' Bank is bankrupt. Because you have spent so much of my money, I feel no remorse at leaving you. The man upon whom you have lavished so much money can now look after you.

Your husband,
Baron Danglars

"Well?" asked Madame Danglars, "what do you think we should do? You realize I am now free to be with you permanently, just as you said we would one day be."

"Hermione, what you need is a chance to get away from all this," Debray said. "You should take a trip out of Paris."

"You will come with me, of course."

"If only I could. However, I must stay here and continue my work."

"Are you saying you are done with me because I can't give you money and buy you presents any more?"

"Of course not. I'm just saying you need to get away from Paris."

"I see," said Madame Danglars, her eyes flushed with tears mixed with fury. "Now that I am no longer rich, you want nothing to do with me! You scoundrel!" With those words, the twice-abandoned woman stormed out of the apartment. Debray shrugged and gathered up his things.

Meanwhile, in another part of the building, Mercedes and Albert de Morcerf were considering their situation. Mercedes was plainly dressed. Her eyes no longer sparkled, and she rarely smiled. When she spoke, she did so in a dull monotone. She now ate from crockery instead of porcelain. Her bed was a lumpy straw mattress, and the walls of her room were covered in peeling grey wallpaper. No carpet graced the floor.

Winter approached. Mercedes had no fire in the cold and naked room—she, who was accustomed to stoves which heated every corner of her house. But she had her son. They were compelled to acknowledge the realities of their situation.

"Mother," exclaimed Albert, "we must leave for Marseilles as soon as possible so that we can retrieve the 3,000 francs the Count of Monte Cristo buried there."

"But how can we afford the journey? We can barely pay the rent here."

Albert reached into his pocket and withdrew 1,000 francs. "This will easily cover the cost of our travel and will leave you with plenty of money for a good while."

"My blessed son, where did this come from?"

"This morning I enlisted in the army. They paid

me 1,000 francs today and will pay 1,000 more in a year. I'll be leaving soon for North Africa."

Mercedes raised her eyes to heaven with an expression it would be impossible to describe. Tears ran down her cheeks.

"The price of his blood!" she murmured.

"Yes, if I am killed," said Albert, laughing. "But I assure you, Mother, I have every intention of coming back to you."

"Merciful heavens!"

"Oh, Mother, think of your joy when you see me return with a handsome uniform bedecked with medals! I expect to look magnificent in it."

Mercedes sighed while endeavoring to smile. Albert saw through his mother's effort to appear cheerful. "Mother," continued Albert, "you will soon have 4,000 francs. You can live on this sum for at least two years. Well before then, I shall become an officer, and I shall make more than enough money for us both."

"As you wish, my son," replied Mercedes.

The next day Albert and his mother left Paris for Marseilles.

CHAPTER 74
The Judge

Villefort accuses the poisoner.

The court where Villefort worked as prosecutor was scheduled to meet the following day. Villefort, shut up in his room, exerted himself feverishly all that night in drawing up the case against the murderer of Caderousse. The evidence was certainly not convincing, since it rested upon a few words uttered by an escaped galley slave on his deathbed. The victim might have been motivated by hatred or revenge in accusing his companion. But Villefort's mind was made up. He was certain that Benedetto was guilty.

Monday morning dawned dull and gloomy. "Today," he said with an effort, "today the man who holds the blade of justice must strike wherever there is guilt."

When he was dressed, Villefort rang for his valet, who brought him the papers and a cup of chocolate. "What are you bringing me?" he asked.

"A cup of chocolate."

"I did not ask for it. Who sent this to me?"

"Madame ordered it for you, sir. She said you

would have to speak a great deal in the murder case, and that you should take something to keep up your strength."

The valet placed the cup on a table and then left the room. Villefort eyed the cup suspiciously. Then, taking it up with a nervous motion, he swallowed its contents all at once. Perhaps he hoped the beverage would be fatal and that he wished death to deliver him from a duty which he would rather die than fulfill.

He then rose and paced his room with a smile too terrible to witness. The chocolate proved harmless, and now the breakfast hour arrived. M. de Villefort had no appetite and thus did not appear at the table.

Later that morning, the valet reentered Villefort's study. "Madame de Villefort wishes to remind you, sir," he said, "that eleven o'clock has just struck, and that the trial commences at twelve."

"Tell your mistress," Villefort answered, "that I wish to speak to her, and I beg she will wait for me in her own room."

"Yes, sir."

Shortly afterward, Villefort entered his wife's dressing room. Madame de Villefort was sitting on a chair, impatiently turning over the pages of some newspapers and pamphlets. She was dressed to accompany her husband to court. Her bonnet was placed beside her, and her gloves were on her hands.

"Ah, here you are, monsieur," she said in her naturally calm voice. "But how pale you are! Have you been working all night? Why did you not come down to breakfast? Well, will you take me to court, or shall I take Edward with me separately?"

M. de Villefort remained mute and cold as a statue. Finally, he spoke.

"Edward," said Villefort, "go and play in the drawing room. I wish to speak to your mother." Madame de Villefort shuddered at the sight of her husband's cold countenance and his resolute tone. Edward raised his head, looked at his mother, and then, finding that she did not confirm the order, began cutting off the heads of his leaden soldiers.

"Edward," cried M. de Villefort, so harshly that the child started up from the floor, "do you hear me?—Go!" The child, unaccustomed to such treatment, arose, pale and trembling, and ran out. M. de Villefort closed and bolted the door after the child left.

"Dear me!" said the young woman, endeavoring to read her husband's thoughts, "what is the matter?"

"Madame, where do you keep the poison you generally use?" demanded Villefort, without any introduction, placing himself between his wife and the door.

A hoarse, broken tone, which was neither a cry nor a sigh, escaped from her. She became deadly pale. "Monsieur," she said, "I—I do not understand you."

"I asked you," continued Villefort, in a perfectly calm tone, "where you conceal the poison you used to kill my father-in-law, M. de Saint-Meran; my mother-in-law, Madame de Saint-Meran; Barrois; and my daughter Valentine."

"What are you talking about?" exclaimed Madame de Villefort, in a trembling voice.

"It is not for you to ask, but to answer."

"Is it to the judge or to my husband?" stammered Madame de Villefort.

"To the judge—to the judge, madame!"

It was terrible to behold the frightful pallor of that woman, the anguish of her look, the trembling of her whole frame. "Ah, sir," she muttered, "ah, sir," and this was all.

"You do not answer, madame!" exclaimed Villefort in his most prosecutorial voice. Then he added, with a smile yet more terrible than his anger, "It is true, then. You do not deny it! Since the death of Madame de Saint-Meran, I have known that a poisoner lived in my house. Dr. d'Avrigny warned me of it. After the death of Barrois, I began to suspect my daughter—a true angel. But after her death, there has been no doubt in my mind, madame, that you are the murderess."

The young woman hid her face in her hands. "Oh, sir," she stammered, "I beseech you, do not believe appearances."

"Ah, but you, who have calculated every step of these deaths, have forgotten to calculate one thing. Hanging awaits the poisoner, even if she is the wife of the king's attorney. There is only one honorable thing for you to do. I assume you still have a few drops of your deadly potion." Madame de Villefort uttered a wild cry, and a hideous and uncontrollable terror spread over her distorted features. "Swallow that liquid, and you will not die at the end of a rope."

"I do not understand! What do you mean?" stammered the unhappy woman, completely overwhelmed.

"I mean that the wife of the leading king's attorney in the capital shall not, by her infamy, soil an unblemished name! I mean that she shall not, with one blow, dishonor her husband and her child."

"No, no—oh, no!"

"Madame, justice must be done. I am on the earth to punish," he added, with a flaming glance. "Any other woman, even the queen herself, I would send to the executioner, but to you I shall be merciful. To you I will say, 'Have you not, madame, put aside some of the surest, deadliest, most speedy poison?'"

"Oh, pardon me, sir! Let me live!"

"No, no!"

"In the name of our child! For the sake of our child, let me live!"

"No, no, no, I tell you. One day, if I allow you to live, you will perhaps kill him, as you have the others!"

"I?—I kill my boy?" cried the distracted mother, rushing toward Villefort. "I kill my son? Ha, ha, ha!" and a frightful, demoniac laugh finished the sentence, which was lost in a hoarse rattle. Madame de Villefort fell at her husband's feet. He approached her. "Be aware, madame," he said, "if, on my return, you have not taken my suggestion, I will accuse you with my own mouth and arrest you with my own hands!" She listened, panting, overwhelmed, crushed; her eyes alone lived, and glared horribly.

"Farewell, madame, farewell!" The finality of that farewell struck Madame de Villefort like the executioner's knife. She fainted. Villefort went out and double-locked the door.

CHAPTER 75
The Indictment

At his trial, Benedetto makes a startling announcement.

The trial of Benedetto for the murder of Caderousse was the talk of Paris. In reality, Benedetto was the young man hired by Monte Cristo, in one of his revenge schemes, to play the role of Andrea Cavalcanti.

At the beginning of the trial, the judges took their places in the midst of the most profound silence. The jury took their seats. M. de Villefort, the prosecutor, sat in an armchair at the front of the courtroom. Spectators noticed his grave and severe face. It was the face of a man who was a stranger to all the softer human emotions.

"Bailiffs," said the chief judge, "lead in the accused."

At these words, all eyes turned toward the door through which Benedetto was to enter. The door soon opened, and the accused appeared.

The chief judge called for the indictment to be read aloud. Villefort proclaimed it without expression. During the reading, Benedetto appeared amazingly unconcerned. The indictment described the crime in all its gory details and also recounted the former life of the prisoner, including all his criminal activities. Benedetto was thus condemned in public opinion before the sentence of the law could be pronounced. At length the reading of the indictment was ended.

"Accused," said the chief judge in a stern tone of voice, "tell us your age."

"I am twenty-one years old, or rather I shall be in a few days, as I was born the night of the 27th of September, 1817." M. de Villefort, who was busy taking some notes, raised his head at the mention of this date.

"Where were you born?" continued the judge.

"At Auteuil, near Paris." M. de Villefort raised his head a second time, looked at Benedetto, and became livid. As for Benedetto, he gracefully wiped his lips with a fine linen pocket-handkerchief.

"Your profession?"

"First I was a forger," answered Benedetto, as calmly as possible. "Then I became a thief, and lately have become a murderer." The calm, un-repentant manner in which he uttered these words provoked an outcry from the spectators. M. de Villefort pressed his hand upon his forehead, which had become red and burning. Then he suddenly arose and looked around as though he had lost his senses—he wanted air.

"And now, prisoner, will you tell us your name?" said the judge.

"I cannot tell you my name, since I do not know it. But I know my father's name, and I can tell you that."

Villefort broke into a fevered sweat. Droplets fell from his face upon the papers which he held in his hand.

"Recite your father's name," said the judge. Not a whisper, not a breath, was heard in the courtroom. Every one waited anxiously.

"My father is the king's attorney, M. de Villefort," replied Benedetto calmly.

An explosion now burst forth like thunder from all those present. Several persons rushed over to M. de Villefort to proclaim their disbelief and express their support. A lady fainted but was revived with the aid of smelling salts.

"Gentlemen," Benedetto exclaimed, "I assure you I had no idea of causing a disturbance in the presence of this honorable assembly. You ask my name, but I cannot give it, since my parents abandoned me. I now repeat that I was born at Auteuil on the night of the 27th of September, 1817, and that I am the son of M. de Villefort. Do you wish for any further details? I will give them. I was born at No. 28 Fontaine Street in a room hung with red curtains. My father took me in his arms, telling my mother I was dead. He wrapped me in a linen marked with an H and an N. Then he carried me into a garden, where he buried me alive."

A shudder ran through the assembly when they saw that the confidence of the prisoner increased in proportion to the terror of M. de Villefort.

"But how do you know all these details?" asked the judge.

"I will tell you, Your Honor. An enemy of my

father stationed himself that night in the garden, waiting to kill him. He saw my father bury something in the ground. Afterwards he attacked my father with a knife and left him bleeding on the ground.

Thinking my father had buried something of value, the man dug up the box that was my coffin and found me still living. He carried me to an orphanage. Three months afterward, a woman came to Paris to fetch me. She claimed me as her son, and the orphanage let her take me to her home in Corsica.

"Certainly, I might have lived happily among those good people, who adored me. However, my wicked nature got the best of me, and I fell into a life of crime. One day, when I cursed God for making me so wicked, my adopted father said to me, 'Do not blame God, unhappy child. The crime is that of your father, who consigned you to hell if you died, and to misery if you lived.' If I have committed an additional crime, punish me. But I beg you to understand that ever since the day of my birth, my life has been sad and bitter."

"But your mother?" asked the judge.

"My mother thought me dead; she is not guilty. I did not even wish to know her name, nor do I know it." Just then a piercing cry, ending in a sob, burst from the center of the room. A crowd encircled the lady who had before fainted, and who now fell into a violent fit of hysterics. As she was carried out of the chamber, the thick veil which concealed her face dropped off. The spectators recognized Madame Danglars.

"Hold on!" said the judge. "Have you any proof that this tale of horror is true?"

"You call for proof?" said Benedetto, laughing. "Just look at M. de Villefort, and you will get all the proof you require."

Everyone turned toward Villefort. The king's attorney advanced staggering into the midst of the tribunal, with his hair dishevelled and his face torn with the mark of his nails. The whole assembly uttered a long murmur of astonishment. "Father," said Benedetto, "is not what I have said true?"

"Yes," the anguished prosecutor said. "Everything this young man has said is true." As he spoke these words with a hoarse, choking voice, he staggered toward the door, which a doorkeeper mechanically opened. An amazed silence enveloped the court room.

"The session is adjourned for the present," said the chief judge. "Fresh inquiries will be made, and this case will be tried next session by other judges." Gendarmes escorted Benedetto out of the chamber.

CHAPTER 76
Expiation

Villefort returns home, where he makes a shocking discovery.

It would be difficult to describe Villefort's feelings as he fled the courthouse. Every pulse beat with feverish excitement, every nerve was strained, every vein swollen. He dashed into his carriage, awakened his sleeping coachman, and ordered him to drive home.

During the ride, he thought of his wife. His wife! He had just acted the severe judge in condemning her. She might at that very moment be preparing to kill herself, as he had suggested! Villefort again groaned with anguish and despair. "Ah," he exclaimed, "that woman became criminal only from associating with me! I carried the infection of crime with me, and she has caught it as she would a fever, the cholera, the plague! But no, she must not die. She shall continue to live, and with me. We will flee from Paris and go as far as the earth reaches. Yes, we will flee. I will confess all to her."

The carriage stopped at the door of the house. Villefort leaped out of the carriage and saw that his servants were surprised at his early return. As he passed by M. Noirtier's room, he noticed two figures through the half-open door. However, he was too anxious to see his wife to inquire who they were.

"Heloise!" he called. He fancied he heard the sound of a piece of furniture being removed. "Heloise!"

"Who is there?" came the answer in feeble tones.

"Open the door!" cried Villefort. "Open! It is me!" But the door remained closed. Villefort burst it open with a violent blow. Madame de Villefort was standing erect, pale, her features contracted, and her eyes glaring horribly. "Heloise, Heloise!" he said, "what is the matter? Speak!" The young woman extended her stiff white hands toward him.

"I have done what you ordered, monsieur," she said with a rattling noise which seemed to tear her throat. "What more do you want?" She fell full length on the floor. Villefort ran to her and seized her hand, which clasped a crystal bottle with a golden stopper. Madame de Villefort was dead. Villefort, maddened with horror, stepped back to the doorway. "My son!" he exclaimed suddenly, "where is my son?—Edward, Edward!" He rushed out of the room.

"Where is my son?" Villefort asked a servant.

The servant replied, "Madame de Villefort sent for him half an hour ago. He went into her room. We haven't seen him since."

A cold sweat burst out on Villefort's forehead. His legs trembled, and his thoughts flew about madly in his brain like the gears of a disordered watch. "In Madame de Villefort's room?" he murmured and slowly returned, with one hand wiping his forehead, and with the other supporting himself against the wall.

"Edward!" he stammered. "Edward!" The child did not answer. Villefort stepped forward two or three paces and saw his child lying on the sofa. The unhappy man uttered an exclamation of joy. A ray of light seemed to penetrate the abyss of despair and darkness. Villefort took the child in his arms, embraced him, shook him, called him, but the child made no response. He pressed his burning lips to Edward's cheeks, but they were icy cold and pale. He felt the stiffened limbs. He pressed his hand upon the heart, but it no longer beat—the child was dead.

A folded paper fell from Edward's breast. Villefort, thunderstruck, fell upon his knees. He picked up the paper, and, recognizing his wife's writing, read its contents.

> You know that I was a good mother, since it was for my son's sake I committed crimes. A good mother cannot depart without her son.

Villefort could not believe his eyes. He dragged himself toward the child's body and examined it as a lioness contemplates its dead cub. Then a piercing cry escaped from his breast, and he wept. He descended the stairs and entered Noirtier's room. The old man appeared to be listening to the priest, Abbé Busoni.

"Why are you in my house, sir?" Villefort exclaimed.

Busoni turned around, "I came to pray over the body of your daughter."

"And now why are you here?"

"I come to tell you that you have sufficiently repaid your debt, and that from this moment I will pray to God to forgive you, as I do."

"Good heavens!" exclaimed Villefort. "Surely that is not the voice of Abbé Busoni!"

"No!" The priest threw off his wig and shook his head. His hair, no longer confined, fell in black masses around his manly face.

"It is the face of the Count of Monte Cristo!" exclaimed Villefort.

"You are not exactly right, M. Villefort. You must go farther back in time."

"That voice, that voice!—Where did I first hear it?"

"You heard it for the first time at Marseilles, twenty-three years ago, the day of your marriage with Mademoiselle de Saint-Meran."

"You are not Abbé Busoni?—you are not Monte Cristo? Oh, heavens—you are, then, some secret and mortal enemy! I must have wronged you in some way at Marseilles. But what did I do to you?" exclaimed Villefort.

"You condemned me to a horrible, tedious

death. You killed my father. You deprived me of liberty, of love, and happiness."

"Who are you, then? Who are you? Wait, I recognize you—I recognize you!" exclaimed the king's attorney. "You are—"

"I am Edmond Dantes!"

"You are Edmond Dantes," cried Villefort, seizing the Count by the wrist. "Then come here!" And up the stairs he dragged Edmond. "There, Edmond Dantes!" he said, pointing to the bodies of his wife and child. "See! Are you well avenged?" Edmond became pale at this horrible sight. He feared that he had passed beyond the bounds of vengeance. With an expression of indescribable regret, he scooped up the child, reopened its eyes, felt its pulse, and then rushed with him into Valentine's room.

A quarter of an hour afterward the door of Valentine's room opened, and Monte Cristo reappeared. Pale, with a dull eye and heavy heart, all the noble features of that face, usually so calm and serene, were overcast by grief. In his arms he held the child, whom he had been unable to recall to life. Bending on one knee, he placed it reverently by the side of its mother, with its head upon her breast. Then, rising, he went out, and meeting a servant on the stairs, he asked, "Where is M. de Villefort?"

The servant, instead of answering, pointed to the garden. Monte Cristo ran down the steps. In the garden he beheld Villefort, encircled by his servants, with a spade in his hand, and digging the earth with fury. "It is not here!" he cried out. "It is not here!"

And then he moved farther on, and began again to dig.

Monte Cristo approached him, and said in a low voice, with an expression almost humble, "Sir, you have indeed lost a son, but—"

Villefort interrupted him. He had neither listened nor heard. "Oh, I will find it," he insisted. "You may pretend he is not here, but I will find him, though I dig forever!" Monte Cristo drew back in horror. "Oh," he said, "he is mad!" He rushed into the street, for the first time doubting whether he had the right to do as he had done.

Not long after, on entering his own house, he met Maximilian Morrel. "Prepare yourself, Maximilian," he said with a smile. "We leave Paris tomorrow."

CHAPTER 77
The Departure

After saying goodbye to Julie and her husband Emmanuel, the Count and Maximilian set out for Marseilles.

The recent events we have described were the talk of all Paris. Emmanuel and his wife, Julie, held animated discussions about them in their little apartment in Meslay Street. Maximilian and the Count paid them a brief visit on their way out of Paris.

"Where are you going, Count?" asked Julie.

"First to Marseilles, madame."

"To Marseilles!" exclaimed the young couple.

"Yes, and I am taking your brother with me."

"Oh, Count," said Julie, "I hope you can cure him of his melancholy."

"I will try to cheer him up," replied the Count.

"Before you leave us, Count," said Julie, "will you permit us to—"

"Madame," interrupted the Count, taking her two hands in his, "all that you could say in words would never express what I read in your eyes. Do not forget me, my kind friends, for probably you will never see me again."

"Never see you again?" exclaimed Emmanuel, while two large tears rolled down Julie's cheeks.

Pressing his lips to Julie's hands as she rushed into his arms, the Count extended his other hand to Emmanuel. Finally, he stepped back and took Julie's hand, just as he had done eleven years before on the staircase leading to Morrel's study.

"Do you still trust Sinbad the Sailor?" he asked.

"Oh, yes," was the ready answer.

"Well, then, sleep in peace, and put your trust in heaven." The Count and Maximilian went out to the waiting carriage. Four powerful horses were already pawing the ground with impatience.

Ali, apparently just back from a long walk, was standing at the foot of the steps, his face bathed in perspiration. "Well," asked the count in Arabic, "have you been to see the old man?"

Ali made a sign in the affirmative.

"And have you given him the letter, as I ordered you to do?"

The slave respectfully signaled that he had.

"And what did he say—or, rather, do?"

Ali placed himself in the light, so that his master might see him distinctly. Then, imitating the face of the old man, he closed his eyes, as Noirtier was in the custom of doing when saying "Yes."

"Good, he accepts," said Monte Cristo. "Now let us go."

After they were well out of Paris, the Count asked Maximilian, "Do you regret leaving Paris?"

"Valentine reposes within the walls of Paris, and to leave Paris is like losing her a second time."

"Maximilian," said the Count, "the friends that we have lost do not repose in the earth, but are buried deep in our hearts. Therefore, they always are with us. I have two friends who in this way never depart from me. Their spirits live in me. I consult them when doubtful, and if I ever do any good, it is due to their kindly counsels. Listen to the voice of your heart, Maximilian, and ask it whether you ought to preserve this melancholy exterior."

"My friend," said Maximilian, "the voice of my heart is very sorrowful and promises me nothing but misfortune."

Before long the travelers arrived in Marseilles. The vibrant city stirred powerful memories within them.

"Here," said Maximilian when they arrived at the port, "here is the spot where my father stopped, when the *Pharaon* entered the port. It was here that the good old man, whom you saved from death and dishonor, threw himself into my arms. I yet feel his warm tears on my face."

At that very moment a groan, expressive of bitter grief, was heard, and a woman was seen waving her hand to a passenger on board a vessel about to sail.

"Oh, heavens!" exclaimed Maximilian. "That youth in the uniform of a lieutenant is Albert de Morcerf!"

"Yes," said Monte Cristo, "I recognize him."

Monte Cristo turned in the direction of the veiled woman, who soon disappeared around the corner of the street. Turning to his friend, "Dear

Maximilian," said the Count, "have you nothing to do in this city?"

"I have to weep over the grave of my father," replied Maximilian in a broken voice.

"Well, then, go—wait for me there, and I will soon join you. I also have a visit to pay."

Maximilian bent his head sorrowfully and left. Monte Cristo remained on the same spot until Maximilian was out of sight. He then walked toward a certain street to seek out a small house that readers were made familiar with at the beginning of this story.

The woman whom the Count had seen leave the ship with so much regret entered this house. The Count followed her. He knew better than anyone else how to open that weather-beaten door with the large-headed nail which served to raise the latch within. He entered without knocking. At the end of a passage paved with bricks was a little garden, bathed in sunshine, and rich in warmth and light. Mercedes had found the money Monte Cristo had buried there twenty-four years ago.

Monte Cristo now saw Mercedes seated beneath a jasmine tree, with her head bowed, and weeping bitterly. Monte Cristo approached her. "Madame," said the Count, "it is no longer in my power to make you happy, but I offer you consolation. Will you accept it as coming from a friend?"

"I am, indeed, most wretched," replied Mercedes. "I am alone in the world! I had only my son, and now he has left me!"

"He possesses a noble heart, madame," replied the Count, "and he has acted rightly. He feels that every man owes a debt to his country. He will increase in strength and honor by struggling with adversity, which he will convert into prosperity. Leave him to build up the future for you."

"Oh," replied the wretched woman, mournfully shaking her head, "the prosperity of which you speak I can never enjoy. The bitter cup of adversity has been drained by me to the very dregs, and I feel that the grave is not far distant. You have acted kindly, Count, in bringing me back to the place where I have enjoyed so much bliss. I ought to meet death on the same spot where I once found such happiness."

Mercedes stood up and extended both her hands toward him. "Look at me," she continued, with a feeling of profound melancholy. "My eyes no longer dazzle by their brilliance, for the time has long fled since I used to smile on Edmond Dantes, who anxiously looked out for me from the window of the house where he and his old father lived. See"— and she exposed her face completely to view—"see, misfortune has silvered my hair. My eyes have shed so many tears that they are encircled by a rim of purple, and my forehead is wrinkled. You, Edmond, on the contrary—you are still young, handsome, dignified."

Mercedes burst into tears. Her woman's heart was breaking under its load of memories. Monte Cristo took her hand and planted a kiss on it.

"Enough," said Mercedes, "enough, Edmond! We must say farewell, Edmond, and let us part."

"Before I leave you, Mercedes, have you no request to make?" asked the Count.

"I desire but one thing in this world, Edmond—the happiness of my son."

"Pray to the Almighty to spare his life, and I will take upon myself to promote his happiness."

"Thank you, Edmond."

"But have you no request to make for yourself, Mercedes?"

"For myself I want nothing. I live, as it were, between two graves. One is that of Edmond Dantes, lost to me long, long since. He had my love! The other grave is that of the man who met his death from the hand of Edmond Dantes. I approve of the deed, but I must pray for the dead."

"Your son shall be happy, Mercedes," repeated the Count.

"Then I shall enjoy as much happiness as this world can possibly grant."

"But what are your plans?"

"I have no longer the strength to do anything but to spend my days in prayer. However, I shall have no need to work, thanks to the money buried by you, and which I found in the place you mentioned. That will be sufficient to maintain me."

"Mercedes," said the Count, "you made an unnecessary sacrifice in giving away the fortune amassed by Fernand. Half of it belonged to you."

"I know what you are going to tell me, Edmond. I know you are going to offer me money—a lot of money. But I cannot accept it, Edmond—my son would not permit it."

"I shall do nothing without the approval of your son, Mercedes dear. But if he is agreeable to a gift of money, would you accept it?"

"Edmond, I am no longer a reasoning creature. If Albert agrees, I will accept whatever you might like to give me." And after pressing her trembling hand upon that of the Count, Mercedes rushed up the stairs and disappeared.

CHAPTER 78

The Past

Maximilian agrees to meet the Count on the island of Monte Cristo on the 5th of October.

The Count made his way to the cemetery to find Maximilian leaning against one of the cypress trees shading his parents' grave markers. Maximilian was overwhelmed by grief.

"Maximilian," said the Count, "you should not dwell so single-mindedly on sorrow."

"Oh, Count, have pity upon me. I am so unhappy."

"I have known a man much more unfortunate than you, Maximilian."

"Impossible! What can be more wretched than the man who has lost all he loved and desired in the world?"

"Listen, Maximilian, and pay attention to what I am about to tell you. I knew a man who, like you, had fixed all his hopes of happiness upon a woman. He was young, he had an old father whom he loved, he was engaged to a woman he adored. He was about to marry her, when fate deprived him of his beloved and cast him into a dungeon. He remained there fourteen years, Maximilian," said the Count, placing his hand on the young man's shoulder.

Maximilian shuddered.

"He also, Maximilian, like you, considered himself the unhappiest of men."

"Well?" asked Maximilian.

"Well, at the height of his despair God came to his assistance. He miraculously escaped from the prison and gradually became rich and powerful."

"And does this man ever expect to be happy?"

"He hopes so, Maximilian. Now remember, on the 5th of October, I shall expect you at the island of Monte Cristo. On the 4th, a yacht will wait for you in the port of Bastia. It will be called the *Eurus.* You will give your name to the captain, who will bring you to me."

"But remember, Count, you promised that on that day you will allow me to die if I wish to do so."

"If you wish to die on that day, I will assist you. Maximilian, farewell!"

"Must you leave me now?"

"Yes, I have business in Italy."

"When do you leave?"

"Immediately. The steamer waits, and in an hour I shall be far from you. Will you accompany me to the harbor, Maximilian?"

"I am entirely yours, Count." Maximilian accompanied the Count to the docks. White steam was ascending like a plume of feathers from the ship's smokestack. An hour afterward, as the Count had said, the boat merged into the mist at the edge of the horizon.

CHAPTER 79
Peppino

Danglars travels to Rome, where he cashes in the Count's IOU for six million francs.

While all this was going on, Baron Paul Danglars was in a carriage heading for Rome. Upon arrival he checked in at the Pastrini Hotel, ordered a good lunch, and arranged for a carriage to take him to the Thomson & French Bank. Secretly trailing the banker was the outlaw Peppino, who was acting on Monte Cristo's instructions. The Count had told Peppino that Danglars would be withdrawing a great deal of money from the Thomson & French Bank.

When Danglars arrived at the bank, a clerk ushered him into the plush office of a high official. Danglars presented identification as well as the IOU Monte Cristo had given him for six million francs.

The Thomson & French Bank was quick to honor the Count's IOU and gave Danglars the money. Overjoyed, Danglars returned to the carriage that was waiting for him. "To the Pastrini Hotel," he shouted up to the coachman with unrepressed gladness. He was a rich man once again.

Tired but happy, Danglars slept well that night, keeping the six million francs under the covers by his side. The next morning he awoke, thoroughly satisfied with the turn of events, and ordered a hearty breakfast. He lingered during the day and ordered a carriage to pick him up at twilight. Because he had failed to pay the Royal Hospital the money that his bank owed them, he was a fugitive from justice. Therefore, he felt it was safest to travel under cover of darkness.

As daylight faded, his carriage arrived. The attendants loaded his trunk into the vehicle, and the baron ordered the coachman to take the road to Ancona. Danglars planned to travel to Vienna, where he would take up permanent residence.

The carriage sped on past the outskirts of Rome, as night descended upon the landscape. Danglars put his head out the window and asked the coachman how long it would be before they reached the next town. "Do not understand!" was the reply in Italian. The carriage moved on. "I will stop at the first inn," said Danglars to himself.

Danglars fell asleep, waking only when the carriage stopped. The banker opened his eyes and looked through the window, expecting to find himself in the midst of some town. However, he saw nothing except what seemed like an abandoned ruin, where three or four men came and went like shadows. The horses were unharnessed and others put in their places. Danglars opened the door, but a strong hand pushed him back, and the carriage rolled on. The baron was completely mystified and not a little put out. "Where are we going?" he yelled up to the coachman. Once again the coachman yelled out in Italian, "Do not understand!"

Danglars saw that men on horseback had surrounded the carriage. He also began to believe that the carriage was circling back to Rome. At first he feared he was being taken back to Paris to be arrested. Then he thought that maybe he was in the clutches of robbers. His hair stood on end. He remembered the harrowing adventures that Albert de Morcerf had related when he was taken by the notorious bandit Luigi Vampa.

The carriage came to a halt, and a rough-looking man yanked open the door and ordered Danglars to get out. Quaking with fear, the baron obeyed. Four men surrounded him and pushed him along a dirt path. The leader was none other than Peppino. Now there was no longer any doubt; Danglars knew he was in the hands of Roman bandits. The path was wide, but dark. Peppino struck a light and lit a torch. Eventually the group came to the mouth of a large cave. A sentinel raised his rifle. "Who goes there?" he cried.

"A friend, a friend!" said Peppino. "Where is the captain?"

"There," said the sentinel, pointing over his shoulder to a wide opening hollowed out of the rock. Peppino grabbed Danglars by his coat collar and dragged him roughly to where the captain sat

"Is this the man?" asked the captain.

"Himself, captain—himself," replied Peppino.

"Very well. Let's see what he looks like." Peppino raised his torch to the face of Danglars, who hastily moved back that he might not have his eyelashes burnt. His agitated features presented the appearance of pale and hideous terror. "The man is tired," said the captain. "Conduct him to his bed."

"Oh," murmured Danglars to himself, "that bed is probably one of the coffins hollowed in the wall, and the sleep I shall enjoy will be death from one of the daggers I see glistening in the darkness."

The banker uttered a groan and followed his guide. A low door was opened before him. Bending low to avoid striking his forehead, he entered a small room cut out of the rock. The cell was clean, though empty, and dry, though situated at an immeasurable distance under the earth. A bed of dried grass covered with goat-skins was placed in one corner. Danglars brightened up on beholding it, fancying that it gave some promise of safety. "Oh, God be praised," he said. "At least it is a bed and not a coffin!"

"Stay," commanded the guide, and pushing Danglars into the cell, he closed the door upon him. A bolt slammed shut, and Danglars was a prisoner.

Lying on the soft bed, Danglars realized he was being held at the catacombs of St. Sebastian, headquarters of the infamous bandit Luigi Vampa

Since the bandits had not killed him at once, he felt that they would not kill him at all. Instead, they would seek a ransom. After calculating what he thought he would be ransomed for, he fell asleep secure in the knowledge that he would still have over five million francs left for himself.

CHAPTER 80
Luigi Vampa's Bill of Fare

Danglars' chicken dinner turns out to be quite expensive.

Danglars awoke to a whitewashed cell that quickly reminded him that he was no longer surrounded by his Parisian luxuries. "Yes, yes," he murmured, "I am in the hands of the thieves Albert de Morcerf spoke about. Perhaps they have robbed me already." He thrust his hands into his pockets. They were untouched. He still had possession of his six million francs in one pocket and the 50,000 in another.

He checked his watch, which he had carefully wound up on the previous night, and it showed half past five. Without this, Danglars would have been quite ignorant of the time, for daylight did not reach his cell. He waited until twelve o'clock. During all this time a guard, who had been relieved at eight o'clock, had been watching his door. Danglars could barely make out the features of his guard by peering through the ill-joined planks of the door.

At twelve o'clock, this man was replaced by another. Danglars, wishing to catch sight of his new guardian, approached the door again. He was an athletic, gigantic thug, with large eyes, thick lips, and a flat nose. His red hair fell in dishevelled masses like snakes around his shoulders. The man took some black bread, cheese, and onions from a small case and began to eat. "Ugh," cried Danglars. "How can people eat such things!" and he withdrew to seat himself upon his goat-skin.

Four hours passed, and the giant was replaced by another bandit. Danglars, who began to experience gnawings in his stomach, arose softly and peered through the crack of the door. He recognized the man called Peppino. Peppino was preparing to stand guard. He seated himself opposite the door and placed between his legs an earthen pan containing chick-peas stewed with bacon. Near the pan he placed a pretty little basket of Villetri grapes and a flask of Orvieto wine. Danglars watched these preparations, and his mouth watered.

"Excuse me, sir," the banker called out, "but are they not going to give me any dinner?"

"Does your excellency happen to be hungry?"

"Happen to be hungry—that's pretty good, when I haven't eaten for twenty-four hours!" muttered Danglars. Then he added aloud, "Yes, sir, I am hungry—very hungry."

"What would your excellency like?" and Peppino placed his pan on the ground, so that the steam rose directly under the nostrils of Danglars.

"Some chicken would be nice."

"As your excellency pleases." Peppino, turning around, shouted, "A chicken for his excellency!" His voice yet echoed in the archway when a handsome, graceful young man appeared, bearing a fowl on a silver dish on his head, without the assistance of his hands. Peppino had the food brought into Danglars' cell. "I could almost believe myself at the elegant Café de Paris," murmured Danglars.

"Here, your excellency," said Peppino, taking the fowl from the young bandit and placing it on the worm-eaten table which, with the stool and the goat-skin bed, formed the entire furniture of the cell. Danglars asked for a knife and fork. "Here, excellency," said Peppino, offering him a little blunt knife and a boxwood fork. Danglars took the knife in one hand and the fork in the other, and was about to cut up the fowl. "Pardon me, excellency," said Peppino, placing his hand on the banker's shoulder. "You must pay before you eat."

"Here you are," Danglars said, throwing twenty francs down on the table.

Peppino looked at the money, and Danglars again prepared to carve the fowl. "Stop a moment, your excellency," said Peppino. "You still owe me something."

"Come, how much do I owe you for this fowl?"

"Your excellency now owes me 99,980 francs." Danglars gasped upon hearing this gigantic sum.

"Come, come, this is very amusing. Go to the devil! You do not know who you are dealing with!"

Peppino made a sign, and the youth quickly removed the fowl, leaving the money on the table. Danglars threw himself upon his goat-skin, and Peppino, reclosing the door, again began eating his peas and bacon.

Danglars' stomach felt so empty that it seemed as if it would be impossible ever to fill it again. After the passage of a half hour, which seemed to him like a century, Danglars arose and went to the door. "Come, sir, do not keep me starving here any longer."

"Your excellency, just tell me what you want, and it shall be yours."

"I will have a piece of dry bread, since the chickens are so expensive in this accursed place."

"Bread? Very well. Hey there, some bread!" he called. The youth brought a small loaf. "How much?" asked Danglars.

"100,000 francs," said Peppino.

"What?"

"We have a fixed price for all our meals, no matter what you eat, or how much."

"And what am I to pay with, brute?" said Danglars, enraged. "Do you suppose I carry 100,000 francs in my pocket?"

"You have over six million francs in your pocket," Peppino snapped back.

Danglars shuddered. "Come," he said, "if I pay you the 100,000 francs, will you bring me back that chicken dinner, and allow me to eat at my ease?"

"Certainly," said Peppino.

Thereupon Danglars withdrew 100,000 francs from his pocket and handed them to Peppino.

"Here is your fowl," said the bandit. Danglars proceeded to carve the bird, which appeared very thin for the price it had cost. As for Peppino, he continued eating his chick-peas.

CHAPTER 81
The Pardon

As the cost of food reduces Danglars to near-starvation, a stranger appears and asks him if he is sorry for the evil he has done.

The next day Danglars was again hungry. The prisoner had planned for no further expenses. He had concealed half of his chicken and a piece of the bread in a corner of his cell. But he had no sooner eaten than he felt thirsty. He had forgotten about that. He struggled against his thirst until his tongue clung to the roof of his mouth. Then, no longer able to resist, he called out. The sentinel opened the door; it was a new face. Danglars asked for Peppino.

"Here I am, your excellency," said Peppino. "What do you want?"

"Something to drink."

"Your excellency knows that wine is very expensive near Rome."

"Then give me water," Danglars begged.

"Oh, water is even more costly than wine, your excellency—there has been such a drought."

"Come," thought Danglars, "it is the same old story." And while he smiled as he attempted to regard the affair as a joke, he felt his temples get moist with perspiration. "Let me have a bottle of the least expensive wine."

"They are all the same price."

"And what is that?"

"Twenty-five thousand francs a bottle."

"Tell me," cried Danglars, "is it your intention to rob me of all of my money?"

"It is possible such may be the master's intention."

"The master?—who is he?"

"The person to whom you were conducted yesterday."

"Where is he?"

"Here."

"Let me see him."

"Certainly." And the next moment Luigi Vampa appeared before Danglars.

"You sent for me?" he said to the prisoner.

"Are you, sir, the chief of the people who brought me here?"

"Yes, your excellency. What is it you want to know?"

"How much do you require for my ransom?"

"Merely the six million francs you have on you." Danglars felt a dreadful spasm dart through his heart.

"But this is all I have left in the world out of an immense fortune," he said. "If you deprive me of that, you might as well take away my life also."

"We are forbidden to shed your blood."

"And by whom are you forbidden?"

"By him we obey."

"You obey someone else, then?"

"Yes, a chief."

"I thought you said you were the chief?"

"I am chief of these men, but there is another over me."

"And did your superior order you to treat me in this way?"

"Yes."

"But my purse will be exhausted."

"Probably."

"Come," said Danglars, "will you take a million?"

"No."

"Two million?—three?—four? Come on, four million? I will give the money to you on condition that you let me go."

"Your excellency, you must surrender all six million francs."

"But what will happen when I have no more money left to pay you?" asked the infuriated Danglars.

"Then you must suffer hunger."

"Suffer hunger?" said Danglars, becoming pale.

"Most likely," replied Vampa coolly.

"But you say you do not wish to kill me?"

"No."

"And yet you will let me perish with hunger?"

"Ah, that is a different thing."

"Well, then, wretches," cried Danglars, "you may torture, torment, kill me, but you shall not have one more franc!"

"As your excellency pleases," said Vampa, and he left the cell. Danglars, raving, threw himself on the goat-skin. For the first time in his life, Danglars contemplated death with a mixture of both dread and desire.

His resolution lasted two days, after which he offered a million francs for some food. They sent him a magnificent supper, and took his million.

After twelve days, during which he spent almost all of his money on splendid dinners and fabulous bottles of wine, Danglars realized he was down to his last 50,000 francs. Then a strange reaction took place. He refused to part with his last 50,000 francs. After three days of starvation, he became delirious.

On the fourth day, he was no longer a man, but a living corpse. He had picked up every crumb that had been left from his former meals and was beginning to eat the matting which covered the floor of his cell. Then, rising in despair, he called out, "The chief, the chief!"

"Here I am," said Vampa, instantly appearing. "What do you want?"

"Take my last coin," muttered Danglars, turning out his pocket. "I only ask to live!"

"Then you suffer a great deal?"

"Oh, yes, yes, cruelly!"

"Still, there have been men who suffered more than you."

"I do not think so."

"Yes, those who have died of hunger."

Danglars thought of Edmond Dantes's father who, in his hours of delirium, he had seen groaning on his bed. He struck his forehead on the ground and groaned. "Yes," he said, "there have been some who have suffered more than I have."

"Do you repent?" asked a new, deep, solemn voice, which caused Danglars' hair to stand on end. His feeble eyes saw a man enveloped in a cloak, half lost in the shadow of a stone column.

"Of what must I repent?" stammered Danglars.

"Of the evil you have done," said the voice.

"Oh, yes! Oh, yes, I do indeed repent." And he struck his breast with his shrunken fist.

"Then I forgive you," said the man, dropping his cloak, and advancing to the light.

"The Count of Monte Cristo!" gasped Danglars, more pale from terror than he had been just before from hunger and misery.

"You are mistaken—I am not the Count of Monte Cristo."

"Then who are you?"

"I am Edmond Dantes!"

Danglars uttered a cry and fell prostrate on the floor.

"Rise," said Edmond, "your life is safe. The same good fortune has not happened to your accomplices—one is mad, the other dead. Keep the 50,000 francs you have left—I give them to you. The 5,000,000 you stole from the hospital has been repaid from the 6,000,000 you have paid us. And now eat and drink. Vampa, when this man is satisfied, let him be free."

Danglars remained prostrate while Edmond withdrew. According to Edmond's directions,

Danglars was provided with the best foods and wines of Italy. Later, when the banker had finished his meal, Vampa lead him out to the road and set him free. Danglars remained in that spot all night, not knowing where he was. When daylight dawned, he saw that he was near a stream. He was thirsty and dragged himself toward it. As he stooped down to drink, he saw that his hair had become entirely white.

CHAPTER 82
The Fifth of October

On the island of Monte Cristo, happiness awaits.

It was about six o'clock in the evening. An autumnal sun shone brightly upon the blue Mediterranean Sea. The heat of the day had gradually decreased, and a light breeze arose.

An elegant sailboat was gliding over the waters as twilight descended. The vessel resembled a swan with its wings opened toward the wind. It advanced swiftly and gracefully. By degrees, the sun disappeared behind the western horizon. The boat moved rapidly on. Standing on the prow was a tall man of a dark complexion. He saw that they were approaching a dark mass of land in the shape of a cone. "Is that Monte Cristo?" asked the traveler in a melancholy voice.

"Yes, your excellency," said the captain, "we have reached it."

"We have reached it!" repeated the traveler in an accent of indescribable sadness.

Ten minutes afterward, the sails were furled, and the crew dropped anchor about six hundred yards from the little harbor. The traveler stepped down into a sizeable rowboat. Instead of sitting down at the stern of the boat, which had been decorated with a blue carpet for his accommodation, he remained standing with his arms crossed. The rowers waited, their oars half lifted out of the water, like birds drying their wings.

"Make way," said the traveler. The eight oars fell into the sea simultaneously without splashing a drop of water, and the boat glided forward. Soon it arrived at a little harbor, where it came aground on fine sand.

The traveler stepped out of the boat and looked around. Just as he turned, a hand rested on his shoulder, and a voice which made him shudder exclaimed, "Good evening, Maximilian. You are punctual. Thank you!"

"Ah, is it you, Count?" said the young man, in an almost joyful accent, pressing Monte Cristo's hand with both his own.

"Yes, you see I am exactly on time, just as you are. But now we both must dress for dinner. You must change your clothes. Come, I have a room prepared for you in which you will soon forget fatigue and cold." Monte Cristo expected his guest to smile at these words. But instead his face remained frozen in grief.

"Then you are not consoled?" asked the Count.

"Oh," exclaimed the traveler, who was none other than Maximilian Morrel. "Do you think it possible that I could be? I come here to die in the arms of a friend. You told me to wait and hope. I waited a month, or rather I suffered for a month! I did hope. Oh, Count, I shall sleep calmly, deliciously, in the arms of death. My friend," continued Maximilian, "you named the 5th of October as the end of the period of waiting. Today is the fifth of October." He took out his watch. "It is now nine o'clock. I have but three hours to live."

"Be it so," said the Count. "Come." Maximilian mechanically followed the Count, and they entered a large vaulted cave. He felt a carpet under his feet. A door opened, perfumes surrounded him, and a brilliant light dazzled his eyes. "Let me try to convince you to live," said the Count. "Maximilian, as you know, I have no family. I have become accustomed to thinking of you as my son. My fortune amounts to tens of millions of francs. I am happy to share that fortune with *you*. What do you say now?"

"I say that I still do not want to live. Do you think I am so shallow that my happiness can be purchased?"

"Very well," said the Count. Edmond unlocked a vault with a key suspended from his gold chain and took from it a silver box, beautifully carved with a praying figure. He placed the box on the table and took from it a little golden box, the top of which flew open when touched by a secret spring. This box contained a powder whose color it was impossible to tell, owing to the reflection of the polished gold, sapphires, rubies and emeralds which ornamented the box. It was a mixed mass of blue, red, and gold. The Count removed a small quantity of this material with a gilt spoon and offered it to Maximilian.

"This is what you asked for," Edmond said, "and what I promised to give you. This will cause your death."

"I thank you from the depths of my heart," said the young man, taking the spoon from the hands of Monte Cristo. Maximilian then swallowed the powder in a single quick gulp. By slow degrees, the light of the lamps gradually faded, and the perfumes appeared less powerful to him. The objects in the room gradually lost their form and color, and his disturbed vision seemed to perceive doors and curtains open in the walls.

"Friend," he cried, "I feel that I am dying, thank you!" He made a last effort to extend his hand, but it fell powerless beside him. Then it appeared to him that Monte Cristo opened a door. Immediately a brilliant light from the next chamber shone upon the room in which he was gently gliding into his last sleep. Then he saw a woman of marvellous beauty glide through the door. Pale, and sweetly smiling, she looked like an angel of mercy. "Is it heaven that opens before me?" thought the dying man. "That angel resembles the one I have lost, sweet Valentine. I am joining her in heaven." Monte Cristo pointed out Maximilian to the young woman, who clasped his hands and smiled sweetly.

"Valentine, Valentine!" he mentally screamed, but his lips uttered no sound.

"He is calling you," said the Count. "From now on, Valentine, you will never again be separated. I gave him a drug that will draw him into a deep sleep for a while. Soon he will wake up, and you will be together for the rest of your lives. Without me, you would both have died. May God accept the preservation of these two lives as atonement for any excesses I have committed!"

Valentine seized the Count's hand and kissed it in gratitude as she knelt down beside Maximilian. "Count," she said, "if ever there is anything I can do for you, please call on me without hesitation. I thank you with all my heart, and if you doubt the sincerity of my gratitude, then ask Haydee! Ask my beloved sister Haydee, who ever since our departure from France, has caused me to wait patiently for this happy day, while talking to me about you."

"You then love Haydee?" asked Monte Cristo, his voice trembling.

"Oh, yes, with all my soul."

"Well, then, listen, Valentine," said the Count. "I have a favor to ask of you."

"Of me? Oh, am I happy enough for that?"

"Yes. You have called Haydee your sister. Let her become so indeed, Valentine. Give to her all the gratitude you think that you owe to me. Protect her, for—" the Count's voice was thick with emotion, "from now on she will be alone in the world."

"Alone!" repeated a voice behind the Count. "Why?"

Monte Cristo turned around. Haydee was standing there, pale and motionless. She looked at the Count with an expression of fearful amazement.

"Because tomorrow, Haydee, you will be free. You will then assume your proper position in society. You are the daughter of a prince, and I restore to you the riches and name of your father."

The blood drained from Haydee's face. Lifting her hands to heaven, she exclaimed in a voice mixed with tears, "Then you leave me, my lord?"

"Haydee, Haydee, you are young and beautiful. Forget me and be happy."

"I will execute your order if I must, my lord," Haydee said between sobs.

"Heavens," exclaimed Valentine, as she held Maximilian's head in her lap, "do you not see how pale she is? Do you not see how she suffers?"

Haydee answered sadly, "Why should he understand this, my sister? He is my master, and I am his slave. He has the right not to notice."

The Count shuddered at the sadness in Haydee's voice. Yet he also took some satisfaction in her lament. "Can my suspicions be correct?" he asked himself. "Haydee," he said aloud, "would it please you not to leave me?"

"I am young," gently replied Haydee. "I love the life you have made so sweet to me, and I should be sorry to die."

"You mean, then, that if I leave you, Haydee—"

"I should die. Yes, my lord."

"Do you then love me?"

"Oh, Valentine, he asks if I love him. Valentine, tell him if you love Maximilian."

The Count opened his arms, and Haydee, uttering a cry, sprang into them. "Oh, yes," she cried, "I do love you! I love you as one loves a father, brother, husband! I love you as my life, for you are the best, the noblest of creatures!"

"Let it be, then, as you wish, sweet angel. God has sustained me in my struggle with my enemies and has given me this reward. Love me then, Haydee! Who knows? Perhaps your love will make me forget all that I do not wish to remember. I have only you in the world, Haydee. Through you I shall live again. Come, Haydee, come!" and throwing his arm around the young girl's waist, he pressed the hand of Valentine and disappeared.

An hour passed, during which Valentine, breathless and motionless, watched steadfastly over Maximilian. At length she felt his heart flutter. A faint breath played upon his lips. A slight shudder, announcing the return of life, passed through the young man's frame. Then his eyes opened, but they were at first fixed and expressionless. Finally, sight returned, and with it feeling and grief. "Oh," he cried, in an accent of despair, "the Count has deceived me. I am yet living," and extending his hand toward the table, he seized a knife.

"Dearest," exclaimed Valentine, with her adorable smile, "awake, and look at me!" Maximilian uttered a loud exclamation, and frantic, doubtful, dazzled, as though by a celestial vision, he fell upon his knees.

The next morning at daybreak, Valentine and Maximilian took a walk arm-in-arm along the seashore. Valentine explained how Monte Cristo had appeared in her room, revealed the crime, and, finally, how he had saved her life by enabling her to simulate death. Maximilian soon perceived a man standing among the rocks and pointed him out to Valentine. "Ah, it is Jacopo," she said, "the captain of the sailboat." She beckoned him toward them.

"Do you wish to speak to us?" asked Maximilian.

"I have a letter to give you from the Count," Jacopo replied.

"From the Count!" murmured the two young people.

"Yes! Read it." Maximilian opened the letter and read:

My dear Maximilian,
There is a boat waiting for you at anchor. Jacopo will carry you to Leghorn, where M. Noirtier awaits his granddaughter, whom he wishes to bless before you lead her to the altar. All that is in this grotto, my friend, my house in the Champs-Elysées, and my chateau at Treport, are the marriage gifts I bestow on you. Mademoiselle de Villefort will share them with you, for I entreat her to give to the poor the immense fortune passing to her from her father, now a madman, and her brother, who died last September with his mother. Tell the angel who will watch over you, Maximilian, to pray sometimes for a man who, like Satan, thought himself for an instant equal to God, but who now

acknowledges with Christian humility that God alone possesses supreme power and infinite wisdom. Know, Maximilian, that he who has felt the deepest grief is best able to experience supreme happiness. We must have felt what it is to die, Maximilian, that we may appreciate the joys of living.

Live, then, and be happy, beloved children of my heart, and never forget that all human wisdom is summed up in these two words: "Wait and hope."

Your friend,

Edmond Dantes, Count of Monte Cristo

The contents of this letter informed Valentine for the first time of the madness of her father and the death of her brother. She became pale, let out a heavy sigh, and tears ran down her cheeks.

Maximilian looked around uneasily. "Where is the Count?" he asked Jacopo. Jacopo pointed toward the horizon.

"What do you mean?" asked Valentine. "Where is the Count?—where is Haydee?"

"Look!" said Jacopo.

The eyes of both were fixed upon the spot indicated by the sailor. On the blue line separating the sky from the Mediterranean Sea, they perceived a large white sail. "Gone," said Maximilian, "gone! Goodbye, my friend! Goodbye, my father!"

"Gone," murmured Valentine. "Goodbye, my sweet Haydee. Goodbye, my sister!"

"Who can say whether we shall ever see them again?" said Maximilian with tearful eyes.

"Darling," replied Valentine, "has not the Count just told us that all human wisdom is summed up in two words? "Wait and hope.""

AFTERWORD

About the Author

"Write about what you know." This advice to beginning writers is surely something Alexandre Dumas would agree with. Although they might seem exaggerated and the material of fantasy, many of the characters and episodes in *The Count of Monte Cristo* were actually drawn from Dumas's own life and family history.

Alexandre Dumas's father, Thomas-Alexandre Dumas Davy de la Pailetterie, was a famous general who served both during the French Revolution of 1789 and later with Napoleon Bonaparte. He was captured in Italy and imprisoned in the Castle of Tarentum, where he remained confined for two years. This traumatic experience, happening before Dumas was born, clearly made an impression on the young Dumas, who grew up listening to stories of his father's exploits. These stories would find their way into the novels he would later write.

Like Edmond Dantes's father, Alexandre Dumas's father was financially hard-pressed. After his release from prison and his retirement from military service, Thomas-Alexandre returned to his wife and young daughter in the village of Villers-Cotterêts, near Paris. Born Marie-Louise Labouret, Thomas-Alexandre's wife was the daughter of innkeepers and had little money. The family had only a small military pension on which to live.

Alexandre Dumas was born in 1802. Reportedly, Thomas-Alexandre was a gentle, loving father, somewhat broken in spirit during his last years. He died at the age of forty-four, when Alexandre was only three years old. The little boy is said to have cried out, "Goodbye, Papa! Goodbye!" For the rest of his life, Alexandre would mourn his father's early death, as Edmond mourns the death of *his* beloved father in *The Count of Monte Cristo*.

In the novel, Edmond is devoted to his father, a widower so poor that he is unable to pay his rent. Alexandre Dumas was similarly devoted to his widowed mother, who also fell into debt. Because the military pension ended with Thomas-Alexandre's death, Marie-Louise tried to earn a living by opening a tobacco shop. She and her children lived on the floor above.

Like his character, Alexandre Dumas had little formal education. In fact, his mother sent him to a local priest, the Abbé Gregoire, to learn the basics, but Alexandre was only a mediocre student—he never got beyond the multiplication tables. In fact, the only subject at which he excelled was penmanship; he had beautiful handwriting. At age 14, he began working for a local lawyer, first as an errand boy and then as a clerk. In 1822 Dumas, aged 20, left for Paris. A general who had known his father recommended him for employment with the Duke of Orleans. Because of his excellent handwriting, Dumas was given a job as one of the duke's copyists. At one point he was assigned the task of copying a secret document, most likely similar to the one Edmond is asked to convey to Napoleon. Interestingly, twenty years later, Dumas visited Elba, the island where Napoleon was exiled. In a rowboat, he circled another island, a small, rocky bit of land south of Elba: Monte Cristo.

While working as the Duke's copyist, Dumas often attended the theater, which he loved. He also read romantic poetry and fiction. He was determined to become a writer. In 1825, his first play opened in Paris. Dumas's first published fiction, a collection of army stories, appeared in 1826. His 1829 play *Henry III and His Court* was a great success. Only twenty-seven years old, Alexandre already was a leading dramatist. He would write many other successful plays, usually with collaborators.

Like the traditional hero of romantic literature, Dumas was highly attractive to women. He had striking blue eyes and resembled his character Edmond in being handsome, black-haired, and tall (about six feet). When he was 22, Dumas and a dressmaker named Laure Labay had an illegitimate son, Alexandre Junior (who also would become a famous writer). Starting in 1832, Dumas had an eight-year love affair with actress Ida Ferrier. They married, but four years later they separated. Throughout his life Dumas would have many love affairs, especially with actresses.

However, Dumas seems to have loved his mother more than any other woman. As soon as he was earning enough money to support her, he invited her to come live with him in Paris. The two took up residence in a rented apartment. In 1829 Marie-Louise suffered a stroke. Initially she was paralyzed on one side and was largely unable to speak. She regained speech and the ability to take short walks. Dumas remained devoted to her, just as, in *The Count of Monte Cristo,* Valentine is devoted to her paralyzed grandfather, Noirtier. Marie-Louise died in 1838 of another stroke. Dumas intensely grieved. Similarly, in the novel, Abbé Faria, who is like a parent to Edmond, suffers a stroke that paralyzes one side of his body. He eventually dies of a second stroke.

The duels in *The Count of Monte Cristo* also have counterparts in Dumas's life. In 1825 Dumas quarreled with a man in a tavern. The two exchanged insults until they agreed to duel with swords. The morning of the duel was cold, with snow covering the ground. Dumas chose to use a sword five inches shorter than his rival's because it had belonged to his father. He inflicted a minor shoulder wound on his opponent, who fell to the ground. The duel ended there, with no further injury. In *The Count of Monte Cristo,* the duel between Noirtier and General Flavien d'Epinay also takes place on a cold day with snow cover. Like Dumas, Noirtier uses a sword five inches shorter than his opponent's. D'Epinay thrusts but misses and falls. However, the fictional duel ends tragically: Noirtier kills d'Epinay. Seven years later, Dumas was involved in a second duel over who should be credited with the authorship of a play. The night before the duel—this time, with pistols—Dumas, like Edmond, wrote instructions to be carried out in the event of his death.

A final similarity between Dumas's life and *The Count of Monte Cristo* has to do with accusation and betrayal. In the book, Danglars, a colleague of Edmond, writes an anonymous letter of accusation against Edmond. Similarly, Dumas considered Victor Hugo, the famous playwright and novelist, a friend. However, in 1833, Granier de Cassagnac, a protégé of Hugo, wrote a pamphlet in which he accused Dumas of plagiarism and fiercely belittled his work. Behind the scenes, Hugo had given the go-ahead for the pamphlet's publication. Clearly, Dumas thoroughly understood what it felt like to be publicly accused of wrongdoing and to be betrayed.

Having quickly become a successful playwright, Dumas also quickly became France's most popular novelist. In 1838, as France was emerging from a period of political instability, press censorship was abolished, and there was great demand for newspapers. To attract readers, newspapers began to publish serialized novels. These easily accessible stories were read by everyone, regardless of social class and gender. It was at this moment that Dumas saw his opportunity. He rewrote one of his plays as a serialized novel for a newspaper. This novel, *Captain Paul*, was especially popular with women and quickly added 5,000 new subscribers to the newspaper. With this success, Dumas took his opportunity one step further and created a studio where writers wrote hundreds of stories under the personal direction of Dumas for publication as plays, serialized novels, and traditional novels. It is believed that Dumas, with the help of 73 assistants, wrote 250 books, of which *The Three Musketeers* (1844), *The Count of Monte Cristo* (serialized in 1844–45), and *The Man in the Iron Mask* (1847) were the most popular. In fact, Dumas's studio is credited with inventing the genre of historical romance.

Like Edmond, Dumas acquired great wealth, which he spent on women and a lavish lifestyle. He sought to create a life for himself straight out of one of his novels. In 1846 Dumas even built an extravagant castle for himself, which he named the Chateau de Monte Cristo. However, the costs associated with constructing and maintaining the building forced him to sell it in 1848, and he soon left France altogether to evade his creditors. He eventually settled in Russia, where his novels were very popular. There he published a newspaper. In 1864, he returned to Paris and continued writing.

When Alexandre Dumas died of a stroke in 1870 at age sixty-eight, he was penniless and living with his son, Alexandre. However, he had become one of the world's best-known as well as most productive authors. In addition to the hundreds of plays and novels, he also wrote travel diaries, children's stories and even a culinary dictionary. Most of his stories involved larger-than life-characters engaging in thrilling adventures set against the backdrop of history—a backdrop that was not often historically accurate, but always exciting.

Since his death, a number of Dumas scholars have unearthed additional unpublished works, most recently in 2005, when Dumas expert Claude Schopp discovered the manuscript of a 900-page unfinished novel, *The Knight of Saint Hermine*. Schopp converted it from its serialized format to a traditional novel and published it as *The Last Cavalier*, adding an ending of two and one-half chapters. Perhaps it was this book that Dumas was referring to on his deathbed. His last words reportedly were, "I shall never know how it all comes out now." Or perhaps he was referring to his life. But the millions of readers who have enjoyed Dumas's gripping historical novels know how the story ends.

About the Book

The Count of Monte Cristo is repeatedly listed as one of the hundred most influential books ever written. What makes this novel so popular? This question actually has four answers. To begin with, it is a human story of betrayal, honor and revenge, wrapped in the cloak of a historical novel and set in a deeply romantic time and place. Second, *The Count of Monte Cristo* offers a commentary on the social classes of the 19th century. Third, it speaks to our tendency to identify with the underdog and our desire for justice. Finally, the book has two great themes: the limitations of human justice and the strength of love over hatred.

In 1807 a French shoemaker named François Picaud, a handsome young man, was falsely accused of being a secret agent guilty of treason. Four men he had regarded as friends made the charge. Shortly before he was going to marry a beautiful young woman, Picaud was arrested. His fiancée and next of kin weren't told what charge had been brought against him. Picaud went to prison for seven years. In prison he became close friends with an Italian priest who told him about a great treasure hidden in the cellar of a deserted Italian palace and then died. When Picaud was released, he found and took the treasure. Then he returned to France and, for the next ten years, tracked down his accusers. Picaud paid a handsome criminal to seduce and marry the daughter of one accuser. Picaud stabbed a second accuser to death and fatally poisoned a third. The fourth accuser, Mathieu Loupiau, had married Picaud's fiancée, who had died grieving her loss of Picaud. Picaud burned down Loupiau's café, and Loupiau fell into poverty. Picaud later stabbed him to death. In time Picaud was arrested and executed.

If much of this sounds familiar, that's because these events inspired the plot of Alexandre Dumas's *Count of Monte Cristo*. As soon as he read the memoir of Francois Picaud in a collection of interesting police stories, Dumas knew he wanted to retell it. Dumas remarked of the story, "A rough, shapeless pearl, of no value, waiting for its jeweler." With his gifts for character development, descriptive language and storytelling, Dumas shaped this simple story into the crown jewel of his literary career.

Dumas had a good eye for a story. Rather than simply relating the tale, Dumas set it against the lush backdrop of French history. While Dumas did not invent the historical novel, he was the first to popularize it. At the time of its publication in the late 1830s, France was enjoying a relatively calm period of political stability and economic prosperity. As a result, the public could enjoy the excitement offered by a historical novel set in a more turbulent time.

Like his contemporaries, Dumas used his novels to criticize the social structure of contemporary France. The French Revolution of 1789, just before the time frame in which *Monte Cristo* was set, marked the beginning of the crumbling of the class system throughout Europe. This created for the first time the idea that a person could rise through society independent of his or her station at birth. *Monte Cristo*, more than any of Dumas's other works, describes the dark side of the upper class in 19th century Paris—characterized by greed, envy, corruptibility, and betrayal. Each character finds status in a different way: Edmond through merit as captain of the *Pharaon* and luck in his ascendancy as Count of Monte Cristo, Danglars through greed, Villefort through hard work and deception, Count de Morcerf (Fernand Mondego) through betrayal, and Caderousse through theft. These characters are, Dumas suggests, typical of 19th century Parisian society. Dumas uses them to show his readers that through the military (Count de Morcerf), through government work (Villefort), through banking/business (Danglars), and even through criminal enterprise (Caderousse), one can change one's social status. However, ascending the social order is never without costs, as each of the characters, including the hero Edmond Dantes, comes to understand.

Social commentary, however, is only the secondary purpose of *The Count of Monte Cristo*. Dumas's primary goal was to entertain his readers. The book's commercial success was due in large part to the themes of the book: justice, revenge, loyalty, and redemption.

Who has not dreamed, like Edmond Dantes, of exacting elaborate revenge for a perceived injustice? When Edmond obtains the huge treasure described by Abbé Faria, it seems in proportion to the great suffering he has experienced; it amounts to millions of dollars. His new wealth empowers him to bring about some of the justice that has so far been denied. In fact, Monte Cristo's limitless fortune and relative anonymity gives him power that Dumas likens to being an "agent of God." Once Monte Cristo reenters society, everything goes right for him. Monte Cristo's perfect timing and his knowledge of everything about everybody verges on the unbelievable. The reader, however, accepts Monte Cristo's invincibility out of a desire to believe in his role as an agent of justice. It is a credit to Dumas's writing that even when faced with the most implausible of circumstances, the reader forgives Dumas and stays fully engaged in the narrative. As Monte Cristo ruthlessly goes about the slow and methodical destruction of all those who conspired to imprison him, he is supremely confident that his actions are morally sound. While the reader may question Monte Cristo's behavior, Monte Cristo remains a sympathetic character because he appeals to the most basic of human emotions—revenge and the victory of the underdog.

While revenge is a major theme of the novel, it is complemented by Edmond's strong sense of loyalty, both to people and to his sense of what is right. It is these two sides of the same coin that define Monte Cristo's actions throughout the novel. Before he sets about destroying those who wronged him, he rewards those who showed their loyalty to him. His first order of business upon his return is to seek out the Morrel family. He rewards the Morrels by replacing the *Pharaon* and providing a very large diamond for Julie's dowry. Only after he has rewarded the Morrel family for their kindness towards his father and their efforts to set him free does he turn his attention toward those who wronged him. After he destroys his enemies, Monte Cristo devotes his energies to ensuring that Maximilian and Valentine can reunite.

Eventually, however, Monte Cristo begins to see the limitations as well as the excesses of his quest for justice. Edmond achieves his objectives, but human justice never is complete. Severe wrongdoing cannot be fully undone. Nothing can bring Edmond's father back to life. Nothing can restore the years that Edmond spent in prison or erase the suffering that he and other innocent people experienced. And his revenge schemes result in further injustice. At the end of the novel, Mercedes—guilty of nothing worse than poor judgment in marrying Mondego— is also punished. She has lost her status, her wealth, her husband, and, to some degree, her beloved son, who has gone off to Africa as a soldier. She still loves Edmond, but he now loves another woman, Haydee. So Mercedes faces a largely dull and lonely life. Similarly, as a result of Villefort's threat to expose his wife's crimes, Madame de Villefort murders their young son. Dumas is telling us that the desire for revenge against the guilty also harms the innocent. It corrupts all who participate in it and leads to further injustice.

The final lesson of *The Count of Monte Cristo* is that love must prevail over hatred. Prior to entering the Chateau d'If, Dantes is depicted as a young man, naïve and trusting, but with an enormous heart full of love for Mercedes and his father and free from any hate. Once Dantes reinvents himself as Monte Cristo, he sets his emotions aside. Even when Dantes visits with the Morrel family, he remains distant and keeps his emotions in check. He is cold and calculating, single-minded and unswerving because he believes his purpose is unquestionably just. Because the quest for justice can lead to further injustice, Monte Cristo must learn that there are limits to the pain he can cause. He realizes this when he reveals his identity to Villefort near the end of the book:

"You are Edmond Dantes," cried Villefort, seizing the Count by the wrist. "Then come here!" And up the stairs he dragged Edmond. "There, Edmond Dantes!" he said, pointing to the bodies of his wife and child. "See, are you well avenged?" Edmond became pale at this horrible sight. He feared that he had passed beyond the bounds of vengeance. With an expression of indescribable regret, he scooped up the child, reopened its eyes, felt its pulse, and then rushed with him into Valentine's room.

A quarter of an hour afterward the door of Valentine's room opened, and Monte Cristo reappeared. Pale, with a dull eye and heavy heart, all the noble features of that face, usually so calm and serene, were overcast by grief. In his arms he held

> the child, whom he had been unable to
> recall to life.

For all the confidence that Monte Cristo exhibits throughout the book, at the end it is clear that Monte Cristo knows that he has gone too far. For this reason, Danglars receives his forgiveness; Monte Cristo realizes that he himself is in need of forgiveness.

Until the very end of the book, Monte Cristo never seems troubled by the suffering he causes to innocent people, such as the families of those he seeks to punish. He does not question his own actions because he believes that the pain he inflicts is the punishment of God for the sins of others. His hatred of his enemies prevents him from sympathizing with the many people who suffer on account of his actions. It is not until he learns that Maximilian is in love with Valentine and he sees young Edward's body that he begins to sense that revenge has robbed him of his humanity. His redemption lies in his rediscovery of how to relate emotionally to other people. This is demonstrated through his extensive efforts to save Valentine, the daughter of his enemy, so she can reunite with Maximilian. Once he has engineered their reunion, Monte Cristo finally is free to enjoy his own humanity through a second chance at love, this time with Haydee. He is no longer obsessed with the revenge that had robbed him of the ability to love.